Praise f[illegible]

T[illegible]

“An absorbing, [illegible] future place in the worl[illegible]”

—[illegible], author of *Deep Sound Channel*, *Thunder in the Deep*, and *Crush Depth*

“If you enjoy a well-told tale of action and adventure, you will love David Meadows’s series, *The Sixth Fleet*. Not only does the author know his subject but [his] fiction could readily become fact. These books should be read by every senator and congressman in our government so that the scenarios therein do not become history.”

—John Tegler, syndicated talk show host of *Capital Conversation*

“Meadows will have you turning pages and thinking new thoughts.”

—Newt Gingrich

“Easily on par with Tom Clancy, *The Sixth Fleet* provides an awesomely prescient picture of the U.S. Navy at war with terrorism and those who support it. It has the unmistakable ring of truth and accuracy, which only an insider can provide. In the aftermath of September 11, this is not just a good read, but an essential one.”

—Milos Stankovic, author of *Trusted Mole*

“Meadows takes us right to the bridge, in the cockpit, and into the thick of battle. Meadows is a military adventure writer who’s been there, done it all, and knows the territory. This is as real as it gets.”

—Robert Gandt, author of *The Killing Sky*

“Meadows delivers one heck of a fast-paced, roller-coaster ride with this exhilarating military thriller.”

—*Midwest Book Review*

Berkley titles by David E. Meadows

DARK PACIFIC
DARK PACIFIC: PACIFIC THREAT

THE SIXTH FLEET
THE SIXTH FLEET: SEAWOLF
THE SIXTH FLEET: TOMCAT
THE SIXTH FLEET: COBRA

JOINT TASK FORCE: LIBERIA
JOINT TASK FORCE: AMERICA
JOINT TASK FORCE: FRANCE
JOINT TASK FORCE: AFRICA

DARK PACIFIC

PACIFIC THREAT

DAVID E. MEADOWS

THE BERKLEY PUBLISHING GROUP
Published by the Penguin Group
Penguin Group (USA) Inc.
375 Hudson Street, New York, New York 10014, USA
Penguin Group (Canada), 90 Eglinton Avenue East, Suite 700, Toronto, Ontario M4P 2Y3, Canada
(a division of Pearson Penguin Canada Inc.)
Penguin Books Ltd., 80 Strand, London WC2R 0RL, England
Penguin Group Ireland, 25 St. Stephen's Green, Dublin 2, Ireland (a division of Penguin Books Ltd.)
Penguin Group (Australia), 250 Camberwell Road, Camberwell, Victoria 3124, Australia
(a division of Pearson Australia Group Pty. Ltd.)
Penguin Books India Pvt. Ltd., 11 Community Centre, Panchsheel Park, New Delhi—110 017, India
Penguin Group (NZ), Cnr. Airborne and Rosedale Roads, Albany, Auckland 1310, New Zealand
(a division of Pearson New Zealand Ltd.)
Penguin Books (South Africa) (Pty.) Ltd., 24 Sturdee Avenue, Rosebank, Johannesburg 2196,
South Africa

Penguin Books Ltd., Registered Offices: 80 Strand, London WC2R 0RL, England

DARK PACIFIC: PACIFIC THREAT

A Berkley Book / published by arrangement with the author

PRINTING HISTORY
Berkley edition / January 2007

Cover illustration by 3DI Studio.
Cover design by Richard Hasselberger.
Interior text design by Kristin del Rosario.

For information, address: The Berkley Publishing Group,
a division of Penguin Group (USA) Inc.,
375 Hudson Street, New York, New York 10014.

ISBN: 978-0-425-21340-7

BERKLEY®
Berkley Books are published by The Berkley Publishing Group,
a division of Penguin Group (USA) Inc.,
375 Hudson Street, New York, New York 10014.
BERKLEY is a registered trademark of Penguin Group (USA) Inc.
The "B" design is a trademark belonging to Penguin Group (USA) Inc.

PRINTED IN THE UNITED STATES OF AMERICA

10 9 8 7 6 5 4 3 2 1

To the first operational F-22A Raptor fighter squadron:
27th Fighter Squadron of the 1st Fighter Wing

Acknowledgments

It is impossible to thank everyone who provides technical advice and support for this and my other novels. I deeply appreciate their advice, support, and technical competence. I also am always appreciative to those who visit *www.sixthfleet.com*, who read my Op-Ed column, and sometimes disagree. Your comments are welcomed and for those who send e-mails, I do try to personally reply to everyone.

Writing a series is different from writing a stand-alone novel. There are characters and story lines that continue throughout the books. I try to make each book a stand-alone, with the following novels bringing the new reader up to date on what has occurred in the books ahead of it. This is my tenth military thriller. Every author appreciates hearing good words about their writing. You readers have given me no greater thrill than knowing you enjoyed my books, whether it is through feedback from the bookstores, publisher, editor, agent, or on my Web site, or from comments posted at on-line bookstores. For each of you, my thanks, and consider yourself as part of my extended literary family as I surely do.

When you are acknowledging contributions, technical advice, and support, you run the risk of failing to acknowledge everyone. If I unintentionally forgot to mention you, please let me know. The F-22A Raptor plays a prominent role in this series, commencing with the second in the *Dark Pacific* series: *Pacific Threat*. I would like to express many thanks to one of the Air Force's finest: Colonel Walter "Waldo" Givhans—"U.S. Air Force Fighter Pilot" as he always introduced himself when we went to school together at the National Defense University. He was kind enough to answer questions about what is easily the most technologically advanced fighter aircraft in the world. All information on the F-22A in this novel is easily available on the Internet. Without reserve, my great respects to the men and women who take this phenomenal weapon of democracy into the hostile areas of the world.

As I did in *Dark Pacific*, I want to recognize again the Master of the USNS *Denebola*, Captain Joe Gargiulo, and Mr. Matthew Cull (PM5 Sealift Surge Detachment), who took time from their busy in-port schedule in Norfolk, Virginia, to guide me around this massive ship. Without them guiding me through this massive carrier-size ship, I would have been unable to capture the true gigantic capabilities of the Fast Sealift Ships of the United States Maritime Sealift Command to support our forces overseas. The *Denebola* and the other seven FSS ships are over 946 feet in length, while the newest aircraft carrier, the USS *George Bush*, is 1092 feet in length—a difference of less than 150 feet. The *Nimitz*-class aircraft carriers, of which USS *George Bush* is one, have a crew of over 5,500 people with ship's company and air wing embarked. The MSC Fast Sealift Ships have fourteen merchant marines assigned when in port, growing to an overwhelming force of forty when they set sail. The staterooms on the Fast Sealift Ships convinced me there are better ways of going to sea than in the open-bay berthing areas belowdecks of a warship. I recommend the Navy ban sailors who are up for reenlistment from seeing the berthing accommodations on these Fast Sealift Ships. Twin beds, a recliner, private bath, desk, and a huge stateroom made me want to up anchor and head out to sea again.

My thanks to Terry Smith, Vincent Widmaier, and William Cross for their security insights. For technical advice and support, my appreciation to Amanda Roberts, Angela O'Neal, Tim Bovill, Jerry Bechlehimer, Cassandra Mewborn, Brenda Williams, Mark Thomson, and Jessie McAliley. And, of course, Patricia McNally, Christine Weston-Lyons (who many believe has known me since she was seven), and Mary Forbes. And to answer your question, Phil, "No, you're not in this book either."

As always, my continued thanks to Mr. Tom Colgan for his editorial support and to his able right-hand person, Ms. Sandra Harding.

Rest assured any and all technical errors or mistakes in this novel are strictly those of the author, who many times wanders in his own world. Please keep in touch. The third and final novel in the *Dark Pacific* series is nearing completion.

David E. Meadows

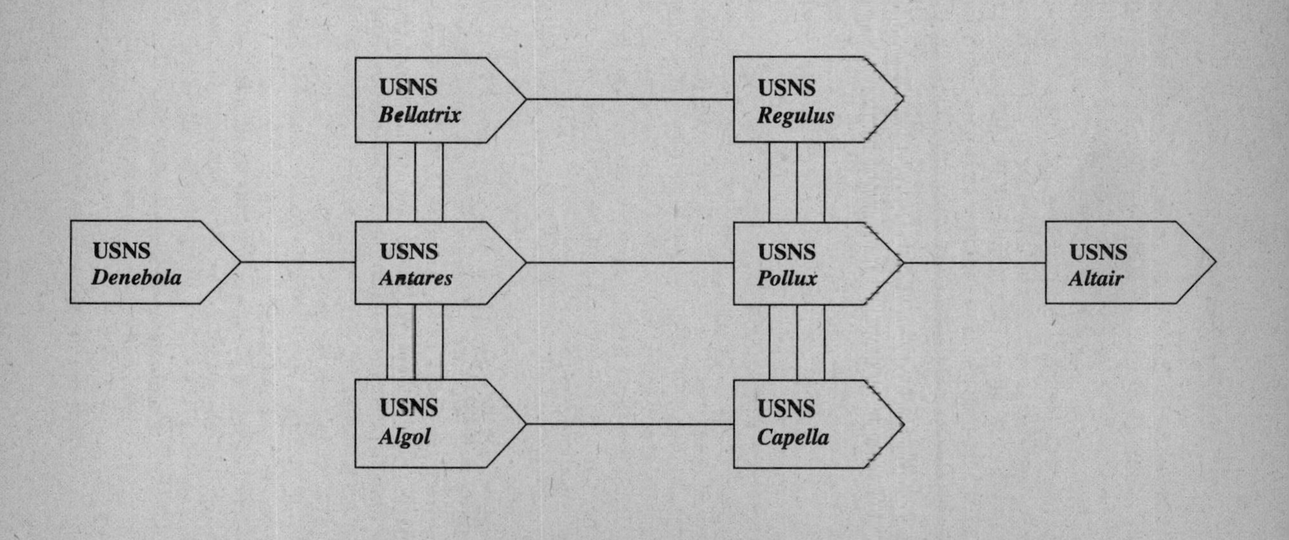

Figure 1. The Sea Base foundation.

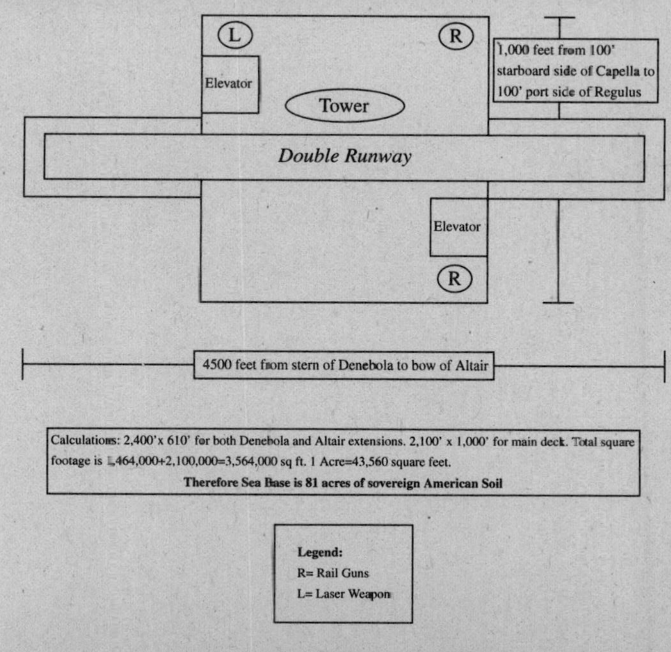

Figure 2. The Sea Base foundation.

ONE

Master Chief Jerry Jacobs flicked ash from his cigar over the safety lines of Sea Base. "Amazing, ain't it, Alistair?" he said to Senior Chief Sonar Technician Agazzi, who was standing alongside him.

"Well, it's true, Jerry. If there is anything I hate to admit, it's that maybe one of your dire predictions is going to come true. When we were told Sea Base was going to get under way and steam northwest toward the Sea of Japan—I mean even the scientists from the Naval Research Labs tried to talk the Skipper into taking Sea Base down and reestablishing it once we were in the SOJ. I think even they had visions of heading downward to the dark Pacific."

Jacobs nodded sharply several times. "I am seldom wrong, my friend. Sea Base is an accident waiting to happen. If not this time, sometime in the future. Let's hope you and I are ashore when it does." He turned and waved his cigar at the scene in front of them. "Look out there. We—you and I and every swinging dick on this floating bucket of bolts—are on eighty-one-plus acres of some sort of tempered metal held aloft by eight ancient Fast Sealift Ships the size of aircraft carriers steaming on engines that would be oohed and aahed in the Smithsonian. And they're towing sea anchors and sonars streaming some thousand feet beneath this contraption, so we . . ."

Agazzi grinned. "Not to mention we're around twenty stories above the ocean."

"I would have gotten to that if you hadn't interrupted me."

"One thing about you, my fine master chief friend: good vibes about future disasters."

Jacobs sucked his stomach in, sighting the ridgeline of his shirt with his zipper. "You want good vibes, go see the chaplain," he said, looking up. "You want the truth, come see me." He turned back to the safety lines, looking at the wake trailing Sea Base, and jammed the cigar back between his lips. "Ain't exactly right seeing multiple wakes appearing from beneath something this awkward. My prediction was near enough to make me lose sleep when we stopped the first time in the middle of the Pacific. I had this great craving for a couple of six-packs when we stood on the *Denebola* and watched eight scrap-metal ships link up and raise eighty-one-plus acres of metal above them." The white puff of cigar smoke was whipped off immediately by the warm Pacific breeze. "The only damn good thing about seeing it set up was we were stationary in the ocean. Making way, under way, but just enough to stay stationary. Now, we're steaming through the deep Pacific shifting our colors from the Pacific Ocean into the Sea of Japan."

"So far, so good."

"So far! Alistair, we've been under way a week, making way. If I didn't think it'd be bad for the morale of my boatswain mates, I'd sleep on the deck, so when this thing crashes and burns, I can at least see the stars on the way down."

"Guess days don't bother you too much."

"Bad things at sea happen at night or in the dark. Bad things wait for God to go to sleep."

"Nothing better than standing out here on a bright sunny afternoon, feeling the breeze on our cheeks, smelling the salt air, and waiting for God to sleep."

"When do you think they're going to straighten out the communications on this thing? We got no intercom; limited capability for my watch-standers to use sound-powered telephones to pass information." He pointed at Agazzi. "You're still having to dial in to Combat Information Center to pass submarine data. Go figure."

Agazzi shrugged. "No, there's been some improvement. We have sound-powered communications with Combat Information Center in the tower, but nowhere else. I can now talk with my guys in ASW control center, which is on the bottom level of the *Algol,* from the Unmanned Underwater Vehicle compartment on the bottom level of *Bellatrix.* Of course, it's only by telephone or via the computer. We don't have the sound-powered phone capability there yet, but the sand crabs tell me they'll have it up and running by next week."

"I can talk with my boatswain mates topside with these little walkie-talkies someone gave us," Jacobs said, patting the small brick riding high in its holster on his khaki belt. "At least, they're not made in China."

"Where they made?"

"Taiwan."

"How do you fight something this size when the internal communications are so screwed up?"

"Our purpose is to test the concept of Sea Base . . ."

". . . a floating island . . ."

". . . for six months and then return to Pearl; not steam from an operational evaluation to an operational mission."

The walkie-talkie on Jacobs's belt squeaked with static as the voice of a female sent a load of profanity soaring across the airways. Jacobs smiled, reached down, and turned the volume lower. "That Showdernitzel, she is going to make life miserable for some fine young man one day. I'm saving up to buy him earmuffs as a wedding present."

After a few seconds of silence, Jacobs asked, "You hear anything about this guy Smith who tried to kill you?"

"A little, but I think I told you," Agazzi said with a nod. "Smith was telling the truth that his name wasn't really Smith. Zeichner . . ."

"You know, I like that NCIS agent Zeichner. I don't feel as bad about this small bulge around my waist when I'm around him."

"You pass the body-fat measurements, Jerry. Wouldn't worry about it."

"If I looked like some forsaken jogger with my ribs showing and head looking like it's on some sort of cornstalk, I'd say the same thing you did."

"Zeichner said the FBI traced the real Smith to a small coal-mining town in Pennsylvania. The real Smith joined the Navy;

the last his family heard from him was when he graduated from boot camp and was awaiting orders."

"Didn't his family have any concerns over not hearing from their son?"

Agazzi shrugged. "They contacted the Red Cross, who sent one of those family notices to the Navy. The family received a reply that their son was fine, heading to sea, and would contact them. He never did, and they never pursued it further. Now, the investigation is on to find out what happened to the real Smith."

"What does Zeichner think happened?"

"He didn't say it out loud, but I think he believes the real Smith is dead."

"I don't understand what this Smith, masquerading as a sailor, expected to accomplish by blowing up Sea Base. I would . . ."

Two F-22A Raptors approaching the landing strip in the center of the man-made island drowned out Jacobs's words. Agazzi noticed the master chief continued talking, ignoring the drone of the Raptor engines blanketing the top of Sea Base.

Agazzi looked past Jacobs as the first aircraft descended toward the end of the double runway that cut through the center of the man-made island. The other F-22A applied throttle, increasing speed, the nose arching up, as it ascended, heading back around the pattern for its landing.

The wheels of the first squealed as the stealth fighter hit the deck, two white puffs of smoke trailing the contact of the tires. The engines wound down, the aircraft slowed as the pilot applied the brakes, and two thousand feet later the aircraft turned off the runway.

An Air Force-blue pickup truck with a blinking sign, FOLLOW ME, led the Raptor toward the parking apron.

"Damn," Jacobs said, wiping his eyes as the whiff of burning rubber and the sting of exhaust flowed across them. "Whatever happened to the pure Navy smell of unburned fuel and bacon grease?"

Agazzi's face twisted in pain for a moment. He reached up with his right hand and touched his left shoulder.

"Bothering you?"

"Doctor said it would for another few months. Looks as if Smith—or whatever his name was—broke the collarbone and knocked the arm out of joint."

Jacobs nodded. "Things like that happen when someone takes a metal rod to you. Be glad it wasn't your head he hit."

"You know, if you hadn't . . ."

Jacobs waved it away. "You tell me one more time how much you owe your life to me, I'm going to start to believe it and demand things like groveling." The master chief's blue eyes glistened for a moment. "I hate it when the fresh sea air is fouled by Air Force pollution."

"I'll try to remember to quit reminding you."

"You do that, why don't you. Between Frieda thanking me and promising me anything I want for saving your life . . ."

"She thanked you, Jerry, and I thank you, but I don't think she promised you anything you wanted."

"Alistair, as a master chief, I am one of the top one percent of the Navy. You don't get there from failing to read the tea leaves when someone is complimenting you."

Agazzi opened his mouth to engage in the good-natured banter, but another twinge of pain caused him to clench his teeth instead. A few seconds later when the pain eased, he said, "I wish I knew what was going through the young man's mind."

"You won't ever know. No one knows what goes through the minds of those who want to die and take as many people with them as possible. It doesn't matter what they think they're dying for; the truth is they're dead and no god or Allah or Jehovah or any god they say they're doing it for is going to be waiting for them on the other side. Most religions blanketing the world would be considered a cult if they started today. It's only because some have been around so long that the world has little choice but to accept them."

Agazzi glanced over Jacobs's shoulder. Richard Zeichner, the NCIS agent in charge on Sea Base, was walking toward them. Zeichner reached in his back pocket, pulled out a handkerchief, and wiped the sweat from his forehead. Zeichner moved slowly, with a gait hindered by heavy thighs that slapped against each other at every step. Zeichner really needed to lose weight, thought Agazzi sympathetically. It appeared to him the NCIS agent was gaining weight instead of losing it, as the man professed whenever they met.

Jacobs's voice droned on about religion as Agazzi continued his observation. If Zeichner were searching for them, then it would be with more information about the bomber that had tried to kill him, or with more questions. White shirt, half in, half out of the man's pants, and a stomach over the belt line hid any belt the man might be wearing.

"Here he comes," Agazzi said, nodding over Jacobs's shoulder.

Jacobs turned. "Damn. You'd think I've answered enough of his questions. Maybe I'll be lucky and it'll be you he'll want today."

"Didn't he interview you this morning about the events in the UUV compartment?"

"Yeah. For the umpteenth time he wanted to go over again what I saw and did when I entered the Unmanned Underwater Vehicle compartment and discovered Smith beating the shit out of you and about to cream your head with that bar. I don't know if he wants me to say I should have tried to reason with Smith before tackling him, or if he wants me to say I intentionally knocked him so he'd fall through the well deck and into the ocean."

"Just tell the truth."

"I have. I told him the sharks leaped up through the opening, grabbed Smith, and jumped back into the ocean. He didn't seem to believe me. I even gave him my theory of those sharks being reincarnated master chiefs. I'm sure I recognized one of them from my early days in the Navy."

"Morning, gentlemen," Zeichner said with a slight wave as he approached, a big smile stretching across his face, causing his jowls to spread.

They acknowledged his greeting and for several minutes commented on the movement of Sea Base from northeast of Taiwan toward the Sea of Japan, the body of water located between the Korean Peninsula and Japan.

The three men stopped talking as the other F-22A completed the racetrack landing circuit and made its final approach to the Sea Base. A minute later the heavy Air Force fighter aircraft touched down.

"Well, Mr. Zeichner," Agazzi said. "What's the latest on this Smith? Figured out who he was or whatever?"

"Ever hear of an organization or a religious group called God's Army?"

"Yeah," Jacobs answered. "Some sort of cult . . ." He pointed his cigar at Agazzi. "What'd I tell you? Some sort of religious group who believes world anarchy is the key to Christ returning."

"Something like that," Zeichner said, running the handkerchief across his forehead and over his sparse hair. "Whew! This heat is terrible. You two want to come downstairs for a chat?"

"Is that a request or an order?" Jacobs asked.

"Just a friendly question," Zeichner said, and then added, "This time."

"Then, I think I'd like to stay out here in the open and enjoy my cigar; watch the sailors work." He pointed his cigar at Zeichner. "It's a grand sight for a master chief to see sailors working. Sends a thrill of chill bumps up my spine; almost makes me want to do something similar, but then I realize that watching me working alongside of them and seeing what a master chief can do would create a hell of a lot of inferiority complexes, so I force myself to stay back and watch. It's better for the sailors that way."

"Master Chief seems to think Sea Base is going to crumble up and sink before we reach the Sea of Japan," Agazzi offered.

Zeichner agreed. "I can hear the groans of the metal in my stateroom. There is a lot more of them now that we're moving."

"Groans? Those aren't groans, Mr. Zeichner; that's every piece of metal on this eighty-one-plus acres of man-made American territory crying for an opportunity to head south. Break apart and hit the dark Pacific."

"We aren't moving fast, maybe . . ."

"Making way is moving and anytime you're moving and trying to synchronize-swim eight ancient ships the size of aircraft carriers connected with makeshift passageways while holding aloft the weight of this metal island over them . . . Well, it's an accident waiting to happen." Jacobs pointed over the side at the ocean. "Neptune is down there, stomping his feet and rubbing his hands with glee, waiting for Sea Base to join him."

"Thanks, Master Chief. I'll sleep better tonight."

"Mr. Zeichner, if you sleep, you'll be doing better than me," Jacobs said softly.

"It's been four months since this guy Smith was killed," Agazzi said, bringing the subject back to his thoughts. "I haven't heard anything that indicates we are any nearer to finding out what happened to the real Smith he was impersonating, why he wanted to blow up Sea Base, and who he was."

"He didn't have to blow up Sea Base," said Jacobs. "He could have waited and the thing would have sunk itself."

"I don't have any additional information," said Zeichner. "No one at Naval Criminal Investigative Service headquarters seems to know what happened to the real Smith and with the imposter dead, we may never know. Whatever happened, happened sometime between when Smith graduated from boot camp and when he reported for sonar training."

Master Chief Jacobs pulled his cigar from between his lips, his heavy eyebrows curling into a V. "It's a far-fetched plan out of common reasoning is the reason why. Why do these Islamic radicals run around trying to take someone with them when they blow themselves up? Why don't they just strap those bombs to their chest, say so long to anyone who would miss them, walk out in the desert, and do the dirty deed? I'll tell you why. They're a cult. And every one of these cults believes some piece of shit, whether it's aliens picking them up to whisk them to heaven located on some ice-covered comet, or waiting for Armageddon when some magic hand will reach down and lift them to heaven. Or when they blow themselves up for some eleventh-century religion, some cab driver in heaven is going to meet them with seventy-two virgins or some shit like that. Religious people make me nervous. Give me a good old redneck with a case of beer any day and I'll show you intelligent design."

"I'm religious."

"Mr. Zeichner, the acceptable religions have grown benign over the centuries, thank God. You don't hear them out there trying to kill everyone who disagrees with how they worship. Unfortunately, some religions are still trapped in the eleventh century, and new cults are trying to head in that direction."

"Mr. Zeichner," Agazzi interrupted. "You were saying about this God's Army."

Zeichner turned from Jacobs, glancing up at the taller Agazzi. "Yes, I was," he said, slightly irritated, looking back at Jacobs, who had turned and walked a few steps away, his back to them. "This group isn't a big one, but has several thousand followers. Innocent enough on the surface, except they subscribe to the belief the world is so modern and efficient that eventually it will descend into anarchy. I would call them some sort of survivalist cult."

"Survivalists tend to weld themselves into some wilderness area and wait for the world to give them a reason to say they're right," Jacobs added over his shoulder.

Zeichner nodded. "Most do. This group apparently has a hard-core center with some sort of plan to hasten anarchy. Their followers believe the sooner they can cause global anarchy, the sooner they, the survivors, can start reforming the world into some sort of agriculture-based, horse-drawn society. Plus, from their religious perspective, they expect the Lord to return to earth sooner."

"What bullshit," said Jacobs.

"So, this Smith was a member of God's Army?"

Zeichner shook his head and shrugged. "Not sure if he was a lone follower trying to hasten Armageddon or part of this senior hard-core bunch."

"He wasn't acting alone," Jacobs said, looking at them from the safety lines a few feet away.

"Why would you say that?"

"Well, Mr. Zeichner, he was young. Too young to know enough shit to fool the Navy to get his young butt sent to sea on Sea Base. Sent to sea and with access to the explosives he needed to blow up the server farm on USNS *Denebola,* blow up the aircraft, and rig the UUVs to blow up and take all of Sea Base with him. He had help. You need to trace his steps backward."

Zeichner nodded. "We agree on that, Master Chief. We are tracking Smith's path to the ship. We know the original Smith—the one who should have been in the Anti-Submarine control center on the *Algol* and trained to work the manual Unmanned Underwater Vehicles on board the *Bellatrix*—disappeared somewhere between boot camp at Great Lakes and the A-school where he learned basic ASW techniques. The real Smith had orders to a ship in Norfolk."

"Then, how did he wind up in Pearl Harbor?"

"Insider help, Senior Chief. In the middle of the real Smith—or by then the new Smith—going through A-school, he received new orders diverting him to Sea Base."

"That happens a lot nowadays," Agazzi said. "We're a smaller Navy so we redirect people when we need them elsewhere."

Zeichner agreed. "You're right, but according to the Bureau of Naval Personnel, they don't usually redirect boot seamen from one coast to another. Not cost-effective."

"So, who cut his orders to Sea Base? Someone inside BUPERS?" Jacobs asked, using the acronym for Bureau of Naval Personnel. He rejoined the two men.

"You're probably right. We have agents in Millington, Tennessee, going through the computer records at the Naval Personnel Command to see who did."

Jacobs nodded. "You find who did that, then you find another piece of this puzzle?"

"Right. Another piece of the puzzle. Plus we find another link to the trail that sent this man to Sea Base."

"Senior Chief!" came a shout from the nearby hatch leading below the deck of Sea Base.

The three men turned. A sailor ran toward them.

"Senior Chief!" he shouted again.

"Slow down, Seaman Gentron," Agazzi said when the young sailor reached them. Sweat poured down the sailor's face to a uniform dungaree shirt already spotted under the arms from perspiration. "What is it?"

"We have a contact, Senior Chief," Gentron said between gasps for breath.

Agazzi moved fast, leaving the two men exchanging glances. He led the way with Gentron following. "What kind and where is it?"

"Submarine bearing two-eight-zero, Senior Chief. Petty Officer Keyland estimates a hundred nautical miles away."

Agazzi started down the ladder. "Approaching?"

"He didn't say, Senior Chief. He just said, 'Go get the senior chief,' so that's what I did."

"Nothing else?"

"Well, he did seem excited."

CAPTAIN Scott "How High" Delaney waited until the canopy opened fully and the hum of the hydraulic ceased before grabbing both sides of the cockpit and pulling himself half up from the seat.

"Good flight, Captain?" someone shouted from the flight deck.

Delaney pointed at his helmet and pulled his helmet off. "Chief Willard, what a great sight for tired eyes. Guess you're out here to train us junior officers?" he shouted at the heavyset man in the Air Force flight suit, the collar devices identifying him as an E-9: chief master sergeant. Only the top one percent of the enlisted military ever achieved the coveted rank of E-9. Chief Willard stood on the deck, legs spread, with both hands on his hips, looking up at him. "I thought you were back at Scott Air Force Base, or was it Nellis?"

"Naw, it was neither, Captain," Willard said, pushing his light blue ball cap back off his bald forehead. "It was Andrews, playing nursemaid to a bunch of politicians and wannabe generals."

"How did you swing this cherry duty?"

"I told the general he needed mature leadership out here with you fighter pilots. Too much uncontrollable testosterone running around . . ."

"Better hope Major Johnson doesn't hear you say that."

The smile left Willard's face. Delaney laughed.

"I heard she's coming out," Willard said.

Delaney turned and nodded toward the second F-22A taxiing into parking position. "None other. And I know you'll join me in congratulating her on being assigned as the Detachment Commander until the colonel arrives with the remainder of the squadron." Delaney remained unsmiling as he turned toward the small ladder leading down from the cockpit to the deck. The hell he and the other pilots expected for the next three to four weeks was nothing compared to how Johnson treated the enlisted. He crawled over the lip of the cockpit and climbed down the small ladder to the deck.

Delaney bent down and touched the metal deck. Then, he jumped a couple of times on it. "So this is what an aircraft carrier feels like at sea?"

"Sir, don't let the swabbies hear you call this an aircraft carrier. I haven't quite figured out what they think of this thing they call Sea Base. Some refer to it as the largest aircraft carrier in the world; others a floating island; and the ones wearing life vests most of the time call it a death trap." Willard glanced over at the second F-22A and the visage of the pilot strapped inside the cockpit. As he watched, she removed her helmet.

"Well, Captain, you couldn't have brought me better news than Major Johnson being the DETCO until . . ."

"I wouldn't call her DETCO, Chief. I did." Delaney looked back at his own butt. "Wow! Must have grown back on the flight over."

Willard pulled the zipper of the flight suit up a little higher, nearer Air Force uniform regulation. "That's what a detachment commander is, sir. Has been for my twenty-six years of active by-God Air Force duty."

"Well, things change, Chief. She prefers to be called Commander."

"She does, does she?"

"Lots of activity here, Chief Willard," Delaney said, changing the subject. "What's that over there?"

Willard looked in the direction Delaney pointed. "That's the tower complex. Within those three stories, it's where they control, fight, and manage everything on this platform from engine rooms on the ships holding it up to the weapon systems you see topside to fight it."

"We going to see those ships?"

"Sir, you're going to live in one."

Major Louise Johnson stood up in her cockpit. She laid her helmet on her seat. She looked around the flight deck, and Delaney knew she was counting the number of aircraft on the tarmac.

"Chief, how many of the squadron birds are here?" Delaney asked.

"Ummm. With yours and hers, sir, we have eight on board. Of those eight, two are boring holes in the sky out front of Sea Base's path, reconnoitering to the northwest. One is down for repairs and—" Damn! He'd failed to check on the status of the parts after lunch. Willard bit his lower lip and shook his head. "The two on the other side of Major Johnson's Raptor are scheduled to launch in about an hour to relieve the pair out now."

Delaney looked at his wristwatch. "Thanks, Chief. I reset my watch en route to Sea Base. I show around 11:20 A.M. Is that right?"

Willard glanced at his. "Close enough, Captain. By the way, I don't have an up-to-date status on the spare parts for Raptor 223, and you probably have a better idea when the squadron commander is coming than I do."

"Thanks, Chief. That may just get me through the next five minutes."

"A chief master sergeant shouldn't have to put up with this shit," Willard mumbled softly.

"What'd you say, Chief Willard?"

"Nothing, sir. Just thinking—with such a lovely day at sea, there has to be a storm over the horizon," he replied, forcing a smile across his face that turned genuine when he saw Delaney's grin. "Plus, my fine young junior officer entrusted with the Air Force's highest-priced, phenomenal stealth aircraft, it's just a pleasure for an old man such as myself to see a bright smiling face. The great news that you brought Major Johnson with you will not be lost on the troops."

Delaney laughed. "It was great news to me also."

Johnson saw the two men, raised her hand, and gave a half-hearted wave. Willard didn't bother returning it. The wave was an acknowledgment to her fellow fighter pilot and subordinate. Willard and the others had learned quickly her dislike for those who wore their ranks on their arms instead of their shoulders.

"I think I need to check the other aircraft and make sure the ground crews did their jobs right, Captain. So, if you'd give my excuses to the major . . ."

"Forget it, Chief Master Sergeant Willard of the mightiest Air Force in the world," Delaney said, tugging at Willard's flight suit. "Major Johnson is going to have questions. She'll expect me to already know the answers because I landed a few minutes before she did. If she asks anything more than number and location of the aircraft, then I'm going to follow the age-honored aviator motto of 'Heat on you is heat off me.' Then I'm going to sidestep quickly behind your hefty bulk for shelter."

"Sir, you are definitely destined for better things," Willard said out of the side of his mouth. For a slight moment, he had thought age and wisdom were going to triumph over youth and exuberance. "You should buy your stars now."

Delaney laughed. "Congratulations, by the way. We were told at Langley you were going to be the First Sergeant when you return," Delaney said, glancing over at Willard.

Delaney was right. He was going to be the First Sergeant. A flush of pride rushed through his body over the honor the Air Force had bestowed on him. The First Sergeant was the senior enlisted person in the squadron, entrusted with keeping the commander fully informed on the morale of the troops, leading the senior enlisted in working together to meet the mission of the squadron, and when necessary, shutting the door with the commander and telling him or her why a certain order or command was a "piece of shit." A chief master sergeant unwilling to step up to the plate and tell a senior officer his or her opinion when it conflicted with squadron policy or actions wasn't much of a chief master sergeant in Willard's mind. You were either part of the top one percent in the military, or you weren't.

"Quite a compliment to your leadership, Chief."

Willard nodded. "Thank you, Captain. I'm the First Sergeant for the detachment, and guess headquarters is giving me the whole kit and caboodle when Chief Reese leaves next month. The orders only arrived this morning."

"That's quite an accomplishment."

Willard watched as Major Louise "Call Me Pickles" Johnson climbed down from her fighter. Maybe the reward wasn't going to be worth the agony of tact facing him in the days to come. He glanced at his watch, looking at the date, wondering how long it would be until the colonel arrived.

Johnson stopped on the small side ladder leading from the F-22A cockpit, reached back inside, and grabbed her helmet. She then quickly scrambled down to the deck, where she motioned to a nearby airman and handed her helmet to the young man.

Willard grimaced. Those helmets cost thousands of dollars and most pilots never let go of them. They baby them. They polish them. Most have their call names embossed on them. He looked at the HGU-86/P helmet tucked under Delaney's left arm. Dark black letters over the dual visors read HOW HIGH. Right now, not high enough.

The HGU-86/P helmet was specially designed for the F-22A. The design reduced the stress to the pilot's neck by twenty percent during ejection over the older HGU-55/P helmet. Each helmet was individually designed and built for each pilot. No pilot had two of them . . . or at least, they weren't supposed to. If your HGU-86/P was damaged or lost, then you could still fly, but you made do with one from the supply locker until Air Force headquarters finished reviewing your statement and your commander's endorsement as to why you needed a replacement. Then, if the Air Force believed your story, you got a second one. No, the helmet was the F-22A fighter pilot's friend. It couldn't sit up and beg like a dog, but it could wrap around your head like the thighs of a lover. Losing or damaging one through misuse or failing to take care of it was something the Air Force did not tolerate well. The Air Force believed anything that showed a lack of attention to detail was a leadership flaw.

The left corner of Willard's lip curled up and his brow wrinkled. He could hardly believe she'd hand the helmet to some airman first class who'd been in the world's mightiest Air Force for all of nearly six months. The young airman looked up, nervously glancing at the two more experienced airmen near her. Willard's eyes widened. "Jesus, Mother of Mary!" he mumbled when he saw the young airman give the helmet to Snaggles, of all people.

"Sergeant Thomas!" Willard shouted, moving away from Delaney.

Delaney reached toward Willard, his fingers barely missing the flight suit of the senior enlisted man. "Chief!" he said sharply.

A tall lanky man, hair peeking from under his ball cap, a set of noise suppressors, commonly called "ears," pushed up onto his temples, waved at Willard.

"Come here," Willard said, his right hand motioning quickly. "I'm not calling you because I like you." He felt the tug on his flight suit.

"Chief?"

"I'm not going anywhere, Captain."

The tech sergeant hurried to Willard's side. Willard leaned over and whispered a few instructions to the man.

Thomas turned and hurriedly walked toward Major Johnson's Raptor, slowing to salute her as they passed. As soon as she passed, he ran to the airman and took the helmet from him.

Willard snapped to attention, his legs coming together and his feet at a forty-five-degree angle. "Afternoon, Major," he said, raising his hand in a salute.

"Uh-oh," Delaney muttered.

"Chief, how many aircraft are supposed to be here?" Johnson asked, returning the salute. She started taking off her gloves as her eyes met his.

"With your two, ma'am, eight. Glad to have you on board, Major."

"It's Commander, First Sergeant. Until Colonel Stephens arrives in a month or so, let's use the term. It will allow the airmen to understand who is in charge. I want no confusion on their part."

"Would the major prefer DETCO to Commander, ma'am?"

"If the major preferred DETCO to Commander, the major would have said DETCO, Chief," Johnson replied with a little laugh. "DETCO sounds . . . well, it makes me think of something a jazz mortician would call a dead body."

"Yes, ma'am," Chief Willard said, thinking her definition made DETCO the more applicable term.

She turned to Delaney. "Where are the rest of the pilots?"

"Maj—Commander, I just landed with you. Chief Willard, do you know?"

"Commander, they are either in their staterooms, the ready room, eating, flying, working out, or . . .," He stopped.

"Or what?"

"Nothing, Commander. We have two flying. The other six are here somewhere."

"Thanks, Chief, but you said 'or.' What was the 'or' for?"

"Fishing, ma'am. The Navy is very big into fishing contests on Sea Base, so some of the pilots and the crew formed their own Air Force team. Yesterday, they—"

"Chief," Johnson interrupted. "Fishing isn't something I find interesting. Send word to everyone that I want to meet with them as soon as possible." She paused as she looked at her watch, then she looked at Willard. "What is the correct local time here, First Sergeant?"

"It's 1134 hours," Willard said. Yep, it was going to be a "rewarding" experience with Johnson in charge.

She looked back at Delaney. "I would have thought Major Crawford would have met me. I'm sure something is going on more important than meeting the new commander." She took her watch off and set it.

"Chief. Tell them I want everyone in the ready room no later than 1200. Think you can do that, First Sergeant?" she asked, staring Willard directly in the eyes as if daring him to disagree.

Stay calm, Willard told himself—think of your ex-wife. Reaching up, he pushed his hat farther back, exposing more of his shaven dome. "Yes, ma'am. I believe I may be able to do that. You want everyone, correct? Does that include the enlisted, because if you do, ma'am, I'll have to pull them off the flight line."

"Don't be ridiculous, Chief," she said with a laugh. "Just the officers, not the enlisted. By the way, Chief Willard, now that you're the First Sergeant, and I hear that you're going to be the First Sergeant permanently because Chief Reese is retiring, you need to look the part. That ball cap is filthy. It has grease and oil fingerprints all over the bib and when you push it back, which by the way is against Air Force regulations, you got sweat marks running all the way out to the edge." She wrinkled her nose as her lips pursed. "Let's set a good example for the airmen and junior officers, why don't we?"

"I'll get on it," he said with a quiet sigh, pulling the ball cap forward. This ball cap had been with him on every deployment since he'd made chief master sergeant. It was his good-luck ball cap. He wondered if it would survive a wash, knowing it would be eviscerated if he tried to send it to one of the industrial laundries on Sea Base.

"Good. You're dismissed."

Willard saluted and walked away. *Dismissed. I'm dismissed?* Blood rushed upward turning his face red. "I'm dismissed! I'm dismissed," he mumbled aloud as he walked away. *This ten-year-career major has dismissed me as if I'm some sort of airman first class . . . no, not even an airman first class. She dismissed me as if I was a basic, a know-nothing Gawldamned airman!* Thank God she didn't represent the majority of the Air Force officers.

In her sharp North Carolina twang, he heard her tell Delaney, "The First Sergeant needs to lose a few pounds, too, Captain Delaney. Have a talk with him. We don't want the colonel arriving to discover he made a mistake."

He knew she meant for him to hear it. *Someday, woman, you'll look down, see a few rolls, and wonder what turning forty did to you.*

"Chief," Sergeant Thomas greeted as Willard approached. "What you want me to do with HNF's helmet?"

"It's Commander to you, Lou. And you make sure your crew knows I want nothing but respect shown to the DETCO."

"Okay, First Sergeant. You don't have to bite my head off. All I want to know is what do we do with her helmet."

"Don't ask a dumb question, Lou." His eyes narrowed and he bit his lower lip lightly. He took the helmet roughly from Thomas, twisted it a couple of times as he inspected it.

"Hey, Chief. What's a matter? Your hemorrhoids acting up or something?"

"Quit your complaining, Lou. You're a sailor now."

"Ah, Chief. Why did you have to go and say that?"

The HGU-86P was perfect, even her personal call sign, personally picked by her, PICKLES, was embossed above the visor.

"Can't believe she left it with Snaggles," Thomas said. "It's a wonder he didn't rush over to the safety lines and toss it in the drink."

"Let's thank his inherent lethargy that he didn't," Willard said, looking at the word "Pickles."

Pilots never picked their own handle. Like ancient tribes, their fellow pilots determined a pilot's handle. Willard heard that Johnson had picked her own handle, "Pickles." Pilots the same rank or senior to her never used the term. The slight wasn't lost on the men.

There were other handles a pilot received. Bestowed by the men and women who had to work for them. The enlisted had bestowed on her the handle "HNF," which stood for "Hard Ass, No Ass, Flat Ass," because of her attitude and the seat of her flight suit that seemed to flop when she walked. Little did they realize how close to her true call sign they were.

His thoughts slipped back to six months ago at Langley when he had run into his old friend Senior Master Sergeant Carl Mortimer of the 510th, who had given him all the dirt over beers at his house. She had been given the call sign "Flat Cheeks" at a fighter-pilot naming session at the officers' club. Things went downhill from there. She complained "Flat Cheeks" was a sexist call sign directed at her lack of a butt.

Willard turned and squinted at Johnson, who was talking with Delaney. His lower lip pushed into his upper lip. Yep, she doesn't have much of one.

Mortimer told him the pilots—some of whom were female—said the call sign was because of her pulling hard G's that flatten buttocks. Either way, the squadron commander let her have her way. Six months later she was gone. Hand-selected for the F-22A program; a promotion that improved morale at her old command. Of course, it didn't do squat for the 28th.

"Look who finally showed up," Thomas said, nodding over Willard's shoulder.

Across Sea Base ran first Lieutenant "Angels" Zimmerman, the junior officer of the detachment and the person in charge of berthing arrangements.

The young officer slowed as he approached Major Johnson and Captain Delaney. Johnson started talking. Willard could hear the voice, but the distance and noise of Sea Base covered what she was saying. It was enough that Zimmerman was nodding furiously, acknowledging every blast from Major Johnson. Willard smiled. *Welcome to the real Air Force, Lieutenant Zimmerman.*

He handed the helmet back to Thomas. "Just follow the major to her stateroom and make sure she takes it."

"Ah, come on, First Sergeant, I'm a ground tech. I shouldn't be the one doing this for HNF. Why don't I give it back to Snaggles and let him follow her down?"

Willard shook his head. "First, I don't want to hear you or

anyone else refer to Major Johnson as HNF or anything other than Commander."

"Ah, Chief, you know what I mean."

"I know what you mean, but you're my number-two person out here on the flight line. The troops are going to be looking toward you for leadership. That means no derogatory comments about the officers. Understand?"

"Yes, Chief Master Sergeant. I understand." Thomas sighed.

"Good. Now you take the helmet to Major Johnson. You just took it from Snaggles and no way we're going to give it back to him. Snaggles gets lost on the flight deck. You send him belowdecks into the cave of the swabbies and it may be the last time we ever see him. Besides, if Snaggles decides it's too hard to do, that helmet will be over the side being fish bait for those sharks swimming beneath us. Besides, Sergeant Thomas, this is good leadership training and an opportunity for some face time with our new commander."

"Oh, I see," Thomas said. "You don't want to lose an airman first class, but you're willing to sacrifice a top-notch E-5 tech sergeant to the jaws of—"

Willard opened his mouth to say something, but Thomas motioned him away.

"Okay, okay, okay. I know, Chief Master Sergeant. I'll go do it, but if I'm not back within an hour, send a rescue party."

"You'll do fine, Lou. Major Johnson is a professional fighter pilot who has just inherited the major responsibility of ensuring our performance on Sea Base achieves what the Chief of Staff of the Air Force has directed—proving we are as capable at sea doing air operations as we are ashore."

"Oh, yeah, I forgot. I'll do fine because she doesn't know we exist."

"Sergeant Thomas, what did I tell you?"

He waved Willard away. "I'm going, I'm going," he complained as he walked off, following the three officers who were heading belowdecks.

TWO

"Captain's in Combat," the Tactical Action Officer, Commander Stan Stapler, announced as Captain Hank Garcia stepped through the hatch leading from the two floors above Combat.

"What you got, Commander?" Hank asked, setting his coffee cup on a nearby chart table. He looked up at the LCD display mounted on the forward bulkhead.

"Those bogies seem to be growing in number, Captain. When I briefed you a couple of hours ago, satellite reflected them leaving the North Korean landmass. At that time, all they did was establish a racetrack pattern about twelve miles off the coast. Satellite radar and intelligence reports indicated a combat air patrol. I think it could be because Sea Base moved into the SOJ," Stapler said, referring to the Sea of Japan. "Original estimates indicated no more than ten formations of two aircraft each."

Garcia picked up his cup and took a drink. "I take it that has changed?"

"Since 1500, when we briefed you, Skipper, we watched the North Koreans fly the same figure-eight pattern over and over again. Every now and then, a formation breaks off and returns to North Korea, probably to refuel. For every formation that breaks off, a two-plane formation replaces them in the pattern.

I should mention that over the past hour the number of formations increased from the original ten to eighteen."

"Yes," Garcia answered morosely. "You should mention it, Commander. You should have told me fifty-five minutes ago instead of now."

"Yes, sir. My apologies, Skipper. It won't happen again." Stapler quickly changed the subject with a laser pointer, highlighting the returns on the bulkhead LCD display. "Since they continued doing the same racetrack, I didn't think too much of it. They're four hundred nautical miles away."

"In the future, Commander, keep me up to date on things as they change," Garcia said, a hint of displeasure in his voice.

"Aye, sir. I didn't want to bother you."

"Bother me, please. I enjoy it."

"A few minutes ago, the formations started having hiccups."

"Hiccups?"

"Yes, sir," Stapler answered. "When aircraft fly close together, it is hard to distinguish how many aircraft actually make up a formation. The radar returns one blip, mashed together because of the proximity of the aircraft within the formation. Even Naval Intelligence units in South Korea reported two fighters per formation."

"Okay. I think I know where this is going."

"Look at this, sir. Chief," Stapler called to the chief petty officer standing nearby. "Take us down."

On the LCD screen above the radar and weapon consoles, images started collapsing until only two radar returns filled the screen. From that vantage point Garcia knew he was looking at a satellite return. The two bogies went into a turn. The bogie on the outside of the turn suddenly split into two pieces of video. The inner bogie inside the turn appeared to elongate as it maintained its position to the outer image.

"Looks like three aircraft," Garcia offered.

Stapler nodded. "It does, but there are four of them. In the turns, it's harder for them to maintain speed and distance. The radar has shown as many as four aircraft in a formation."

"Eighteen formations?"

"Yes, sir. Eight more formations than the original ten, but instead of thirty-six aircraft out there, we may have as many as seventy-two, sir. . . ."

"Seventy-two," Garcia interrupted. "Why in the hell would

the North Koreans want seventy-two fighters buzzing around off their coast? It isn't as if they couldn't launch in time to stop anything coming from the east."

"That's not all, Skipper," Stapler said. "Chief, show the large ones."

"Large ones?"

The displayed image shifted. The image dropped away as the focus zoomed outward. Then the display panned toward the west for a few seconds before starting to zoom inward. When the shift of the satellite radar stopped, Garcia was watching four images of radar video in a flight pattern.

"What am I looking at?'

"Sir, these four bogies are flying lower than the eighteen fighter formations orbiting at eighteen thousand feet. They are flying near the Korean landmass at around ten thousand feet. The land smear complicates the radar return. But they are individual aircraft, larger than the four-aircraft formations, and slower."

On the screen four aircraft trailed one another as they executed an oval racetrack a few miles off the upper North Korean peninsula.

"What are they?"

Stapler shrugged, then said, "I think they're heavy bombers."

The sound-powered phone talker, standing near the Electronic Warfare AN/SLQ-32 suite, pushed his mouthpiece out of the way. "Commander, sonar reports they have a submarine contact."

"Whose?"

"They didn't say, sir. Just said an unidentified submarine bearing two-four-zero degrees true, directly off our starboard beam. Beam?" the young seaman repeated, wondering for a moment where the beam was on something such as Sea Base. On a ship, it would mean directly off the left or right side of the ship; in this case off meant in the right-hand direction to Sea Base.

"Ask them range."

"They have no estimate at this time, sir."

"Tell them to give me an estimated range!" Stapler shouted. He turned to the chief. "Chief, I want a sound-powered phone talker right there beside the Skipper's chair," Stapler ordered, pointing to an empty space between Garcia's chair and the plotting table. "I don't want to have to shout over the weapons and radar consoles to relay orders via the sound-powered phones."

"We still haven't straightened out the communications problems on Sea Base, Commander. Are sound-power telephones all we have?" asked Garcia.

"No, sir. I have regular telephones and some limited intercom, but the most reliable and most widespread comm at this time is the sound-powered telephone system the chief engineers managed to rig."

"The submarine bothers me, Stan. We need more information on it. The aircraft are four hundred miles away and we'd know if they decided to get froggy."

Stapler turned to Garcia. "Sir, the submarine is the immediate issue, but whenever the North Koreans are doing something, it makes me nervous."

"Makes two of us, Commander."

"You never know what they're going to do."

Garcia nodded. "Whatever it is, it is always something dumb, arrogant, and unexpected. What do we have out there?"

"We have a two-F-22A Raptor formation—distance, Chief?"

"Raptor formation is 140 nautical miles, bearing three-four-zero degrees, sir!" He ran his hand through his rich crop of blond hair. "They've been out there a couple of hours. We'll have to relieve them sooner than I expected. Raptor 10 is already complaining about fuel consumption."

"Do what you have to do, Stan," Garcia said softly. His eyebrows furrowed as he asked, "What's the weapons status of Sea Base?"

"Sir, laser and rail guns are in place, but we've only done limited testing of them since the engineers finished the installations. The fire control radars for them are up and running. I had the fire-control spectrum for the rail guns switched from gunfire support to antiair-warfare mode."

"So, they're activated—up and running?"

"Not yet, Captain. I have them manned, but I have them powered down. I was concerned about keeping them activated for too long."

"But if we wait until we need them to turn them on, Stan, we run the risk of discovering problems we could have corrected. Let's activate them and have the crews do their diagnostics. We want them up and ready for use. Just in case, you know—no other reason, so don't let the crew get nervous about it."

"Sir, you want to go to general quarters?"

Garcia's lower lip pushed up against the upper and his eyes narrowed as he thought about the question. The prudent thing would be to call GQ, but if he called it and the North Koreans only continued posturing off their coast, then Sea Base would be locked down. The work of the platform would come to a halt. Sea Base might have to fight for its survival if the North Koreans did their "Let's show our teeth and be arrogant" thing. Meanwhile, Sea Base still had a lot of work to be done to reach full warfighting capability. When Garcia failed to respond to Stapler's question, the taciturn Tactical Action Officer continued.

"Unless you have other orders, Skipper, I intend to launch our SH-36 LAMPS and lay some sonobuoy patterns around Sea Base. See if we can locate this unidentified submarine sonar has."

"The submarine is probably Chinese."

"Yes, sir; probably is. I would prefer it be Chinese and not North Korean."

Garcia's eyebrows furrowed deeper at the thought. He shook his head. "The North Koreans only have a bunch of old 1970s-era Soviet submarines. I'd be surprised if they sent them out of sight of land."

"But they could."

"Any weapons anyone has can be used for things you'd never expect," Garcia countered. "That's what we're doing with Sea Base."

"I hope it's Chinese," Stapler said, gritting his teeth. "Even so, Skipper, we're going to have to do something about it. We can't have it tailing us wherever we go."

Since the encounter a few weeks ago, everyone up and down the chain of command had speculated that the Chinese were keeping a submarine nearby observing them. Why, after all this time trailing them, would the Chinese let themselves be detected? Garcia's eyes widened. Unless the submarine wasn't Chinese, but North Korean? Even though he had just argued the North Koreans would never chance sending their submarines far from their coast, maybe they had. Maybe the North Koreans intended to activate their total war plan against the South Koreans and the United States. Worst case for Sea Base would be if the North Koreans wanted to make a statement and launch a preemptive attack against them. America had been attacked unexpectedly in its history, and each time it was because of the refusal to expect the unexpected.

Garcia took a deep breath. "Go ahead and lay the sonobuoy patterns, Commander Stapler. Have Senior Chief Agazzi send some UUVs out to see what he can find. It'll give them a chance to practice some underwater ballet on those things. As for GQ, hold off on calling general quarters until we really have to do so, Commander." He clasped his hands behind his back and rocked back and forth a couple of times. "Let's keep the Air Force out in front of us until I tell you differently."

"Yes, sir. Raptor Formation . . ."

"Raptor Formation?" Garcia asked seriously. "You're calling them Raptor Formation? That's what the Air Force uses?"

Stapler's eyes shifted back and forth. "Sir, I didn't ask them. Just gave them the formation title recommended by Combat, Captain."

Garcia nodded. "In the future, ask them what they would prefer and as long as it doesn't conflict with doctrine or security, we'll use their preference."

"Yes, sir."

"Meanwhile, keep them between us and the North Korean CAP. Let's see what the North Koreans do."

Stapler smiled. "They don't know the Air Force fighters are out there. According to Naval Intelligence, the North Koreans aren't showing signs they have detected the F-22A formation. If the North Koreans do some macho-shit thing, those 22s will wipe the skies of them."

"Let's hope you're right, Commander, and this stealth technology works, huh?"

"Wish we had some on Sea Base right now."

"Hard to hide over eighty acres of metal riding eight stories above the ocean."

"Thought it was four."

"Four stories above the Fast Sealift Ships. I like to add another four stories to account for the ships' height above the water. You think that's okay, Commander?" Garcia asked in a nice tone.

"Yes, sir, Skipper. You are the Captain."

Garcia smiled, thinking of how his mother would have beamed at such a statement. "Yes, I am, aren't I?" he said softly as he picked up his coffee. "Stan, I'm going up to the tower for a few minutes; then I'll be back in my quarters. If the North Korean aircraft break the CAP and turn toward us, sound general quarters. If the submarine turns out to be anything other than Chinese, then sound general quarters."

"Could be Japanese."

"Wish it was, but we both know it isn't."

Stapler acknowledged the order and watched as Garcia headed toward the ladder leading up one floor to the Skipper's stateroom directly below the air tower on the top level.

At the foot of the ladder, Garcia stopped. "Commander Stapler, contact that nice young pilot who's been in charge since the Air Force arrived and ask him to join us in Combat."

"Yes, sir. Will do, but I think their new detachment commander arrived an hour ago."

"HEY, Alex, what would you think of doing this for a career?" Ronny "Fast Pace" Walters asked. "Just think—every day those Navy pilots fly over the same scene. Day after day. Look below us. No matter how high we go, it's the same thing. Nothing but ocean. We're so far out in front of Sea Base, we can't see anything but the wake of a few freighters below us."

"I was thinking the same thing. No trees, no hills, no golf course, no herds of sheep to buzz so we can watch them run together knocking over the herdsman. It isn't fitting for fine outstanding Air Force fighter pilots to be doing what we're doing. Nope, I think this is a Navy trick and we fell for it."

"What trick?"

"We used to argue we could replace those hotshot Navy pilots, so they've given us our chance. They knew we'd see how boring it is. Meanwhile, they're back with our wives and girlfriends telling them what hotshots they are. Just hope they're not using my clubs. Nope, I've decided to support the Navy. They can keep their carriers and their air wings. They can stay out at sea as long as they want. They can drink that—what do they call it?"

"Bug juice," Walters answered.

"They can drink their bug juice forever until it turns their liver pink. Besides, Fast Pace, the two most important things to us Air Force fighter pilots is missing—no officers' club and no golf course."

"It's a shit life sometime, Blackman. Where do they expect us happily married men to help you young, lonely single bachelors get hitched—"

"What? And have me come home to the same—"

"Don't say it or I'll tell Connie and you will have had your last free home-cooked meal in our house."

"I don't know, Ronny. I've eaten Connie's cooking for nearly a year now and I seem to be losing weight."

"I never said she knew how to cook."

"Raptor One Zero, this is Raptor Haven," came a voice over the radio.

"Raptor Haven. I'm going to be sick," Alex "Blackman" Franklin said, looking at Fast Pace through his cockpit window and making the one-finger gesture toward his mouth. "We are going to have to talk to the Navy about their call-sign etiquette."

"Raptor Haven, Raptor One Zero, standing by."

"Not much chance of disguising what type of fighter aircraft we are," Franklin broadcast in Fast Pace's other ear.

"Weapons check."

"Weapons check! How often do they want us to do weapons check? Must be a Navy thing. They think the weapons fell off and dropped in the ocean and we forgot to mention it?"

Fast Pace reached over and switched the radio off for a moment. "Can it, Blackman, while I put salve on whatever ails them. They don't have the downlink capability up and running yet."

"Roger."

Walters flicked back to the main channel.

"Weapons check. Do you copy?"

"Copy fivers, Homeplate. Full load-out: two Sidewinders and six AMRAAMs." AMRAAM was short for Advanced Medium Range Air-to-Air Missile. Sidewinders were the venerable active and infrared-seeking air-to-air missiles that had been in the U.S. military inventory since after the Korean War, nearly seventy years ago. Walters pressed the icon on the control panel. "Electronics show weapons ready."

"Raptor Two Zero, Raptor Haven. Weapons check."

"Raptor Two Zero. Full load-out: two Sidewinders, six AMRAAM missiles, and a fully loaded M61A2 cannon." Blackman looked through the cockpit window at Walters and touched his helmet with a two-finger salute.

"Roger, Raptor Two Zero."

"Raptor Formation, check secure comms."

"Secure comms functioning," Walters replied.

The bagpipe sound of the cryptographic systems synchronizing echoed across their earpieces. A few seconds later, the slight background buzz of a secure voice circuit replaced the earlier voice communications. Several transmissions went back and forth between Walters and Sea Base to ensure the secure link was up and functioning.

Satisfied, the Sea Base communications person was replaced with the earlier voice. "Raptor Formation. Fuel state?"

Ronny looked at one of the two Up-Front Displays reflected on the front of his cockpit. An Inter/Intra-Flight Data Link (IFDL) connected the two aircraft so the two F-22A fighters automatically shared fuel and weapons status and, during combat, target data without any voice communications. The IFDL reflected this data on the windshield of the cockpit so the pilot's eyes never left the direction the aircraft was flying.

The United States Air Force had taken the science of information technology and leaped ahead of every fighter aircraft in the world. The IFDL was just one more element contributing to the stealth qualities of the world's most lethal and hard-to-detect fighter aircraft.

Once a formation broke apart in the heat of combat, keeping track of the other members of your formation as well as other friendlies in the battle became nearly impossible—only the shouting through the airways echoing in your earpiece gave any indication of how your fellow fighter pilots were doing.

That changed with the F-22A. The IDFL allowed each pilot to operate autonomously, but no matter at what point or where they were in a combat situation, they knew where each of their fellow pilots were. They also knew the fuel and weapons status of every F-22A Raptor in their formation, and if necessary, each pilot could tell when it was time to break off and haul ass home or do a series of coordinated victory rolls over the combat scene.

"Fuel sixty-five," Ronny broadcast.

"Roger, stand by."

CAPTAIN Garcia opened his stateroom door. "My apologies, Admiral," he said as he shut the door. "Looks as if the North

Koreans are playing operational deception with our radar and our intelligence."

Vice Admiral Dick Holman, Commander, United States Seventh Fleet, rose from the deep comfort of Garcia's personal chair and walked to the nearby sink, pouring the remains of his coffee down the drain. "What are they doing now? Trailing banners from their tails screaming and hollering how no one gives them any respect? They're the Rodney Dangerfields of the world, only they actually believe everyone is out to get them."

Garcia nodded as he moved to one of the four straight-back chairs shoved under the small oval table used for everything from work to eating. "Being paranoid doesn't necessarily mean you're wrong. They sleep at night convinced the big, bad Americans are going to be streaming through their streets when they wake up."

"That's what their government keeps beating into the heads of their citizens. I think their citizens are beginning to realize that a full stomach is more important than who is in charge of their country."

Garcia set his cup in the sink. "Could be, Admiral, but would we put our stomachs before our freedom?"

Across the compartment, a first-class petty officer wiped his hands as he stepped back from the eight-cup coffeepot. "Admiral, Skipper, the coffee will be ready shortly."

Garcia thanked him as the sailor left through the door on the forward bulkhead of the combined living room and kitchenette of the Skipper's cabin.

"I think we've been down this argument before, Hank. You are the most liberal Navy captain I know. It's a wonder they even let you past the gates in the morning."

Admiral Holman sat back down in Garcia's chair. Garcia sat down at the table. "Being liberal does not mean being unpatriotic."

"Okay," Holman said, motioning the argument away. "We can argue this later, preferably over a cigar and a drink."

"The drink sounds good. Now, aren't you glad that we have merchant marine ships holding up Sea Base? Means we can have a beer or two every week."

"For every Navy misfortune, there is some silver lining in the clouds. Now, enough of this shit, Hank. What are the NORCOMs up to?"

"Seems the original two aircraft in ten formations is more

like eighteen formations with each formation composed of four aircraft. We also have a submarine contact off our starboard side. About a hundred miles according to ASW control center. We'll watch him. I'm not too concerned with the contact. We had a Chinese submarine identified on the western side of Sea Base when we first started our test and evaluation four months ago. Plus, Naval Intelligence sent us a message speculating the Chinese have been surveilling us since that close encounter. We have had a couple of contacts since then. Most times the contacts are sporadic and then disappear as the undersea environmentals change. I expect ASW control center to report their loss of contact soon."

Holman nodded, patting his pocket to ensure his Padron 3000 cigar was still there. "I'd keep a close eye on the submarine, especially if it has any kind of underwater missile launch capability."

"I think if they had wanted to attack us they would have by now."

"Things change and shit happens, Hank."

"I have authorized ASW to launch a couple of UUVs to guard against the submarine. I'll keep them down there as long as their fuel lasts and replace them if the submarine threat continues to exist."

"It's the North Korean fighters that bother me more. The explosions last week in Ottawa and New York have stirred up their little hornet's nest. The fact they've tried to hide the number of aircraft tells me they're up to something. Usually the NORCOMs bluster and flex their military might without any guile. They want everyone to know what they're willing to do. How far away from North Korea is Sea Base?" Holman leaned back and drummed his fingers on the leather arms of the chair.

"We're nearing the four-hundred-nautical-mile range. Our—pardon me—*your* orders have us setting up an area of operations at the three-hundred-nautical-mile range. Right now, we are on a course of three-three-zero, eight knots."

"What do you think of us stopping Sea Base right here? Setting up operations a hundred miles farther out. Would you have any problems with such an order?"

"No, sir," Garcia replied, straddling the chair he had pulled out from the table. "I think it would be perfectly acceptable. At four hundred miles from North Korea, I don't think their aircraft can reach us. What adds to this 'bother' I feel is that nearer the coast—somewhat obscured by land smear—are what we believe to be four heavies flying their own lower-altitude racetrack."

Holman bit his lower lip and stood. He began to pace the floor.

Garcia watched, remaining where he sat. Holman never sat still for long. The short, slightly overweight admiral had a reputation for never resting and always making quick, decisive decisions—most of which were good. The thick thighs of the admiral stretched the cotton of the khaki trousers as the man walked back and forth. Garcia had heard of the man and Holman's quick rise through the ranks from captain to three stars in less than six years. Holman was both a pariah and a role model, depending on which side of political correctness you stood. He had shown up out here at Sea Base when they received orders to move into the Sea of Japan, immediately after the bombings of North Korean embassies. Garcia had quickly learned that Admiral Holman believed in knowing everything that was going on, then asking your advice for the orders he was going to give.

Maybe this was how those in combat reacted to the possibility of having to fight? A major combat action at sea was something the "talking heads" and "deep thinkers" of academia had said would never happen again. Reduce the size of the Navy, they argued. Put the money into health care. *The Navy was an anachronism in the twenty-first century. Wars would be fought with asymmetric warfare—economics, terrorism, drugs, cyber wars—but never a war at sea. Nope, academia argued, "Read my paper." Warfare would be out of sight; fought from and on the land. The Navy was only good for transporting soldiers to the fighting.*

Holman and he had had several arguments over what the Navy should look like and what its mission should be in the changing geopolitical world of the twenty-first century. The discussions had seldom been heated, but for Garcia they had revealed a lot about the man some called the last true Navy warfighter. Garcia smiled as he watched the man pace. One thing he had learned from their discussions. When Garcia was winning a discussion, Holman always fell back on his "thirty-plus years of being a military officer" argument.

Some of those canned replies were insightful, such as whenever a decision is made that changes the direction of the military, serendipitous events will always change that decision.

Holman sighed and turned. "You don't know what you don't know," he said softly.

"Sorry, Admiral?"

"Nothing, Hank. Just thinking out loud."

The gurgling sound of fresh coffee finishing perking reached both their ears. Garcia stood, grabbed his cup from the sink, and quickly poured himself a cup of coffee, keeping quiet as Admiral Holman flopped back down in the chair. The admiral brought clasped hands under his chin.

Holman was a controversial figure in the Navy. He had as many detractors as he did supporters. The day would come when one side outweighed the other and he would either go home or go up. His actions in combat had earned him his first two stars. He had personally taken the U.S. Navy into the Mediterranean when the North African nations decided to close it, fighting a carrier strike force through a mined Strait of Gibraltar without a single loss.

Less than two years after being awarded his first star and the Silver Star for this combat action, Holman was assigned as Commander, Amphibious Group Two. He was directly responsible for securing the western side of the African continent from becoming a new frontier of terrorism. His squat appearance, his ever-present battle of the waistline bulge, and his ever-present cigar were cited by those of the Navy's fitness mafia as proof of his incompetence. He was quick to point out that "being fleet of feet is not a good leadership trait." Flames of emotion burned around the Navy's most controversial admiral. Near the bottom of his Naval Academy class with a barely passed degree in electric engineering, he had risen through the ranks slowly until the Mediterranean actions. The second star was more of a surprise than the third one. Rumor had it that Holman was already processing his papers for retirement when at the last minute—for reasons unknown—he was given his second star and diverted to Naval Net Warfare Command as the vice commander. Within a year his third star was pinned on his collars. It's hard to argue against someone who wears the Silver Star.

Garcia cleared his throat, drawing Holman's attention.

"Maybe we should ask for some Navy F/A-18 Hornet squadrons to bingo aboard, Admiral, until . . ."

Holman shook his head and waved his hand back and forth a couple of times. "Nothing would give me greater pleasure, Hank, but my hands are tied."

"But, Admiral, I have eight—no, seven Air Force fighters available to protect Sea Base." He held up one finger. "One is down for spare parts. Hopefully, they're coming aboard the afternoon C-130." He glanced at his watch.

"Hank, Congress approved funds for this floating island with the express direction that it function as a joint operation. Our beloved and ancient Chairman, Bulldog Hulley, approved the Air Force as the air arm on board Sea Base."

"Yes, sir, but he is Air Force, Admiral."

Holman laughed. "Three years ago, Hank, I would have thought the same things you do, but Bulldog would bleed purple if you cut him now instead of Air Force light blue. The man is more 'joint' than 'Air Force.'" He leaned forward, both hands on his knees. "I think working at anything joint, whether it's on the Joint Staff or with one of the component commanders—the warfighting commands such as Pacific Command, which we are under—whatever you want to call those organizations manned and operated by military members from all the services, it tends to corrupt their service-oriented focus. It broadens the spectrum to where the merit of working as a combined military team exponentially improves our nation's warfighting capabilities." He leaned back. "For the record, Hank, I am one-hundred-percent behind him."

"How about off the record?"

"Ninety-five-percent," Holman said with a grin. "It's more important the fighters perform their mission than who is piloting them. Wouldn't you agree?"

"Sir, the Air Force presence on Sea Base is going to be a success. If Navy pilots can do it, they can also. The fallout is we are going to prove we don't need aircraft carriers or the Navy doesn't need an air wing."

"Hank, bite your tongue. As a fighter pilot to my illustrious surface warfare skipper, you are right that the Air Force experiment will be a success. I don't think it means proof we don't need aircraft carriers, and it sure as hell won't mean we do away with the Naval air wing." He pulled his cigar halfway out of his pocket, and then released it, letting it slide back in. "It has never been a secret how to conduct flight operations on an aircraft carrier. It just takes the gumption to set a three-hundred-knot bullet on what looks like a postage stamp from the air."

Garcia looked past Holman to the television set mounted on the bulkhead behind the admiral. He pulled the controls across the table to him and hit the mute button, restoring the volume.

". . . third bomb thirty minutes ago in London at the North Korean embassy. The explosion destroyed the front of the embassy. Fire is raging through the building as London firemen watch helplessly from the streets and sidewalks. The surviving Korean diplomats have refused the firefighters entry. We take you to London and CNN reporter Carline Postanalie."

"Tom, we are about a block from the latest explosion in what is more and more appearing to be a worldwide action against North Korean political missions. The London firefighters are working to keep the blaze from spreading from the North Korean compound to the nearby shops and buildings. London Metropolitan Police have cordoned off the streets, diverting traffic. We know there have been some casualties, but until the North Koreans allow the British firefighters and police into their compound, the number may never be known."

Holman stood, watching the television with Garcia. "That's the third one. Sounds like the same thing from last week in New York and Ottawa. I was watching while you were down below. Naval Intelligence reported this morning that the French, Italians, and Germans are deploying security forces around the North Korean embassies . . ."

"We interrupt for a news bulletin. Moments ago, French police reported the arrest of three Americans near the North Korean embassy in Paris. An unidentified source within the Paris police has told CNN the men were apprehended as they were driving a van filled with explosives. CNN Atlanta is interrupting further newscasts to follow these developments. We will have our expert on terrorism, retired Army Special Forces Lieutenant General Donnelly, in a few minutes to discuss this . . . this . . ." The newscaster looked off to the right. "What do I call it? I don't know what to call it."

"Just what we need," Holman said, jabbing his finger at the television. "Another talking head."

"For those who may have just joined us, a few moments ago

reports have been received of the French police arresting three Americans who allegedly were caught in a van filled with explosives, heading in the direction of the North Korean embassy in Paris." On the screen a hand laid a sheet of paper in front of the announcer, who reached up and pushed his earpiece tighter against his ear. The man stared at the camera as he listened to the voice in his earpiece.

"Looks scared to me," said Garcia.

"Unexpected violence always frightens someone," Holman said, pulling his cigar out. "It's the fear-factor syndrome that makes you want to run, take a crap, and scream with your eyes shut, all at the same time."

The rumors were true. When Admiral Holman was nervous or upset, he had a cigar in his hand. Garcia looked back at the television, thinking, *Guess everyone has their own version of the security blanket.*

Holman caught Garcia's glance. "Don't worry, I'm not going to light it."

"Aye, Admiral."

The announcer took a deep breath. "Ladies and gentlemen, we have a new report of explosions at the North Korean embassy in Copenhagen, Denmark. We will take you to the scene as soon as possible. Meanwhile, back to New York for the reaction from the United Nations. Stay tuned to CNN. We will be interrupting as necessary to bring you the latest on the ongoing and what appears to be coordinated bombings of North Korean embassies in the Western World."

A map twirled across the television screen, showing North Korea, outlines of the countries where its embassies had been bombed, and graphics of flames jetting up from each of those countries. The two in Ottawa and New York were included.

"Hank, stop Sea Base here. We're going no farther into the SOJ. Keep a close watch on those North Korean fighters. The normal North Korean paranoia, combined with these bombings, is going to convince them that the United States is attacking them. Everything bad that happens to North Korea, they blame us for it. If the report of Americans being involved turns out to be true, they'll believe it validates their belief."

"I would think the North Koreans would want to know the facts before they reacted."

"North Koreans aren't the normal world. They have never let

common sense and facts stop them from being irrational and fanatical. It's not in their makeup. Their idea of good politics is blackmail, bluster, and fear—like an arrogant ten-year-old who has a football, but wants everyone to pay him for the privilege of him not using it."

"Yes, sir, but we don't know who is responsible for the bombings."

Holman nodded. "Do you know what the North Korean military doctrine is for war with the United States?"

"I would presume to fight us to the last man."

"You're right, but they call it their total war doctrine. If attacked by the United States, North Korea intends to use every weapon, every person, everything they can to fight us, and they intend to be preemptive in their actions. They know they won't win, but they intend to take everyone and everything with them." Holman pointed at the television. "If it is true that Americans were behind the bombings, North Korea won't give a shit whether they're part of an action planned by our government or something a bunch of nutters did, like this God's Army."

"We believe the sailor who was killed trying to blow up Sea Base was part of this God's Army group."

Holman stood. "And I'll bet they're behind this also. Nothing would give them greater pleasure than to see the North Koreans launch a nuke missile at the United States. They know we'd have no recourse but to retaliate."

"It would turn North Korea into a parking lot."

"Which would cause the Chinese to retaliate against us, and then for a couple of days the skies would be filled with raining missiles as other countries joined the fray. Then, this God's Army would have what they want—Armageddon and anarchy. A survivalist's dream and a sane person's nightmare." He shook his head. "We are not going to let this happen, Hank."

"I told my Tactical Action Officer, Commander Stapler, to hold off calling general quarters until we had to do so. Otherwise, I was afraid we'd lock down Sea Base and bring the continuing work on her to a standstill."

Holman nodded. "You are the Skipper, Hank. I'd recommend you bring your weapon systems up to stand-by or ready or whatever you call it with these damn laser and rail-gun things. Christ!" Holman said, pointing his cigar at Garcia. "What is the Navy coming to when you can't have a good explosive sound when you fire a weapon?" he asked, trying to lessen the seriousness of the situation.

Garcia forced a smile at Holman's outburst, his mind racing to figure out what he could do without going to full general quarters. "I believe the rail gun makes a gigantic noise when it fires."

Holman grunted and went back to the coffeepot. "We need to be ready, Hank. Keep a keen eye on those fighter aircraft."

"The Air Force . . ." Garcia started.

"Damn straight, Hank. I would recommend you have the Air Force make arrangements for a ready launch. They need to be fully armed and fueled. I would further recommend they go to a ready-room alert. How many you got on board?"

"Eight, counting the one down hard for parts. Two are about a hundred fifty miles out in front of our path. I had CIC redirect them between the North Korean fighters and us. Figure they'd give . . ."

". . . early warning. Smart move. Last night while I was on the USS *Boxer,* I ordered the USS *George Bush* to join the Sea Base fleet, but I have not heard from Washington whether they'll even send it or not. If they decide to, it's going to have to go back into San Diego and outfit. It'll take two weeks for it to arrive once Washington decides what to do. So, don't expect any help."

"Thanks, Admiral. It'd help to have a heavy carrier in the strike group."

"Additionally, the British have their carrier, the HMS *Elizabeth,* only two days away. It's leaving an official port visit to Japan."

"I knew the British carrier was in the Pacific, but had not been keeping track of its voyage," Garcia said.

"Every now and again, the British flex their Naval might and send it around the world." He waved his cigar at Garcia. "Don't ever discount the British in a fight. Did you know that since World War I, over a hundred years ago, the United States Navy has never sailed into battle without the comfort of having the Royal Navy steaming alongside?"

"Don't see much of them nowadays."

"Don't see much of us either. Things change," Holman said wistfully. "Empires come and go in the wink of an historical eye."

"Should we ask for their assistance?"

"Already have, Hank. Bulldog said to only put Air Force fighters on board Sea Base. He didn't say anything about allies flying aboard or conducting combined air operations, nor did he say I couldn't have one of our aircraft carriers show up in our area of operations."

"I don't think he'd care, would he, Admiral?"

Holman shook his head. "Naw, this Chairman would consider it a tribute to my ingenuity and leadership to be able to obey his directions while simultaneously building a force to be reckoned with."

The familiar CNN music announcing a news bulletin drew their attention.

"This is Robert Ketchum from CNN headquarters in Atlanta. A few minutes ago German and Italian authorities announced the arrest of American citizens on terrorism charges. CNN has been told that London police have detained three Americans at Heathrow Airport who were attempting to board a United Airlines flight to Dulles Airport. While London authorities have refused to say why the three were detained, it appears similar to the operations ongoing in France, Germany, and Italy. The State Department has refused to make any comments at this time on the ongoing European actions. CNN will continue to bring you up-to-date news as events unfold."

"Let's hope this is a European overreaction and isn't true," Holman said.

"Homegrown terrorists."

"Homegrown terrorists who think they know how to take the world's anti-Americanism into their own hands. Unfortunately, if these assholes turn out to be part of God's Army, then they understand the damage they are doing and the havoc their individual actions may foster," Holman said with a sigh. "If they are Americans, I hope they toss them into jail and throw away the key. Revoke their citizenship."

"Now, we are going to New York, where we have been told the North Korean ambassador to the UN will be addressing an emergency session of the United Nations Security Council in the next few minutes."

"You know what this reminds me of, Hank?"

"No, sir."

"It reminds me of how events unfolded when the Japanese attacked Pearl Harbor."

"Sir, the North Korean aircraft couldn't reach any American territory."

"Hank," Holman said with irritation. "It's their doctrine of total war and the less-than-hidden fact they have nuclear weapons. Even Naval Intelligence says they have the missile capability to deliver them."

Someone knocked on the door. Before Garcia could say "Enter," the Combat Information Center watch officer entered. "Sorry, Skipper, Admiral. Commander Stapler asked me to give you this," he said, handing a message to Captain Garcia.

Garcia read it and then handed it to Holman, who finished it quickly.

"Admiral, think this is true?"

"We'll know shortly," Holman said, glancing back at the television.

THREE

Sea Base was the brainchild of retired Admiral Bushnell, who foresaw more than individual ships as the genesis for sea basing. He saw the day coming when the global leadership of America was waning while the threats to its national security were increasing. The Navy was old and growing older, with few shipbuilding projects being authorized by Congress. The Base Realignment Commission had cut shipyards through the years until in 2021, only one remained capable of building an aircraft carrier or cruiser or any warship.

The eight Fast Sealift Ships of the Maritime Sealift Command were even older than most of the warships. Designed in the 1970s by German and Danish engineers, the eight ships were still capable of providing logistic support to American forces overseas. An aircraft carrier the size of the USS *Nimitz* measured 1,101 feet, 2 inches in length with a beam of 134 feet. It was capable of carrying over one hundred aircraft and performing stand-alone air operations for three days. Two aircraft carriers could do five days; and three could perform continuously. The days of three-carrier operations had passed years ago. Fully loaded, the *Nimitz*-class aircraft carrier displaced over 97,000 tons.

The FSS's of the *Denebola* class that made up the eight ships holding aloft the eighty-one-acre metal canopy known as Sea Base were a few feet shorter than the *Nimitz*. The *Denebola,* positioned directly under the aft end of the runway that stretched the length of Sea Base to extend fore and aft an additional one thousand feet, was 964 feet, ½ inch; not much shorter in length than the USS *Nimitz*. Her beam was shorter by 106 feet, and the FSS could only displace 55,350 long tons. A long ton was a British measurement equivalent to 2,240 pounds, compared to the American two-thousand-pound tons.

Bushnell had used Congressional contacts to force through the funding for this controversial Office of Naval Research project: eight aging Fast Sealift Ships, their every movement controlled by a bank of central computers, holding aloft tons of metal, creating a man-made metal island capable of sailing anywhere.

"SENIOR Chief," Keyland said when Agazzi entered the Anti-Submarine Warfare Control Center located on the bottom level within the Fast Sealift Ship USNS *Algol*.

"What you got, Petty Officer Keyland?" asked Agazzi.

Seaman Gentron followed close behind Agazzi, turning as Agazzi and Keyland walked across the compartment. Gentron pushed the long metal lever of the hatch down, restoring watertight integrity to the compartment and shutting out the white light of the lowest passageway.

The blue overhead light of the control center accented the multicolored consoles arrayed against the port bulkhead on the lower level.

"We still have contact with the submarine. The bearing, 240 degrees, remains the same and the signal strength remains constant."

"Gentron said the contact is about a hundred miles out. How can we have contact with a submarine that far away? You sure about that?"

"I didn't say a hundred miles out, Senior Chief," Keyland said, glaring at Gentron as the young seaman walked past.

"I thought you said it was a hundred miles out, LPO," Gentron whined, pronouncing each letter of the abbreviation for "Leading Petty Officer" separately.

"I said . . . never mind. Get your butt down there with

MacPherson and practice operating the UUV console," Keyland ordered, jerking his thumb toward the array of consoles.

Keyland turned to Agazzi. "That Tactical Action Officer in Combat kept trying to pin me down to a distance. *Is it twenty miles out? Is it thirty miles out? How about fifty miles out, Petty Officer?* He kept rattling off distances, so I told him it could be thirty to a hundred. He didn't say anything, so I said nearer a hundred, I guess." He glanced at Gentron's back as the sailor clambered down the short ladder to the lower level. "I guess Gentron overheard the conversation."

"Well, it's the story circulating through Combat also. One of the CIC chiefs stopped me as he was heading back to Combat from a quick sandwich. Told me Commander Stapler told the Skipper the submarine contact was Chinese and we had him about a hundred miles out."

"Damn," Keyland said, putting both hands on his hips, looking angrily up at Agazzi. "Senior Chief, how in the hell can I tell how far out a submarine is using only passive contact? And I sure as hell didn't call it Chinese, though it probably is."

"Passive plot?"

"I have Bernardo doing one now. Hard to get a true distance because the submarine is maintaining constant speed and bearing. Signal strength doesn't indicate whether it's closing us or going away from us. It'd help if the submarine did a maneuver so the physics and math of the calculations would focus . . .."

Agazzi walked by the first-class leading petty officer, patting the stocky but shorter man on the shoulder as he passed. "Not to worry. Let's leave it alone and work the problem. What you got right now?" he asked as he lifted his feet and with his hands on the railing slid down the short four-rung ladder to the console area. Directly in front was the Unmanned Underwater Vehicle operator, Petty Officer Jenkins MacPherson—Agazzi's number-one liberty risk; not from alcohol but from pissed-off boyfriends and husbands who had been cuckolded by the handsome sailor from New Jersey. One of these days, MacPherson was going to wake up in the hospital with a load of buckshot in his butt.

Agazzi looked at the small cam picture in the upper left-hand corner of the console screen. The image came from a small computer cam mounted in the UUV compartment, which was two ships away on the USNS *Bellatrix*. *With information tech-*

nology, who needs collocation—go figure! Just once he'd like to meet a scientist who had fought something while wearing a Navy uniform.

When he needed someone in the UUV compartment, it took nearly thirty minutes for the person to go from here to the compartment, unless *he* had to go. His bad knees turned the time more into forty-five minutes. Since the near-death experience in the UUV compartment four months ago, his healed shoulder had failed to return to full use. He rolled his left shoulder, wincing slightly as he heard the bone grate against bone.

He turned his attention back to MacPherson's console. The cam pointed directly at the UUV firing cartridge. The white lights inside the UUV compartment lit up everything so the stationary camera could watch the firing cartridge.

"They all ready?" he asked, touching MacPherson slightly on the shoulder.

"Senior Chief, ran the diagnostics," he said, pushing a wisp of black hair back off his forehead. "All eight loaded UUVs check out. The well deck below the firing cartridge remains closed. Running checklist again now."

"How soon could we launch if asked?"

"From where I am right now, Senior Chief . . ." He paused, then said with confidence, "Five minutes. That includes opening the well deck."

"Good. Any way to shorten the launch sequence?"

"Of course. We can open the well deck now. Lower the UUV down to launch position, and then it's just a matter of hoping the security cameras are functioning to give us the safety visuals we need to launch." MacPherson turned in his seat and nodded at the security panel on the upper level, located alongside the maintenance table.

"They're working!" Petty Officer Taylor said with irritation. "Just because they fouled up one time . . ."

"Once! What you trying to say, Po Boy?" Petty Officer Second Class Pope Bernardo exclaimed from the AN/SQR-25 sonar console located across the compartment from the maintenance table. "And that once nearly got the senior chief killed."

"The security cameras are working now. Besides, they were working then. Smith just . . ." Taylor grumbled.

"Stop it," Keyland said, motioning his hand downward.

"Time?" Agazzi asked MacPherson. The mention of Smith

brought back memories of that afternoon in the UUV compartment. The slight pain in his left shoulder never left him. It intruded on his thoughts daily. Agazzi had woken in cold sweats from dreams of him raising his arm to stop the metal rod Smith swung as he lay helpless on the metal walkway. It was the fierce expression of hatred on the sailor's face he'd never forget. Agazzi's eyes shifted slightly, noticing the metal walkway in the UUV compartment running along the bottom edge of the cam display.

"About a minute, if we did all the other stuff ahead of time," MacPherson replied.

Agazzi shook his head, bringing his focus back to the situation. "The problem will be, Senior Chief, if we have a malfunction or something, then we're stuck with an armed UUV packed with five hundred pounds of explosives, hovering over open water inside the *Bellatrix*."

"Then we can drop it," Bernardo volunteered.

"Yeah, once you drop it, then you better hope we have control of it."

"Why?" Seaman Calvins asked. Calvins was the maintenance man Taylor's helper. The young eighteen-year-old sailor had stepped aboard Sea Base the day the ships sailed from Pearl Harbor. From the small town of Oxford, Pennsylvania, he'd gone straight to boot camp, spent a few weeks in ASW school—the same one the false Smith had gone to—and now was learning on the job how to perform maintenance on ASW equipment and weapons. Equipment and weapons were separated on two ships.

"Because when the logic head inside the nose cone recognizes the UUV is in the water, it's got no propulsion, and it's sinking, then it's going to turn into a Gawlawful depth charge right under the ship," said MacPherson.

"Thanks," Agazzi said.

"Give Seaman Calvins a break, Jenkins," Taylor sniped back. "It ain't as if he has a lot of time at sea."

"Sorry, Tommy," MacPherson mumbled. The second-class petty officer slipped his earpieces back down across his ears, hit an icon on the screen, and watched the numbers run across the screen. As part of a software upgrade from the contractor, the UUV launch console now ran a constant check on the UUVs. Agazzi watched the numbers. He lightly bit his lower lip.

Sometimes too much safety was like too much detail—it slowed down the process of anything being achieved.

"Everything okay?" Bernardo asked MacPherson, leaning back from his console so he could see the UUV screen.

MacPherson turned and smiled. "So far, so good."

Agazzi looked at Bernardo. Bernardo had been the primary UUV operator, but with a minimum complement of seven reduced to six, Agazzi had even stood a few watches to give some of the men time for a long sleep. Commander, Seventh Fleet had interceded after the explosions on Sea Base and managed to have five hundred additional sailors identified for assignment. Sea Base originally had 1,500 sailors as the main crew; with embarked air wings and a few Marines this had doubled in size. The additional five hundred sailors would become part of "ship's company" as they say—a permanent addition to Sea Base. Three of those new sailors were going to be his.

"Petty Officer Bernardo, so where is this submarine?"

Bernardo pointed to the long rainfall of colors running down the left side of the screen. "Right here, Senior Chief. I believe the submarine has an internal engine running somewhere on it. Something like a water purifier or an oil sump or a bilge pump—though I haven't heard the whish of anything being pumped overboard."

Agazzi walked the couple of steps to the AN/SQR-25 console and leaned over Bernardo's shoulder.

"You know, Senior Chief, that I hate the SQR-25," Bernardo mumbled. "Give me something . . ."

"Has the database given us any choices?" Agazzi interrupted.

"The Office of Naval Intelligence database hasn't done shit. All I can tell you is it's some sort of engine. It could even be an air-filtering system."

"No engine noise?"

"No engine noise, Senior Chief. It's a diesel, whoever's submarine it is."

"Chinese," Keyland said from behind Agazzi. "They've been trailing us since we arrived on station. Maybe they're closing to see if our defenses have improved or how close they can come before we detect them. Want to send a UUV out against them again?"

Agazzi shook his head. "Not unless the Skipper tells me to."

"I would have thought last time they would have gotten the idea we didn't want them around," Bernardo said.

"I think they did," Agazzi said. "But the Joint Chiefs of Staff were not amused over the confrontation. Said we should have left them alone. So, now we leave them alone."

"Well, I don't think the Chairman banked on Admiral Holman flying out to take charge," Keyland said, a hint of amusement in his statement.

Taylor walked from the maintenance desk area, wiping his hands on a rag. Short black hair, lean trim, with wiry muscles that warned even the largest of bullies to stand clear. When Taylor wanted, his rich Southern accent from his roots of Newnan, Georgia, could beguile most anyone. Agazzi thought of Keyland's remark the other day about Taylor. "The man has never met a schematic he didn't like." Which for them was good.

Taylor leaned over the top rail running above the console deck. "I think they're testing stuff inside the submarine to see what we can and cannot detect."

Agazzi looked up at his maintenance technician. Taylor wasn't known for intuitive comments. "Why do you think that, Petty Officer Taylor?"

"I was thinking . . ."

"Uh-oh," retorted MacPherson, pulling his earphones down. "Watch out, everyone, his head may explode."

"MacPherson, I'd throw you overboard, but it might scare the sharks away and ruin everyone's fishing tournaments."

"Enough, everyone," Keyland commanded. "Answer the Senior Chief, Taylor."

"I was thinking that if someone really wanted to know the capability of Sea Base to detect him, he would come at Sea Base with different noise configurations. One time he'd have the oil sump powered up; the next time he'd have the bilge pump working. Or he'd have combinations of internal machinery working. He'd be watching for any kind of reaction from us." Taylor made a motion with his hand as if he was writing. "He'd note them down. And as he learned more about his own deficiencies and our capabilities, the better he could use them when he decided to attack."

Wow, Agazzi thought. *That's great, Taylor.* He looked at Keyland. "We've had some faint registering of noise from possible submarines since the Chinese fired the torpedo at us. Maybe Petty Officer Taylor is onto something?"

"Senior Chief, you told us to forget they fired a torpedo at us.

That we couldn't prove they had fired a torpedo. Office of Naval Intelligence couldn't even confirm the revolutions in the water belonged to a torpedo," Keyland added.

Agazzi nodded. When the Pentagon wants to hide something, they want to hide it from everyone. Even when it means changing people's memories of an event.

"Good work, Petty Officer Taylor," Agazzi said.

"Oh, God," MacPherson said. "There'll be no living with him now."

A grin beamed across Taylor's face. He wiped his hands faster. "Yep, it just came to me as I was watching y'all."

"This is the strongest return we've gotten," Keyland said.

"Any time you guys need help, just ask," Taylor said, strutting back to the maintenance table and security console. "Yep, just ask. That's what we're here for, ain't it, Calvins?" he asked the young seaman squatting beside the maintenance desk, arranging the tools.

"What?" Calvins asked, looking up. "I'm nearly done, Petty Officer Taylor," he said, a slight whine in his voice.

"Senior Chief," MacPherson said, waving his hand at Agazzi to get his attention. "I need to physically check the UUV firing cartridge. I was going to do it before lunch, but it's just hard to tell with only a cam for a visual. . . ."

"Wait a minute!" Taylor interrupted. "We got a security camera looking that way also." He tapped the twelve-inch screen on the security console. "See. It has a larger picture than that tiny thing."

MacPherson hit a button; the cam picture filled the screen. "If I wanted a bigger picture, Jeff, I have it." He hit the button again, downsizing it back to the top left side of the screen. He turned to Agazzi. "I need to do my safety inspection on the safety latches holding the UUVs in the firing cradle, Senior Chief. It's something I can't do visually, using just cameras."

"I thought you already did it," Keyland said.

MacPherson sighed and lifted a slim black notebook, flipping it open. "According to the safety checklist, the latches are to be inspected once every twenty-four hours." He flipped the book closed and laid it aside. "I'm sorry, but it's been over twenty-six hours."

"How did that happen?" Petty Officer Keyland demanded. "You know you're supposed to do them."

Agazzi touched Keyland's arm. "When were they last inspected, Petty Officer MacPherson?"

"Yesterday, Senior Chief. I thought I did them in the afternoon. I thought I did them around 1500 before my break, but if I did them then, I made the wrong entry in the log because it says 1300."

"I think 1500 was the right time," Bernardo offered.

"Why?" Agazzi asked.

"Because," Bernardo said with a pause. "Because MacPherson is always making mistakes such as log entries. I'm sure he did it at 1500 like he thinks."

MacPherson slid his seat around, his back to Agazzi, and stood up. "Quit trying to be helpful, Pope," he said to Bernardo. "When you're in a hole, quit digging." MacPherson set his earpiece on the small panel that jutted out along the console array. "It won't take long, Senior Chief."

Agazzi looked at MacPherson for a few seconds, then said, "I'll go. I haven't been in the compartment today. It'll give me a chance to do a walk-through. What are you looking for on the firing cartridge?"

"The safety latches that run alongside the UUVs, Senior Chief. If the red tab is showing, then they're okay, but if you can't see the red tab, then it means they've come unsnapped." He shrugged. "It happens sometimes. Movement of the ships; strain of staying in synch with Sea Base. Just happens sometimes."

"I know, Petty Officer MacPherson." Agazzi made a motion with his thumb sticking out in front. "Just press it back down until I hear a click and they're ready to go. Right?"

MacPherson's face turned darker in the blue light. Agazzi had embarrassed the sailor, who was already disappointed he had forgotten to inspect the UUVs as safety doctrine required. "Sorry, Senior Chief."

"Don't forget again, will you?"

MacPherson shook his head. "Won't happen again, Senior Chief."

"I'll go with you, Senior Chief," Taylor offered. "That way, if you find something broke, I'll be there to fix it."

"We may need . . ."

"Ah, LPO," Taylor interrupted. "You got Calvins here. He's bright, fun, and how else is he going to learn how to fix things when they break if he always has to have me here to slap him upside the ears?"

"Yeah, I'll be here," said Calvins.

"Okay, but don't use anything other than a screwdriver."

"A screwdriver?" Calvins asked, looking questioningly at Taylor.

"Yeah, that way you can't screw anything up I can't fix later."

"It'll be okay, Petty Officer Keyland," said Agazzi. "Come on, Petty Officer Taylor, let's go see how the UUV compartment is looking."

"Let us know when you get there," Keyland said.

"You should be able to see us on the security console," Taylor replied.

JACOBS walked to the safety lines and tossed his cigar overboard. He leaned over the railing. Zeichner stood beside him, peering down at the ocean.

"I thought we'd lose them when Sea Base started moving."

Jacobs shook his head. "Sharks are smart, Mr. Zeichner. They know a good thing when they see it. Beneath Sea Base is a good thing for them. We burn our plastic and compact our cans and such. But we dump the organic stuff like leftover food over the side."

"Some big ones."

"Leading the small ones."

The two men stood back from the edge of the platform, looking across the two runways that stretched parallel to each other across the center of Sea Base. Sea Base was an unbroken metallic island and the runways made up the longest portion. From the *Denebola,* the runways crossed over the ships *Antares* and *Pollux* before ending over the forward ship, the USNS *Altair.*

"The tower seems almost out of place on top, doesn't it?" Zeichner asked.

"Don't know. Looks like an aircraft tower to me with how the top deck flashes outward from the main tower, is covered in large windows, and you can see the people walking around inside it. Yep, reminds me of a small airfield tower like the one in Frederick, Maryland."

Zeichner noticed Jacobs had slowed his pace so he could

keep up. "The Skipper is the lucky one. His stateroom is on the third floor, above Combat and below the aircraft control tower."

"Skippers are always the lucky ones."

"I thought master chiefs were luckier."

"We do get to wear two stars. Only one other rank has a similar privilege."

As they neared the hatch leading down, Kevin Gainer came up the ladder. "Mr. Zeichner," he said, seeing the two men.

"Kevin, you looking for me?"

"Yes, sir," he said from the ladder. "NCIS headquarters has sent some information on the man Smith, the one the master chief . . ."

Zeichner glanced at Jacobs. Jacobs had tackled the false Smith as the man was raising a metal bar to finish off Agazzi. The broadside hit had knocked the metal bar out of the man's hand and sent the smaller false Smith rolling under the safety line around the UUV firing cradle. Smith had hit the well deck and rolled into the water. The sharks had done the rest.

Jacobs's face went rigid as he recalled the dark gray scales of the shark as Smith disappeared into the waters.

"Thanks, Kevin. I'll be right there. Head on back to the *Denebola;* I'll catch up."

Gainer went back down the steps. The clanging sound of the metal steps echoed through the tunnel leading down to one of the Fast Sealift Ships.

"Sorry about that, Master Chief," Zeichner said to Jacobs. "Unless you've been there and done it, you can't know the effect of what you did."

Jacobs waved him off. "I had little choice."

Zeichner nodded. "If you hadn't done what you did when you did, your friend Senior Chief Agazzi would have been the one dead. The fact is, you stopped him from killing the senior chief and you saved Sea Base. He had those underwater torpedoes."

"They're called Unmanned Undersea Vehicles. . . ."

"The explosion would have occurred in *Bellatrix* and not out to sea. We were lucky you followed the senior chief down to the UUV compartment."

Jacobs nodded. This conversation was making him feel uncomfortable. "I need to get back to my boatswain mates, Mr. Zeichner. I appreciate what you're trying to say, but I was there. I saw how bad Alistair had been beaten and I saw the sharks pull Smith under." He shook his head. "I don't feel bad about what happened to Smith—or whatever his name was. I feel bad because I lollygagged around following Alistair and by the time I got to the compartment, the fight had been decided."

"It's just that some people—"

"I'm not some people. And I don't feel bad about Smith. If he hadn't rolled onto the well deck and into the open ocean, I might have tossed him in myself." Jacobs turned and started walking away, saying over his shoulder to the NCIS agent, "I have to get back to my boatswain mates. You have a nice day, Mr. Zeichner."

Zeichner watched Jacobs saunter across Sea Base, wondering if the man was truthful. He had seen several agents during his career who had killed suspects; all of them had been cleared, but each had had a different reaction. Each had felt remorse over the killing and each had spent some time wondering whether he should have done things differently. Zeichner raised his head, the soft breeze across the deck cooling the sweat trapped beneath one of his two double chins. Turning, the NCIS agent headed down the ladder, his hands holding onto both railings, helping him guide his heavy frame as he carefully moved down the ladder. He hoped the master chief was comfortable with his own self-assessment. From his viewpoint, the master chief was right, but being right and being comfortable with your actions are seldom compatible.

AGAZZI and Taylor emerged on the main deck of the *Algol*. Above them the bottom of Sea Base shadowed the huge ship from the hot rays of the sun. The top also trapped the fumes from the eight Fast Sealift Ships until a stiff ocean-level breeze blew through, taking the exhaust with it.

"I hope they do something about this exhaust, Senior Chief."

"Let's get across and get belowdecks on the *Bellatrix* and we'll be out of this air."

The passageway creaked and groaned as the men walked along it. Huge rubber gaskets every fifty feet shifted slightly as the computers fought the ocean waves, current, and winds to keep the eight ships moving in the same direction at the same speed while keeping the same relative location. It was something no human could do.

"One of these things is going to fall in the water, you know, Senior Chief."

"They kind of remind me of those swinging bridges you see in some of the old Tarzan movies."

"I hate walking along these things," Taylor said. "I can't find enough fittings at each end to be holding them this steady. Naw, Senior Chief, I hate walking through these things."

"But you do it. Otherwise, you have to go topside. That's another four stories. So you have to walk through them."

"Uh-uh, I don't usually, you know," Taylor replied shaking his head. "Usually, I run through them."

THE passengers disembarked from the C-130 Hercules aircraft. Kiang Zheng shielded his eyes from the bright sun, using the butt of his hand to push strands of hair away. He grabbed his suitcase from a line of luggage where the flight crew was off-loading personal items from a pallet and setting them alongside the rear of the aircraft. A petty officer in a flight suit kept the passengers away from the props and the front of the aircraft. A lone propeller turned out of sight on the other side of the C-130. Exhaust fumes blew under the wheels of the aircraft enveloping the passengers as they hurried away from the lowered ramp.

The sooner he was belowdecks in his stateroom on USNS *Regulus,* the sooner he could shower and scrub the effects of travel off his skin. Three weeks away had been good. He reached to pick up his lone travel case.

A hand reached down and picked it up before he could.

Kiang looked up into the face of a sailor. Black mustache accented a craggy face where smooth skin seemed stretched over a sharp bone structure.

"Here, sir, I'll help you carry your luggage."

Kiang reached out and grabbed the handle. "No, I can carry it."

The man tried to pull the luggage back. "I really don't mind, sir."

Kiang refused to let go and tugged it back, his eyes widening. No one else was offering to help the others. The man let the luggage go and stepped to the next passenger, offering to help him. Kiang quickly stepped away from the aircraft, taking a deep breath and feeling the beating of his heart.

No one stopped him as he walked away from the aircraft with the other passengers. He glanced back at the sailor, but didn't see him. He had probably disappeared belowdecks, helping some other traveler. Everyone split up in different directions as the new arrivals followed the young lady with the clipboard. The returning Sea Base veterans talked among themselves as they headed in their own directions toward familiar destinations. Kiang spoke to no one. A group of three men, talking and laughing at something someone said, followed him as he headed toward the hatch leading down. Considering where the C-130 was parked, the ship beneath this far hatch would be the USNS *Pollux*.

The *Pollux* was the most important ship of Sea Base. It held the massive server farm and information systems that synchronized the ships so Sea Base could remain aloft and functional. The *Denebola* had originally been the ship destined to control Sea Base, but an early explosion barely days out of Pearl Harbor had destroyed everything within the main cargo hangar. Kiang had barely made it out of the cargo hangar when the explosion occurred. He had heard that the person responsible for the explosion as well as rigging the aircraft to explode had been killed when NCIS had tried to arrest him after catching him rigging the UUVs to explode.

Kiang saw the helpful sailor enter the UUV compartment and barely avoided being seen by him. He made a mental note to find out more about the man. His handler would want to know. He wanted to know.

Kiang set the suitcase near the hatch, pulling a handkerchief out to wipe the sweat from his forehead. He squinted against the bright sun as he looked around Sea Base. The number of F-22A Raptors had grown to six since he left. He wondered if more were on board. His experience on Navy carriers told him at least two would be airborne at all times.

"Excuse us," one of the men said as the three who had been behind him went down the ladder single file, disappearing quickly into the shadows that covered the eight Fast Sealift Ships below.

The laser weapon was on the far port aft side. The two rail guns were on the far forward port and starboard sides. Only the starboard aft side of Sea Base lacked any visible weapons topside. That was something for his next report. He would have to retrain himself to speak like normal Americans after having to speak "Navy" for six months.

When he flew out to return for discussions with the Institute, the only weapons Sea Base had deployed were the rail guns. He shielded his eyes as he glanced toward the forward port side—*front left* for civilians. His eyebrows curled inward into a V. Why were sailors swarming over the rail gun?

He turned to the aft starboard side—*front right*—and saw the same activity around that rail gun. He shrugged. Kiang would store his suitcase, shower, and change into something more comfortable. Then he would see if the Navy was preparing to conduct some tests on the weapons.

His handler would want to know details. But his handler wasn't here, thank God. He took a deep breath, grabbed his suitcase, and started down the ladder. The *Pollux* was inboard to the *Regulus,* but it still meant a long trek up and down ladders, and across the enclosed passageway between the ships.

ZEICHNER swiveled his chair around and with one hand bracing himself on the desk, he sat down. "Well, spit it out, Kevin," he said to the former Army captain turned NCIS agent.

He had grown attached to Gainer's inexperience in the months they had been at sea. After the Smith incident, headquarters had offered to send a more experienced agent to replace Gainer. Zeichner saw through the ruse. Headquarters hadn't been able to find an agent to volunteer for this six-month experimental deployment of Sea Base before the experiment set sail, so Zeichner had been "volunteered." Too close to retirement to say no.

He stared at the young man and grunted. He doubted Gainer had volunteered either, so he wasn't about to let a bunch of Johnny-come-latelies show up trying to steal the show. When something becomes important, the A personalities came out of the woodwork like cockroaches at night. To hell with headquarters—he was here and they were there and, if he had his way, never the twain shall meet.

"You okay, Boss?"

"Why wouldn't I be?"

"Just curious, sir. It's awful hot to be topside too long," he said, handing a sheet of paper to Zeichner.

"Boss, headquarters is still insisting their original report of a foreign agent on board Sea Base stands."

"Yeah, and we both know what they're saying about our own American homegrown terrorist Smith."

"They agree. It was Smith they missed; not the spy."

"Spy. Hell of a short name for something that sounds so ominous, Kevin. They didn't get Smith. They didn't even know about Smith. Smith nearly blew up this contraption built by the lowest bidder and sent every one of us to the bottom." His eyes looked at the ceiling for a moment before he continued. "What is it the boatswain mate chief calls it?"

"The deep Pacific."

Zeichner shook his head. "No, he calls it the dark Pacific. That part of the ocean depth where sunlight can't penetrate. Where flesh, blood, and man-made objects"—he made a fist—"are crushed into crumpled balls on their way down."

"Yes, sir," Gainer acknowledged. He leaned against the bulkhead, a couple feet from Zeichner's desk. "They still say we should continue our investigation."

Zeichner sighed. "Kevin, for an ex-HOOAH type with the 19th Infantry, don't you think it's time to loosen up a bit?"

Confusion was etched on Gainer's face. "Loosen up?"

"You know, Kevin. Let the 'high and tight' haircut go by the wayside."

The man smiled. "Boss, I've grown used to the hair. Besides, it wouldn't be me without the Army haircut."

"Okay, don't say I didn't try." Kevin would come along. He had a lot of good insight for a new agent but: *Methinks he takes things too literally is what methinks.*

"Boss, you think they're right about us having a spy on board?"

"Well, they have been right before. And it isn't as if we have stopped our investigation. The challenges are there's only the two of us and we are still tying up the loose ends with this Smith investigation. I think it has priority."

"Yes, sir. I understand," Gainer answered, his forehead wrinkling. "Maybe we should take headquarters up on their offer to send more agents out here. If we show headquarters how far along we are . . ."

". . . Then headquarters will definitely send someone out here, Kevin."

"I don't understand."

"How long were you in the Army?"

"Eight years."

"And you never had someone try to take credit for your hard work or ideas?"

"All the time."

"Same here."

"I was thinking we should show them we are working their leads along while we continue completing the Smith investigation. When I was in the Army, I worked for this colonel who was leading a battle near Ghandar, Iraq. He assigned this young captain to do nothing else but write situation reports to his generals. I always thought it was to show his bosses what a great job he was doing, but later discovered it was to keep his bosses off his back while he won the battle."

Zeichner took a deep breath. "And you think we ought to do the same thing?"

Gainer nodded. "It would keep headquarters off our backs."

"Or it would cause headquarters to ask more questions."

"Could be, Mr. Zeichner, but if we are the genesis of the questions, then we control the actions."

Zeichner grinned. "Kevin, I didn't think Army HOOAHS were sly and devious."

Gainer nodded without a grin. "As you pointed out, sir. Eight years can teach you a lot about politics and ambition. Besides, I think the Army would take great exception to good leadership being called sly and devious, sir."

"Well, you stick with NCIS. You'll pick up those spin traits the Army missed. As for sly and devious, wait until you've met some of the criminals we arrest. They'll teach you what the Army didn't."

Zeichner leaned forward, his arms on the desk and his hands clasped together. "Ghost-write an e-mail that brings headquarters up to date on the bomber. Tell them what we're doing in regards to the possibility we have a foreign agent on board."

"Yes, sir."

"Kevin, I know I should know, but what is the status of our espionage effort? You've been working the bulk of it while I've been tied up with the Smith case."

"We have ten on the short list, sir. One of whom departed Sea

Base three weeks ago for San Antonio." He covered a slight cough. "He returned today. I'll follow up on him later."

"Why did he leave?"

"I was told his company—no, his institute—asked him to return. According to the program manager over at the Office of Naval Research quarters in the tower, it had to do with some new software for the radar systems on Sea Base."

"I'll bet when you finally find the ground truth on him, you'll find it all has to do with business development. My former wife's nephew works for a defense contractor. He has a degree in computer science and is a certified information security systems professional, but he is expected to identify new business and keep old business growing."

"Yes, sir. You are probably right," Gainer said, then continued. "I am watching the older man—the naturalized citizen from Thailand. He seems okay, but I think he knows I'm on to him."

"Why would you say that?"

"He has given me the slip a couple of times. I would like to sit down, go over his file with you, and ask for your guidance on when to start interviewing people who work with him. See if he is doing anything he shouldn't be doing."

Zeichner nodded. "Once we go down that path, it's only a matter of time before your suspicion of him being aware of you becomes an established fact."

"I understand, but I need to see if we're missing anything, and interviewing others may provide us information we need," Gainer argued. "It's the only way to either clear him from our list or . . ."

Zeichner clenched his lips together. Gainer was right. Complicating the headquarters directions on chasing down what Zeichner believed was a mythical agent was his personal desire to show headquarters they had chosen the right man to be the head of the NCIS detachment for Sea Base. If you could call the two of them a detachment.

Gainer opened a folder. "Here are the photographs of the top two contenders."

"Sounds like a prizefight."

Gainer laid the photographs of the man from Thailand and Kiang Zheng on the table in front of Zeichner. Zeichner picked up Kiang's photograph. "We searched his stateroom and didn't find anything."

"We searched the other one's stateroom and didn't find anything either. Fact is, Boss, we didn't find anything out of the ordinary in either stateroom. Usually there is something unusual in everyone's living room, and these staterooms were bedroom, living room, and bath. We should have found something leading us further into espionage or away from it."

Zeichner nodded. "I don't know if I agree with you, Kevin, but with only ten names on the list, we should be able to do one a day to start fattening out the files you've already started."

Gainer picked up the photographs. "Thanks." He looked up. "I understand the NCIS agent from USS *Boxer* wants to come over and help also."

"Screw him and screw headquarters. They put four NCIS agents on the amphibious warship *Boxer* filled with sailors, Marines, and helicopters, while assigning us two with a young yeoman as an administrative assistant for Sea Base. Let the *Boxer* agent have his glory and we will have our plodding work they think we do."

"WHAT'S this?" Bernardo asked, pointing to a slight trace that had appeared right of the noise signature from the unidentified thought-to-be-Chinese submarine.

Keyland sidestepped a couple of feet to the passive sonar console to look over Bernardo's shoulders. Bernardo's finger pointed to a faint trace tracking down and to the left, breaking the vertical lines of the rainfall. The faint noise signature turned red as he watched it.

"Hostile," Bernardo said.

"Or unknown," Keyland added.

When a noise broke the pattern, it disturbed the electronic rainfall, creating a different intensity and parting the fine grain of the rainfall to show the noise to the operator. This latest variant of the AN/SQR-25 displayed in colors the noise signature before the operator ran the signals through the Office of Naval Intelligence database. A red noise signature told the operator the contact was hostile or unknown; blue, and the contact was friendly; and gold was ambient noise. The base color of the rainfall remained computer-green.

MacPherson leaned over, bracing himself with his left hand on the small worktable that ran along the consoles. "What you got?" he asked, craning his neck to look at the passive sonar display.

The entire screen was covered with what most would think of as static when you first looked at it. But like a massive, hard-to-see-through rainfall, the signals from passive sonars deployed at varying depths beneath the ships holding up Sea Base trickled down the screen.

Rolling the ball of the console mouse, Bernardo positioned the cursor over the noise signature.

The mouse engaged the massive computer power of the databases supporting the AN/SQR-25 passive sonar. The system immediately identified the signal strength in hertz—a common measurement of noise. Different engines, different pumps, even different marine animals made different noises, and each noise had its own frequency as a signature.

The Office of Naval Intelligence database converted the data now flowing into its analytical cells into base qualities of noise, frequency, and speed, searching for a specific platform, system, or ambient noise to identify the source of the noise on Bernardo's sonar.

Sea life, waves, and currents caused ambient noise. Most people thought of the undersea environment as a quiet, mute place where fish swam and life was snuffed out quickly. To the contrary, the ocean was a cacophony of noise—all that was needed was the right instruments to hear it, but life still could be snuffed out quickly.

Bernardo pressed the left earpiece against his ear as he kept the cursor on top of the sound trace. "I can't hear anything."

"What does the database say?"

"It's searching."

This time the ONI database was quick to answer and the answer was flashing red. Loud beeping startled the three sailors. "Christ!" shouted Bernardo, slapping the mute button.

"It's a fucking torpedo!" MacPherson exclaimed.

"Bearing?" Keyland shouted, rushing up the ladder to the higher platform, heading toward the telephone.

"Three-three-zero degrees!"

"CBDR?" Keyland shouted back, using the abbreviations for "Constant Bearing, Decreasing Range." CBDR was the nautical term when a contact was moving in such a fashion that it was going to collide with your ship. He lifted the telephone, dialing Combat Information Center. "Calvins! Get your sound-powered headset on!" He looked at the back of Bernardo's head. "CBDR or not?"

"No! Definitely not coming at us. I have a left-bearing drift. It's not heading toward us. It's on a collision course with the unidentified submarine."

"Bernardo, hit the buttons. Get the data into the Naval Tactical Data System so everyone can see it."

"Hello, Combat?" While Keyland relayed the news of the torpedo heading toward the Chinese submarine, the noise signatures on the AN SQR-25 sonar were being electronically translated into symbols on the NTDS.

The Naval Tactical Data System was the command and control system for the Navy and Marine Corps. It was capable of connecting every platform across thousands of miles so the battle group commander could see the tactical profile surrounding his or her area of operations. Almost immediately, the V symbol of an unidentified submarine appeared southwest of Sea Base. A dotted line traced toward it, representing the torpedo.

FOUR

"Raptor 10, Raptor Haven. We're going to keep you in the pattern right where you are," the voice on the secure communications suite said.

"Raptor Haven, Raptor 10. Roger, be advised we will have to start our return in . . ." Walters paused, glancing at the fuel level reflected in the heads-up display. "About thirty minutes. According to my navigation readout, we are about 175 miles from Sea Base. Request advise."

"We have got to teach them how to come up with some good call signs, *Raptor 10,*" Franklin said on their private circuit.

"Raptor Formation, we will try to relieve you on station. Be advised you have hostiles at your twelve o'clock."

"Hostiles?"

Walters glanced up, looking ahead of the aircraft. He looked to his port side and saw Franklin with a raised hand, palm up. He mimicked the gesture. He didn't know either.

"Raptor Haven, what hostiles? Are they inbound? Who are they? I need more information than just they're at my twelve o'clock."

"Raptor Formation. Seventy-plus North Korean fighters remain in a combat air patrol racetrack, bearing three-three-zero degrees true, distance two hundred miles."

"Roger, Raptor Haven, are they inbound?" Walters asked, his voice rising an octave. "Last information showed about half that number and they were flying routine patrols off their coast. Has this changed? Are some or all of them flying a racetrack; are they headed toward Sea Base? Give us more information. From thirty-five or forty to over seventy is quite the jump. Why are you calling them hostiles?"

"Raptor Formation, weapons tight. Hostiles in figure-eight DEFPAT at this time. Forming up."

"Raptor Haven, hostiles to me means we can shoot them down."

"Negative, Raptor One Zero. Weapons tight; I repeat, weapons are tight. Authority to engage denied."

"Fast Pace, we have to work on our communications with these Navy types."

"Raptor Haven, this isn't the time to hold back information. Are we expecting them to come after us?"

"Raptor Formation," the Air Intercept Controller said, ignoring Walters's question. "Come to course two-four-zero; maintain angels twenty. Weapons tight. *Possible* hostile formations bear three-three-zero true from your current position; range two hundred."

"Well, this makes it clearer, Fast Pace. Now, they're possible hostiles," said Franklin.

"Let's go," Walters said sharply, easing his Raptor fighter into a right-hand turn. Something was up. He was confident the stealth qualities of the F-22A would keep the North Korean MiG-29s from detecting them. A ready deployment intelligence unit from Air Force Intelligence Command had briefed the squadron before they deployed that the North Korean Air Defense system was antiquated and they doubted it was capable of detecting the Raptor. Doubt was a word Walters discovered to be as reliable as "possible" and "probable"—not much difference. The North Koreans were probably just overreacting again as they usually did.

"You think the bombings in Ottawa and New York have anything to do with this?" Walters asked as the formation turned smoothly onto course two-four-zero.

"Wouldn't surprise me in the least," Franklin responded. "I don't think they need much encouragement to stir up their little hornet's nest."

"Raptor Haven, Raptor Formation; steady on course two-four-zero, Angels twenty."

Several seconds after Sea Base acknowledged Walters's transmission, Franklin said, "If we are going to take on seventy enemy fighter aircraft, the least Raptor Haven could do is send us a third F-22A to even the odds."

LOUISE "Pickles" Johnson thanked Captain Garcia as he departed the briefing given the Air Force fighter pilots. She quickly turned to the other Air Force pilots and shouted, "Attention!" The ten Air Force personnel snapped to attention as Garcia exited the small ready room of the tower.

"At ease," Johnson said when the door shut. "Chief Willard, what is the status of the fighters available?"

"Commander, two are airborne in a defensive fighter patrol—"

"I know that, Chief. Tell me about the ones on the apron," she interrupted bluntly. "Are they fueled? Are they armed? If armed, what is the load-out?"

Willard took a deep breath, straightened his back, rising to his impressive six-foot-four height. "Ma'am, we have six aircraft on the flight deck. One is down hard; the other five are fully fueled. Major Crawford . . ." He nodded at the bull-necked former Air Force Academy tight end, who was standing quietly to the left of Johnson. Who also, up until earlier in the day, had been the acting detachment commander, and who, in a space of minutes after her arrival, had made all of them miss his quiet leadership. Willard paused, clearing his throat. "Major Crawford had us fully arm all the F-22As yesterday, Major."

"Thank you, Chief," she said coldly.

Willard looked down; she wanted to be called Commander, but it'd be a cold day in hell before he called her that—well, unless he had to, Willard thought rudely. In the Air Force she was the detachment commander, DETCO, and he'd call her DETCO or he'd call her Major. What in the hell else could she do to someone who was as high as he could go in the enlisted ranks of the world's mightiest Air Force? When he looked up, Captain Delaney smiled and winked at him. Maybe the young man wasn't all fun and frolic.

"Myself and Captain Delaney will take the first formation out," she said. "We've had some time flying together and . . ."

Willard smiled as he watched the shocked expression on Delaney's face.

"DETCO," Major "Tight End" Crawford interrupted. "You two just finished a six-hour flight here. Don't you think you should take the second wave? How about . . ."

"Major," she said, turning her eyes on Delaney. "I am fully rested and ready to get out there. If Captain Delaney feels he needs some crew rest until the next relief on station, then . . ." She left it unsaid.

"No, ma'am," Delaney said with gusto, rubbing his hands together. "I'm raring and ready to go."

"See?" she offered. "I think we can handle another four hours flying a DEFPAT, don't you?"

"It's not that you can't, Major Johnson; it's just that there are those of us who are better rested. Crew rest and all that."

"Thank you, Major Crawford, but I am the Commander. I need to be out there to see what we are facing. All of you have had some time boring holes in the sky off of Sea Base. We haven't. The decision is made."

Crawford nodded and stepped back.

Bravo, bravo, Willard thought. He didn't think Tight End had it in him. Willard moved to the door. Just because he looked as if he could rip a watertight door off its hinges didn't necessarily translate to moral courage.

"Chief, where are you going?" Johnson asked.

"I was going to check on the aircraft, ma'am. Wouldn't want anything holding up the launch."

"Go ahead," she said with a dismissive wave of the hand.

This was going to be a long deployment, and with only eighty-one-plus acres to hide from her, Master Chief Jacobs's offer to use the Navy chiefs' mess when he tired of the ready room suddenly grew very attractive. As he closed the door behind him, he wondered how he was going to protect the men and women who worked for him. Without him between her and them, life would be worse than the seasickness plaguing Yates and Wilcox.

TEN minutes later, Johnson and Delaney emerged from the tower, their helmets tucked beneath their arms, running toward their aircraft. Johnson was a couple of steps ahead of Delaney, who hurried to keep up with her. They split apart nearer the flight line, with Delaney scrambling up his ladder a few seconds ahead of Johnson.

Ten minutes later, Willard, with his hand shielding his eyes from the bright sun, watched the fresh F-22A formation rise off the end of the runway, flying directly ahead of Sea Base for about a mile before twisting slightly left. Afterburners hid the aircraft in that moment. The formation must have pulled several G's, thought Willard, as the aircraft turned tight, their noses pointing straight up. A few seconds later, they disappeared into the clear sky, leaving a long contrail behind them.

He dropped his hand. *Have to give it to the DETCO,* he thought. *She really knows how to show off for the spectators. Hope she knows how much fuel she wasted.*

WILLARD turned toward the remaining four aircraft, nearly tripping over the airman kneeling on the deck. Willard jumped reflexively. "Snaggles, what in the hell are you doing?"

The young airman ran his fingers through the slightly raised X above the tie-down depression. "Nothing, Chief. I was just thinking how much this would make our life easier back at Langley if we had these things on our—"

"Snaggles, aren't you supposed to be helping Lou and the others fix 223?" Willard asked, pointing at the aircraft where Sergeant Thomas and several other technicians were working.

The lanky airman from Chicago stood up, brushing the knees of his trousers. "Right, Chief. Sergeant Thomas told me to take a break."

"He did, did he? What did you do this time?"

"Ah, Chief, I didn't do anything this time. He rewarded me for accomplishing a mission against all odds."

Willard started walking toward 223, where the technicians were busy installing the new part. Snaggles fell into step with the chief. "Snaggles, I'm almost scared to ask what you did."

"It was nothing, Chief. Lou—Sergeant Thomas asked me to go get the spare part." He pointed to the Hercules aircraft parked across the runway. "It was on board that C-130, which landed about a half hour ago." He shook his head. "They didn't want me to take it until they checked it into supply. Said something about keeping a log on it."

"I take it you were able to talk them out of doing that?"

"Naw, Chief. They're squids. You can't talk them into doing anything that makes sense."

"I take it they wouldn't give it to you?"

"I couldn't get them to see it my way. It was a small part, so when they went back to unloading the aircraft, I opened the box, took out the part, and resealed the box."

Willard grinned, reached over, and lightly slapped the young man on the back of his head. "You know, Snaggles, you ever thought about seeking a commission? You might be officer material."

"Ah, Chief, why would you want to say something like that?"

Loud bongs from the deck speakers startled the two, bringing Willard to a stop as he searched the main deck of Sea Base. His eyes locked on the broken aircraft.

On 223, the working party stopped what they were doing, glancing toward Willard. Chill bumps broke out on Willard's legs and arms. "What the . . ." he said, realizing what he was hearing were the sounds of a United States Navy warship going to general quarters. He recalled similar sounds from some of the old movies.

"General quarters, general quarters," boomed the voice over the continuing bonging sound. "All hands man your battle stations."

"Is this real?" Snaggles asked.

Before Willard could answer, the voice over the megaspeakers broadcast, "This is not a drill. I repeat, this is not a drill."

People ran across Sea Base. Seemingly in a helter-skelter lack of pattern they ran, sometimes knocking into each other as they rushed to assigned stations in preparation to fight Sea Base. Some walked slowly, strapping on life vests. Others uncurled the fire hose along the aft edge of Sea Base. Across the runway on the port side of Sea Base, Navy crewmen ran from one helicopter to the next, jerking chocks from beneath the wheels, preparing the four SH-36 Anti-Submarine helicopters for liftoff.

Willard started walking again, his pace quickening until he was nearly running. Old war movies had no impact such as this. The bonging continued, along with repetitive commands from the announcer. Willard had never expected to hear it in real life.

He was Air Force; what in the hell were they doing out here in the first place?

He looked at 223. The airman on the ladder crawled down to the deck to join the others. They shrugged. Willard knew they were preparing to bolt for belowdecks. "When in doubt, always take cover" was a good mantra for a ground crew.

"Don't you dare!" he shouted, pointing at them. He knew. He'd been there—the explosions in Bahrain. When you were scared or confused, you fled. People ran. When one ran, usually they all did. It was a survival instinct to run with the pack. Lemmings and humans had the same instinct.

"Come on, Snaggles. Stay with me," he said, his heart pounding.

"No sweat on that, Chief."

What in the hell is the squadron's GQ mission? he wondered for a fraction of a second before realizing his job was to get these aircraft ready for launch. His pilots would be here shortly. A slight sense of easiness flowed over him. He had his job. With Johnson in the air, Tight End was back in the saddle. He visualized the major controlling the melee occurring in the ready room. The pilots would be here soon. His job was to have the Raptors ready for launch.

Willard was about fifty feet from the broken F-22A when Thomas ran toward Willard.

"Snaggles, get over with the others."

Thomas and Snaggles passed each other without a word.

"What do we do, Chief?" Thomas asked as he reached Willard. The young sergeant's breathing was quick, his eyes wide in alarm.

I know how you feel, Willard thought, coming to a stop. Chill bumps raced down both arms.

"What's going on?" Thomas added.

"Seems we have some North Korean aircraft buzzing off their coast, I believe. This man-made island is getting closer, so I think the Navy has decided to take some defensive actions."

"Are they coming this way? How far away are they? And most important, Chief, what do we do?"

"I don't know if they are heading our way or how far away they are. We'll let the Navy and our pilots worry about that. For us, we need these bad-ass fighters ready for immediate launch, Lou. Then, we fix this broke-dick one. Now, tell me: What's the fuel load-out and what's the weapons load-out?" he asked, draping his arm for a moment over the young sergeant's shoulder as they walked toward the ground crew.

"The three good ones are fully loaded and armed, Chief. You know that. We did it yesterday and you had us recheck them this morning as if maybe the Navy unfueled them and unarmed them during the night. Christ! Is this a dream or what!"

"Stay calm, Sergeant."

"Stay calm! Chief, I'm a fucking airman. I don't know how to swim and I'm smack dab in the middle of the Pacific with all this World War II noise going on." He turned, his eyes wide. "Have you seen the sharks underneath this thing? There are so many sharks under this damn thing that if you fell overboard you could walk across their backs. No way I can be calm," he said in an emphatic whisper, shaking his head back and forth. "No way."

"Well, Lou, then at least try to look calm," Willard said, leaning over until his head was nearly touching Thomas's. "Now is the time to do what we're trained to do, do it quickly, and do it right." He raised his head and nodded toward the troops around 223. "You see them. They're scared shitless . . ."

"Good. Then, I'm not the only one."

". . . and they're looking to you and me to reassure them there's nothing to be scared about. I think you and I can do that, don't you?" Willard asked, lifting his ball cap to run his hand across his bald pate. "Think you can fake it and look calm?"

Thomas smiled. "OK, Chief, if you can look calm, I can look calm," Thomas said, jabbing his thumb in his chest, his voice slightly steadier.

"Then let's get those bad-ass Raptors ready to kick ass and take names, Sergeant." He slapped Thomas on the back. "Yep, if they're in the sky when these wannabe bad-asses get here, the North Koreans will be below sea level when the smoke clears."

The two walked together the few feet remaining to the ground crew.

Willard pointed to the sets of huge mobile fire canisters parked between each of the aircraft. "Snaggles! You see those canisters? Pull them farther away from the aircraft and I don't mean half the distance to China."

"How far?"

"Far enough if one of the aircraft takes a hit we can fight the blaze. Right now, they're so close, they'll go up with the aircraft."

Snaggles took off in a run toward the nearest fire canisters.

"Parker!" Thomas shouted to the woman standing near the nose of 223. "Give Snaggles a hand shifting those fire canisters. The rest of you help. Now move it!"

Parker jammed her ball cap over her short, cropped hair and ran after Snaggles. "Wait up, asshole!" she shouted.

"Okay, Lou, start with the ready aircraft. Get those canopies opened, ladders down, and check the chops. I don't want them trapped by a wheel when we have to jerk them away. When the Air Force's best fighter pilots come roaring out of that hatch, I want them to keep roaring right into an aircraft ready for launch."

"Right, Chief," he said, turning to give the orders.

Willard touched his shirtsleeve. "Lou, put Danny and Snot-Nose on 223. We'll need that one up as soon as possible."

Sergeant Thomas gave a half salute. Moments later everyone was busy, but they were busy in an organized way. A way Willard understood. They were doing things they knew how to do. *Comfort things* came to mind as he watched them move quickly, but confidently, about the aircraft. In the midst of confusion and panic, the comfort of executing familiar tasks calmed nerves and helped control fear. It focused the mind and the energy. If this Goddamn alarm would stop . . .

As if hearing him, the bonging stopped and across Sea Base, with the exception of the flight crews, turning helicopters, and the race to get the F-22A Raptors airborne, the top of Sea Base had become a ghost town.

Willard glanced at his watch, then at the hatch where his pilots should be emerging any minute. What was keeping them?

"WOW! Guess they decided it was time for GQ," MacPherson said.

Keyland slid down the ladder to the lower level, a deep thud vibrating along the deck as he landed on the rubber matting.

"Left-bearing drift, Petty Officer Keyland," Bernardo said, his voice strained.

Keyland, Bernardo, and MacPherson—leaning across from his console to the right—watched the two noise signatures continue to close.

The hatch opened and Seaman Gentron stepped inside. "What the hell is going on?" he asked, tucking in his shirt and starting to button it. "One moment I'm asleep getting ready for my watch, and the next thing I know, I'm bumping my head on—"

"Keep quiet and take the sound-powered headset from Calvins. You're it now," Keyland said, jabbing his finger at Gentron.

"Long-range torpedo. Guess no one wants to do any underwater dogfighting," MacPherson said.

"Yeah," Bernardo replied. "The torpedo isn't moving fast, but it's definitely a torpedo and whoever fired it isn't even on our sonar."

"Torpedo?" Gentron asked, reaching for the sound-powered headset from Calvins. "What's going on?"

Calvins leaned down and brought the other seaman up to date on events as they exchanged the sound-powered telephone headset and mouthpiece.

"Why aren't the Chinese doing anything? Surely they know they have a torpedo heading toward them," Keyland said aloud, his voice strained.

"Maybe they've dropped a decoy behind them and their noise spike is blocking it from us? Maybe the torpedo is approaching in their baffles and they haven't detected it," MacPherson offered. "Besides, we don't know the target is Chinese," he added softly, stress lines visible across his brow.

"They're definitely Chinese. No one else has this kind of a noise signature as the Chinese Han class," Bernardo said, his tongue flicking across his lips. "I don't know why they're not doing anything."

"They ought to be maneuvering. Going up or down or something," Keyland said, running his hand across his chin. "Ought to be doing something."

"Who shot is what I want to know," Bernardo said.

"What type of torpedo did the database say?" Keyland asked.

"I didn't ask it. I saw from the noise signature it wasn't one of ours, but—"

"Hit the database."

Bernardo reached up and touched the MORE INFORMATION icon.

Everyone stopped talking as they watched the database display. Their eyes moved from the display to the rainfall, waiting for the database to identify the type of torpedo and watching the torpedo close on its target. Seaman Calvins ran over to the railing on the upper level and leaned down to watch, just as the database pinged.

"Russian?" Bernardo exclaimed. "What the fuck are the Russians doing out here?"

"Doesn't have to belong to a Russian submarine," Keyland answered, shaking his head. "It could be another Chinese submarine or even the North Kor—"

"Koreans! We have a North Korean submarine out here?" Calvins shouted. "Wow!"

"Shut up, Calvins," MacPherson said. "This isn't the zoo and you're not a kid."

Bernardo shifted the mouse so the cursor stayed on the noise signature of the torpedo. "Can't be. Why would the North Koreans fire on the Chinese? Besides, their submarines are thirty-forty-fifty years old. They wouldn't send them out, would they?" Bernardo asked, turning to look at Keyland.

"They have the fourth largest submarine force in the world. Granted they're a bunch of old Russian diesel Foxtrots and Golf II submarines, but they're submarines."

"The Golf II class carries cruise missiles," Bernardo added.

"Why would the North Koreans fire on the Chinese?" MacPherson asked. "They're friends."

"He's moving!" Bernardo shouted. "Damn, the Chinese have detected the torpedo. They know they have a torpedo coming up their ass."

As the four sonar technicians watched the rainfall display, the running lines of noise changed. The larger one of the Chinese submarine curved to the right.

"Right-hand turn. Didn't do much! The torpedo is turning with him." He touched the screen between the torpedo and submarine traces. "Decoys. There they are. The CINCOMS are ejecting decoys into the water." He touched the screen where the rainfall curved around slight deviations in the underwater noise.

For a moment it looked as if the decoys were going to pull the torpedo away from its track, but the torpedo drove through the multiple decoys, emerged on the other side, and quickly reacquired the maneuvering Chinese submarine.

I know why they fired," Keyland said, his voice distant. He pushed MacPherson back into his seat. "Get that UUV ready to launch. Open that damn well deck!" He ran up the ladder, stopping at the top of it to point at MacPherson. "Get the senior chief's attention as soon as he and Taylor enter the UUV compartment."

"Look!" Calvins shouted, pointing at the security console. "The senior chief and Petty Officer Taylor are inside."

AGAZZI placed his hand on the biometric reader, conscious of the Marine standing nearby, watching him and Taylor.

"Damn, he makes me nervous," Taylor whispered.

"General quarters probably didn't help either."

"They're psychotic enough without giving them the heavy metal of GQ. Hurry up, Senior Chief. The sooner we're in there the better." When Taylor glanced over at the Marine sentry, the man met his eyes, lifting his eyebrows and slowly stroking his M-16 while running his tongue lightly over his lip.

"Damn, Senior Chief . . ."

Agazzi hit the combination lock after the biometric reader gave the clear signal. The sound of suction breaking when the hatch opened was accompanied with a burst of air jetting into the passageway. Agazzi was barely inside the hatch before Taylor pushed him.

"Taylor, stop that shit. That hurts, you know," Agazzi said, rubbing his left shoulder.

Taylor pushed the hatch closed and secured it. "Sorry, Senior Chief, it was just the Marine gave me the willy jeebies."

Agazzi nearly asked him what *willy jeebies* were, but instead said, "Petty Officer Taylor, get down and check the latches on the UUVs. I'm going to link up with Petty Officer Keyland and the others."

Taylor scrambled down the two inner levels within the UUV compartment; a leapfrog using the ladder rail to the second deck, before sliding down to the well-deck level.

Watching, Agazzi's memories flashed of that late afternoon when he stumbled on Smith rigging the UUVs to explode. If it hadn't been for Jacobs being his nosy master chief self, Agazzi would have died that day. No one would have known because thousands of those on Sea Base would have died minutes later.

Directly in front of the hatch where they entered was a long double row of cells where inactive Unmanned Underwater Vehicles were stored. A series of overhead tracks ran from those cells to the firing cradle. A large crane carried the two-ton-plus UUV from storage to the firing cradle above the well deck. The automated overhead rail system could only carry one UUV at a time. It was not a fast process, for the UUV had to travel down three levels from the cells to the firing cradle.

The firing cradle was a large complicated piece of machinery. Located directly over a well deck that opened to the Pacific, it reminded most who first saw it of a huge pistol chamber. The firing cradle rotated with each UUV release so the next weapon was ready for firing. The firing cradle held eight UUVs. Each weapon held five hundred pounds of explosives along with the impressive array of sensors to help the remote operator guide it.

Agazzi recalled the comments of the master of the *Bellatrix* the first time Agazzi told him they were going to open the well deck.

The master said the folks from Office of Naval Research had opened it numerous times during open-ocean testing prior to this deployment. *"It worked then and the ship didn't sink. It'll work now, and the* Bellatrix *will still stay afloat. Besides, even if something went wrong, all we're talking about, Senior Chief, is a small compartment on board a ship that when full can carry over 55,000 long tons. A few tons of seawater won't even change the draft of the* Bellatrix."

Since then, Agazzi had only notified the bridge of the ship when they were opening, closing, and testing the well deck. He never bothered the master, who seemed to appreciate the small kindness.

Agazzi followed Taylor down to the second level, stopping there as the maintenance technician continued onward to the firing-cradle level.

"Be careful of the well deck," Agazzi said, his memory reeling to the moment when Jacobs tackled Smith, sending him flying into the well-deck area. He shivered.

"Sure thing, Senior Chief. Besides, they wouldn't dare open it while I'm here. Who else would do all the shit-work keeping everything going?"

Agazzi stepped in front of the computer console, waved at the cam on top, knowing the team could see them inside the compartment. He slipped on the set of earphones plugged into the computer. "Agazzi here, anyone hear me?"

"Got you, Senior Chief," MacPherson replied. "We got problems up here."

"Why are we at general quarters?"

MacPherson relayed the news of the torpedo heading toward the suspected Chinese submarine and the recent order by CIC to prepare to launch the UUVs.

"Senior Chief," Taylor said, his voice echoing in the compartment. "Latches secure!" As he climbed up from the well deck, he added, "Tell Jenkins he can open the well deck."

"Petty Officer MacPherson," Agazzi said. "Latches are checked. You are clear to open the well deck. We'll stay here and monitor."

"YES, sir, Admiral," Garcia said over the handset. "The torpedo isn't inbound against us, but it appears someone has fired a torpedo at our Chinese shadow. Sonar reports one torpedo."

The Tactical Action Officer, Commander Stapler, handed Garcia a life vest. He laid a helmet on the Skipper's chair. Garcia nodded at him and mouthed the word "thanks."

"Hank, how much longer before Sea Base comes to a stop?"

"We started the parking commands soon after you flew off, Admiral."

"Let me know as soon as Sea Base is in a . . . Hank, what do you call it? A loitering position; a parking position?"

"What would the Admiral prefer?"

"I would prefer for it to be out of harm's way. Away from any actions that occur so I don't have to worry about defending such a target chunk. That's what I would prefer."

"The Sea of Japan doesn't give us many options for that, Admiral. Narrow strait behind us separated by South Korea and Japan. Now, we're wedged between the Korean Peninsula to our northwest and our ally Japan to our east."

"What's the status of the fighters?"

"We have four airborne. Combat informed me the K-135 tankers are due in the area by late afternoon, but they won't arrive soon enough before I have to recover the two out there."

"Sea Base?"

"We are slowing our progress to two knots. Once the computers have modeled the currents, waves, weather into a common profile, they will adjust the individual speeds of the eight Fast Sealift Ships so we remain motionless. You might say we will be under way, making way, but our speed will be zero. We'll still drift, but Sea Base will drift as a unit and the computers will compensate so we drift in a predestined direction."

"Well, whatever that means, Hank, make sure you drift southeast, away from the Korean landmass. Every mile means less legs for those North Korean aircraft if they decide to storm out like angry hornets. Call me if you need anything else. I have dispatched the cruiser *Anzio* outward to take position one hundred miles in front of us as an early warning and first line of engagement. The two destroyers, *Gearing* and *Perry,* are already maneuvering to take positions on the port side of *Boxer* and the starboard side of Sea Base. That'll help provide antisubmarine protection for *Boxer* and Sea Base."

"Yes, sir. Where are you positioning your flagship, the USS *Boxer*?" Garcia shut his eyes and winced. Why did he ask a question the answer of which his Combat Information Center would know? He envisioned Holman's thick eyebrows twisting into a V as they did when someone asked him a question he expected them to know the answer to.

"Five nautical miles off your port beam," Holman answered a few seconds later. "This amphibious warship has some limited air defense capability, but it's only good for close-in support. She doesn't have enough to survive a massive attack. What else do you have out here? You have better satellite comms than I do."

Captain Garcia shrugged. He didn't know. If the sensors didn't pick it up or some tidbit of intelligence didn't filter to him, they were blind. He hadn't realized how blind the Navy had become until Holman asked the question. It wasn't as if Sea Base had a robust intelligence apparatus on board. In fact, it had none. The Navy had transformed itself out of most of its support disciplines, deciding by 2009 it would depend on the joint forces, other services, close allies, and national agencies for any intelligence it needed. What it got was CNN.

"I don't know, Admiral. The first-class leading petty officer in the ASW control center thinks the torpedo may have been fired by a North Korean submarine." It was a lame response. The most miraculous technology and weapon the world had ever seen and he was relaying the opinion of a first-class sonar tech about who had attacked the Chinese. He cringed, waiting for the blast from Admiral Holman.

A couple of seconds passed before Holman asked in a calm voice, "Why in the hell would they fire against the one country that keeps feeding and fueling them?"

The sound-powered telephone talker released the mouthpiece button and looked up at the TAO. "TAO, sonar reports the Chinese submarine is releasing decoys and taking evasive maneuvers."

"I'm watching the action on NTDS," Garcia said. His stomach contracted. He had never been in battle. Was this what it was like? He touched his left shoulder and rubbed it. His job was to test the concept of Sea Base. Test the concept of eight gigantic ships holding aloft eighty-one-plus acres of tempered alloy platform capable of conducting air, amphibious, or at-sea warfare. *Not actually demonstrate its warfighting capability! Not this time out! And not in a real-world scenario.*

A half minute later, after Admiral Holman had passed on several other instructions, the two leaders hung up.

Stapler touched Garcia on the shoulder. He nearly jumped at the unexpected touch.

Stapler picked up the life vest Garcia had laid on the Captain's chair. "Sir," he said, handing it to him again. "I think all of us are a little nervous. Sir, you heard?" he asked, nodding toward the sound-power phone talker. "The report from sonar?"

"Yes, I heard, Commander. Give me a couple of seconds," Garcia said. He was concentrating on Holman's instructions.

"Long conversation, Captain?" Stapler probed, ignoring Garcia's request. The TAO glanced from Garcia to the large geographical display projected on the bulkhead screen above the consoles. "The North Korean formations have started returning to the landmass. Only a few formations remain flying the racetrack, Captain."

"Maybe they've given up and are going home for the day," Garcia offered.

"I doubt it, sir," Stapler said uneasily. "The North Koreans are like petulant children. They're going to do something to show they're angry. They want the world to know they're angry. They're planning something, Captain. And when they're being petulant and angry, they always blame the U.S. for their problems."

Garcia put on his life vest.

Stapler continued. "Just flying defensive fighter patrols along their coast is them beating their chest. Eventually they're going to do something."

"Then why are they heading back to base?" Garcia asked, unconvinced. "Maybe they've finished their little show of force?"

Stapler shrugged. "Maybe topping off fuel before they pitch their fit."

"How about those four heavies?" Garcia asked, referring to the large aircraft orbiting near the North Korean coast.

Stapler shrugged. "They disappeared a few minutes ago. We haven't seen any reflections of them. I think they've already returned to base for the afternoon."

"Could they have turned out to sea?"

Stapler shook his head. "If they had, satellite would have picked them up. They're so close to the beach the land smear hid them well, so they've either returned to base or they're orbiting over land. If they're orbiting over land, then eventually one of the Air Force recce birds will pick them up."

"Let's go through the drill of preparing to launch the fighters. But don't man the cockpits yet."

Stapler put his hands on his hips, biting his lower lip. Garcia wondered when the man was going to bite through that lower lip. It was Stapler's way of weighing his orders.

"They're going to do something, sir," Stapler said finally. "It wouldn't surprise me to see them cross the 38th parallel. Start an all-out war."

"Let's hope you're wrong."

"Yes, sir. I've been wrong before." Stapler turned to take care of Garcia's orders.

Garcia weighed Stapler's words. Commander Stapler was a good officer. Not one he'd want to spend a long time at sea with. The man was given to adding his opinions while focusing on executing orders effectively. What if Stapler was right? What if the Koreans were preparing to do something such as cross the 38th parallel? As Admiral Holman pointed out a couple of hours ago, the North Korean doctrine for war with the United States was one of total war. Everything was on the table . . . even their nukes, he thought with horror . . . even their nukes.

After a few seconds, Stapler said, "The pilots are in the ready room, Skipper. I'm holding them there. The Air Force ground crew is topside and have the remaining three F-22As ready for launch. Anything the admiral wants us to do?"

"We seem to be okay," Garcia said slowly, his face pensive in the blue light. He looked up at Stapler. "He wants to know when we have brought Sea Base to full stop. Also, the admiral recommended we set the security detail. Wants to make sure we don't have another Smith incident."

Stapler nodded. "I can do that, sir, but it means taking sailors from damage-control parties to mount the security detail. We only have the minimum number of sailors on board."

"How about the Marines?"

"Only have a handful of them, Skipper. You have one with you at all times, and they rotate another one outside your stateroom at night. We have three rotating on the UUV compartment for security. I don't know what the other eight or nine are doing. If we need more, we can probably get some from the *Boxer*. They have seven hundred Marines embarked."

Garcia sighed. "Set the security detail. Have the Marine Detachment officer come see me. We may ask *Boxer* to send us a detachment or two."

"Aye, sir. One other thing, Skipper. Right now, every bit of over-the-horizon information is coming from outside sources. We don't have a reconnaissance aircraft nor do we have any intelligence detachments on board. If we lose satellite communications, Captain, we are going to be one blind formation. It'd be nice to have some intelligence."

Garcia nodded. "The same thoughts crossed my mind a few minutes ago, Commander. By the way, Admiral Holman mentioned the Royal Navy aircraft carrier *Elizabeth* may be heading our way."

"Yes, sir. We established comms with her a few minutes ago. She sailed from Hakodate, Japan, around noon. The *Elizabeth*, CVA-01, is about four hundred nautical miles northeast of our position."

"How soon could she provide us air support if we request it?"

"The *Elizabeth* has forty Joint Strike Fighters embarked. She's in range now, but we'd have to recover them if they were launched from that distance."

The operations specialist manning the surface console took her earphones off, reached over, and touched Stapler on the arm. "TAO," she said, "I show *Anzio* thirty-two knots on course 330, distance twenty-five nautical miles, sir." A voice from the earpiece drew her attention; she raised it, placing it against her ear. "Commander, *Anzio* fire-control radars are activated."

"Thanks, Bonicella," he replied.

She smiled, her shoulders twitching from side to side as she casually placed the earphones back on her ears.

"How far away are we from the North Korean landmass, Commander?" Garcia asked.

"You mean where the aircraft are flying or the closest point, sir? Their aircraft are flying DEFPATs about a hundred miles north of the DMZ—off the coast of Hamhung. That's about 350 nautical miles, but the DMS is only about 250 nautical miles. Either way, Skipper, if they want us, they can come after us."

Garcia turned without speaking and climbed up into his command chair. No sooner had he sat down than a young petty officer handed him his cup full of coffee. He glanced at it. Steam rose from it and the acrid smell of old coffee hit his nose. He could tell by the color of the powdered cream that the coffee had been sitting on the burner for a while. He sipped it anyway, the bitter tannic-acid taste curling his taste buds. Stapler stood watching.

"Commander, set the security detail."

He breathed a sigh of relief when Stapler walked away. He needed to talk with Holman again. What were his orders if the North Koreans invaded the South? He set the cup down, resting his arms along the chair arms, his hands curling over the ends where his fingers drummed the metal with a light rhythm.

Around the new Combat Information Center, sailors manned the warfighting consoles. Against the forward bulkhead was the venerable AN/SLQ-32(V) Electronic Warfare suite—he had no idea what variant it was. A vintage, proven system originally introduced to the fleet in the seventies. Most likely the original engineers were long dead, but the contractor kept turning out new variants year after year. The polar display never changed, but the system continued to evolve.

Directly in front of him were the air and surface search operators managing the radar returns as information technology sorted the contacts into air or surface targets. Almost immediately, the information was automatically transmitted across Naval Tactical Data Systems to the other ships and aircraft in the battle group. With every new contact, the icon representing it would flash until manually overridden. The large high-dimensional displays on the bulkhead allowed him a battle sphere that stretched from the Korean Peninsula on the west to Japan on the east. It wasn't much good if he couldn't populate it with sensor information.

Behind Sea Base was the narrow channel separating the East China Sea from the Sea of Japan. He had always thought of the Sea of Japan as a huge body of water, but it seemed awfully small right now. He would much prefer to be in the middle of the Pacific. His arm fell off the chair arm, draping for a few seconds down the side of the Captain's chair before he raised it.

The Captain's chair was in the center of CIC, raised off the deck so the Skipper could look anywhere in Combat and see what was going on. The fire-control radars and weapons-control consoles were to his right. He had to turn slightly in his chair to see them, but the six sailors manning the weapon systems were aligned in a row, their heads bent over their consoles.

From where he sat, they were going to be looking to him to give the command to fire. He gripped the ends of the chair arms. For a fleeting moment, he nearly climbed down with the intention of giving the warfighting control to Commander Stapler. After all, he was the Tactical Action Officer. He was one of four officers Garcia had given a letter authorizing each to fight the ship—Sea Base—if he wasn't available. There were lots of excuses he could give. He eased forward and noticed Commander Stapler staring at him as if the man could see into his thoughts. Garcia nodded, slid back into his chair, and crossed his legs. Some responsibilities are yours and no matter how much you want to pass them to someone else, you have no choice.

"Commander, how long until we come to rest?"

"About thirty minutes, Captain," Stapler said, turning his attention back to the consoles in front of him.

"KEYLAND!" Bernardo shouted. "The sub's gone beneath the layer. It's off the scope."

Keyland leaped to the safety railing, standing near Gentron. They both watched as the torpedo disappeared also.

"The torpedo followed it! They're out of sight."

"Can you hear them?"

Beside him, he heard Gentron passing the latest news to Combat Information Center.

"Not a damn thing."

"Shit. MacPherson!"

"I'm right here, Petty Officer Keyland."

"Get that UUV into the water. We need to know what's going on beneath the layer."

"Sea Base is stopping, LPO," Bernardo said, "but it won't be completely stopped for a while. I can't lower the sonar arrays from the ships any farther until we stop."

Everyone looked at the rainfall display of the AN/SQR-25 sonar. The rainfall display continued the slow pattern down the screen, the noise signatures of the submarine and the torpedo having disappeared. Within a couple of minutes, any sign of the unseen combat had disappeared from their view. Somewhere out of sight, a fight for survival was occurring, and it was possible no one would ever know the outcome. They needed those dipping sonars from the Fast Sealift Ships down beneath the layer.

FIVE

Kiang hurriedly tied his shoes. The general quarters alarm had quit, but he'd needed the quick shower. His left cheek twitched. He dropped the laces long enough to rub the spot, shifting his lower jaw back and forth. The twitch continued. It was tension, he told himself. The more intelligence he provided, the more his handler demanded, and the more his parents' lives were threatened. He grabbed the laces, ignoring the twitch, and finished tying his shoes.

Pushing himself up off the edge of his rack, Kiang reached across to the metal desk and lifted the radio. Since the secret search of his quarters by Zeichner and Gainer nearly four months ago, no one had entered the compartment, sifting through his things. Nothing out of place. No odor of a stranger. His nostrils widened as he took a deep breath and smiled. The two were amateurs.

Armed with new instructions that easily increased the danger of exposure, Kiang was confident of his advantage over these two NCIS agents. If this was the best the Navy could send, then two months from now when this experimental deployment was over, he'd be skipping down the gangplank while they were still trying to decide if they'd had a foreign agent on board Sea Base or not.

He glanced at the shower. Even two amateurs such as Zeichner and Gainer would be scratching their heads at the small device hidden in the ventilation shaft. He shrugged and smiled. *When guilty, deny, deny, deny.*

He pushed open the back of the radio and grabbed the barely visible end of a wire protruding from inside the body. The casual observer would have thought the wire was part of the battery chamber. He stretched the wire and watched it unreel. Kiang set the radio on the table, unwinding the wire as he walked slowly across the compartment. Near the reclining chair, he wrapped the end around the electrical cord of the lamp, and released it.

He crossed back to the radio, careful not to touch the thin wire running through the middle of the compartment. Without lifting the radio, he turned it on. Kiang crouched to see better, and pushed the locking toggle for the battery compartment to the "open" position. He slipped his small earpiece into the radio and waited for a few minutes, listening for instructions. Kiang glanced at the clock. It had been nearly five minutes since the GQ alarm had ceased to bong.

His face twisted in anguish. He was a loyal American, Kiang told himself. He was forced to do this because of the threat to his parents, who were being held in China. "No, don't even think it," he said aloud. He could never tell anyone what he was doing. His life in America would be over. His parents would die and he would never hear of them again. But then it would matter little, for his life would be over also.

He recalled listening to his father telling the story of when the first wave of Chinese came to California during the Gold Rush. How they were invisible as long as they "stayed in their place." He intended to stay in his.

Kiang pulled the desk chair out and sat down. He looked at his watch and nodded curtly. He was still within the five-minute window.

He was a contractor. Contractors were invisible as long as they stayed in their place. "Sand crabs" was the nautical colloquial slang the sailors used for contractors. The Navy expected them to do what they were contracted to do, as well as anything else that seemed like work. During general quarters, contractors were expected to stay out of the way. He intended to honor that unwritten dictum . . . for the most part.

Footsteps along the passageway outside his stateroom drew his attention. He held his breath until the footsteps receded. Kiang looked back at the radio. His fingers drummed the desk. Sea Base wasn't your normal warship at sea, so breaking Condition Zebra, as the Navy called the GQ lockdown condition of watertight doors, should be easy.

Kiang had noted the hatches of the eight Fast Sealift Ships were not even connected internally to a damage-control console, much less to a wide-area network capable of monitoring the status of general quarters. He had even listed it as a business opportunity to the Foundation. He'd also passed the information to his handler. The Institute's business development people would follow up on it. His handler, the colonel, would incorporate the information into the Sea Base file at the Ministry of State Security. He assumed there was a Sea Base file.

The five minutes passed slowly with no transmission. He removed the earpiece and less than a minute later, the radio was back to its normal state. He set it on the table, aligned with the faint pencil marks.

Kiang grabbed binoculars from the closet along with his camera. Initially, when they sailed from Pearl Harbor, he had been concerned the camera would draw attention, but soon discovered nearly everyone on board, including the average sailor, was taking photographs of Sea Base. Not everyone had binoculars, but no one took notice of them. His only worry was belowdecks in the sensitive areas such as near the UUV compartment.

He recalled how he had nearly stumbled into this mysterious Smith that day in the UUV compartment. The hatch to the compartment had been jimmied. He didn't do it, but he did take advantage of it by shorting the security cameras long enough to take some great photographs inside the high-security compartment. As he approached the hatch to leave, it swung open and this lanky sailor entered. Kiang had hidden near the row of UUVs until the sailor passed, and then quickly exited through the hatch. Later, rumors told of how the sailor was responsible for the explosions on Sea Base.

Kiang's handlers wanted to know more about this Smith. They believed he was connected some way to this radical American God's Army. Another task from the colonel was to get information about Smith.

He patted his pockets, making sure he had everything. Kiang opened the door to his stateroom and stuck his head into the passageway. Seeing no one, he stepped out and pulled the door shut, checking to ensure it was locked. Kiang was confident no one would stop him as he ambled upward, working his way to the top of Sea Base, opening and closing watertight hatches as he moved. Even when he reached the hatch leading to the top of Sea Base, he didn't hesitate to open the watertight hatch and push it open. The sound of it hitting the metal deck reverberated down the ladder, the noise echoing along the ladder well leading up from the USNS *Regulus.*

Topside, he lifted the heavy hatch, letting it drop close. He looked around, surprised to discover dozens of sailors rushing around the top of Sea Base. Near the F-22A fighters, the Air Force ground crews were scrambling over the aircraft. He squatted and spun the watertight hatch. Someone might have noticed him breaking Condition Zebra, but as long as he closed the hatches behind him, he doubted they would waste the energy to even shout at him, much less take his name.

At a brisk pace he headed toward the four-story tower. On top of the tower was the gigantic mast where banks of antennas and radars dotted the structure like electronic ornaments on a leafless Christmas tree. Near the main transmission antenna at the top of the tower was a small platform where he could stand and watch everything. Since he was assigned as the senior Tech Rep responsible for the performance of the more complex antennas, his presence could be easily explained. More importantly, from this vantage point he could see everything occurring topside on Sea Base.

As he walked, his eyes roamed Sea Base, resting for moments on the laser weapon before shifting to the rail guns. It was important his observations were never obvious, never noticed. He walked with a briskness fast enough to blend in with the activity going on around him, but not so fast that it made him stand out from the others. The sights and sounds of Sea Base shifting to a warfighting stance filled the air.

A curse drew his attention to the forward port-side rail gun, behind him on his right. "Gunner's mates" the sailors who manned the three weapons systems were called. Whatever had caused it, the curse faded, lost in the tenseness of the activity surrounding the weapon. Kiang had never experienced the stress of preparing for battle, even as his own anxiety soared with the thought of what the next few hours might hold. The tenseness, the fear, the unknown over the horizon. He didn't even know why Sea Base was at general quarters, but assumed it was real. Everything at sea was real to him.

While his eyes absorbed the activity around Sea Base, he failed to notice the continuous glances of the sailors toward the horizon, combing the sky, their minds a cauldron of nightmares and fatalistic fantasies.

He tripped over a raised tie-down on the deck, quickly regaining his balance. "Gunner's mates," he said aloud. He had shared a cup of "bug juice"—the horrible name sailors used for the too-sugary flavored water flowing through transparent plastic containers on every mess desk. The petty officer had been very proud of his job on the rail guns.

The principles of electromagnetic rail guns had been understood for decades. It wasn't necessary to have a PhD in mechanical engineering such as his to understand them. But theory and design are abstract concepts. Those who operate such a high-tech weapon are the ones who really understand the nuances of the weapon.

Rail guns worked on the principle of a rapidly moving electromagnetic field that started at the bottom of the barrel behind the shell, propelling the shell ahead of the field as it expanded up the barrel at many times the speed of sound.

He had seen the firing results shared by the Office of Naval Research scientists. They were very proud of their scientific accomplishment. *Well, they should be,* he thought. No other country in the world had anything such as rail guns, with the exception of Canada, England, and Australia. Three countries with whom America shared everything, even its sailors when the opportunities arose.

The electromagnetic field expanded so fast that within the fraction of a second it took to propel the shell out, the shell was exceeding ten thousand mph. Satellites and fire-control technology were so accurate, targets hundreds of miles away could be hit with pinpoint accuracy by the smaller shells arriving at many times the speed of sound.

Kiang was impressed. The gunner's mate was appalled. What was his Navy coming to? No more gunpowder. No more smell of cordite drifting across the deck of a warship. No more slapping his dungaree shirt and smelling the odor of a true gunner's mate. Instead, when he slapped his shirt, the ozone odor of an electrical fire swept up around his nose. *"Shit, man,"* he had said, *"I smell more like an electronic technician in a whorehouse than a gunner's mate in a bar brawl."*

The gunner's mate had been more helpful than he would ever know. Very helpful, confiding how the smaller shells were harder to store.

The more bug juice the gunner's mate drank, the more he talked. Kiang regretted the lack of alcohol on Sea Base, though he doubted the gunner's mate could have told him anything more than he confided on the mess deck. The gunner's mate told "Dr. Zheng," believing Kiang to be part of the Office of Naval Research team on board, that the loader couldn't keep up with the rail gun. Too many "misfires." If the gun fired too fast, the loader froze, causing a complete failure to fire.

To unfreeze it, the gunner's mates had to unload the shell in the weapon. Not only was it a "misfire," but they had to treat the whole failure to fire like a "hangfire," where a shell fails to fire and remains in the barrel. Hangfires scared the shit out of gun crews, the gunner's mate said. The scientists may believe hangfires were a thing of the past with rail guns, but *"by God, we know better."*

He recalled what the gunner's mate said about hangfires. "You run the risk of the high temperatures of the barrel cooking off the shell. Once you have a cook-off, then you have to sweep up the body parts."

The rail gun fired shells so fast and at such speeds that the very first shell created a high enough temperature within the barrel to cook off. Multiple firings sent temperatures soaring. Good information, thought Kiang as he transcribed the conversation later that evening.

Information such as this filled his laptop, written in such a way that anyone reading it would consider it a treatise for correcting the problem. It could even be argued that Kiang was seeking business opportunities for the Foundation.

Kiang reached the outside of the tower. He slipped his arm through the strap of the binoculars so they were on his side instead of in front on his chest. He grabbed the ladder leading up, and began to climb. The binoculars bounced off his side as he moved up the tower, heading to the platform at the top. This should please the colonel. "Fuck you, Colonel," Kiang said through heavy breathing, seeing the image of the crooked teeth, the heavy eyebrows, and the bright scar that ran from the top of the right eyebrow to the edge of the hair over the left eye. The face was quickly replaced by the red-blotched toe of the Army boot that had filled his vision for so many days. Kiang stopped for a moment halfway up, wrapping his arm through the railing, catching his breath.

He glanced up. The ladder led directly to a small opening in the solid metal deck of the platform. Kiang took a deep breath and continued climbing. Several minutes later when he reached the opening, Kiang stuck a hand inside the opening and pulled his head through. Standing there watching him was a sailor wearing a sound-powered telephone headset and a life vest. Kiang felt a rush of unexpected heat to his face. What was the sailor doing here?

"Hi," the sailor said, squatting and grabbing Kiang's hand.

Kiang gripped it, allowing the sailor to help him through the small opening.

"Guess we're going to be in a tight fit for a while," the young sailor said.

"Yes, I didn't expect to see anyone up here," Kiang said, his eyes narrowing. "Haven't we met before? Didn't you meet the aircraft?"

The sailor stomped the platform deck a couple of times, smiling broadly. "You were on the C-130 that landed a couple of hours ago. I was part of the working party helping to unload the aircraft."

Kiang nodded. "I thought you looked familiar. What are you doing up here?" Kiang asked, trying to sound innocent.

"My GQ station according to the master chief. Is this your station?"

"Yes. I am in charge of the antennas up here," Kiang said, his mind racing. Should he stay or leave?

"Well, good, because it's not a nice place to be by yourself," the man said. He held out his hand. "I'm Petty Officer Taleb. My friends call me Jaime."

Kiang shook the hand too quickly, barely touching it before he dropped the handshake.

"You're the one with the PhD, aren't you?" Taleb asked.

Before Kiang could answer, the young man held up his hand,

pushed the button on the mouthpiece of the sound-powered headset. "Combat, Tower; all clear. GQ set."

"Sorry," Taleb said, smiling. He touched the bulky sound-powered telephone outfit. "These things make me feel like a robot or something."

"They remind me of warrior ants," Kiang offered. He'd stay here with the sailor for the time being. It might create suspicion if he left so soon after arriving. It was going to be hard to take pictures with the man watching.

"You mean the wide helmets," Taleb said, a broad smile stretching across his face. The sailor reached up and slapped both sides of the huge light-gray helmet that held the earpieces. "I know what you mean. I don't think the Navy has changed these since they were invented centuries ago. Sometime around World War II, I think."

Kiang shifted a couple of feet to the far side from the sailor and lifted his binoculars. *How young,* he thought, *and how ignorant. What are they teaching in school today? Centuries ago indeed. World War II was what? About seventy-five years ago.'*

"You're the doctor from San Antonio, aren't you?"

Kiang gave Taleb a long, searching look. He nodded slowly. "Yes, I am from San Antonio. I am surprised anyone knows this. How would you know it?"

Taleb laughed, his brown eyes twinkling. "Sorry. I didn't mean to be so nosy. I'm studying for my bachelor degree on board. A couple of months ago I helped you and the other scientists get settled on board." The sailor shrugged, the smile disappearing. "You wouldn't remember me. Sailors tend to blend into the background. Unless we're acting up on liberty or being forced to talk with officers, we could be burning the place down and the only ones who'd notice would be the guys who have to clean up the mess. I think we sailors are the background noise to life at sea. There—but not there. You know what I mean?"

"So, you helped me to my stateroom?" Kiang asked, knowing no one had helped him. He'd carried his own suitcases from the pier, up the equivalent of four stories along the swinging gangway of the USNS *Regulus.*

Taleb shook his head. "Naw, I didn't help you. I was part of the working party on the pier when you and the others arrived. I heard someone call you Doctor." He touched his chest. The smile returned as well as the excitement in the man's voice.

"I'm working on my bachelor's right now. The chief told me to get my associate's first. . . ." He stopped, pushed the talk button on the mouthpiece. "Yes, Combat. Communications check fivers."

Taleb released the button and looked at Kiang. "Then I'm going to go and get my master's. All compliments of the Navy."

Kiang raised his binoculars and started working his way around the top of Sea Base, watching the activity and mentally noting it for later. Beside him, the sailor continued to talk about his plans for his life, how he was going to eventually study for a doctorate like Kiang, leave the Navy, raise a family, though he didn't have a girlfriend yet, but he'd find one eventually. After five minutes of Taleb's never-ending commentary, the sailor's voice faded into background noise. Kiang promised himself he'd leave the platform as soon as circumstances allowed before the sailor's monologue drove him mad.

Kiang twisted the binoculars, focusing on the F-22A Raptors. Pilots were climbing into the cockpits of three of the aircraft. Airmen scrambled over the fourth aircraft. The side of the fourth aircraft was open. He touched the electronic toggle, increasing the magnification. Two airmen had their hands inside the open panel. One held a piece of dark gray equipment, while the other worked what looked like a screwdriver.

With four aircraft on the deck, it meant four aircraft must be airborne. It also meant two of those aircraft airborne must either be low on fuel or . . . He turned and faced where the end of the runway extended outward over the sea, away from the main body of Sea Base. Beneath that forward end of the runway was the Fast Sea Lift ship USNS *Altair*. If anyone could say Sea Base had a bow, it was the USNS *Altair*, hidden beneath the end of the runway. Maybe somewhere up there, over the horizon, Air Force KC-135 tankers orbited.

These Raptor fighters were of much interest to his handler. Their stealth technology and multiple-target-engagement capability were things China wanted desperately. All the cyber espionage by the People's Liberation Army had failed to penetrate the computer network defenses of the Air Force or Department of Defense.

Kiang lowered his binoculars. The sailor was still talking—saying something about a deceased father and fishing on a family creek. A shock of anxiety raced through Kiang. The man's features were composed, almost angelic, but the eyes . . . The young man's deep-set eyes seemed to be appraising, scrutinizing Kiang. He turned, keeping his face expressionless and raised his binoculars again. Taking a deep breath, he told himself to quit being paranoid.

"THE submarine's back!" Bernardo shouted, drawing everyone to his screen. "It's above the layer."

"Where's the torpedo?"

"Second torpedo in the water!" Bernardo yelled, touching the screen slightly right and above the submarine signature. "Target is submarine. Left-bearing drift away from Sea Base."

"First torpedo must have run out," Keyland added, his face paler than usual in the blue light. "I don't understand why it doesn't fire a spread of torpedoes. Why just one at a time?"

"Maybe the first torpedo is still circling beneath the layer," Gentron offered from the upper level. "How far away is the submarine?"

"Pass the info," Keyland commanded.

"Won't know distance unless we go active or everything steadies up so we can do a passive maneuvering board on it," Bernardo answered. "How the hell can I do a passive plot on the damn thing if it keeps twisting and turning every few seconds?"

"If it quits twisting and turning with those torpedoes after it, you won't need to do any plotting," MacPherson said.

"Oh, be quiet."

Gentron pushed the talk button on the sound-powered telephone. "Combat, Sonar; I have you fivers. Contact regained on possible Chinese submarine; bearing one-nine-zero degrees; distance unknown. New torpedo signature in the water. Target remains submarine. Lost contact with first torpedo. New torpedo bearing two-three-zero degrees."

"We have multiple torpedoes fired from the Chinese submarine," Bernardo said, his voice dry. He grabbed a half-empty plastic bottle of water and took a quick swig. "Minimum of three in the water."

"Gentron, tell Combat the submarine is firing torpedoes," Keyland said, his arms blossoming with chill bumps.

"What if the Chinese think Sea Base was the one who fired the torpedoes?" Calvins asked, his voice shaking.

"Course of the torpedoes, Pope?" Keyland asked Bernardo.

"Keep quiet, Calvins," MacPherson said softly, motioning at the sailor. "We'll be the first to know if they're coming this way."

"They're on a reciprocal course to the inbound torpedo," Bernardo announced, relief in his voice. He reached up and tweaked the rainfall reception. "Decoys in the water."

"What's that?" Keyland asked, touching a faint spot below the submarine signature.

Bernardo leaned forward, his head blocking Keyland's view. "I don't know. . . ." he said, squinting. He jumped reflexively, his back hitting the back of his seat. "Christ! It's the other torpedo. It's above the layer!"

"Petty Officer Keyland," MacPherson said. "UUV ready for launch. Senior Chief says launch when you give the word."

"Above the layer!"

"Above the layer and it's heading for the submarine."

Everyone watched as the noise signatures of the submarine and the original torpedo headed toward each other. Bernardo took off his ears, reached above his console, and turned the volume up on the speaker.

Above them, Gentron kept a running commentary on what he was hearing, passing the information to another seaman who stood near the Tactical Action Officer in Combat. In Combat, a similar group of silent people hunched over the Naval Tactical Data System and watched the data return disappear.

The noise signatures merged. From the speaker a rising noise like boiling water brought everyone to sudden silence. No one moved. Then a sound as if someone was crushing empty cans and running fingers down chalkboards echoed through the compartment. Then, silence.

"Jesus Christ," MacPherson moaned. "This can't have happened."

"Wow!" Calvins said. "It's like . . ."

"Shut up," Bernardo said quietly, his voice quavering. "We just watched a hundred and something sailors die."

"Focus," Keyland commanded, putting his hand on Bernardo's shoulder.

The only passive signatures on the scope were of the torpedoes, the Chinese torpedoes passing the lone remaining hostile one. Soon rainfall lost contact with all of them.

"Scratch one Chinese submarine," Calvins said aloud, breaking the silence.

"Somewhere, someone is going to blame Sea Base for this," Keyland said, straightening up.

"You ready to launch the UUV?"

"Gentron, tell Combat we are launching the UUV." Keyland turned to MacPherson. "Tell the senior chief what happened. Tell him we're going to launch and unless he wants me to do something differently, I intend to wait a minute to give Combat time to countermand the order."

Two minutes later: "Launch the UUV, Jenkins. Tell Senior Chief we need a second one prepared for launch," Keyland said to MacPherson, his voice wooden, distant.

SIX

"Raptor 10, Raptor Haven; come to course one-eight-zero, angels fifteen. Raptor 30 Formation approaching Combat Air Patrol area. You are cleared to return to Homeplate."

"About f'ing time," Alexander "Blackman" Franklin said on the private communications channel. "I don't think this piddle pack would last much longer."

"Roger, Raptor Haven; turning to course one-eight-zero," Ronny "Fast Pace" Walters replied. "Okay, Blackman, let's go take care of that piddle pack. Wouldn't want the aircrew to think ill of their number-one stud." Walters eased the throttle left. The right wing of the stealth F-22A rose as the fighter twisted into a lazy left-hand turn.

"Okay, okay, Fast Pace," Franklin replied. "I got you so don't go and try any of that *'Let me see what I can do to confuse Blackman'* shit."

Together the two F-22A Raptors twisted right, Ronny "Fast Pace" Walters leading the pair—Blackman riding Walters's left wing, a half-aircraft length back. A few seconds later the formation emerged from the turn, wings leveling. Walters watched as Franklin eased his F-22A forward until the two aircraft were flying alongside each other, separated by about fifty feet from wingtip to wingtip.

"Raptor Haven, Raptor 10; on course one-eight-zero, angels fifteen."

"Roger, Raptor 10. Maintain course and altitude."

"I told you not to drink so much coffee and what did you do? You brought a thermos of it with you," Walters chastised.

"Piddle packs are supposed to soak up urine for hours," Franklin retorted.

"Maybe it's one of those recycled ones?"

"Don't give me that shit, Ronny. They don't recycle piddle packs. They destroy them. You been trying to convince me from day one they recycle them."

"Not only do they recycle them, they test the urine without our knowledge to see if we are abusing—"

"Man, you are so full of shit your eyes are brown."

"It is true they are brown, but that's so everyone will think we're twins."

"Yeah, you tried that in Virginia. Nearly got both of us killed."

"How did I know it was a redneck bar?"

"I would have thought the tractors parked out front would have told you."

"Did you read the latest Air Force bulletin on the updated Patriot Act? They can have our medical records and covertly take our urine and other bodily fluids to see if we are terrorists. I understand the Air Force is turning over our piddle packs to the FBI."

"Raptor 10, Raptor 30 Formation passing down your left side, forty miles, angels twenty."

"Roger, Raptor Haven."

"You see them?" Walters asked.

Both pilots looked up, searching the skies to their left.

"I don't see any contrails," Franklin said finally.

"Well, you wouldn't, would you? I mean we are stealth aircraft."

"According to my calculations, Fast Pace, we should be back on board within thirty-five minutes."

"You never did answer my question. Have you seen the latest Air Force bulletin?"

"No, I haven't and I heard what you said. I don't believe it for a minute."

"Fact is, Blackman, some of those young lovelies you been shagging from the officers' club at Langley are probably FBI informants. They probably wanted your body fluids to match against your library card. The chaplain told me they have discovered a person's DNA can tell them whether they're a terrorist or not."

"Cut the crap, you two," a female voice erupted across the airways. "This is the Commander and this a war zone, not a college frat party. Give me your situation report."

Walters looked out his cockpit at Franklin. He pantomimed across his helmet as if wiping sweat from his brow.

Franklin pointed at him, raised his hand, and twisted it as if changing a lightbulb. Walters flicked him off.

"Fast Pace, this is Pickles; did you copy?"

Walters's lips curled upward with indignation. Flat Cheeks was what everyone called her behind her back, and not with the camaraderie of a teammate. Pickles went against the anointing tradition of fellow pilots.

Walters was awarded his call sign at Langley. His fellow pilots gathered in the officers' club and around several pitchers of beer awarded him the call sign "Fast Pace."

A pilot did something that caught the fancy of the other pilots, or like Franklin, was so squared away, that they played the call sign name game on some characteristic of the pilot. Walters's was because of a bad case of the trots on his first deployment to Aviano, Italy. *"Man, he set a fast pace from that cockpit to the toilet, didn't he?"* someone had said with a laugh. The name stuck and as long as he was in the Air Force, he would have it. He wondered briefly how "Halfpenny" Baines, the Chairman of the Joint Chief of Staff, got his.

"I said, Raptor 10, situation report," Johnson growled.

"I copy, Major," he replied dryly.

"We're on secure comms, Captain. You can call me Commander or you can use my call sign or you can call me Raptor 30."

"Roger, Raptor 30. Nothing to report. We've been out here three hours. Bogies are outside of our radar range, but the Navy has been relaying the picture via tactical data system."

"Roger, Raptor 10; we have the link up and operating. What is your fuel state?"

Walters glanced at the heads-up display on the front portion of the cockpit window and reported his fuel state to the detachment commander. Walters was furious by the time he finished the status report to Johnson, which, because of his dislike of her, he viewed more as an inquisition.

"You are cleared to return, Fast Pace. How High and I have relieved you. Be advised on your return that we are on strip alert aboard Sea Base. Do what you have to do when you return, do it quickly, and be prepared for immediate turnaround."

"Roger, ma'am."

A few minutes later, he held up his hand passing a new frequency to Franklin. A moment later the two pilots were able to talk without anyone listening. They turned right, heading back to Sea Base with Franklin riding Walters about being pussy-whipped—threatening to tell his wife—and Walters riding Franklin about the FBI keeping tabs on him with those women they kept sending for him to pick up.

"Hey, man," Franklin said, "I got some blips off to our left. Low-flying ones. You got anything on your radar?"

Walters's eyes narrowed as he scrutinized his heads-up display; the sunlight coming through the right side made the display hard to read. "Wait one, Blackman," Walters said, squinting against the sun glare to read the heads-up display. After a moment, he said, "I don't have anything on mine."

"I had them on mine."

"How many?"

THE UUV dropped three feet from the cradle, the sharp sound of metal on metal echoing through the compartment at the release. It fell into the water, the nose pointing slightly downward in the few seconds it took to hit.

Taylor stood on the small walkway encompassing the aft and starboard side of the firing cradle. He saw it coming, but could do nothing. "No, no, damn it!" he shouted as the splash from the two-thousand-pound-plus UUV leaped above the well deck, saturating him from head to foot.

Senior Chief Agazzi stood on the third level near the computer, staring at the well deck. "Clean release. Petty Officer Taylor, let's rig one from storage so we can replace the one released."

"Why don't we wait, Senior Chief, and see if we are going to recover this one?" he asked, holding his arms out by his side and shaking the water from them. He shook his head.

"Recovery has to be done by one of the small boys and then, it'll be days before we are able to work it back down to here, do the diagnostics, and get it ready for another launch. No, we're going to have to reload the UUV firing canister from the ready storage." Agazzi grabbed a towel draped over the railing running alongside the walkway and tossed it to Taylor. "Here, dry yourself."

THE ton of weight dragged the UUV down quickly. One hundred feet below the hull of *Bellatrix*, the propeller started to spin, picking up revolutions fast. The fins turned, using the increasing speed of the UUV to level out.

"I've got control," MacPherson said. "Bringing it onto course two-three-zero. Hopefully, this will bring us close enough to the other submarine so we can identify it."

"Senior Chief says to prepare to launch a second one," Keyland said from his desk, holding the telephone away from his ear.

"LPO, I'm going to need Gentron. I can drive two of these things from this console, but it'd be an awful lot easier if he's helping."

Keyland spoke into the telephone with Agazzi for a few seconds before hanging up. "Calvins, relieve Gentron on the sound-powered telephone," Keyland said, jerking his thumb toward Gentron. "Gentron, you get your butt down there with Jenkins and give him a hand."

"Torpedoes have passed each other," Bernardo said. "The salvos from the Chinese submarine are fading; I think they're going out of passive range."

A minute later, Gentron sat alongside MacPherson as the two brought the second console up to an operational state. A single console could control four UUVs, but two divided the work, still controlling a maximum of four UUVs. MacPherson ran his tongue between his lips. The problem was they had never handled more than one UUV at a time in an exercise, and here they were about to handle two.

"I hope the senior chief doesn't want more than two in the water," MacPherson said.

Keyland shrugged, ran his hand through his thick hair, and said, "Pope, you still got contact with the torpedoes?"

"Right now, I have strong contact on the single torpedo fired by the unidentified submarine. The contact on the torpedoes from the probable sunk submarine is sporadic. I think we're going to lose them." The man's eyebrows wrinkled. "I think we'll lose them about the place where the other torpedo first appeared."

"Calvins, tell Combat we have one UUV in the water and that we are preparing to launch a second. 'UUV One' is being steered on a course of two-four-zero degrees, searching for unidentified submarine. Speed, ten knots."

"Let's bring the speed up and get the weapon on station ASAP," Keyland said.

"If I bring it much above ten knots—twelve max, we're going to lose passive capability."

"We have passive capabilities with the dipping sonars from the Sea Base ships. We need the UUV out about fifteen miles to give us some over-the-horizon capability. Hike it up to twenty-five knots and let me know when we're fifteen miles out."

"Okay, you're the LPO, Petty Officer Keyland," MacPherson said with a shrug, "but I won't have any sensor or targeting capability until we get it on station."

"I understand," Keyland said, wondering if he was doing the right thing, but his comprehension of the overall underwater picture told him he was.

The soft murmuring of Seaman Calvins, his finger holding down the talk button, passing information to the Combat Information Center inside the tower, blended with the low background noise of electronic gear operating in the closed confines of the blue-lighted Anti-Submarine Operations Center. The others were silent as they watched the consoles.

Bernardo glanced at Keyland standing on the upper level, glad to see the experienced leading petty officer appearing so calm. He saw Keyland's eyes narrow, an expression of steely confidence. Bernardo swallowed dryly, grabbing the nearby water bottle and chugging half of it, thinking how grateful he was Keyland was here and the senior chief was only a button away.

MacPherson's mind raced, his fingers a fraction of a second behind it as he concentrated on the UUV, bringing online the various sensors of the Unmanned Underwater Vehicle. The cameras designed to show real-time what the UUV was seeing had been found useless when the speed of the water over the lens blinded the cameras. The thermal detectors worked regardless of speed along with active sonar. The slower speeds of the UUV allowed MacPherson to add the television cameras and passive sonar to the array. He glanced at the UUV speed, clicked on the speed icon increasing revolutions for the shaft, bringing the speed up to twenty-five knots. He paid little attention to Gentron as the young sailor worked his way through the checklist for the second console. It wasn't as if this was Gentron's first time.

Gentron saw the sideways glance from MacPherson. You'd think MacPherson would trust him to be able to do this without looking over his shoulder. He wiggled in his seat, mentally clamping down his bladder muscle. He had to pee. And he had to pee really badly. His stomach was a twist of fear from not knowing what was going on and what was happening. Why did he join the Navy? He should have stayed in the Pocono Mountains, hunting and fishing. Better facing a bear in the open than being crammed on the bottom deck of a fifty-year-old ship where he stood no chance of escaping. In the reflection of the CRT, he saw Keyland standing calmly on the second level, the LPO's hands gripping the top safety railing. Keyland's eyes narrowed, causing Gentron to look away, wondering if the LPO was angry.

Keyland's thoughts wove a maze of anxiety, worrying if he had the knowledge and experience to be leading this team of sailors, all of who were near his age. Why in the fuck did the Navy decide they didn't need officers for division officers; just chiefs and first-class petty officers would do fine? He looked at the four sailors surrounding him. Four sailors with varying degrees of experience, crammed into the ASW operations center, with the senior chief and their lone maintenance person on the other side of Sea Base. His palms were sweaty and clammy, gripping the railing.

He caught Bernardo glancing at him. Turning his head, he caught the reflection from the CRT of Gentron looking in his direction. His eyes narrowed with disgust over his own lack of confidence, knowing the two sailors saw the depth of his doubts. *"Damn it,"* he said silently to himself, slapping the top railing. *"I'm it and we're going to do it right by the book."*

"Petty Officer Keyland," Bernardo said. "I've lost the Chinese torpedoes. They disappeared along bearing two-three-zero from us, traveling on a course of three-three-zero. Jenkins, your UUV is cavitating; it's churning up the water like a crazy man.

I got a passive signature on it that makes it look like a massive torpedo."

"That's what it is, Pope: a massive torpedo."

"Calvins," Keyland said, nodding at the sound-powered phone talker.

Calvins passed the data to his counterpart in Combat.

"Jenkins?" Keyland asked, calling MacPherson by his first name.

"UUV One is on course two-three-zero, speed twenty-five knots. I have no passive contact at this time," MacPherson announced, then in a softer voice added, "And I won't until I can slow it down to around ten or twelve knots."

"Recommend we change the course of the UUV to Three-zero-zero," Bernardo said. "The current course is taking it to the location of the Chinese submarine. There's nothing out there right now. Three zero zero will tweak it more toward where the Chinese torpedoes disappeared and maybe nearer the possible submarine out there."

"Time remaining until we're ready to launch the second UUV?"

"Gentron?"

"I'm nearly done with the checklist."

"Petty Officer Keyland," MacPherson said. "I agree with Pope. I'm changing course to three-zero-zero degrees."

"Okay."

The telephone rang. Keyland held up his hand and walked briskly over to the desk. It was Senior Chief Agazzi. For the next couple of minutes, Keyland relayed the information on the hostile torpedoes off the port beam of Sea Base.

"I think you should come back over here, Senior Chief. Combat is on our backs. I've got Calvins on the sound-powered phone keeping them abreast of what we're doing, but I think they'd rather be dealing with you."

A minute later, Keyland hung up.

"Is he coming back?" Calvins asked.

Keyland shook his head. "No. Says we're at general quarters. It'd take him about forty minutes to work his way from *Bellatrix* to *Algol,* opening and closing locked hatches along the way. Doesn't think the time out of contact is worth the risk."

"We got confidence in you, LPO," Calvins said with a smile, his voice quaking slightly.

Keyland stared at the young sailor for a moment. "Good, damn it, because this is what war is like," he said, his knees shaking, hoping no one noticed. He walked back to the safety railing along the upper level, peering down at the consoles. He wondered if his voice had been firm when he'd said it. He concentrated on several short breaths, calming himself. He could hear his heart beat. Keyland hoped they believed his words because he had no idea what war was like. He glanced at the digital readout on MacPherson's console. The UUV had been in the water approaching eight minutes.

"I just had a slight hit, Petty Officer Keyland. I couldn't tell if it was a torpedo or possibly a submarine," Bernardo said.

Keyland bolted from his observation perch, sliding down the railing of the ladder to Bernardo's console.

"I don't have anything on my sensors," MacPherson added, his tongue protruding slightly between his lips as he reached up and started tweaking the sensors. "Of course, I'm doing twenty-five knots."

"How far out are you?"

"About five miles, LPO, based on speed and direction."

"Slow it down to ten knots and make sure the passive sonar is operating."

"Oh, it'll work all right," MacPherson said.

"Second UUV is ready for launch," Gentron said.

"Senior chief said not to launch it until he says so and Combat authorizes it."

"Slowing down to ten knots; passing twenty knots now."

"Maybe we should ask Combat for permission and then we can launch, it when we want to."

"Gentron," MacPherson said. "That isn't how it works. Once Combat sticks their head into the picture, we have to do what they tell us to. If we ask for permission to launch and they say launch, we have to be ready to launch.

"I'm ready to launch," MacPherson said, turning to Gentron. "Right? You ready?"

"I'm ready."

"Let's leave it to Senior Chief," Keyland said, making a downward motion with his hand.

"Passing fifteen knots, bringing passive sonar online."

"I have steady contact now on one torpedo. The other torpedoes must have run out of steam," Bernardo said.

"Maybe they sank the other submarine?" Calvins asked.

"The information is coming from your UUV, Jenkins," Bernardo said.

"I don't have anything here. Passing twelve knots speed," MacPherson announced. "I've got something! I've got something!" he shouted, his hand rolling the mouse cursor.

"Turn on the camera!" Keyland said, his eyes widening.

SEVEN

"Two, maybe three bogies. They were definitely aircraft. I've seen enough to know aircraft radar returns when I see them," Franklin said emphatically, while glancing at the heads-up radar display projected on his front cockpit window.

Walters watched his wingman searching the airspace beneath them and knew Franklin was hoping for a visual on the unidentified aircraft. Spotting an aircraft in the sky was harder than most surmised. Unless you spotted the glare of sunlight off the fuselage, or a contrail, or were just plain lucky, seldom did you see an aircraft with the Mark-1 Eyeball until it was right up on you.

"I think we ought to go down and take a look. What do you think?" Franklin finally asked.

"Want to swim back to Sea Base?" Walters asked sarcastically, still unsure if Franklin really had a radar return off aircraft, or if it was one of the ocean quirks the Navy would know about, but forget to tell them about.

"Ah, Fast Pace, it's on the way. We have enough fuel for one pass," Franklin argued.

"I didn't see anything on my radar."

"Maybe my aircraft is blocking your radar."

"Let's contact Raptor Haven and see if they have anything

out here. You have any sort of speed on it? Your electronic warfare suite telling you anything?"

"No, I don't have any EW readings, but the quick look by the radar indicated they were traveling about 250 knots."

"Kind of rules out helicopters . . ." Walters added.

"Or fighters."

"Too low for commercial aircraft."

"Don't have anything such as an oil rig in the area," Franklin said, "but then we've already ruled out helicopters."

"How long did you have them on radar? They hitting it sporadic or what?"

"They're gone now. A couple of hits," Franklin replied defensively. "Man, let's turn left and open up our radars. See if they're still out there, or if it was a bogus return."

"We'll do it together. Let's warn Raptor Haven," Walters said after a long pause. If he didn't let Franklin prove himself wrong, he'd have to listen to his wingman bitch and whine all the way back to . . .

"And it's not bitching and whining, Fast Pace. I know what you're thinking. If we go back to Sea Base and later they discover aircraft out here and we didn't intercept them . . ."

"Or if we go down and discover it's some sort of sea return Navy pilots would know but us starched-flight-suit zoomies didn't recognize!"

"We don't have to tell them why we're going down."

"Okay." Walters sighed. "You win. I can't win against a bitching and whining maneuver."

"I'm going to tell your wife when I see her next time."

Walters smiled. "Let me talk to Raptor Haven. Sea Base is painting us with their air search radar. We start doing a bunch of maneuvers, changing our altitudes, or whatever, they're going to want to know why. You think your radar could have caught some sea returns?"

"Maybe it was sea returns. All I know is that I don't have them now. But they sure as shit looked like low-flying aircraft returns."

"Raptor Haven, Raptor 10; request permission to modify our course slightly and descend a couple of thousand feet. Air's a little rough at this altitude."

"Roger, Raptor 10; cleared to descend to angels ten."

"Guess they don't know what a couple means?"

"Roger, Raptor Haven; descending to angels ten."

"Raptor 10, come to course two-zero-zero."

"Wrong direction, Fast Pace . . ."

"Raptor Haven, request right turn to course."

"Raptor 10; right-hand course takes you off track for Sea Base. Come to course two-zero-zero."

"Roger Raptor Haven."

"That won't help . . ."

"Let Raptor Haven worry about it. Bottom line is when we finish our turn, we steady up on two-zero-zero. No reason we can't do a full circle, turning right to steady up on two-zero-zero," Walters said buoyantly.

"Man, you are one smooth cookie. They gonna eat your ass for lunch."

"Okay, let's start a slow right-hand turn through the compass to two-zero-zero."

Walters turned slightly, watching Franklin in his peripheral vision since the maneuver hid his wingman from view. Franklin tilted his F-22A fighter right, watching the belly of Walters's aircraft as the two stealth Air Force fighter aircraft started a slow around-the-compass turn to two-zero-zero.

"ALL right, you bunch of God-fearing, best damn great-looking boatswain mates the Almighty has ever put on an American warship—quit your Gawl-damned fidgeting and get your Gawl-damned gear on right!" Jacobs shouted to the twelve sailors in front of him. The sailors, standing in the two rows, buckled their life vests, taking turns while the buddies beside them held the shotguns.

The heavyset female sailor at the end of the front line in the formation turned and pushed the sailor behind her. "Stop it, Shit-head, before I—"

"Snawzernitz, Potts, quit your grab-assing!"

"Not me, Master Chief," Potts stuttered.

"Master Chief," she snarled. "It's Showdernitzel. How many times do I have to tell you." Then with a smile, she added, "Why don't you call me Stella?"

"*I* called you Stella," Potts said shakily.

Jacobs ignored the question. "I'm going to divide you—"

"I'm gonna divide you, Potts," Showdernitzel said in a loud

whisper. "You're trying to park in my brain and you ain't even paying for it."

Jacobs gave her a hard stare.

Showdernitzel looked down and put her hands behind her back.

"—into pairs—that's groups of two, and for those who are trying to obtain a higher level of calculations, that's six pairs." He started a slow walk down the formation. As he meandered along the formation, the sailors stood to attention and the conversation stopped. Jacobs turned at the end and started back in the other direction. "Let me tell you what I know, okay?"

The twelve shouted in unison, "Okay, Master Chief!"

"What a great bunch!" He laughed. "Now, listen to me, because this is important. We aren't chipping paint, painting decks, or checking lines now. *You-me-we*"—he punched his chest with his thumb—"are at a real, live general quarters. That means we could be attacked with bombs and shit, spraying fire and hot metal all over this eighty-one acres of a floating crapshoot designed by the lowest bidder."

A hand went up in the back row. "Why are we at general quarters, Master Chief?"

"Yeah, Master Chief, if we're at general quarters, why ain't we at our stations?"

"Seaman Leary, I'm glad you asked that question because it is the very one I am trying to answer, if I could get all of you to be quiet." He stopped and faced them, his voice taking on a serious tone. "You twelve were pulled off the damage-control teams because the Skipper wants security patrols while we are locked down. You six teams are it. Every one of you have been *expertly* trained on the weapons you're carrying—shotguns. In fact, you are such experts I want them kept unloaded unless you need them. I can't think of any reason why you'd need them, but if you do, then load them, then think twice before you flick off the safety, and if you have to fire them, remember two things: First, the bullet comes out the small hole at the end of that long barrel. . . ."

"Ah, Master Chief, we know that," Petty Officer Third Class Echels said with a laugh, his Southern accent drawing the words out. "You're just trying to scare us."

"And he's doing a damn fine job of it."

"Who said that?" Jacobs asked.

The group stopped smiling and straightened.

"Okay. Stop the BS'ing and listen to me," he ordered, his finger shaking at them. "We're at general quarters and this isn't the time for grab-assing and smart-mouthing." Jacobs clasped his hands behind his back and continued his walk along the row. "The second thing everyone of you no-loads better remember is that you're going to have to explain to a bunch of investigators—"

"Police," Showdernitzel mumbled loudly.

Jacobs shot her a hard glance and continued. "Who will want to know why." He waved his hand back and forth in front of them. "That's not to say you're not to use them if you have to. I just want you to know that your very presence with these weapons should be sufficient to maintain security. I've never seen a sailor who failed to understand why it was bad juju to piss off a boatswain mate; especially one who is armed. Any questions?"

Leary raised his hand.

"What is it, Leary?" Jacobs sighed.

"Why are we at general quarters, Master Chief?" he asked, two fingers unconsciously tracing a line of acne down his left cheek as if looking for something to squeeze. His voice shook. "Are we about to be attacked?"

Jacobs shook his head. "As long as I've been in the Navy, and that's nigh on twenty-seven years . . ."

"I was four years old when he came in," Potts said.

"You still act it," Showdernitzel ad-libbed.

"I've never known one of our warships to be attacked on the high seas." Jacobs pointed at the sailors. "Remember this, my favorite bunch of rogue warriors, we are over four hundred miles from the nearest land. If anything is going to hit Sea Base, it's gotta cross open ocean under the radar surveillance of our warships and aircraft." He shook his head. "The only thing that might reach us is a cruise missile or a torpedo."

"But, Master Chief, surely they have a reason for putting us at GQ?"

Jacobs's eyebrows went up and he opened his mouth to speak, before shutting it as a mental sigh brushed away a legacy of canned responses. He shook his head. "I'm not sure myself. As I said, let me tell you what I know and what I think. You recall all the explosions in New York and Canada last week?"

"New York and in Canada? What explosions?" Leary added, his fingers finding a target.

Showdernitzel reached over and slapped him on the shoulder. "Don't you ever watch the news? And keep those fingers away from your face," she added with disgust in her voice.

"About an hour ago," Jacobs continued, "our European allies in France and Denmark caught some American Holy Roller do-gooders with explosives heading toward the North Korean embassies. I've been a PAC-Fleet sailor my entire career—*wouldn't have it any other way*—and I can tell you the North Koreans are the most xenophobic and paranoid people on our planet. Sometimes, I don't even think they are from our planet. Regardless, right now they're slapping their military into step, marching them up and down the 38th parallel, and rattling their shields as if they're going to invade the South."

"Does that mean we're going to be wearing these life vests and helmets for a while?" Showdernitzel asked, her free hand pulling on the strapped-down vest. "It's going to mess up my hair."

From the snickers someone yelled, "That'll be an improvement."

"Who said that?"

"Cut the crap," Jacobs said. "Next person who speaks while I'm speaking will be confined to Sea Base for the duration of the deployment."

"We're already confined to Sea Base."

"Showdernitzel, when GQ is over, come see me," Jacobs said angrily. Everyone went quiet. He never threatened. If he'd learned one principle of leadership that stuck with him through the years, it was to be consistent. Every one of his boatswain mates knew when Jacobs asked to see them alone, it was not going to be a pleasant experience.

Jacobs took a deep breath and let it out. "We'll be wearing the vests and helmets until the Skipper secures from general quarters or relaxes it."

"So, Master Chief . . ." Leary started.

Jacobs held up his hand. "You've had your quota, Leary. Okay, everyone. I'm dividing you up. Those in front are the petty officers in charge. Your teammate is directly behind you. This is an important detail you're being assigned. I don't need to remind each of you of how that animal 'Smith' nearly sent everyone of us to the bottom; to the dark Pacific where light is an anomaly. So be alert. If you do discover someone skylarking or otherwise doing something other than staying where they're supposed to be, get their names, find out why they're there, and if you believe them, send them on their way. Make sure their explanation makes sense."

For the next five minutes, he pulled the pairs forward one at time, explained their orders meticulously again, and pointed them to their area of responsibility. He sent a pair to the laser weapon and the two rail gun systems. When each pair marched off, carrying their weapons at port arms across their chest, Jacobs called forward the next pair, and so Navy tradition through the years of leading sailors continued in the United States Navy of the twenty-first century. Simple, direct instructions designed to reduce erroneous interpretation.

Twenty minutes later, finished, he turned and watched the security details fan out across the top of Sea Base. He was told the ships had their own security teams among their merchant seamen crews. He pulled a cigar from beneath his vest, glanced both ways to ensure no one was looking, and then unbuckled the top part of the vest before unzipping it down the middle.

"LOOKS as if my shipmates are gonna be part of the security team," Taleb said to Kiang, pointing toward the aft port side of Sea Base.

Kiang turned his binoculars across the runway running down the middle of Sea Base, looking left where the boatswain mate pointed. He watched as a pair of armed sailors walked across Sea Base heading toward the rail gun on the starboard side. A second set of armed sailors stood in front of a tall, heavyset man in khakis, nodding to his words and looking to where he was pointing. Minutes later, the two ambled away, heading toward the laser gun mount.

"What are they doing?" Kiang asked.

Taleb patted the sound-powered telephone helmet on his head. "The Skipper wants security details patrolling Sea Base while we're at general quarters."

"Why?" Kiang asked, running his tongue across his dry lips.

"I don't know," Taleb answered, the left side of his mouth rising up in confusion. "Maybe they want to make sure we don't have anyone causing explosions while we're all locked down?"

Kiang nodded, noticing Taleb's words emerged from the right side of his mouth. The man's right lips separated farther apart, with the left side sometimes failing to open at all. Kiang shook his head slightly at the observation.

"No, it's true," Taleb said, causing Kiang's eyes to raise at how lopsided the man's face seemed from this manner of speaking.

Kiang nodded. "I believe you."

"Good." Taleb reached up and pushed the talk button, responding to some unheard question from Combat Information Center.

Kiang used the moment to start a slow sweep with his binoculars along the top of Sea Base. From this highest vantage point in this modern-day crow's nest, he could see every inch except for directly beneath him. Kiang wasn't looking for anything in particular, but he had his camera, and producing photographs of how something like Sea Basc goes to general quarters would be useful.

The thought of him running traitorous errands until caught caused a rush of fatalism to sweep across him. To stop doing it meant the sure death of his parents, but eventually they were going to die, whether through old age and poor health or at the hands of the colonel. Either way, death was inevitable. But death should come at a moment when you and the Supreme Being have decided your learning experience on earth is completed. Not at the murderous whim of his handler.

Several deep breaths, along with the continuing sweep of the binoculars, brought his thoughts back to the here and now. Two people emerged from the hatch leading up from the *Bellatrix*. *Bellatrix* was the Fast Sealift Ship located directly beneath the laser weapon on the aft port side of Sea Base. He nearly grinned at the thought of "aft port" instead of the civilian description of "rear left side" he would have used ashore.

He swung his binoculars onto the two. He squinted at the two men. Zeichner stood above the hatch, all 280-something pounds of him, while his more physically adept helper—Gainer—eased the hatch back down, pulling the lever around, securing the watertight seal. It had taken a few seconds to recognize the two. This was the first time Kiang had seen them without coats and ties.

Kiang lowered his binoculars. Were the two NCIS agents looking for him again? From where they emerged, he doubted they had been through his stateroom again. His stateroom was on USNS *Regulus,* directly in front of *Bellatrix.* A lone encapsulated passageway that ran from the bow of *Bellatrix* to the stern of *Regulus* connected the two ships. Most avoided the multiple passageways connecting the eight ships. Most doubted their safety.

Kiang glanced toward the hatch leading down to *Regulus,* located along the front left side of Sea Base. One of the security details walked past the hatch. As he watched, one of them squatted and checked the lever before the pair continued their patrol.

Kiang turned back to the two NCIS agents, raising his binoculars and focusing on Zeichner. Zeichner was looking up at the crow's nest. For a moment, Kiang was looking directly into Zeichner's eyes. He dropped the binoculars, moving his hands away as if scalded.

"You okay?" Taleb asked. "You gonna break those glasses if you don't keep a good hold on them." The sailor slapped the metal railing running around them. "No cushioning on this damn thing."

Kiang nodded. "Hands wet. Too hot up here."

Taleb tapped his helmet. "Try wearing one of these for a while." He looked over the edge. "Reminds me of sitting in something like this while deer hunting. Only no 'squitos."

" 'Squitos?"

Taleb slapped his arm. "You know, mosquitoes."

Kiang raised his binoculars and looked again at the NCIS agents. Both were shielding their eyes and looking up at him. For a wild moment, Kiang considered scrambling down the ladder. He was trapped here. How did they know? He had discounted Zeichner as a buffoon, but the man knew exactly where he was.

"WHAT you looking at, Boss?" Gainer asked.

"The tower. You see those two people up there?"

Gainer shielded his eyes and looked. "Yeah. Long way to fall."

Zeichner looked down. "I was thinking how much I'd hate to have a job that high up."

Gainer nodded, dropping his hand and turning to Zeichner.

"Someone has to do it, I guess. From the helmet, looks like a sound-powered phone talker."

Zeichner dropped his hand. "Damned job, if you ask me. Well, let's go see the Skipper and find out what's going on. Seems we're the last ones to find out."

"Did you release the message to headquarters?" Gainer asked as they walked toward the tower.

One of Jacobs's security details stopped them for a moment, but after Zeichner and Gainer showed their NCIS badges, the security detail allowed them to continue.

"Yes, I released it," Zeichner said as he stuffed his wallet into his pants pocket. "Told them what a great and wonderful job they were doing supporting us. I didn't change much of your draft. I made some grammatical changes and strengthened our request for more information on this supposedly foreign agent that may be on board. If there was a foreign agent on board, we would have found him by now."

"What if it's a her?"

"If there is one, then I doubt it'd be a woman. Either way, we'll have to continue our investigation until it proves them or me wrong."

"I'm working my way through the list. We had another suspect return earlier today on the C-130—"

"Kiang Zheng?"

Gainer nodded. "We should pay him a surprise visit when this GQ is done. If the man brought anything back with him, a quick visit by us so soon after his return and before he can hide anything might cause him to stumble."

The 1MC roared to life. "Attention all hands topside. Stand clear of the runway as we launch the C-130."

The two men stopped and looked at the end of the runway where the C-130 that had landed earlier revved its engines up. Zeichner put his hands over his ears. A minute later the transport aircraft roared past them, and halfway down the runway lifted off the flight deck. Zeichner dropped his hands as the two men watched it for another minute. The lumbering aircraft continued outward ahead of Sea Base, then did a slow turn to the right, heading back toward Japan.

"Okay," Zeichner agreed. "We'll pay a visit to his stateroom when GQ is secured, unless the Skipper decides the four positive urinalyses that came back with the C-130 outweighs it."

They reached the tower, Gainer reaching forward and opening the hatch. "I can handle those, Boss. It's more paperwork than investigation. Whip out the appropriate papers; read them their rights; seem sympathetic to their excuses; and hustle them off to legal. By this time next week, they'll be standing outside the gates at Pearl Harbor wondering where their paychecks went."

Two helicopters flew along the front of Sea Base, passing right to left.

"Wonder where they're heading," Gainer said.

"One of them has a torpedo loaded on it."

"What does that mean?"

Zeichner shrugged. "Don't know where they're heading, but in an Anti-Submarine Warfare scenario, one of the helicopters would use its dipping sonar or sonobuoys to locate the submarine and the one with the torpedo would buzz in and drop it."

"Can't just one helicopter do both missions?"

"Could, but looks as if they're using two. Never can tell—we might have a submarine off"—Zeichner shielded his eyes as he followed the helicopters—"our port side somewhere, maybe targeting Sea Base. In this day and age of information technology, someone is always targeting something."

"I would hope they would drop the torpedo before the sub attacked Sea Base."

"I'M getting passive noise signatures from the UUV," Bernardo interjected.

"What's it showing?"

"Give me a few seconds for the system to correlate the signatures, Petty Officer Keyland."

"I'm not getting much on my console," MacPherson said.

"It may be the data relays between the UUV and the SQR-25 are better attuned . . ." Bernardo went quiet, leaning forward, his head and shoulders blocking the view of his screen. Suddenly, he jerked back. "Shit! It's a submarine. A Goddamn submarine."

"How far out is the UUV?" Keyland asked, lightly biting his lower lip. A submarine. This was the one that had sunk the Chinese submarine.

"Fourteen miles."

"Can you get closer so we can see him on camera?"

"I show the submarine commencing evasive maneuvers," Bernardo said. "I've got trace all over the rainfall!"

"Calvins, you passing this to Combat?"

Calvins nodded at Keyland's question, murmuring into the mouthpiece as he relayed the information to the sound-powered telephone talker in the Combat Information Center.

"Jenkins, tell the senior chief. Where are we in launching the second UUV?"

MacPherson leaned over toward Gentron's console. "We can launch whenever Senior Chief gives us a safety thumbs-up from *Bellatrix*."

Senior Chief Agazzi's face filled the small cam vision at the upper left side of MacPherson's console. Keyland watched as Agazzi put on the ear- and mouthpiece, then listened as MacPherson brought him up to date on detecting the submarine threat. Keyland could tell from Agazzi's expression that the senior chief wanted to bolt from the UUV compartment in the depths of *Bellatrix* and race back to *Algol*, but they both knew general quarters complicated such a move. This minimal-manning bullshit was dangerous.

"Okay, Senior Chief says it's ready for launch."

"Calvins! Tell Combat we want permission to launch a second UUV."

"LPO, Combat says the destroyer *Gearing* is heading toward the submarine's location, plus another SH-36 LAMPS helicopter is being launched. The two airborne have already been diverted along the line of bearing. One of them is armed with a torpedo."

"Tell them not to sink my UUV," MacPherson offered.

Keyland stopped Calvins before the young sailor could pass MacPherson's comment to Combat.

"Roger, Seaman Calvins. Tell them we have a UUV in the vicinity of the unidentified submarine and we are requesting permission to launch a second."

Calvins nodded and passed the information. While the tense, excited ASW team waited, Bernardo continued a running report on the changing courses of the submarine. MacPherson kept trying to close the distance sufficiently so the camera could catch an image of the submarine. And sitting beside him, shaking slightly, the novice seaman Gentron waited for the order to push the launch button.

"Sub is in a turn."

"Wow!" MacPherson said, "Look at the bubbles in her baffles." He reached and pushed the talk button. "What did you say, Senior Chief?"

While he listened to Agazzi speak, MacPherson started making changes to the speed and depth of the UUV. A few seconds later, MacPherson whipped around in his chair toward Keyland. "Senior Chief says to bring the UUV to all stop and let her float in place."

"Why?"

MacPherson nodded at Bernardo. "He thinks the submarine is maneuvering because it may have detected the UUV and thinks it's a torpedo."

"It is," Keyland protested.

"And since it is in a turn, the UUV is hidden by the baffles. When the submarine comes out of its turn, the UUV will have disappeared from detection."

Keyland leaned down, looking over MacPherson's shoulder, watching the low-light scene of the deep Pacific, and hoping Agazzi was right.

"I still don't have any reflections," Walters said, easing up on the throttle of the F-22A. Then he added, "Passing one-five-zero degrees." He ignored Raptor Haven bombarding them with questions as to what they were doing.

"I'm telling you, man, I saw them. Only for a moment, but I've seen too many air bogies to not recognize them."

"But it isn't as if we have a lot of experience with operating over the water. I'm told radars sometimes pick up waves and identify them as ships or aircraft."

"I have a bogie to the east of us, outbound," Franklin said.

"That's the noon transport heading back to Japan and cold beer. Could you have mistaken it?"

"No way and the returns weren't waves. This wasn't a single aircraft, so it wasn't the C-130, and if they were waves, then the waves were flying in formation. . . ." He stopped. "There they are! What in the hell did I tell you? Dis the Blackman, eh?"

"I don't . . . Wait, damn it. Okay, okay, I have them now." Walters straightened up in his seat, looking at their heading. "Steady on course one-four-zero."

"Let's go down."

"Slowly," Walters said, easing the nose downward.

"We should have better returns on them."

The wings of the two Raptors leveled in unison—a precision ballet of formation flight. The result of two fighter pilots flying months together in all types of weather, performing tandem maneuvers needed to fight as a unit, and functioning with the confidence that creates meticulous performance.

"I have them on course one-six-zero; no altitude. They're too close to the water."

"Raptor Haven, Raptor 10; we have bogies heading course one-six-zero toward your position. Minimum two to three. Raptor 10 Formation has steadied."

"Raptor 10, what are you doing? You're supposed to be steadying up on course two-zero-zero—"

A second, calmer voice interrupted. "Raptor 10, Air Traffic Control. This is Raptor Haven Air Intercept Control. I am assuming control. Raptor 10, I show you on course one-four-zero, in descent. Do you still have the bogies on your scope?"

"We have them. We are turning slightly right to align ourselves with the bogie formation. Do you have them?"

"That's a negative. We have the cruiser *Anzio* twenty-five nautical miles ahead of Sea Base. They show no indications of air traffic in your vicinity. Can you confirm definite air targets?" In a softer voice, the AIC offered, "You know about waves."

"Roger, Raptor Haven, we are familiar with false positives from sea states. These are minimum three bogies, traveling about 350 knots, heading your direction. How far out do you have us?"

"We show you one hundred miles, but your present course will increase return flight. Come to course one-six-zero at this time. Report fuel state."

"Raptor Haven, Raptor 10; turning to course one-six-zero. Request permission to intercept."

On the private squadron net, Detachment Commander Johnson called, "Raptor 10, this is Raptor 30. Are you sure about your contacts? We don't want the Navy to have some reason to rib us."

"Major," Walters replied with emphasis on the rank. "We are sure what we have is a three-aircraft/in-line formation, flying around 350 knots on a course of one-six-zero that will take them directly over Sea Base."

"I hope you're right, Captain," she replied tersely. Then added, "For your sake."

"I hope we're right, too," Franklin added on the private line between him and Walters.

"Roger, DETCO. We hope we're right, too. I think they're going to let us do a pass and identification flyby." He looked at his fuel. "I think one pass is all we can do if we want to reach Sea Base safely."

"Raptor 10, Raptor Haven. You are cleared to intercept the bogies. Weapons tight. Pass and identification only. We are processing your links into Naval Tactical Data System. We have your bogie icons being transmitted. *Anzio* is attempting to gain contact."

"What the f . . .!" Franklin cursed.

"They're gone," Walters added shakily. He shook his head, envisioning the "I told you so" smiles of the Navy.

"Raptor Haven, bogies have . . ."

"Raptor 10, we only have your returns. No electronic warfare hits; no other radars in battle group showing anything."

". . . have disappeared."

"Roger, Raptor 10. What do you want to do?"

EIGHT

"Skipper," Commander Stapler said, "the combat air patrol off the North Korean coast is growing again. Guess the KORCOM fighters refilled their tanks and are back trying to scare everyone with their angry-hornet scenario." He shook his head, glanced at the large familiar Navy analog clock on the aft bulkhead. "I figured they'd go home for the afternoon, but looks like they plan on continuing it."

Garcia leaned forward from his chair. "What about those bogies Raptor 10 reported?"

Stapler lifted his hands, palms up, from his side. "Who knows, Captain? No one else has them on their radar. *Anzio* is an Aegis ship; got an advanced radar system capable of burning through any kind of electronic warfare or environmental smear to find a target. And she's reporting empty skies."

Garcia leaned back; his fingers drummed the arms of his high chair. "How many North Korean fighters off the coast this time?"

"Minimum of twenty formations, but the Air Force has launched a RC-135 reconnaissance aircraft to patrol the 38th parallel. Reports from it are showing a lot of military activity."

"Um," Garcia said, his lips clenched. "That doesn't sound good." His eyes narrowed. "How many aircraft to a formation?"

"Anywhere from two to four, sir."

"And the status of the F-22A Raptors on our deck?"

"Major Crawford reports three of the fighters manned with pilots in the cockpit, ready for action. He says the fourth fighter will be repaired and ready within the hour. They're replacing a broke part with a new one that arrived on the C-130 today."

"Hanger queen?" Garcia asked, referring to the practice of using one aircraft within the squadron as a spare-parts bird.

"Don't think so, but don't know. I would think you'd need more than eight aircraft to relegate one to hangar queen status. But what do I know, Skipper? I'm just a surface warfare officer in an aviation world."

"Think it'll be ready for action in an hour?"

Stapler shrugged. "Major Crawford said they only needed this spare part."

Stress lines formed on Garcia's brow as his eyes took in the high-definition screens mounted on the bulkheads around CIC. Reams of information rolled across them like rushing tides of unexpected waters. Everything pointed to something about to happen. But what? The report by the Air Force reconnaissance aircraft of increasing military activity; the North Korean combat air patrol; the sunk submarine somewhere to the west of Sea Base—*the Chinese are going to blame us for that one*—and those possible slow-flying bogies heading toward Sea Base. He took in a deep breath and let it out.

The first-class petty officer standing near the communications console lifted the red secure telephone, said a few words, and turned to Garcia.

"Captain, Admiral Holman would like to speak with you."

The small hairs on the back of his neck stirred and Garcia's stomach knotted. The admiral was going to want to know what in the hell he was doing. He hadn't done anything but put some boatswain mates on security patrol to augment the few masters-at-arms on board. He had to tell him something.

"Commander, launch two of the ready fighters to check on those bogies," Garcia said, his voice struggling slightly to control any quavering.

"Sir, we are diverting the two inbound to an identification pass on their way back. They're the only ones with anything on radar," Stapler replied, his voice bridling as if from a rude remark. "I think they're confusing wave returns—"

"What is the sea state?" Garcia asked, his voice normal. He motioned to the leading petty officer for the handset. He wiped the sweat from his palm as he took it.

"Sea state is three, Captain, but that doesn't mean it isn't churning a hundred miles northeast of us."

"Admiral, Hank Garcia here."

A voice on the other end asked him to wait one while the admiral came on the line. Garcia leaned back. "That may be, Commander Stapler, but you tell the Air Force to taxi two of their aircraft to the end of the runway. When I give the word, I want them in the air within seconds." He pulled his handkerchief from his pocket and ran it across his sweaty forehead. What if Stapler was wrong? What if there were bogies coming this way? What can slow-moving bogies do?

"Hank, Admiral Holman here. What you doing over there?"

For the next few minutes Garcia brought Holman up to date, receiving praise over having the Air Force fighters ready for immediate launch and for diverting low-on-fuel aircraft to do an identification pass on their return. Holman updated Garcia on minutes-old news via back-channel communications that indicated North Korean troops massing along the demarcation line.

Stapler handed Garcia a piece of paper on which he had written something. Garcia turned it slightly so it was under the faint reading light. He nodded at Stapler. "Admiral, we have comms with the Royal Navy fighters. A four-fighter formation is joining our two Raptors in the defensive fighter patrol area of operations. I'm being told they will rendezvous in the next ten minutes."

"Do you know their weapon status yet, Hank?"

"Not yet, Admiral. I think *Boxer* is on the circuit also, so we should hear it about the same time."

"Hank, just got told the same thing. Well done to your combat team. What are your plans if these bogies turn out to be real?"

His eyes widened. What were his plans? "I was waiting for the identification pass, Admiral," he said, his voice straining. A well of acid bubbled up in his stomach, causing him to reach for his antacids.

"Hank, what are your plans if they're North Korean?"

His breathing picked up in tempo. "We will warn them away, Admiral," he said, mentally crossing his fingers he had picked the right answer.

"Good, Hank. I'd do the same thing," Holman said, his voice steady, strong.

Why couldn't he have the same confidence this cigar-smoking, cursing combat veteran had? Maybe it was because he'd focused on a career that kept him away from action, a career that centered on building and proving new weapon systems, and a career that gave him more time with his family.

"But what if they don't heed your warning?"

He took a deep breath. "Admiral, unless you have different directions, my intentions"—his voice quavered slightly—"my intentions are to launch the ready CAP and shoot them down."

"Consider it approved, Hank," Holman said. Then, after a slight pause, Holman added, "Hank, I know all of your people are tense and a little scared. They are right to be. You and I have to be strong, and even as nervous and worried as we both are, we're going to put on a confident bravado for the troops. Right?"

"Right, Admiral," Garcia said, his breathing returning to normal.

"I don't have to tell you how tight my stomach is right now, Hank. No matter how many times you enter a situation where you might find yourself defending your battle group, it doesn't get easier. If you need anything, anything at all, you call me. You understand?"

Garcia let out a deep breath. "I understand, Admiral."

"TAO! *Anzio* reports three bogies to her northeast and one to her northwest; distance 125 nautical miles!" the air search radar operator shouted at Commander Stapler.

MASTER Chief Boatswain Mate Jerry Jacobs sauntered up alongside Chief Master Sergeant Johnny Willard, who was standing near one of the portable CO2 extinguishers.

"How long can those pilots sit in their cockpits before their bladder starts crying foul?"

"As long as they have to," Willard replied. "What brings you over here, Jerry? Thought all you sailors would be locked down for this general quarters thing and you chiefs would be sipping coffee in the goat locker."

Jacobs tucked his unlit cigar into his open khaki shirt pocket beneath the half-secured life vest. "My men and women are scattered between damage-control party and six security teams. Seems the Skipper is concerned we may still have a mad bomber on board."

Willard nodded. "Good. I don't sleep well at night since those explosions. Granted, the person they say did the bombings is dead, but in this day and age of terrorism, most of them work in teams."

"Homegrown terrorist in this case."

A young airman holding a walkie-talkie ran over to the two senior enlisted men of the Air Force and Navy. "Chief," he said, referring to Willard. "Combat says we are to put two Raptors at the end of the runway for a ready-alert launch."

The two E-9s exchanged looks.

"Ready alert, we call it in the Navy."

"Looks as if we may see some action after all," Willard said softly to Jacobs.

"You want some weapons for your people?" Jacobs asked, thinking if six security teams were good, then arming these Air Force types who had nothing better to do but babysit a few aircraft would be better. "I can get you some riot shotguns."

"If you're going to arm my airmen, then get us M-16s. They're trained to use them."

Jacobs looked at the airmen working on F-22A side number 223, wondering why they were trained on the M-16 and his boatswain mates had to settle for riot shotguns.

"Tell me how many you want," Jacobs answered, wondering if he was going to be able to deliver.

"Let me think for a moment," Willard said, hurrying off toward Major Crawford, who was standing with several other officers near the aircraft being repaired.

Jacobs heard someone walking up behind him and turned. It was Showdernitzel and Potts. The lovesick seaman and the Wicked Witch of the East. What in the hell did Potts see in her? He shrugged. To each his own. "I thought I told you to stay near the laser weapon."

Showdernitzel shook her head. "No, Master Chief, you told us to walk the deck and shoot anyone who looks suspicious."

"Petty Officer Showdernitzel, you are the last person I would tell to shoot anyone."

"Thanks, Master Chief," she said smiling. "That's a great compliment."

"Then I need to look into how I said it," Jacobs mumbled. "If you're not guarding the laser weapon, who is?" He shaded his eyes and looked aft toward the starboard side. The tower blocked most of his view of the laser weapon.

"Petty Officer Timmons has the laser weapon. Thought we'd come over and see if you were lost."

"Snowandsnitzels, I'm not lost."

"It's Showdernitzel, Master Chief. I know you know it. You just like to bug the shit out of me by missaying it. Don't think I don't know what you're thinking." She winked.

"Okay," he said, more important things overshadowing the slight perverse pleasure the two found in riling each other.

Several seconds passed before Showdernitzel sighed and said, "Okay, Master Chief, if there's nothing we can do, then we're going. . . ."

The sound of jet engines revving up drowned her words. The two fighters at the end of the row started a right-hand turn. Those engines were going to be pointed right at them unless they moved. "Come on," he said, touching Showdernitzel on the shoulder. "Let's you, Potts, and me shift our bodies out of the way of those engines."

The three boatswain mates walked hurriedly to the right, passing through the windblast for a few seconds before the turning aircraft aligned with the runway. The three stopped and watched the fighters taxi quickly along the runway, heading toward a series of long white lines marking the end of the runway.

"What are they doing? Are they going to launch?" Potts asked.

"Ready alert," Jacobs said, his eyes squinting from the heated exhaust cascading across the runway, the smell of burning fuel filling his nostrils. "Take a deep breath, you two. Just like a carrier, except with Air Force blue on board." He pointed at the light blue pickup truck. "And that piece of garbage they call flight line equipment."

Willard stood with seven other airmen watching the aircraft taxi. Jacobs turned to Showdernitzel. "Okay, Petty Officer Showdernitzel, go to the armory, you and Potts. I want you to draw out another four shotguns and issue them to Chief Willard."

"He's only a chief?" Potts asked.

"He's an Air Force chief. That's the same as a master chief in the Navy."

"Master Chief, Dickens is manning the armory. He ain't gonna want to issue us arms."

"I have no idea who Dickens is and tell him Master Chief Jacobs sent you."

Showdernitzel laughed. "I know that will put the fear of God in him. He'll probably give us the whole damn armory."

"Showdernitzel, your days are numbered. Now go get the arms for the Air Force."

"Shotguns?"

"Wait a minute. Not shotguns. Get him . . ." Jacobs paused, his eyes squinted. "Get him four M-16s."

"Sure, Master Chief. I'm going to walk up to Dickens and say, 'Hey, bud, Master Chief Jacobs wants to give the Air Force four M-16s.' What you want me to say when he throws me out the hatch?" She waved. "Bye-bye?"

"Showdernitzel, go do what I say or you're going to find yourself on bread and water."

"Aye, aye, Master Chief," she said with a heavy sigh. "Come on, Potts, and quit looking at me like that. Jesus Christ." She slapped him on the shoulder hard enough to move the thin sailor. "Let's go get arms for the Air Force," she said, slapping him lightly upside the head. "And don't ask dumb questions. Arms for the Air Force? Now, there's a good title for a book."

Jacobs watched as the two boatswain mates turned toward the runway. The slight wind across the deck carried their conversation for a few moments.

"I have a question."

"Potts, it's a dumb question."

"You don't even know what it is."

"I don't have to know. I know you."

"The master chief said the only dumb question was a question not asked."

"In your case, Potts, you're the exception."

"RAPTOR 10, Raptor Haven. Steady course two-zero-zero. Continue descent. Permission to increase rate of descent to maintain radar contact."

"Well, at least we have some say-so," Franklin complained.

The common fighter voice frequency squeaked as a new voice joined the circuit. "Raptor 30, this is Commander Lester

Tyler-Cole, Royal Navy 801st Naval Squadron. Request permission for four F-35 fighters to join your pattern."

"Think the NORCOMs can speak English with that type of accent?"

"Looks as if the Joint Strike Fighters from the British aircraft carrier have arrived," Walters answered on their formation link.

"Think they can fight?"

"How long has England been around? You still got those bogies?"

"I still have the bogies, but it's only the rear two that seem to stay steady. By the way, my friend, I know your mother is British. I wasn't taking potshots at our allies. It's just that in the Air Force manual there's this section about how cynical, good-looking Air Force fighter jocks are supposed to act." Franklin paused for a few seconds, before adding, "Fact is, I'm glad they're here. While I like the idea of fighting a righteous fight against insurmountable odds, I prefer to do it with overwhelming force."

"I'm glad to see you didn't read anything in this manual you keep referring to about us having to reject anyone's help," Walters said with a laugh.

"I think I read it someplace in there, but I'll have to wait until this is over to double-check it."

"Roger, Blackman. Wait one while I get us some privacy. Raptor Haven, Raptor 10; request channel change."

A couple of transmissions later, Walters and Franklin were on a separate channel with the Air Intercept Controller. The comms chatter between the Royal Navy F-35 Joint Strike Fighters and "Pickles" Johnson and "How High" Delaney about joining in the defensive fighter patrol pattern remained on the main tactical frequency.

Walters smiled at the thought of how Major Johnson was going to be one pissed-off DETCO when she discovered they had switched off tactical main. It must be hard on micromanagers when some of their inmates escape.

"Hey, I'm getting good solid returns on the bogies. There are definitely three. Distance twenty miles," Franklin said.

Walters relayed the information. "Did you hear Raptor Haven?" he asked Franklin.

"What?"

"Said their boat *Anzio* reported another contact north of our position. Only had it for about a minute before it disappeared."

"Lots of funny radar shit out here. One moment you got bogies and the next moment you got nothing. Think we ought to ask them if maybe the *Anzio*—is that its name? What in the hell is an Anzio?"

"Ask them what?"

"Ask them if maybe *Anzio* had a sea state return?"

"You don't think they'd let the boat fire in our direction if we have to take these bogies out?"

"If they do, then we'll see how good those Navy ship missiles are. By the way, don't let the swabbies hear you call their ship a boat. They seem to get upset about it."

"Boat-ship-paddle-oar—"

"Hush! There's the rear one. I got sunlight reflection. Man, oh, man, we have a visual!" Franklin shouted.

"Take the lead and I'll follow you down." Walters relayed the information to Raptor Haven, who authorized them to make the pass and identification approach based on their radar and visual. The AIC reemphasized his weapons-tight instruction. Last thing the U.S. wanted was to inadvertently shoot the wrong guy down.

Walters continued following Franklin. Three minutes into the descent, sunlight reflection drew his attention to the unidentified aircraft. "I see it."

"My radar shows they're following each other. Like ducks waddling toward the water. Man, oh, man, if they're making an attack run on Sea Base, they are suicidal."

"The others are probably directly ahead of this one's nose. I estimate altitude at less than five hundred feet."

"Five hundred feet?"

"I don't think we want to go that low," Walters said.

"What's five hundred feet among friends? What do you say to us doing a visual interception now?"

"Looks like a C-130 to me," Walters offered, unsure of himself.

"Could be. You see that ramp below the large tailfin? Same transport configuration. Lower the ramp and offload supplies."

"We use the C-130 to drop the mother-of-all-bombs, MOABs."

"The famous GBU-43—I want a photo for my desk," Franklin said. "MOAB weighs over 21,000 pounds with over 18,000 pounds of explosives jammed into it. They roll it out the back of a C-130 without a parachute, unlike the Daisy Cutters of Vietnam. Lets the aircraft be ascending when the winged angel of death MOAB rolls out the rear."

"I saw one of those dropped once. In Afghanistan, back at the beginning of Operation Enduring Freedom after 9/11. It leveled a Taliban position. An area about the size of a football field."

"I don't think we have the same thing here, though. The aircraft are flying too low."

"Hold on while I tell Raptor Haven."

"I gag every time you say Raptor Haven."

Walters held up one finger through his cockpit window at Franklin.

"I wouldn't mention the MOAB discussion, Fast Pace. I trust the Navy like I trust your mother-in-law; therefore, I would hate for them to decide, without our participation, for this *Anzio* ship to fire missiles."

Walters relayed the description back to Combat Information Center on Sea Base, becoming aware the cruiser *Anzio* had joined the circuit. Sea Base reported no C-130 transports due for another two hours, and that would be the late-afternoon mail run from Japan.

"Okay, Blackman, I'm taking the lead."

"Fifteen miles to interception, Raptor Haven," Walters broadcast after moving slightly ahead of Franklin.

"Roger, Raptor 10; you are cleared for pass. Be advised to keep distance well enough away from aircraft during your approach to reduce air turbulence."

"Well, now," Franklin said derisively, "last thing I'd want to do is to disturb a bunch of unidentified, possibly hostile bogies approaching the only place I can land before my fuel runs out."

"I'll take right. You pass down the left side. One pass, and we continue ahead to the next bogie. After last bogie, unless Sea Base directs otherwise, we ascend to ten thousand feet and head for home. I'd like to land on something other than fumes from an empty tank."

"Roger, breaking left."

"Blackman, if we become separated, continue to Homeplate alone."

"We aren't going to become separated unless you start daydreaming again and forget I'm supposed to be with you."

Eight miles from the bogie in front of them, it appeared more and more like an American C-130 from the rear. "Looks as if someone is in for the chewing of his life when they land."

"If they don't get shot down first."

They flew in silence for a few seconds. Then Franklin said, "Fast Pace, I know it looks like a C-130, but there's something not quite right with it."

"Guess we'll find out for sure in the next few seconds. Here we go," Walters said.

The two aircraft flew down the port and starboard side of the bogie, both pilots taking in the insignias painted on the side of the fuselage.

"Those are Russian markings," Walters said with disbelief in his voice. "The copilot is waving at me."

"If they're Russian, what in the hell are they doing out here?"

"Their nation does border the Sea of Japan."

"Yeah, but we're out here, North Korea is slinging its tiny willie around as if it's the biggest man at the urinals, and we're armed to the teeth."

"Raptor Haven, Raptor 10; pass and identification complete. Aircraft is a Russian AN-12."

"Russian?"

"Russian markings."

GARCIA stepped down from his chair to stand near the Air Intercept Controller. Stapler came up on his left side. "Commander, we know anything about the Russians being out here?" Garcia asked, running his hand through his short black hair.

"First I've heard, Skipper," Stapler answered pensively. "There shouldn't be anything out here near us that we don't know about. Maybe the Russians are doing a reconnaissance mission."

"Three transport aircraft flying together? I don't think so," Garcia said, his tone short.

The red speaker mounted overhead the main operator consoles blared, "Sea Base, Task Force 72."

The two officers looked at each other.

"Looks as if the admiral wants to know what's going on," Stapler offered.

"Task Force 72, this is Sea Base; go ahead."

The speaker crackled for a moment before the broadcast

echoed, "The admiral would like to speak to Captain Garcia, over."

The leading petty officer looked at Garcia and handed the handset to him.

Garcia pointed at the speaker. "Turn the speaker off."

Garcia pressed the privacy button before answering. Holman did want to know what was happening. The admiral was an impatient leader quick to point out how he liked to tell his subordinates what he expected and then let them get on with it. Unfortunately, the admiral's idea of knowing the status of a situation was getting it minute by minute. Garcia repeated the identity of the AN-12s as Russian to Holman, knowing the admiral had heard the Raptor broadcast on *Boxer* at the same time it was echoing through Combat on Sea Base.

"Hank, you warn those Russians away from Sea Base. During the Cold War, we never had Russian aircraft this close to an aircraft carrier. We used to intercept them a thousand miles out."

"Aye, aye, sir," Garcia answered, motioning Stapler to come nearer. *More like two hundred nautical miles out.* He grabbed a nearby piece of paper and scribbled the admiral's instructions on it, handing it to Stapler, who nodded and hurried over to the Air Traffic Controller.

"What's our fighter status?" Holman asked.

"Two returning—they're doing the identification pass en route back. Two are on CAP, three are on ready alert, and one is down, but we expect it up shortly."

"That's the one awaiting spare parts?"

"The spare part arrived on the C-130 that landed earlier."

As the two senior officers talked, the overhead speaker for the ATC boomed with Sea Base calling the Russian cargo aircraft, warning them away from the area. With one ear listening to Holman, Garcia waited for the response from the Russians. Glancing at the clock, he watched the red second hand tick away—second after second after second. *What in the hell are the Russians playing at?* he asked himself. *Holman would shoot them down in a nanosecond and worry about questions from Washington later. Is that what he wants me to do?*

"I haven't heard a response from them," Holman said, the bagpipe sound of the public key infrastructure synchronizing to keep their conversation secure and private.

Garcia pointed at Stapler, making several circles in the air with his finger. Stapler nodded, touched the ATC on the shoulder, and told him to transmit again.

"You still got those fighters on standby?"

"Yes, sir, Admiral."

"Launch two of them, Hank. Tell them to intercept those bogies. What's the status of our two fighters inbound?"

"They're short on fuel, Admiral. We're going to bingo them directly to Sea Base after they fly past the third bogie. Otherwise, we may be picking them out of the drink."

"I understand. We're ramping up our defenses rapidly, Hank, but those Russians aren't part of the game plan. Let's get those fighters launched. Four Royal Navy F-35G Joint Strike Fighters have joined our Raptor defensive fighter patrol. My people tell me that the Air Force KC-135 tanker has taken station west one hundred nautical miles of our fighters. Now, let's get those damn Russians out of the area."

Garcia acknowledged the orders, and quickly handed the handset to the waiting petty officer. It'd be another few minutes before Holman was uncomfortable enough or thought of something else he needed to suggest, recommend, or pass along to Hank.

"Commander Stapler, launch the ready-alert fighters. Vector them to intercept the Russian AN-12s heading our way. Also, have ATC warn the Russians they are in danger of being shot down. Then, swing one of our rail guns in their direction."

"The laser might be more effective," Stapler offered.

Garcia nodded. Technology, new weapons, test and evaluations: Those were subjects he was comfortable with. "Yes, it would be more effective, but unfortunately lasers reach from the weapon to the target. Anything flying between the weapon and the target is toast—history—gone." He let out a deep breath.

Around the immediate area, the chief petty officers and enlisted sailors watched Garcia and Stapler. Each knew whatever happened in the minutes, hours to come depended on the decisions these two made.

Garcia tried to hide a slight smile from the others who he knew watched him from the shadows of the blue-lighted Combat Information Center. His decisiveness surprised him, until he realized all he did was repeat Holman's directions as if they were his. The smile quickly disappeared, replaced by a slight bubble of acid welling up from his stomach.

This wasn't what he was supposed to be doing out here. His job in the Navy was taking new weapon systems and platforms to sea, assessing how they performed, and making a *thumbs up—thumbs down* decision on whether the Navy should put more money into development. He was assigned to test the Sea Base concept, prove it worked, and then go back home to hot dinners, Little League games, and early bedtimes.

Garcia turned and climbed into his chair, propping his elbows on the arms, resting his chin on his clasped hands. Barely comfortable before he realized he should have made a head call before sitting down.

KIANG raised his hands to his ears as the thunderous noise of the jet engines revving up increased in decibels. Mentally, he envisioned the pilots pushing the throttle forward, urging the engines to full bore.

The F-22A Raptor: He knew a lot of details about them. His job was to furnish as much information as possible on these stealth fighters. He knew the politics. The Pentagon wanted every fighter to be an F-35 Joint Strike Fighter because allies were buying them and the military services under different leadership years ago had agreed to them. But both the Air Force and Navy had fought for their service equities: Air Force got the F-22A Raptor and the Navy got the latest version of the F/A-18 Hornet.

As he watched the Raptors, hot exhaust rippling the air behind them as the engines continued to accelerate, his thoughts went to what he knew about the Air Force stealth fighter. The F-22A had an internal 20mm cannon mounted where the right wing met the fuselage. He couldn't see it, but that was because a gun door covered the cannon, opening when the pilot pressed the firing trigger and immediately closing when the pilot ceased firing. Over four hundred rounds the Raptor carried. It was as deadly in close-in combat as its missiles and stealth radar configuration made it at long distance.

He assumed the aircraft were configured for air-to-air combat, but the stealth design of the fighter hid the missiles within the internal weapons bays of the fighter. The F-22A had four weapons bays. Two bays were flush along the mid-fuselage, and the other two were hidden along the air-intake sides. He pushed his hands harder against his ears. These two Raptors should have two Sidewinder and four AIM-120C AMRAAM missiles. Each aircraft could engage multiple targets simultaneously. He nodded once, then raised his head up—proud that the People's Republic of China had nothing that could touch the technology his company helped design.

He had nothing to do with the Institute's work on the F-22A, which was good because the colonel would have known and most of the technology that kept this fighter number one in the world would be in Beijing by now. For that fleeting moment, Kiang forgot the threat to his parents that forced him to spy against the country he loved.

Kiang lowered his binoculars and glanced at the sound-powered phone talker beside him, surprised to see the man staring at him. The sailor smiled and tapped his helmet a couple of times, letting him know the noise from the aircraft was muffled.

Kiang lowered his hands. His brows furrowed deeply; his face grew pinched as the pain from the noise slammed against his ears. Wincing, he lifted the camera and took photographs of the fighters as they started rolling down the runway, picking up speed. He kept snapping photographs, tracking the aircraft with his camera as they roared by the tower, catching some good photographs as the noses lifted and the two Raptors shot off the end of the runway, racing into the sky. He turned the camera up, hoping to catch the two Raptors as they turned to a nearly ninety-degree angle, racing for altitude.

His face and brow relaxed as the noise quickly disappeared.

"You're going to have some good photos, Doctor," Petty Officer Third Class Jaime Taleb said. "What's the chance of me getting copies?"

Kiang put the cover on the lens and dropped the camera, letting it hang around his neck by the strap. "We'll have to see," he said, patting the camera. "Belongs to the company and they don't like us giving out free photographs."

"Why? They're photographs made of our stuff," Taleb whined. He pointed at the camera. "Besides, it's a digital camera. Digital photos are easy to download and easy to transmit, wouldn't you say?"

Kiang smiled. "That's right, but it's our organization's camera and they worry about perceptions of influence when we give out things free. Even digital photos."

"To a lowly third-class petty officer? I don't think so, Doctor." Taleb pulled out his wallet and lifted a dollar. "Here's a dollar. You tell them I paid you for copies."

Kiang laughed nervously. "I am so sorry," he said with a sigh. "I will check and make sure it is okay to give you copies. All right?"

Taleb tucked the dollar into his dungaree pants pocket. "In that case, I'll keep my dollar." He winked at Kiang as he pressed the talk button on the mouthpiece. "Roger, Combat. I read you fivers. Everything is okay here on the highest point on Sea Base."

"COMMANDER," Operations Specialist Second Class Grace Bonicella called.

"What you got, Bonicella?" Stapler asked, looking at her from where he stood near the Air Intercept Controller.

She turned, her body rippling under the loose dungarees. *How does she do that?* Garcia asked himself. He had seen sailors stumble into bulkheads when she passed, and had had to remind a couple of junior officers to keep their minds on their job.

"Captain, I think I have a low flyer off our starboard side about fifty miles."

"No way," Stapler snapped, stepping hurriedly over to her position. "A low flyer?"

She touched the radar screen. A square with the bottom line missing rode atop radar video. "Right there, Commander. See the line showing the direction it's flying?" She touched the mouse, stretching the line from the unidentified aircraft outward. The line went directly over the aft portion of Sea Base. "I think it's the aircraft *Anzio* reported earlier, but lost when they thought it turned toward South Korea." She clicked on the symbol. A small box blossomed, showing course, speed, and an unknown altitude. "It's doing three hundred knots, Commander," she said with a slight trill in her voice. "I'd say the altitude is near sea level. Has to be for my surface search radar to be picking it up."

"Ask *Anzio* if they have anything, then pass the information to the *Boxer* with guidance to inform Task Force 72."

"Already transmitted, Commander."

Bonicella was a professional in her job. One of the best operations specialists on Sea Base. She also seemed impervious to the unintentional havoc she wreaked on the men around her.

Garcia wished he had gone to the head earlier. "What does *Anzio* have?" He had this overwhelming desire to wipe nonexistent sweat from his brow.

"If they have anything, we'll know soon. They lost the earlier contact nearly ten minutes ago. About the time the returning fighters made their first pass on the other three bogies."

"Commander, have the laser weapon lock on the approaching low flyer." Garcia snapped his fingers at the leading petty officer. "The red phone," he said just as the speaker transmitted a call from Task Force 72. He already knew who was on the other end.

"It's gone," she said. "It was there one moment and now it's gone." Even Garcia felt more empathy with her disappointment than with the fact that the radar had lost contact.

Stapler patted her briefly on the shoulder. "You sure you had a return? Maybe it was a false positive?"

Bonicella shook her head, her black hair flowing with the motion. "Commander, I know what I saw and I know it was a valid contact." She touched the screen. "Right here. Right here, I saw it and I tracked it. The system even tracked it. You saw course and speed. That wasn't no false-positive shit. It was a valid contact."

"Okay, I believe you," Stapler consoled. "Where do you think it is now?"

"It either went up, or it's hugging the surface."

Garcia listened to the exchange and watched as Stapler asked the air search radar operator if he had anything. The operator shook his head. Garcia let out a deep breath and leaned back in his chair, wondering if an aircraft was out that way. *Anzio* had had a contact earlier in that direction, and now Sea Base. Too many radar contacts against disappearing targets for something not to be out there.

NINE

"There she is!" MacPherson shouted, nodding toward the cam vision on his console. Both hands worked on the controls. One hand worked the camera on the UUV while the other piloted the Unmanned Underwater Vehicle.

"Where?" demanded Keyland, equally excited.

MacPherson touched the screen. "See? She's coming out of the haze now."

Gentron leaned over and glanced for a moment before returning his attention back to his UUV.

"I want to see," said Bernardo, jumping up from his seat. He took the few steps toward MacPherson and Keyland so fast that the short wire trailing from the headset dangling around his neck reached its limit and jerked the headset off. "Damn."

Keyland leaned back so the AN/SQR-25 operator could see.

"Never thought I'd ever see a hostile submarine."

"We haven't identified it as hostile," Keyland interrupted.

"What about the Chinese submarine we chased away last month?" MacPherson asked. "It was hostile."

"We never saw it," Bernardo objected. He pointed back at the passive sonar screen. "All we saw and heard was noise from it. When the UUV exploded, it turned tail and ran." He nodded at

MacPherson's screen display. "But this is truly seeing it, not just hearing it or detecting it—truly seeing it."

Keyland touched Bernardo on his arm. "You've seen it; now back to your seat." Keyland turned to Gentron. "Where's your UUV?"

Bernardo picked up his headset as he sat down, looking it over to see if anything was broken before he jammed it back around his neck.

"I've got the second UUV easing under *Bellatrix* to starboard side, Petty Officer Keyland," Said Gentron.

MacPherson leaned over, glancing at the displays on Gentron's console. "You're doing good, Mertz," he told the young seaman. "Bring her up to twenty knots and give her a course toward my UUV." He glanced at Keyland, who nodded.

"But not directly to it," Keyland added, afraid of the two colliding. He could hang up on ever making chief if that happened. He looked around the compartment. Come to think of it, he told himself, this could be just the thing in his performance evaluation to make him chief. A brief moment of giddiness replaced apprehension before the realization of what they were doing shocked him back to reality. His career was the least of his worries right now.

"Hey!" MacPherson said. "I can see her torpedo tubes."

"How many tubes?" Keyland asked, squatting between the two consoles to pull out the latest *Jane's Fighting Ships*.

"Six," MacPherson said.

Keyland opened the book.

"Three on each side of the bow. I can only see the starboard side ones clearly."

Keyland quickly flipped through the pages to the North Korean section. "Open or closed?" he asked as his fingers rapidly scanned down the pages of the submarines.

"I don't think that it's going to help, LPO," Bernardo said. "Most submarines have either six or eight torpedo tubes on the bow. Where at on the bow might be a better—"

"I think they look closed, but the bow is pointed toward Sea Base," MacPherson interrupted.

Keyland's finger stopped moving. His lips moved slightly as he read. He slapped the heavy book down on the small shelf between Bernardo and MacPherson. "It could be anything. It could be a Chinese Xia or a Han class."

"Chinese wouldn't sink their own boat," MacPherson said.

"Or it could be a Russian or North Korean Golf- or Kilo-class submarine."

"It's a North Korean," Gentron said.

"How do you know?"

"The Russians don't have any Kilo or Golf submarines left in their inventory. They sold all of them ages ago. Those classes of submarines are from the 1970s. They're ancient. They're coffins waiting for burial. Both classes, like most submarines, have six torpedo tubes."

"Some have eight," Bernardo interjected.

"How do you know this?" Keyland asked Gentron.

"They taught it to us in A-school."

"No," Keyland said, waving his hand back and forth. "Not how you know about the submarines; how do you know they're North Korean?"

Gentron kept his attention on the UUV he was controlling as he spoke. "Number one, the Chinese didn't sink their own submarine. Number two, both the Kilo and Golf-class submarines are diesel-electric-powered, so they had to come from somewhere within their range. And number three," he said, his voice rising as held up his left hand with three fingers raised, "is the North Koreans have both classes, are within range, and are preparing for war. Ergo, it's North Korean."

Everyone exchanged glances. Bernardo shrugged with his lower lip pushed out, his expression wide-eyed. He nodded at Keyland and said aloud, "Mertz Gentron! I am truly impressed."

Keyland noticed the seaman smile as his face darkened slightly in the blue-lighted compartment.

On the half-level above them, Seaman Tom Calvins passed to his fellow sound-powered phone talker in Combat the assessment that off the port side of Sea Base, a North Korean Kilo- or Golf-class submarine had turned toward them.

"You got the acoustics turned on?" Keyland asked MacPherson.

MacPherson nodded. "They come on automatically." He reached up and flicked the switch on the speakers. The noise of the ocean flowed through the compartment. "How about that?" he said with amazement. "You can hear the soft turn of the propellers, even though the UUV is sitting off the starboard bow of the submarine."

"You know the Golf class," Gentron interjected, "has cruise-missile capability."

"The North Koreans don't have cruise missiles," Keyland argued.

"They say they do," Bernardo replied.

"Jenkins, how far away from the submarine is the UUV?"

"About a hundred yards." MacPherson laughed. "He doesn't even know we're there. You have to hand it to those Navy scientists to develop smart torpedoes that we can stop so dead in the water, they drift."

"Petty Officer Bernardo is right. They say they have cruise missiles. They have nuclear weapons and they have missiles," Gentron added. "We have no way of knowing they haven't developed a cruise-missile capability."

"Okay, Gentron," MacPherson said good-naturedly, "you've had your moment in the sun; now get that UUV out there with mine."

"Already accelerating number-two UUV. Bringing it up to twenty knots."

Bernardo leaned toward Keyland and MacPherson. "You know, he'll hear the second UUV at that speed. He doesn't know they're UUVs. He'll think he dodged the first torpedo, and he'll detect this second UUV and think we've fired at him again."

"But they're not torpedoes," Gentron said.

"They are!" MacPherson objected. "They're just smart torpedoes that someone decided to call Unmanned Underwater Vehicles. Both UUVs and torpedoes are explosive devices. Both are designed to sink a ship or a submarine. The difference is we have more control over a UUV than a wire-guided torpedo."

"As I was saying," Bernardo continued, looking at Keyland. "Since Gentron's UUV is heading toward MacPherson's, what if the submarine thinks he's dodged a first torpedo and now has what he thinks is a second torpedo inbound?"

"Guess he'll go into deep maneuvers again," Keyland answered.

"Well, what if he has orders we don't know about? What if he has orders to stay where he is and defend himself if attacked? What if his orders are to sink Sea Base? What if he feels he has to attack Sea Base so he can run from the torpedoes?"

"He would have already done it," MacPherson replied.

"Not necessarily. He had the Chinese submarine to get rid of."

"The Chinese wouldn't have stopped him. They would have watched, recorded everything that happened, and hurried back to the homeland to share with their buddies over sake and rice."

"Sake? That's Japanese," Gentron said.

Keyland straightened and looked at Bernardo. "What makes you think that?"

Bernardo turned in his seat and leaned forward, his hands clasped in front of him. "If he was concerned with his survival, wouldn't he have continued away instead of turning back toward Sea Base?" Bernardo's face paled, his voice as cold as death as if he just realized where his thoughts were leading.

A sucking noise echoed from the speaker above MacPherson.

"What was that?" Keyland asked.

On the screen, bubbles cascaded around the bow of the unidentified submarine.

"He's opening his torpedo tubes."

"HERE comes the second aircraft," Walters said.

"They're about five miles apart."

"Visual formation."

"Could be, but they're still transports."

"I recall from our preflight briefing that the Russians were conducting reconnaissance missions north of us, located a few hundred miles off Kamchatka. Far enough away to stay out of any fight, but close enough to monitor everything."

"Well, I would say they are a little off course, wouldn't you?" Franklin asked incredulously. "Not to question if they would have the legs to do a round robin from Kamchatka to Sea Base and back."

"They'd have the legs. They're transports. Transports and four-engine jobbers can fly forever." Walters inched the F-22A to the right slightly. "Here we go."

The two Air Force Raptors zoomed down the sides of the second transport. A face appeared in the small porthole near the rear of the aircraft. Just like the first aircraft they had flown by, the pilots in this one waved. Ahead, Walters could already see the lead aircraft. As the two men flew past the nose, heading toward the last transport, Walters realized the face staring back at him from the small window had been Asian.

"Hey, Blackman, Russians have Asians in Kamchatka?"

"Is that some kind of trick question, Fast Pace? Of course they have Asians in Kamchatka. Kamchatka is in Asia. Duh!" After a slight pause, he asked, "Why'd you ask?"

"I saw someone who looked Asian staring at me from the rear right porthole as I flew by."

"I don't think your eyesight is bad. It's just Russia stretches from Europe across nearly a third of the globe to end at the Pacific Ocean. It's got people of all ethnic, religious, and political classes living in it. The farther east you go, the more their eyes slant."

"The farther east you go, the more their eyes slant? Is that some kind of Franklin theorem?"

"Naw. The spin of the earth is faster on this side, hence the slanted eyes caused by the spin."

"Bigot."

"Raptor 10, Raptor Haven; report."

"Roger, Raptor Haven. Same markings, same AN-12. Am proceeding toward lead transport. They remain steady on course two-zero-zero, altitude five hundred feet."

"How's your fuel?" Franklin asked Walters on their closed circuit.

"Roger, Raptor 10. After final pass, you are cleared for immediate landing. No aircraft are in landing pattern. We will switch you to air traffic control after final pass and identification. Be advised Raptor 50 and 60 heading your way. Estimate arrival your area four minutes."

"Roger, Raptor Haven." Walters flipped to the formation frequency. "My fuel needle is barely off the red. Yours?"

"In the red."

"It's this altitude. It's eating up what little fuel we had."

"How far to Homeplate?"

"Raptor Haven, Raptor 10; request distance to Sea Base."

"Raptor 10, we hold you sixty-five miles."

"Blackman, think we can do it?"

"Downhill we can, but if we have to stay down here much longer, we might as well practice our swimming techniques. Mine is called splash and shout."

For the next forty seconds the two men flew in silence, watching the lead transport bogie grow bigger in their cockpit windows as they closed the distance. Then, suddenly, they were past the lead aircraft and without words both pilots started climbing.

"Notice anything different on the first aircraft?"

"No. You?"

"You're going to laugh, but I could swear I saw an old Lockheed logo painted over beneath the Russian marking," Franklin said.

"Lockheed? Why would Lockheed be on the aircraft, and Blackman, if it was painted over, how did you see it?"

"I'd say sunlight hitting it, but the sun is on your side. Black letters and bad paint job?"

Walters passed along the information to Sea Base as the two aircraft climbed to six thousand feet, turning slightly to align their flight path toward Sea Base.

"LOCKHEED?" Garcia asked. "Lockheed designed the C-130, but they didn't have anything to do with the AN-12. Did they?"

"I have no idea, sir. I'm a surface warfare officer. I don't even know who built the Hornet," Stapler answered. When Garcia shook his head, Stapler added, "I've asked *Boxer* if their Intel department has any insight. Reach back for intelligence is such a great innovation," he said skeptically.

Garcia glanced at the clock on the bulkhead and sighed. "Hand me the secure handset," he said, holding his hand out. The petty officer handed it to him. He held it loosely by his side.

A few seconds later, the speaker announced a call from Task Force 72. Admiral Holman was on the other end.

"I am concerned about the aircraft approaching us, especially with this tidbit that 'Lockheed' may have been painted over on the lead aircraft."

"Admiral, we're scratching our heads on that also."

A young petty officer third class approached Garcia, offering him a cup of coffee. He nodded, mouthed thanks, and set the cup in the holder at the end of the right arm.

"I've got our Intel department researching it now," said Holman.

"Admiral, they're continuing toward us. I don't recommend shooting down the Russians, but I've got those three coming toward me and *Anzio* had a sporadic detection on what he thought was another sea hugger off my port side—northwest of us. The three confirmed Russian bogies are crossing the sixty-five-mile range now. At their speed, they're going to reach us within the next ten minutes, depending on headwinds."

"Hank, you're having the same feeling I'm having, aren't you?"

Garcia's eyes widened. *What feeling is that?* he asked himself. He didn't know, but if the admiral had a knot in his stomach, then they both had the same feeling.

"I'm not sure, Admiral," he said hesitatingly.

"I think you are," Holman said with confidence. "Those aren't Russians coming our way. They're hostiles. They've broken the hundred-mile rule . . ."

Hundred-mile rule? Garcia mouthed, his eyes widening.

" . . . and they continue inbound. Transport planes don't do overflights. They . . ." And Holman ceased talking.

"Admiral, you still there?" Garcia asked.

"Shit! They're not Russian and they're not reconnaissance aircraft! They're North Koreans and they're not going to do a flyby. It's a bombing run, Hank!"

"But they're transports, Admiral."

"Listen to me, Hank. You get the other fighter airborne now! You tell the Air Force to splash those three bogies."

"But, Admiral, what if they're Russian? What if they have Americans on board?" *Why in the hell did he say that?*

"Hank, trust me. If there are Americans on board, they shouldn't be there. If they're Russians, then we'll let the State Department apologize and it's my decision. If you don't splash them now, then you're going to have some gaping holes in Sea Base."

Stapler appeared as the admiral finished his warning. He handed Garcia a handwritten note.

"Admiral, my TAO has some information back from your intelligence."

"Hank, I just got something from my intelligence people. Lockheed was hired by the Chinese back in the late 1960s to help them design their Shaanxi Y-8 transports. The Y-8 is the Chinese variant of the Russian AN-12. The Chinese gave those old aircraft to the North Koreans. Now, shoot the sons of bitches down; that's an order!"

* * *

"PULL those chocks, Sergeant Parker!" Chief Master Sergeant Johnny Willard shouted, running from the nearly repaired Raptor toward the lone remaining alert fighter.

Everyone shouted along the flight line. The man-made ear protectors shielding their hearing from the inherent aircraft noise created a situation where everyone shouted to be heard.

Major Andy "Tight End" Crawford looked down at him, spinning his finger in the air for the ground crew to hurry up. Parker and Snaggles Cole ran from beneath the lead F-22A Raptor, dragging the wheel chocks behind them.

Technical Sergeant Lou Thomas stood to the right side of Tight End's fighter and twirled his finger at Tight End. The engines on the F-22A Raptor revved up in decibels as the major pushed the engine to full. The fighter leaped from stationary and in seconds was racing alongside the Sea Base runway, heading toward the aft end for takeoff.

Willard stood there, tears leaking from squinted eyes brought about by the wash of fumes blowing across him. But he stood, watching the former Detachment Commander head for action.

Several seconds passed before Willard turned and ran toward the broken 223, shouting at Technical Sergeant Grossman, but the roar of the fighter and protective ceramic muffs over Grossman's ears drowned out Willard's words.

At 223, Melanie Parker and Snot-Nose Johnson had joined Grossman. Everyone turned to watch the Air Force fighter as it reached the end of the runway. The aircraft did a rolling turn, slowing slightly, before the major applied maximum power.

Willard shielded his eyes as he watched the Raptor lift off two thirds of the way down the runway. He took a deep breath. There was something awesome about watching the meanest fighter aircraft in the world take off. The wheels lifted, melding into the smooth body of the Raptor that gave it the stealth capability to disappear from most radars.

The fighter continued steadily over the runway, quickly ascending until it reached the end of Sea Base and was over the Pacific Ocean. Then, Tight End turned the aircraft on its tail, reaching nearly a ninety-degree angle. Willard was impressed; most pilots enjoyed using their afterburners once airborne. The two Pratt & Whitney engines powering the Raptor gave the fighter over 39,000 pounds of thrust. Even without afterburner, the Air Force fighter could reach up to Mach 1.5. With afterburner, the fighter could tack on another .3 Mach. In Willard's opinion, the extra three-tenths of a Mach wasn't worth the fuel.

The noise across the flight deck quickly dissipated with the last fighter aircraft. Everyone turned back to the lone remaining Raptor parked on the flight line, watching as the lead F-22A technician worked on replacing the broken part.

Across Sea Base, the two boatswain mates Willard's friend Jacobs had sent for arms walked toward them, weapons arrayed "ever-which-away" in their arms. That had to be a heavy load and there was no doubt, Willard thought with a smile, that sailors were carrying them. If there was a hard way to do something, trust the Navy to find it.

"Snot-Nose," Willard said to the youngest airman. "You and Melanie go help those sailors before they drop those M-16s. Those are our M-16s," he added as an afterthought. Willard grimaced. He had asked for the M-16s months ago and the Navy had refused. He had never been at an airfield where the flight line was left unguarded until he arrived on Sea Base. "Looks as if the Navy finally decided we could have our weapons."

"I know what you mean, Chief," Thomas said. "Not only are there a lot of sailors running around, but you got civilians, too."

"SENIOR Chief says he's going to leave Taylor in the compartment and come back here," MacPherson said. "Says Taylor is premissioning two more UUVs, but it'll take a couple of hours to load them."

Keyland looked at his watch.

"What are we going to do?" MacPherson asked, staring at the picture of the submarine bow on his screen.

Keyland turned to Calvins. "You got anything from Combat? They tell us what to do?"

"I don't think the guy I'm passing this information to has been able to interrupt them to tell them about the open torpedo tubes."

Keyland realized his breathing was coming fast. He shut his eyes for a moment, concentrating. His breathing slowed. What in the hell was he going to do? The ones who were supposed to give him his orders weren't. They were preoccupied with the inbound bogies or hostiles or whatever the fuck they're calling them, and he was stuck here with a submarine pointed at Sea Base with opened torpedo tubes. Torpedo tubes only opened when they had torpedoes in them. They taught at ASW School and during training exercises that opening tubes was a hostile act. An act that gave permission to attack first. Navy rules of engagement said you couldn't attack until the Captain gave the order; or his Tactical Action Officer gave it.

"It'll take the senior chief twenty to thirty minutes to get here from *Bellatrix,* Petty Officer Keyland," Bernardo added. "And that's on a good day. If that sub fires every tube, we aren't going to be able to decoy every one of them."

Keyland's eyes widened. A smile nearly broke through his expressionless face. He didn't have to attack the sub. "Jenkins, how far away is your UUV from the submarine?"

"It's about one hundred feet off the starboard bow."

"Can you move it so it's in front of the torpedo tubes?"

"The submarine is also moving, you know." MacPherson gave the UUV power, using the camera to guide the UUV toward the submarine.

"Do it very slow, so he can't detect it."

"Gentron's UUV will mask the noise, or it should. If I position it directly in front, he could run into the UUV. That's the same thing as us attacking it, you know."

Keyland leaned down. Keeping his voice level, he said, "It's up to you not to let it run into your UUV. Put it in front of the tubes. You can turn the camera around so you can see behind you, right?"

"Yeah, but the bubbles from the cavitations . . ."

"I know. The bubbles may obscure the cameras, but if you're in front of it . . ."

". . . he either won't know what's in front of him . . ."

". . . or he'll think it's another submarine," Bernardo finished.

"The question will be whether he will fire or not," MacPherson said.

"If he fires, the question will be whether he will be firing at something he thinks is a submarine or at Sea Base."

"Won't matter," Gentron said. "His bow is pointed in our direction. If he misses the UUV, he'll hit Sea Base."

Keyland straightened up, clasping his hands in front of him. "Nope, if he fires, Jenkins' UUV will be so close that one of those torpedoes is going to hit it."

"And when it hits the UUV, there is going to be one gosh-awful explosion," Bernardo said cheerfully. "Petty Officer Keyland, you are one bad mutha. Yeah, one bad mutha."

The Anti-Submarine Warfare technicians grew silent as MacPherson maneuvered the UUV forward quietly toward the North Korean Golf-class submarine. Six minutes later, the UUV crossed the submarine's bow and began turning. MacPherson used the compass to align the UUV so the propeller pointed at the center of the bow between the two rows of tubes.

Keyland wondered what the sonar operator inside the submarine made of the sound coming off their bow. He tried to put himself in the operator's place. The operator, who in most Navies other than the English-speaking ones was a young officer, would think the passive detection was either an unidentified American submarine or an underwater convergence zone anomaly. Convergence zones were areas where underwater noise sine-waved as it traveled through the waters. The noise could be over a hundred miles away and sound as if it was directly off their bow. He smiled at the irony.

"Here goes the cameras," MacPherson said

They watched as the television cameras on the UUV swung from forward to aft so they faced the North Korean submarine. The bow filled the screen. Two rows of opened torpedo tubes ran along the edges of the picture.

"Shit! How close are you to it?" Bernardo asked.

"Good maneuvering," Keyland said.

MacPherson glanced at the readings. "About fifty feet in front of it. If he increases speed, then we won't have to worry about him launching torpedoes to explode the UUV."

"AH, man! Give me weapons free for a few minutes. We can shoot them down and keep on track to Sea Base. Why can't we?"

"One word, Blackman; no fuel."

"That's two."

"At a time like this, who's counting?" Walters asked, switching channels to air traffic control. "Raptor Haven, Raptor 10; request immediate clearance to land. We are running on fumes."

"Raptor 10, you are forty nautical miles away, on course two-four-zero, angels six. Maintain course, speed, and altitude until twenty miles and then I will vector you on board. You have two Foxtrot-22s in your vicinity. They are at your eleven o'clock, angels eight on reciprocal course."

"Roger, Raptor Haven." Walters switched to the common fighter channel. "Raptor 50, this is Raptor 10. Do you copy?"

"Fast Pace, Blackman; this is Werewolf and Zimmerman. We have you visual below us."

Walters acknowledged the broadcast. He had no pleasant or insulting repartee for his fellow fighter pilots. He licked his lips, aware for the first time how dry they seemed. He had never shot down an adversary in real life and while it was every fighter pilot's dream, he didn't envy Fairwell and Zimmerman their opportunity.

"This is Tight End. Werewolf and Angel, you have the targets. I'll take the CAP overhead."

"Roger, Raptor Leader," Fairwell acknowledged.

"Good hunting," Walters replied. He didn't know why they needed a combat air patrol overhead, but with all these enemy aircraft running around out here avoiding radar protection, he was confident Major Crawford knew what he was doing.

"We have them on our fire-control radar. Did you see any signs of electronic warfare capability on them?"

"Nope. Nothing but pure sitting duck transports, flying in a row, waiting to be shot down. But we only did an identification pass."

"Yeah, that's all we got to do," Franklin said with frustration.

A deep sigh came across the tactical channel. "Oops, sorry about that. Forgot I had the button pushed."

"That's okay, Blackman," Walters answered. "Werewolf, Zimmerman, you stay with the man, you hear?"

Two pushes of the button came back in acknowledgment. The young second lieutenant's throat was probably constricted over this baptism he was about to receive. If he was scared about attacking unarmed transports, then he better get over it quickly, Walters thought, recalling the seventy or more North Korean fighters orbiting off the Korean Peninsula. Walters took a deep breath. For a moment he felt empathy with the young officer.

Sure, every one of them had splashed each other in mock aerial combat. *The major,* he said silently, referring to Tight End Crawford, *has dropped bombs in support of the Army in Indonesia, but no one else in the deployment has been in combat.*

The logical trail of his thoughts raced to the conclusion that the squadron had chosen them for the Sea Base test and evaluation because they were the most expendable. He grimaced. It could be true. They weren't the most seasoned veterans of Langley. A wry smile crossed his lips. The fact that the squadron had sent the least-liked officer in the squadron, Major Johnson, as the DETCO only served to confirm Walter's theory. Back at Langley, he imagined the going-away party they gave for her after she left.

"Man, what are you laughing about?"

"How do you know I'm laughing?"

"Your head is bobbing like those things in the back of some redneck's muscle car. Your head bobs like that when you're laughing."

"Can't a man have some privacy in his cockpit?"

"Well, if you ain't laughing, then whatever you're doing requires you to zip up that flight suit. They are going to shoot down our targets. They're going to have three splashes X'd out beneath their cockpit windows and we're going to have to listen to them describe every arc, every maneuver, every muscle twitch of the trigger finger when they return."

"What's your fuel remainder?"

"My FUREMS is so low, the readout is in the minus area."

"Raptor 10, Raptor 20; descend to angels two. Raptor 20, drop back. . . ."

"Raptor Haven, this is Raptor 10; request Raptor 20 first to land. His FUREMS is lowest."

TEN

Garcia eased out of his chair, excusing himself as he passed behind the leading petty officer. He stopped alongside Stapler, crossing his arms as he joined him. Both watched the Naval Tactical Data System screen. The background murmur of voices that rode the atmosphere of a Combat Information Center had transformed to a tense silence as everyone strained to hear the voices of the Air Force pilots coming from the tactical air speakers mounted over the center consoles where Garcia and Stapler stood.

Stapler nodded. "Sir, they're approaching the bandits. We still don't have the low flyers on our air search radar, but surface search is tracking them." He nodded toward Petty Officer Bonicella just as she ran her index finger along the left edge of her hair. For a fraction of second both men were distracted.

Garcia cleared his throat.

Stapler motioned to the hostile air targets on the NTDS, their video returns highlighted by triangles with no bottom. Lines from the edges of the icons showed the direction of travel while the length of each line represented speed.

"They're bearing zero-two-zero degrees true from us, traveling around 350 knots," Stapler said softly to Garcia. He glanced at the clock on the bulkhead. "Five minutes to Sea Base."

"Raptor 50 Formation, Raptor Haven; bandits bearing twelve o'clock from you, altitude under five hundred feet. You are cleared to engage. Weapons free at this time."

The sound-powered phone talker interrupted. "Sir, topside watch in the tower reports visual on inbound aircraft."

Garcia shivered for a moment. If they were visual, they were closer than the thirty nautical miles five minutes would put them. At five hundred feet altitude . . . *To hell with it,* he thought, and immediately quit trying to calculate the distance.

"Thought they were farther out," Garcia said to Stapler.

Stapler leaned down. "How far are the bandits?" he asked the Air Intercept Controller.

"I hold our fighters at thirty nautical miles, sir, and they have them on visual."

Stapler straightened and looked at the sound-powered phone talker. "Tell the topside watch to confirm."

One of the tactical air speakers mounted overhead blared, "Raptor Haven. Bandit One in sight. Making single pass. Two Sidewinders followed by cannon. Continuing firing run."

Sea Base acknowledged the transmission. On the radar screen, Garcia and Stapler remained riveted to the scenario unfolding, watching digital icons approaching each other. Garcia made a mental note to argue for the newer holograph display in the funding for Sea Base upgrade. On board the USS *Boxer,* Holman would be watching the same scene on a three-dimensional display with virtual aircraft replacing the icons Garcia and Stapler were watching. The admiral could walk around the display taking in the scenario from every perspective: right, left, top, bottom. The Tactical Holograph could even display a subsurface scenario simultaneously with an ongoing air battle and amphibious landing. If the officer in charge wanted, he or she could zoom in or zoom out on the action. Here he was with 1990s technology trying to fight in a twenty-first century where information determined who won or lost battles.

Icons representing the three North Korean bandits continued single file toward Sea Base—same course, same speed, no changes since the Raptor 10 Formation intercepted them. Approaching them dead-on at near Mach speed were the two F-22A fighters launched minutes ago from Sea Base. Beneath the top-half circle, computer icons on the Air Intercept Controller screen overlaid the radar return, telling everyone in the battle-group they were seeing friendly aircraft.

"Raptor 60, ease left one hundred feet," the AIC ordered, giving the aircraft a few more feet of separation for firing their missiles.

"I have lock-on."

Garcia wondered which pilot had reported lock-on.

"Sea Base, Raptor 50 Formation. We have lock on target. Raptor 60, on my command: Launch one . . ."

"He's turning right!" shouted Raptor 60.

"Maintain lock-on," Raptor 50 mumbled over the speaker. "Five . . . four . . . three . . . two . . . one. Fox one."

"Fox one," came the near-simultaneous transmission of the wingman.

"Sir," the sound-powered telephone talker said, touching Stapler's arm.

"What is it?" Stapler asked irritably, his head turned slightly so his right ear remained toward the speakers.

"EW reports airborne radar bearing three-zero-zero degrees."

Garcia's head snapped up, his gaze toward the SLQ-32 electronic warfare suite against the forward bulkhead. "Three-zero-zero?" he said sharply to Stapler. "I thought you said the bandits were at zero-two-zero?"

"They are," Stapler snapped, bumping Garcia slightly as he stepped to the other side of the surface search radar operator. "Bonicella, you got anything at Three-zero-zero?"

The operations specialist slid her cursor over to the top left-hand side of the polar radar screen. "There's nothing out there but the USS *Boxer* off our port side, sir. The USS *Gearing* is northwest of our position about twelve miles, conducting the ASW operation. No other ships."

"Not ships. Aircraft?"

"Sir, the only aircraft I have are these three low flyers." She shrugged. "The *Gearing* has helicopters up, but they're too low and too far out for surface-search to pick up."

"TAO!" the sound-powered telephone talker shouted. "Topside watch confirms low flyer with left-bearing drift—range approximately ten miles."

"Sea Base, this is *Boxer*. We have an unidentified aircraft off our port beam. Confirmed by topside watches, but we have no radar confirmation. EW reported a sporadic hit on a APSO-504 surface-search radar."

"Sounds American," Garcia said.

"What type of aircraft is it?"

The red telephone rang. Garcia looked at it and without waiting for the leading petty officer to pick it up, he reached over and answered. "Sea Base here."

"Hank, this is Admiral Holman. Something's not right here, shipmate. The TAO on *Boxer* is telling me we got a bandit, which our radar doesn't seem to reflect."

"We have a visual from our topside watch, Admiral."

"He's out of *Boxer*'s range to engage. It's up to you, Hank. Take the unidentified aircraft out. Shoot him down."

The sound-powered telephone talker voice boomed, "Topside says aircraft looks like a C-130."

"Shouldn't we try to contact him first, Admiral? He might be a friendly."

"What . . ." Admiral Holman stopped suddenly. A few seconds later, he continued. "Hank, you can try to contact him while you're shooting him down. If he talks quick, so be it. Give him one warning, then splash the son of a bitch."

Garcia hung up. "Commander Stapler, tell the laser battery to line up on the unidentified target. Then start broadcasting for him to turn away from the battle group or be shot down."

"Aye, sir." Stapler turned to Bonicella. "Ask EW if the radar is a C-130."

"**I** don't think they believe me," Petty Officer Taleb said to Kiang.

"Probably too low for the air search radar to see," Kiang replied without lowering his binoculars. His fingers worked the focus controls as he lined the glasses up with the unidentified aircraft flying down the port side of Sea Base.

"You see him yet? What type of aircraft is he?"

Kiang caught a glimpse of silver as he searched, quickly bringing the glasses back, and finally lining up the aircraft in the lens. His fingers moved fast as he focused on the aircraft. It looked like a C-130, except the body seemed longer. "It's a C-130," he said.

"A C-130," Taleb repeated back. "Must be the mail plane arriving early or something?" He pressed the button and reported the aircraft type to Combat.

Kiang tracked the aircraft until it passed the aft port edge of Sea Base. "Looks as if it may . . ." he started to say, but the aircraft tilted left slightly, veering its course toward Sea Base. After several seconds, Kiang said slowly, "I think he's in the landing pattern. He's turning toward Sea Base."

Taleb pressed the talk button and passed the information along to Combat. A few seconds passed before he looked up at Kiang. "They want to know if we see any markings on it."

Kiang squinted. What if the aircraft was Chinese? What would he do? What would his handler expect him to do? He squinted as he tried to focus on the blurry letters along the fuselage of the aircraft. "I can't quite see them," he said, drawing out the words as he concentrated. His handler would want him to protect his cover. As if resolving the anguish of a decision, the letters focused for a few seconds before the aircraft leveled again. "It's Air Force. It's got 'USAF' embossed in black along the side of it."

Hydraulic noise and the slight grind of gears caused him to lower his binoculars. The laser weapon on the rear left side of Sea Base shifted its barrel in the direction of the approaching aircraft.

Taleb let out a deep sigh. "Thank God." He fumbled a moment in his attempt to push the talk button before he passed the information to Combat.

Kiang watched the laser gun. A sound-powered phone wire trailed from the base of the laser weapon. The sailor wearing the helmet hurried to put distance between him and the laser weapon. Kiang wondered why. The sound-powered phone talker stopped when the wire reached its limit. The sailor was closer than he would have wanted to be. Kiang had tons of photographs of the laser weapon, but none of it firing. He touched his camera. Combat must believe the approaching aircraft is a danger if they are lining up a weapon against it.

GROSSMAN straightened up, glancing down from the top of the ladder. One hand held a screwdriver while the other rested lightly on the skin of the F-22A fighter. "Chief, she's fixed. Should be able to fly this bucket of bolts to China and back with no problems," Tech Sergeant Danny Grossman said, his deep North Carolina nasal twang drawing out the sentence.

He slipped the screwdriver into his tool belt and came down the ladder. Grossman stepped away to allow Thomas room to scoot up to perform the quality-assurance check. Grossman wiped his hands on the rag tucked through a loop on his flight suit and smiled. "You won't find anything wrong with it, Lou," he said loudly, the pride in his work obvious in his tone. He wiped his forehead with the back of his hand, leaving a streak of dirt or grease across it.

"Good job, Danny. Now let's get this aircraft ready for launch," Willard added.

Above the two men, Tech Sergeant Thomas shut the panel door. "Checks out, Chief. She's ready."

"Told you so."

Willard turned, hands on his hips. Three pilots stood to one side, watching the events and talking. Probably about their golf swing, Willard thought. He crouched to peer beneath the repaired aircraft. On the other side some of his ground crew stood, their toes pointing toward each other. One stumbled back. He recognized the long legs.

"Parker, quit giving Snot-Nose a rough time. Find a place for those M-16s before you shoot each other and get your butts over here," he shouted, his voice carrying easily across the flight deck. Out of the corner of his eye he saw an officer approaching.

"Chief," First Lieutenant Neil O'Roarke asked, "I take it 223 is fixed?"

Willard straightened. O'Roarke was one of the better junior officers Willard considered his responsibility to train. The young officer stood a head shorter than the burly chief master sergeant. Smooth shave, short crew cut, and an expression that always seemed to be asking if he should be asking. Willard shook his head slightly and smiled. Where was the Air Force finding its officers nowadays? High school?

"Yes, sir," Willard replied. "We'll need to run a systems check on it, but . . ."

The brick beeped on Willard's belt. "Excuse me, Lieutenant." He jerked the radio free. "Willard here."

"Flight line, this is Combat. How soon until you can launch the Raptor?"

Willard and O'Roarke's eyes met. The lieutenant's tongue flicked lightly across his lips.

"Sir, we just finished repairs. We need to run . . ."

A new voice came on the circuit. "This is the TAO."

What in the hell is a TAO? Willard thought.

"Do the checks while taxiing. We have three hostiles inbound and an Air Force C-130 trying to land. Get that aircraft into the air."

Without waiting for Willard to finish his reply, O'Roarke jammed his helmet on his head and started climbing. Four steps and the young fighter pilot was at the cockpit.

"Sir, we need to do the diagnostics," Willard said as he put the brick back in its scabbard.

O'Roarke had one leg inside the cockpit and the other on the small foothold. "Ah, Chief, you heard the man. They need this aircraft in the air. I can run the diagnostics as I taxi. Honest."

The other two pilots rushed up. "What the hell is going on?" Captain Henry Nolan asked. "What's Butthole doing up there?" he asked, pointing at O'Roarke, who was buckling his harness.

Willard didn't care too much for Nolan. Nolan could conjugate any verb in the English language, as long it only required the first-person pronoun. "He's about to launch, Captain."

"Well, you can tell him to get his ass down, Chief. I'm taking this aircraft aloft."

Willard's lower lip curled upward to the left and his eyes narrowed. He patted the radio on his side. "Sir, the Captain of Sea Base ordered Lieutenant O'Roarke into the saddle." He turned to Parker. "Get those chocks away from the wheels!"

The F-22A engine started revving up. In front of the aircraft, Technical Sergeant Thomas held his hand in the air, rotating it counterclockwise.

Willard pointed to his ears and shook his head. He motioned Nolan away from the aircraft, giving Thomas more time to get the Raptor moving. On the other side of the aircraft, Parker and Snot-Nose stood holding the chocks in their hands.

Nolan was talking.

Willard pointed at the aircraft, then his own ear protectors, and shook his head.

Sooner than he expected, the fighter aircraft was rolling. Mentally, Willard inventoried the weapons, the fuel, and the oxygen on the aircraft, knowing the repetitive thoughts echoed the repetitive checks he and the ground crew had been doing all day. Checks, checklists, repetitive checks, quality checks . . . life on the flight line was one heavy day of checks—*check this, check that.* Fact was "check" was the most used verb in the Air Force vocabulary. *"Check that out!"*

Nolan put his hand on Willard's chest and gave it a slight shove. "Stop him!"

Willard leaned down to the pilot and shouted above the din of the engines as the aircraft taxied toward the end of the Sea Base runway. "Can't, sir. He's doing his checks."

"Chief, that's my aircraft," Nolan snapped angrily, his face red as he pointed at the fighter.

Willard leaned toward the officer. Their faces were less than six inches apart. "Sir, even if I wanted to call him back, Combat wouldn't let me. Nor would they let you, Captain, unless you can give them a good reason!" Willard shouted above the noise.

Nolan stepped away, turning his back to Willard.

Willard grinned.

Suddenly, Nolan turned back. "Chief, tell Combat we haven't done diagnostics and that the lieutenant is unqualified!"

Willard's breathing increased in tempo, his eyes widened, and his nostrils flared. "Captain, that would be a lie," he said angrily, jerking his brick out. "Here's the radio. All you have to do is hit the transmit button and you'll be talking to the man in charge of this Navy thing we're riding. You tell him whatever you want."

Nolan drew away, his eyes widening as he looked at the radio. "That's not my job," he replied.

"And I don't think you want me to twist the truth about this, do you, sir?"

Nolan nodded. "My apologies, Chief. It's just that . . ."

"I know what it's about, Captain," he replied, his voice mellowing. "You'll have your opportunity, sir. War will always be with us."

From the direction of the tower, three sailors pushed a large cart in their direction. Willard looked around. Not a damn aircraft in sight other than the C-130 tied down across the runway. Nothing but a group of airmen and two pilots—*Nolan obviously venting his anger with the other junior officer—what is the other officer's name?* Nothing to do but mill about smartly near four mobile CO2 canisters. Gravitating into small groups as if being alone on empty apron space was something to be avoided. The enlisted shifted slowly toward the end of the parking line where 223 had been parked. The two officers stood watching the end of the runway. Everyone watched the taxiing fighter. Willard stood in the center alone, as if his job was to keep the two groups separated.

Everyone turned when the decibel level of the Raptor roared upward. Inside the cockpit, Willard envisioned the young officer watching his rpms rise, waiting for the magic moment when he could release the brakes.

The fighter moved. Picking up speed as it headed down the runway, bringing the noise closer to them as he neared the halfway mark. Willard crossed his fingers that Grossman had done his usual meticulous and thorough repair job. Though, sometimes the real problem is never the obvious one.

As suddenly as it started, the F-22A lifted off the end of the runway, its wheels disappearing into the fuselage, and the tail turning toward the ocean before it quickly disappeared into the sky. A rush of pride, a feeling of well-being flooded over Willard. It was a feeling he first felt as a young airman many years ago, and something that never failed to happen every time one of his aircraft took off. He had never fully understood why, but the rush was worth a career that jerked him and his family around the globe at the whim of the United States Air Force.

The brick beeped. Willard pulled it from his belt. "Chief Willard here."

He listened to Combat for a few seconds before interrupting. "Sir, the Air Force doesn't have any C-130s out here. Only the Navy does." Willard went on briefly describing to the voice on the other end that Air Force C-130s were part of the Air National Guard homeland security response teams Stateside. They were ancient, dilapidated, and many Air Force active-duty personnel watched with awe anytime one of them took off without a fire on board.

"RAPTOR Haven, Raptor 10; request permission to enter the pattern," Walters transmitted.

"There goes two-two-three," Franklin said on their private circuit.

"Raptor 10, Raptor Haven; you are cleared for immediate entry. Be advised we have an Air Force C-130 in the pattern. No comms with the friendly at this time."

"What's an Air Force C-130 doing out here?" Franklin asked. "Air National Guard has all of them. I didn't know they were doing any active-duty time out here and who would be foolish enough to take one over water?"

"Roger, Raptor Haven; passing turn one at this time."

"I said, I didn't know they were doing active-duty time out here."

"I heard you, but I was talking with the air traffic control."

"Well, did Tight End say anything about them coming out? The Commander," Franklin continued, referring to the squadron commander at Langley Air Force Base, "has been using Navy C-130s. Kind of a left-handed bone to show joint operations."

"HE'S turning away from Sea Base," Kiang said, his fingers rolling the focus knobs on the binoculars as he followed the aircraft heading toward the stern of Sea Base.

"Why is he doing that?" Taleb asked, squinting at the approaching aircraft.

Kiang shrugged. He lowered his binoculars. "It doesn't look like any C-130 I remember seeing. The fuselage looks too narrow; the engines look too small."

Taleb glanced at the aircraft turning from Sea Base, now heading away. "It looks like a C-130 to me."

Kiang smiled. "It's not. It's an old Russian AN-12 cargo aircraft." Amazing how that information seemed to come to him as if waiting for the proper moment.

Taleb passed the information to Combat, his eyes never leaving Kiang's face as the doctor lifted his binoculars and started searching for the AN-12 that had disappeared.

INSIDE Combat, Garcia sensed the restlessness of the officers and sailors manning the nerve center of Sea Base. The tension of the moment had reached the point where the silence was disappearing. Little things told him—the shifting in the seats; the quick whispers snatched between the sailors; the glances toward him. He focused on the action in front of him, listening to Stapler give the orders.

Oh, yes, they are restless, he told himself, afraid the sweat on his brow, his own nervousness, and his body language were visible to all. In times of combat or in times of facing the unknown, physical display of courage is expected of the leader.

"Fox two!" came a transmission from the fighter aircraft engaged with the approaching transports.

The sound-powered phone talker voice drowned out the next transmission over the speaker as he passed the information relayed from Taleb to Stapler.

"AN-12! Is he sure? How does he know?" Stapler blasted. "And why in the hell did he turn away?"

Stapler had barely acknowledged the report when the electronic warfare operator stood at her position and shouted across Combat. "Sir, I got hits! I got hits! The airborne radar is definitely the Chinese variant of the AN-12; it's a Shaanxi Y-8."

"What are the Chinese doing out here?" Garcia asked.

Stapler ignored Garcia's question. "Bonicella, you got contact?"

"Too close, sir."

"If we have his radar, then he's not heading out now. He's heading toward us," Stapler said irritably.

"I got him, Commander," the Air Traffic Controller spoke up. "The contact is back on final. Two miles out. It's in the approach phase."

Garcia was half-listening to the sound-powered phone talker reporting the status of the .50-caliber machine guns mounted on the sterns of the aft Fast Sealift Ships. The .50-caliber machine guns were the weapons of choice for close-in fighting against such threats as a Zodiac raft or a bomb-laden suicide terrorist. Not much effect on an aircraft unless the gunner was lucky.

Stapler turned to Garcia. "Sir, the bandit has reached fourth and final. It's turning in toward Sea Base and is too close for the laser weapon. We only have the fifty-cals on the stern of the *Denebola*."

"You told me we couldn't shoot down a friendly. I argued with—"

"Skipper, it may have Air Force markings on it, but it's not a friendly. I was wrong. The admiral was right."

"What do we do?"

"Laser can't lock on it. I ordered them to engage, but the aircraft is too low and we have ships between us and it."

"Sir," Bonicella offered. "We have the two Raptors returning. ATC has them off our bow."

Garcia moved back to his chair, leaving Stapler to fight Sea Base. Holman was going to have his nuts for garters when this was over.

Stapler took several steps past Bonicella to the ATC, where he told the second-class petty officer at the ATC console to vector the armed aircraft toward the inboard bandit—weapons free—and not to allow the aircraft to pass overhead.

"Splash one bandit!" came an excited squeal over the speaker.

"RAPTOR 10, this is Raptor Haven! You are cleared for an immediate overhead pass of Sea Base. Previously identified Air Force C-130 is not friendly; I repeat not friendly. You are cleared weapons free."

Chill bumps flowed up Walters's spine and raced along his arms and legs. His eyes clouded for a second. It was what every fighter pilot was trained to do: respond with little notice and destroy the enemy.

"Jesus Christ! I told you, man, I told you. Ain't no fucking Air National Guard out here. Besides, they'd get lost if they ever got out of sight of land, not to mention having to land on a floating bucket of bolts like this Navy contraption."

"Roger, Raptor Haven."

"Raptor 10 Formation, come to course two-zero-zero. Do not allow him to pass over Sea Base!"

"Let's roll, Blackman."

"Roll is what I'm going to have to do and hope the maneuver shakes loose some fuel hiding in these fumes keeping me aloft."

"HEY, Chief," Thomas shouted. "Looks as if a Navy C-130 is in approach."

Willard put the brick back on his belt. "Lou! Get everyone away from the runway. Run!" he shouted, waving his hand, noticing everyone standing, staring at him.

"What's the problem?" Captain Nolan asked, hurrying toward Willard.

"That's not a friendly! It's enemy! Bombing run! It's a fucking bombing run!" Willard shouted over his shoulder as he passed Nolan.

The ground crew ran, their M-16s at port arms, putting as much distance as possible between them and the runway. Runways were always primary targets of an air attack, but all of Sea Base was a runway.

Machine-gun fire echoed from somewhere off the rear of Sea Base. Willard looked toward the stern. Tracers arced upward from beneath the Sea Base canopy; someone on the ship beneath the protruding end of the runway was firing at the aircraft. That would be the Fast Sealift Ship *Denebola*—the ship firebombed months ago when the components of Sea Base had set sail from Pearl Harbor.

Ahead of him, Thomas dropped to one knee, bringing his M-16 up, pointing toward the aircraft. The tech sergeant started firing, empty shells ejecting onto the deck like locusts landing.

Willard watched the shells bouncing on the deck. They were going to have to pick them up before his fighters returned.

Parker stopped alongside Thomas, a broad grin across her face. She squatted on one knee and started firing.

Willard's breathing came in deep draughts and he made a quick promise to start jogging again when—if he survived this. He looked over toward the inbound aircraft and saw the wheels coming down. No one made bombing runs with wheels lowered.

He reached the two airmen. "Stop firing," he gasped. "Wait until it slows. It's too far out for bullets to do anything."

ELEVEN

"Senior Chief!" Keyland shouted, turning with the others toward the hatch. "Are we glad to see you." He was glad, but he had mixed feelings about knowing that with the arrival of Senior Chief Agazzi his leadership had been instantly supplanted.

Agazzi sealed the watertight hatch. "What are you talking about, Petty Officer Keyland? I've never been out of contact except for the time it took me to get here. You guys have been stupendous. Wonderful!" he said as he hurried across the compartment and down the ladder to the console area. "Bring me up to date and tell me where we are in prosecuting this contact."

Keyland walked Agazzi through the events of the past twenty minutes, including the repositioning of MacPherson's UUV in front of the North Korean submarine's bow tubes. When he finished, Agazzi grinned. "See, you don't need me. You are spot on, LPO." He looked at the others who were watching. "Every one of you has done a great job. But we are engaged and now is not the time for patting ourselves on our backs.

"What's the estimated distance to the submarine?" Agazzi asked Bernardo.

"Roughly fifteen nautical miles," MacPherson answered.

Agazzi turned to the UUV operator.

"It's roughly the distance my UUV has traveled. I think he is waiting to sink Sea Base," MacPherson added, pointing to the submarine in the camera.

"Could be," Agazzi said. "But what guides your thinking?"

MacPherson shrugged. "He sank the Chinese submarine that's been watching us, he ran from my UUV when it approached him, and he returned. Once pointed at Sea Base, he opened his tubes. There's no other submarine out there with him. No other reason to have those tubes opened."

Agazzi nodded and turned to the AN/SQR-25 console. "Bernardo, what's the contact doing now?"

Bernardo spoke up. "I hold the contact under way, Senior Chief, but barely making way. Passive contact is very sporadic from our sonar. The dipping sonars beneath the Fast Sealift Ships aren't much help either, but he's still moving."

"Where is the best signature coming from?"

Bernardo nodded toward MacPherson. "The strongest noise signatures are coming from Jenkins's UUV. With his UUV off the bow, there's no interference."

"Bearing and speed?"

"Bearing two-zero-zero degrees . . . I'd have to estimate speed at less than four knots. At that speed it's more of a hover than being under way. It's almost as if it's watching and waiting for something. Something or someone to tell it what to do next."

"It's been less than an hour since the contact sank the Chinese submarine and it has already shifted bearing from around one-nine-zero to two-two-zero. He can't be that far out," Keyland added.

"Watching and waiting, that's what submarines do best," Agazzi said. "He's got something up his sleeve. He has to know we know he sank the Chinese submarine that had been tailing us since we reached the west Pacific."

"You're right, Senior Chief. And he knows we know where he is at," Gentron said softly, drawing everyone's attention.

"Why do you say that?" Agazzi asked.

"I'd be careful if I was you," Bernardo said to Agazzi. He pointed toward Gentron. "Seaman Gentron is after your job."

"Yeah," Keyland continued. "Thanks to him we know the sub is North Korean."

Gentron leaned closer to his console, his face turning dark

once again in the blue light as they explained to Agazzi how he'd determined the submarine was North Korean.

"Why do you think he knows we have him?" Agazzi asked, waving the comments of the others away.

"Senior Chief, the UUVs make too much noise in the water. Even barely moving, they cavitate like a torpedo."

"So the UUV is telling him we know he's out there," Agazzi said.

"Yes, Senior Chief, but there's more. The contact is a Golf-class submarine—granted . . ."

"How do we know it's a Golf-class submarine?"

"Look here, Senior Chief," MacPherson interrupted, flicking the screen on his console to show the television picture of the submarine bow.

"It's an old outdated class, but it's a diesel-electric propulsion," Gentron continued while Agazzi leaned over MacPherson's shoulder looking at the gray bow of the contact. "While submerged, it's on its electric power, which means no noise except the shaft and propeller turning." Gentron pointed toward Bernardo without raising his head to look toward Agazzi or anyone else. "If it had not fired the torpedo and we had not had a vicinity to search, most likely we would never have picked him up. When we launched the UUV, it went directly toward it. The contact took evasive action, which means it was evading the UUV, thinking it was a torpedo."

After several seconds of silence, Agazzi said slowly, "Good job, Seaman Gentron. You've given this a lot of thought. Sounds like good analysis to me, but it may still be unaware we have contact," Agazzi said.

"Oh, he knows, Senior Chief. Otherwise, he wouldn't have taken evasive action when he did."

"But he came back," MacPherson said.

"If he hadn't returned—probably an underwater Anderson turn," Gentron continued, "we would have lost him. If the contact had gone elsewhere, changed its depth a little more to take him beneath the layer, or just reemerged from beneath the layer on some other compass bearing, we would have lost him."

"But he didn't," Keyland added.

Gentron shrugged, leaned closer to his console, and started talking. "Something—maybe his orders—told him to be where he is at. Exact location."

Agazzi put his hand on the young seaman's shoulder. "Good job, Gentron. Where is your UUV right now?" he asked.

"It's four nautical miles from the contact and closing at twenty knots, Senior Chief."

Bernardo laughed. "That North Korean skipper is probably shitting his pants right now, Boss. Probably thinks Gentron's UUV is another inbound torpedo."

"You're right." Agazzi turned to Gentron again. "We should slow it down—take some of the angst off the NORCOM skipper's shoulders. What do you think?"

Gentron's Adam's apple bobbed as he swallowed. "If we don't, Senior Chief, the contact is going to disappear again and when he does, he won't make the same mistake of returning to this spot."

"I think you're right, Seaman Gentron. We need to make him think it's disappeared."

"I thought it might be best to have the second UUV out there with mine as soon as possible," MacPherson said.

"You may be right, Petty Officer MacPherson, but as you said earlier, it won't matter if he has orders to sink Sea Base. If those are his orders, when he believes he's run out of options, he'll fire."

"Then he's going to wake up in the dark Pacific. That UUV directly in front of his bow has over five hundred pounds of high explosives. There isn't going to be a bow when his torpedoes hit my UUV."

"Probably right, Petty Officer MacPherson, but if even one of those torpedoes survives the explosion and hits one of the Fast Sealift Ships, then Sea Base is going to go down like a line of dominoes." Agazzi shook his head. "We don't want him to fire. He needs to think Gentron's UUV has gone *tits up*—then, it'll increase his options. If he's preparing to fire, this may delay it."

"USS *Gearing* is out that way, Senior Chief, leading three SH-60 LAMPS MK III helicopters," Seaman Calvins said from the level above them. "All three have a full complement of sonobuoys. One of them has an MK-46 torpedo."

"Time to datum?" Agazzi asked.

"Any time now, Senior Chief," Keyland replied.

"Calvins, ask Combat to tell the LAMPS not to drop the sonobuoys. Tell them to use their dipping sonar. If they drop the sonobuoys, the contact may hear them hitting the water. The dipping sonar has a depth in excess of 1500 feet." Agazzi looked at MacPherson. "What is his depth?"

"I hold my UUV at five hundred feet, Boss."

Calvins acknowledged the order and passed it along to Combat. Agazzi watched. They had to straighten out the internal communications on Sea Base. It was like fighting blind without any immediate comms with Combat, the other ships, or even the capability to listen to the other communications such as the tactical air. The reason lay with why Sea Base was in the west Pacific. Sea Base was deployed to test the concept—to show that computers could fight the elements of the sea to keep a man-made island afloat. A man-made island designed to go anywhere to meet the tasks of national security. It was not ready for a fight, but here it was in the middle of one.

"What if the contact fires anyway?" Keyland asked.

"Then, MacPherson's UUV sinks or cripples the submarine." Agazzi nodded at Gentron. "Then, Gentron attacks with his to finish him off and we cross our fingers none of his torpedoes survive the explosion."

"Bring the speed down to four knots," Keyland said.

"Aye, LPO," Gentron replied, reaching over with his right hand and bringing the speed down.

"Bring it down sharply. Bring it to all stop," Agazzi corrected. "Make him think the inbound torpedo he believes heading toward him has had a mechanical failure or reached its limit."

Gentron brought the speed down to zero. "Bringing it to zero." On the digital speed gauge above the console, the figures raced downward as the speed started to decrease.

"Zero?" MacPherson asked. "Thought . . ."

"It'll continue along the same course for a few seconds. That way, the sonar operator on the submarine will believe . . . " Gentron took a deep breath and continued. "Will believe what the senior chief said."

"Then he can put speed back on a knot at a time. At four knots speed, it'll reach the submarine in less than an hour," Agazzi said. "Hopefully, by then the submarine will have closed its bow tubes and departed the area."

"And if it hasn't?" Keyland asked.

"Then Admiral Holman and Captain Garcia have a decision to make. If the sub fires its torpedoes, then it's made its own decision to die." Agazzi looked up sharply. "Has Combat given us orders?"

Keyland shook his head. "We told them what we did and they rogered it; about all we've gotten from them. The approaching enemy bombers are taking all their attention right now."

Agazzi nodded. "I suspect approaching bombers would make me more nervous. I'm sure," he continued, "they know you have corralled the enemy submarine."

"What do we do?" Calvins asked from above him.

Agazzi turned. "We wait. That's what we do." He touched Gentron on the shoulder. "And we see how well Gentron glides his UUV undetected up against an old, yesteryear North Korean submarine."

"I'm getting data from sonobuoys," Bernardo said. He touched several buttons on the AN/SQR-25 sonar console. A side screen appeared, lined with numbers across the top. "Looks as if the SH-60 LAMPS helicopters are sowing a barrier."

"Damn," Agazzi said, looking up at Calvins. "Didn't you tell them . . ."

"I told them, Senior Chief. I passed it to Combat," Calvins protested.

Agazzi moved over to Bernardo's console. "I wish they hadn't done that. If the sonar team on board the Golf is worth its salt, they will have picked up the splash of the sonobuoys entering the water."

"Looks as if one of the LAMPS has lowered its dipping sonar, Senior Chief," Bernardo said.

"We don't have comms with them, do we?"

"Kind of hard for us to have communications, Senior Chief, when all we have is a sound-powered telephone connected only to Combat and a regular telephone," MacPherson said. "We're blind and we're on the bottom deck of a ten-story ship. On the positive side, we're fighting."

"Calvins, tell Combat to warn the helicopters not to go active on their sonar. All we want is passive input."

"Active will help them locate the submarine better, Senior Chief," Gentron said.

"An active sonar pinging off the skin of the submarine will tell the contact a LAMPS helicopter is overhead. Helicopters are the bane of submarines. They can hover directly overhead, zoom forward of the contact, or aft to drop a torpedo that has little chance of missing."

"Wouldn't the presence of sonobuoys tell him the same thing?"

"Could be, Petty Officer Keyland, but sonobuoys can be launched by P-3C Orions or even surface ships, and as much as I wished they hadn't dropped a pattern, the noise is low and there is a chance they missed it."

"I'd say slim to nil is the chance," Keyland said.

"Gentron, when you're ready to launch a conventional torpedo, going active is the best way to refine the data. Helicopters and P-3Cs do it in their attack phase. Surface ships don't. If the Skipper of the contact is convinced his minutes are numbered . . ."

". . . and if his orders are to attack Sea Base, he'll launch."

"On target, MacPherson."

"Sounds like a good mantra for our patch, if we live long enough to design one," Bernardo sniped.

"Seaman Calvins, tell Combat about the sonobuoys and see if they have comms with the helicopters."

Calvins nodded and pushed the talk button on the mouthpiece.

"How do we know there's only one contact out there? What if he's the honeypot, intentionally keeping us occupied while others creep closer?" Gentron asked.

"We don't, but we have a couple of destroyers and we have the *Boxer* somewhere up there. They have a total of six SH-60s and with only one submarine detected so far . . ."

"Combat said only the *Gearing* and the three SH-60s were involved in the prosecution," Calvins added.

"Guess we really don't know if we have only one submarine out there," Agazzi said. The Golf-class submarine was diesel-electric-powered. Diesel submarines historically hunted in groups of two and more. Maybe Gentron was right, but North Korea wasn't a sea power. It was an angry little country rushing around the political environment flexing muscles of mass destruction.

"It's the only one we've detected, Senior Chief," Bernardo said. "We've got our sonar here. We're also getting feed from the dipping sonars beneath each of the ships holding up Sea Base, and now we have a sonar pattern near the contact." He shook his head. "I think this is the only one we have out here. The Chinese submarine is scattered on the ocean floor, surrounded by the dark Pacific."

"What do you think they feel, Senior Chief?" Calvins asked.

"Who?"

"The North Koreans," Calvins answered, nodding toward MacPherson and Gentron, "on board the submarine. You think they're scared?"

Agazzi nodded as he replied softly, "Anyone in combat who says they're not scared is full of it, Seaman Calvins." Agazzi nodded at the submarine on MacPherson's screen. "Right now, every sailor on that submarine is scared—frightened, adrenaline racing through their bodies with action moving so fast that only afterwards will they realize how close to dying they came."

"Like me."

"Like all of us."

"Hate to say this," Bernardo said, "but this action doesn't seem to be moving fast to me."

"FAST Pace, I've lost an engine. I can't execute the intercept. I have to land!" Franklin said, his voice high.

"Say again!"

"I'm going to land; my right engine just cut out."

Ahead of them, less than a mile, Sea Base filled the front vision of his cockpit. Walters glanced at his fuel gauge. His was in the red, but the engines were still running.

"Let's take her up another hundred feet, Blackman."

"I don't know that I can, Fast Pace. I need every bit of fume to reach Sea Base."

"Need to get a little altitude. Blackman, if you cut out now, you got no glide room to the field."

"Glide? Raptors glide like a rock, Fast Pace. This fighter isn't even going to skip across the waves; it's going to hit the top and keep on going."

"If you can get some altitude, then at least you'll be a rock landing on Sea Base instead of in the ocean."

"Raptor 10, bandit is lowering wheels; TAO believes it could be a suicide run. I hold you forty seconds to intercept."

"Raptor Haven, Raptor 10; I have bandit in sight; unable to lock on. Too much Sea Base between it and me. I'll be going cannon. Raptor 20 is declaring in-flight emergency for immediate landing."

"We have no runway for landing."

"You don't understand, Sea Base. He's landing. All of Sea Base is a runway in an emergency. I have the bandit."

"Fast Pace, I got that extra hundred feet; lowering wheels. Thirty seconds to Sea Base."

In the background of the transmission, Walters heard the hydraulics in Franklin's aircraft—the sounds of the wheels being lowered. Franklin was above and behind him. Sea Base was approaching too fast for him to glance back and confirm three wheels. A visual courtesy, but not a required one. Franklin's console would tell him if anything was wrong.

Ejection seats were only slightly less dangerous than crashing headfirst into the ground. Pilots had been paralyzed from bad ejections. Spines torn apart; skulls broken; insides ripped apart. Dangerous, yes, but most lived. But there were so many things to go wrong when ejecting, pilots had an unwritten golden rule to avoid grabbing the brass monkeys except when death was imminent. As Earnest Gann, the mid-twentieth-century adventure writer and pilot, once said, "If an airplane is still in one piece, don't cheat on it. Ride the bastard down." Air Force pilots subscribed to that philosophy.

"WHAT the hell were you two thinking? We don't fire just because it seems to be the thing to do! Now, hold your fire until I tell you to fire or you see blood on my chest," Willard said. They were only a little more scared than he was. What in the hell were they all doing out here on top of some damn Navy experiment? What in the hell was the Air Force thinking?

"You mean until we can see the whites of their eyes," Parker added, her voice shaking through the bravado.

"I mean you can't go firing willy-nilly around here, Parker. Look about you. What do you see?"

When she didn't say anything, Willard continued. "Every bullet you fire has to go somewhere and everywhere you look is Sea Base. If you're lucky, those bullets you and Lou ejaculated went off into the wild blue yonder."

"Hey, Chief!" Snot-Nose shouted, pointing toward the front of Sea Base. "We got two fighters inbound!"

Willard looked to where the young airman pointed. One fighter was slightly higher, its wheels lowered. The other was heading full bore toward Sea Base, leaving the other one behind.

"We got two aircraft inbound, airmen!" he shouted. "And from the way the first one is moving, I don't think you're going to need those M-16s."

"That's the Raptor 10 Formation!" Captain Nolan shouted.

"There're inbound, sir," Willard said.

"Only one's inbound, Chief, and that's the one with the wheels down. The other is on an attack run."

Everyone's eyes went from the inbound fighters to the enemy transport approaching Sea Base from the stern.

"We got three inbound, Chief!" Parker shouted, pointing aft toward the approaching North Korean transport.

"What you want us to do?" Thomas asked.

"Lou, that second fighter of ours has something wrong with it or else its wheels wouldn't be down. You take Grossman with you when it hits the deck. I want you and—"

"We got it, Chief," Captain Nolan interrupted, nodding toward Lieutenant Sipes. "Give us one airman and we'll take care of the fighter. You should get your people off the flight deck now."

Willard's eyes widened. Moments ago these two were hugging the deck with the rest of his ground crew. He nodded, turning to Grossman. "Danny, you're the tech. You go with the captain. Taxi that fighter as far away as you can"—Willard pointed toward the laser weapon—"in that direction. Keep it out of harm's way." The young technical sergeant turned with the officers, but Willard put his hand out and grabbed the airman's shoulder. "Danny, when you've secured the aircraft and have it chocked, you do what you have to do to get that Raptor ready for immediate launch."

"Chief, it'll take more than me and those officers to rearm her. We can refuel—"

"Don't rearm, but get her ready for launch."

Nolan shook his head. "Won't need rearming," Nolan said. "This is Raptor 10 Formation returning. They haven't fired anything."

The increasing decibels of Fast Pace's Raptor approaching the front of Sea Base drowned out the turbine engines of the North Korean transport approaching from the rear. *What is going on?* Willard asked himself. *What in the hell has the Air Force gotten us into?*

"Go!" he shouted, slapping Grossman on the shoulder. "I'll be right behind you as soon as I get everyone below."

The two officers and the technical sergeant took off running toward the row of fire extinguishers near the empty apron where in the early morning hours six Raptors had been parked. *Time changes everything,* Willard thought.

He looked aft as the North Korean transport crossed the stern.

JACOBS was running. Two masters-at-arms ran ahead of him heading toward the tower. His breathing came in short, rapid breaths, his lungs crying for him to stop.

His eyes searched as he ran, looking for his boatswain mates, trying through force of will to wish them away from wherever the bombs were going to hit. Praying everyone would come through this bombing run alive. As much as he chided Agazzi about Sea Base being an accident waiting to happen and how everyone was going to head to the dark Pacific, he'd never expected it to happen. No one expects the worst, and fewer are prepared when it arrives.

The screaming noise of jet engines broke through his thoughts, causing him to look forward. He squinted against the setting sun, able to make out the outline of an F-22A with its wheels down. A quick motion caused him to look lower. A second Raptor, wheels up, crossed the bow, making a low-level pass over Sea Base. He quickly glanced between the enemy aircraft crossing the stern and the fighter streaking across the bow. They were heading directly for each other.

Chill bumps flowed down his spine and through his extremities. Without thinking, he came to a stop as he turned to watch the tableau unfold. He never expected to know the true feeling of seeing the cavalry come over the hill. Maybe God was smiling on them.

His next thoughts were of the sharks swarming beneath Sea Base. That split second of joy was washed away by a tide of fear.

He heard someone screaming, "Master Chief." Near the far rail gun on the fore starboard side of Sea Base, Showdernitzel stood, her shotgun balanced on her hip with the barrel pointing upward. Alongside her stood Potts, trying to balance his piece off his bony hips as she did, but the gun kept slipping. She waved at Jacobs. It seemed to him as if she stood stubbornly unafraid of what the next few seconds were going to bring.

Showdernitzel motioned Jacobs toward her, pointing past him. He ran toward the two sailors, glancing over his shoulder toward the stern. The enemy transport was descending! One moment, tracers from the M-50 mount on the *Denebola* trailed upward toward the enemy aircraft, and the next, its wheels slammed down on the runway. Bursts of smoke from the friction of the rubber hitting Sea Base billowed from beneath the transport.

"What the f—!" he shouted. Mesmerized, he watched the C-130 lookalike sail down the runway. On the other side, Willard's airmen were filling the aircraft with M-16 fire as it sailed by them. Damn, they're shooting in this direction. As if listening to his thoughts, the whistle of a bullet passing near him galvanized Jacobs into moving. He was running toward Showdernitzel and Potts. Like angry hornets, M-16 bullets passed harmlessly around him.

A new, louder noise joined the cocophony of sound drowning out the normality of the day. Cannon fire from the Raptor stitched down the runway, hitting the enemy aircraft. Jacobs dived for the deck, his M-16 clattering beside him as he lost his grip. He rolled twice before coming to a stop. Lifting his head, he watched with mixed emotions as the cockpit on the Shaanxi Y-8 shattered. For a fraction of a second he thought he saw the red of blood hurling outward with the metal of the aircraft. A few feet away, his shotgun lay. Jacobs crawled quickly to it and pulled the weapon against him.

With the cockpit gone, the enemy aircraft continued moving, drifting off the runway, as its engines wound down, turning toward them as its speed diminished. The F-22A Raptor pulled up as it reached the stern of Sea Base. An explosion inside the destroyed cockpit sent flames leaping into the air. The engine nearest them fell from its casing, hitting the deck, burying itself a couple of inches. Jacobs put his head down, expecting another explosion. When none came, he looked up. The front of the aircraft was encased in flames, dark smoke roiling into the air. The thick smell of burning fuel filled his nostrils as the slight southwest wind blew across the aircraft, blowing the smoke away from them.

A second F-22A immediately followed the first; only this one had its wheels lowered. Jacobs glanced from the slowing transport turning to the left toward them to the jet fighter as it touched down along the far side of the runway, avoiding the gaping holes along the runway where cannon fire from the first fighter had ripped open the deck.

His attention quickly came back to the enemy aircraft. The nose wheel was frozen to the left, causing the burning transport to continue veering in that direction.

Jacobs pushed himself off the deck, holding the shotgun by the middle of the stock. *What now?* he thought. The scenario was winding down. Whatever bombs the North Korean transport had tried to deliver had nearly made it. Inside the aircraft, those bombs were still there. A siren rode over the noise of the burning transport and F-22A engines winding down.

"Get the hoses!" he shouted to Showdernitzel and Potts. He turned toward the nearest cache of fire hoses. The danger wasn't over. If they didn't stop the fire from reaching the explosives in the rear of the Y-8, the North Koreans would still achieve their objective of sinking Sea Base.

From the other side of Sea Base, nearly a mile and a half away, came the siren of the A/S 32P-25 Shipboard Firefighting Vehicle. That fire truck would be the key to stopping the fire from reaching the transport section of the burning aircraft, if it could get here in time.

Jacobs fell to his knees, reached down, and twisted the two locking mechanisms on the deck-level door. "Here!" he shouted. He pulled the door up and then pushed it back, a loud clang drowning out his first few words as the door slammed down on the metal deck. ". . . the hose as I pull it out!"

Potts and Showdernitzel squatted behind him. Jacobs freed the brass nozzle and quickly stood, the hose unrolling behind him. "Come on!" he shouted. "When we get the hose unwound, Potts, you turn on the water."

Water would do nothing for a fuel fire but spread the flames, but right now the fire was confined inside the burning frame of the cockpit. He didn't want to think what would happen when the heat reached the fuel tanks in the wings.

The rumble of the yellow shipboard firefighting vehicle with its siren blaring heading their way was a comfort. All they had to do was stall the progress of the fire until it arrived. The P-25 could blanket the burning aircraft with AFFF, quickly smothering the fire.

As he led the three of them pulling the hose toward the burning aircraft, Showdernitzel said, "I don't think I've ever been as scared as I have been these past minutes, Master Chief. Never been."

Jacobs nodded. "Me, too."

"I feel as if I've run twenty miles," she said, grunting with the effort of pulling the fire hose. "Twenty miles."

"Potts, you okay?" Jacobs asked, his eyes watching the damaged transport come to a stop less than a hundred feet from them. Smoke boiled from the cockpit area. He hoped the fire hose was long enough to reach it.

The sailor nodded. Jacobs knew the young man couldn't speak. Fear grabs your throat, twisting it closed, making breathing difficult until the fear passes. Then the closed throat is still there, but the knowledge you're still alive tears through normal attempts to hide the emotional release.

From the stern area of Sea Base, he caught the glimpse of a fire team rushing toward them. It would take them fifteen minutes to reach this area of Sea Base. While one of the values of Sea Base was its huge eighty-one-acre size, it was also a disadvantage in responding to an isolated crisis. This was just one more example of efficiency gone wild.

"Stay with me, Stella," Jacobs said, concentrating on the burning cockpit in front of them. Not much farther.

"You hear that, Potts? He called me Stella. Damn, Master Chief," she said through clenched teeth. "You keep that up and you'll have me thinking of you as my father."

The sound of hydraulics brought him up short. The ramp at the rear of the Y-8 jumped open a few inches. Showdernitzel ran into him and Potts into her.

"What the fuck, Master Chief?" she said, bouncing away from Jacobs and dropping her hold on the hose.

The rear ramp started down.

TWELVE

"Raptor Haven, touchdown!" Franklin broadcast. A burst of bluish smoke cascaded from beneath the aircraft from the friction of the tires hitting the runway. The fuel-warning light continued flashing on the control panel, but he still had power to both engines. He pushed forward on the brakes, hearing the squeal as the tires gripped the runway and, unseen by him, more friction burn shot out beneath the aircraft. The aircraft slowed quickly, so by the time he was a third of the way down the runway, he had taxi control.

To the right of the runway, he saw Captain Nolan motioning him toward him, using two wands normally wielded by one of the enlisted ground crew.

"Raptor 20, Raptor Haven; taxi off the runway ASAP, shipmate. The main portion of the runway was damaged during Raptor 10's attack. Bear right toward the apron crew for parking assignment."

He squinted at the runway ahead of him, glancing quickly out the left side of the cockpit window to see a small crater where one of Fast Pace's 20mm shells had hit. Quickly looking forward, he saw where he was only yards away from running into a heavy patch of 20mm holes. He expected to see clear sky beneath the runway, but it looked as if the gunfire had only blown away the top part of the metal island.

Franklin jerked the stick to the right. The Raptor moved easily off the runway onto an undamaged part of Sea Base. Ahead of him, Nolan motioned him onward.

A minute later, when Franklin was about fifty yards from the spot the ground crew had selected as his parking spot, the engines coughed and died. The F-22A rolled a few more feet before the weight of it brought the aircraft to a stop. Nolan continued motioning him forward, his hand signals increasing, but all Franklin could do was throw his hands up in a questioning gesture. Franklin hit the controls and the cockpit rolled back and open.

The odor of the burning Y-8 transport wisped across Franklin, causing him to look left at the scene. The rear ramp was halfway down and smoke poured over the top of it, but not down around the open sides. His impression was that some of the smoke from the burning cockpit was rolling through the transport section of the aircraft much like a horizontal chimney, venting out the top of the opening ramp.

"RAPTOR Haven, Raptor 50; splash first bandit. Second bandit in sight," came Zimmerman's transmission from the overhead speaker.

After a few seconds' pause, Crawford broadcast, "Lock-on second bandit."

"Roger, Raptor leader; Fox one."

Garcia glanced up at the speaker. He had more stuff going on with Sea Base than he had ever handled at one time. The CAP with the British was continuing two hundred miles out between them and the North Korean defensive fighter patrols off their coast. His fighters—*his!* That's right—they were his fighters who were shooting down inbound enemy transports that intelligence kept telling him were North Korean. He hoped they were right.

He had a burning North Korean transport on his deck and a North Korean submarine poised to fire on them somewhere to the northwest. He hoped that intelligence was right also. What more could go wrong?

"Skipper," the young operations specialist said, holding the secure red handset in his hand. "The admiral would like to speak with you, sir."

He shut his eyes for a moment before taking the handset.

"Charlie Oscar here," Garcia said.

"Hank, what in the hell is going on over there?" Holman asked. "I have no . . ." The admiral's voice was loud enough that Stapler standing nearby could hear both sides of the conversation.

"Admiral," Garcia interrupted. "I have aircraft engaged thirty miles northeast of me and closing. I have a burning enemy bomber on Sea Base." He took a deep breath and continued. "Raptor 10 shot the Y-8 transport up as it landed. It's now burning on the forward starboard side."

"Raptor 10's burning?"

"No, sir, the enemy transport is burning. Raptor 10 attacked it as the bandit made its approach and took it out. Raptor 10 should be landing . . ."

"No explosion when it landed?"

"No, sir. No explosion, but it is burning and we are responding. Right now, the fire is contained around the cockpit. We are trying to stop it from reaching the fuel tanks in the wings or the explosives in the rear; then we . . ." His voice trailed off.

"You need anything from me?" Holman asked, his voice conciliatory.

Stapler leaned down, shook his head, and whispered, "Not yet, Skipper. Everything is under control."

Garcia nodded. "Admiral, we have everything under control right now, but I would ask you to have fire teams and medical personnel standing by in the event we are unsuccessful."

"If it explodes, Hank, what's the worst case?"

"Worst case is a cascading effect with Sea Base collapsing. A rapid collapse could take the whole thing down."

"Okay. We should add preparing for an evacuation to the request for additional medical and fire teams. I'm going to have every helicopter we got standing by. You fight the fire, but have any unnecessary people muster on your port side in the event we have to pull them out. I'm going to send a company of Marines over to help with the organization."

Stapler rolled his eyes, grabbed a piece a paper, and started writing furiously.

"Thanks, Admiral. My concern right now is that I still have two inbound possible bombers. We can start . . ."

Stapler handed him the paper. Garcia stuck it under a nearby low-wattage reading light. He read it while the admiral picked up the conversation on the other end.

"Hank, I don't think the North Koreans intend to cross the Demilitarized Zone along the 38th parallel. I think all along they have intended to sink Sea Base as a sign of their belligerence. A sign to the world to not fuck with them."

Garcia finished reading the note and handed it back to Stapler. "Admiral, you most likely are correct. Right now, sir, let's put the evacuation to a planning stage. Let me continue to fight the engagements I have," he said, regurgitating what Stapler had written. When he finished, he felt a moment of apprehension, wondering if he had overplayed his hand.

After a few seconds, Admiral Holman responded. "Hank, I couldn't have said it better. You need anything, you let me know. Good luck."

Garcia pulled the handset away from his ear.

Stapler took the handset and handed it to the nearby sailor. "Skipper, topside watches report the ramp is coming down."

"What ramp?"

"The ramp of the burning transport." Stapler shrugged. "Probably the fire has burned the hydraulic lines causing the mechanism to free the ramp. The on-scene damage-control leader is concerned the fresh air will enable the fire, causing it to spread. The P-25 fire truck should be there any moment. Once it fills the rear of the transport with AFFF foam, it'll stop the fire from spreading, but . . ."

"Until it can do that, we are in peril of the aircraft exploding."

"Aye, sir. That we are." Stapler turned back to the Air Intercept Controller.

"Raptor Haven, this is Raptor 30; we are four strong on CAP. Two Royal Navy F-35 fighters integrated into formation. Two Royal Navy F-35 fighters on afterburner, heading your direction. No contacts held this area."

"Air Search," Stapler said, walking up beside the third console. "What's the status on the North Korean defensive fighter patrol?"

"Sir, they're circling just like they've been doing all day. Most times a racetrack pattern; every now and again some of the formations do a figure-eight to break up the monotony. Hard to keep track of how many there are. Seems to me they are reducing the number of aircraft again, sir. Most likely heading to their bases for refueling."

"Pass along information when the tactical situation changes, sailor," Stapler said sharply.

The sailor's back hunched over as he concentrated on the circular motion of the radar sweep. "Sir, sometimes we get the returns from the satellite and sometimes we get them from our land radars. Most times we get both simultaneously. Our radars don't have the reach to paint the bogies. The picture jerks and jumps because of the two radar images overlapping. . . ." the sailor responded, his voice trailing off.

"And every time they change, I want to know," Stapler snapped. Pausing a moment, he took a deep breath. "How many are in the pattern and what's the change from a quarter hour ago."

"Commander, the system is tracking forty-two returns. That's down from sixty a few minutes ago."

"What happened?"

"Just what I said, Commander," the sailor said with a shrug. "I think some of them are returning to base. It's hard to tell when they leave and rejoin. Naval Tactical Data System updates by the second. That's when I know if we have had a change in number. Too many to count manually."

"Keep an eye on them. We don't want them deciding to head this way."

"Another thing, Commander Stapler." Emboldened, the sailor continued. "Because we have two different radar systems providing us data, there's no deconfliction. I think we have a lot of false positives; dupes."

"What does that mean?"

"It means we could have less than what we are seeing. I don't think it means more, but it could mean that also."

"Well, stop it. I don't want any more false positives. We don't have false positives in this CIC."

"RAPTOR Haven, Raptor 10; I have a problem," Walters broadcast. He leaned forward, blinking sweat from his eyes, trying to get a visual on his left engine.

The low-fuel alarm beeped incessantly in his ears. His fuel had disappeared with the low-flyover attack against the approaching transport. He had smiled when his shells stitched the enemy cockpit. A feeling of euphoria had washed over him when the cockpit exploded, destroying the front of the transport. The idea of people dying in it was not part of the ethos of fighter-pilot satisfaction. But the smile had quickly vanished when he flew into the cloud of the explosion. Shrapnel had hit his fighter. Some foreign object had been sucked into the intake of his left engine as he zoomed over the exploding Y-8 transport.

He had exhausted the fire extinguisher in the left engine. The fire-warning light flashed on the control panel, accompanying the beeping in his ears. If scientists ever wanted a mechanism for stimulating stress in a pilot, the fire-warning light deserved a first-place award.

The right engine was still running, but pilots knew their aircraft. The least change in performance radiated through them as if they were part of the aircraft itself. Even though the control panel showed the right engine was fine, performing to standards, there was a subtle change to it. He wanted to believe the change was the loss of the left engine. He took a deep breath, his mind and body performing a routine he had done over and over in training. Intense Air Force training overrode fear in situations such as this. Every action was a practiced rote in Walters's fight to bring the aircraft around and land on Sea Base before the left engine exploded—worst case—or the right engine decided to quit also—another worst case. Franklin was right about one thing; an F-22A glided like a rock and at two-thousand-feet altitude, it was going to be a quick rock hitting the ocean surface. He'd be a hundred feet below the surface before the aircraft slowed.

Walters tugged the stick to the left, using the good engine to ease into a turn. There it was again! A soft hiccup in the right engine. He glanced at the control panel, seeing no sign of a malfunction. The low-fuel and fire-warning alarms beeped off synch with each other. He reached over and switched both off. The flashing lights were still there, and he needed no extra noise blocking out his comms with Sea Base.

He was faced with the quandary of keeping an aircraft aloft with little fuel. Complicating the low FUREM was the fact he was flying a damaged aircraft in danger of exploding—worst case again—or dropping from the sky. Everything depended on luck and fuel right now. As his instructor told him at flight school, "In a situation where your aircraft is about to crash, it is important to know that the primary thing that will allow you to use the skills you've learned to save yourself is luck."

A long turn toward the safety of Sea Base was a better tactic for a damaged aircraft, but he had no idea how much longer the right engine would continue to operate.

Walters touched the pedals. The aircraft bounced a couple of times as he moved it a few feet up and down. At least he still had vertical control. Right now, any good news was appreciated. Was it luck or skill keeping him aloft? he wondered.

"Raptor 10, Raptor Haven; you are cleared for immediate landing. Be advised the runway is closed due to damage. You are going to have to touch down at the end of the runway at an angle. An angle that will take you off the runway as soon you reach the Sea Base apron. The runway is too damaged for you to land on it. Once off the runway, you are cleared to steer parallel to it."

"Roger, Sea Base," he replied nervously. "Be advised I have fire-warning light on left engine. I think it took some FOD from the explosion. I also have low-fuel warning light."

"Roger, Raptor 10. I show you five miles southeast of Raptor Haven in a right-hand turn. How is your visual—"

"I have visual on Sea Base," Walters interrupted. *Shit! The thing takes up most of the ocean at this range! You can't help but see it.*

"Roger, Raptor 10. Report engine status."

"Roger. I say again, left engine has fire-warning light. Right engine, according to the control panel, is within parameters, but there's something not quite right with it. I think . . ."

The Raptor jerked as the right engine coughed out, caught, and fired up again. His body pulled inward as if the aircraft had squeezed him. "Jesus Christ!" Every light on the control panel flashed a couple of times, went out, and then returned to normal. The aircraft rocked hard to the right. He tugged the stick to the left, and for the fraction of a second that the control panel was out, he had no response. Then the aircraft reacted immediately to the hard tug, righting itself. Walters caught the reaction and corrected, bringing the aircraft level. He was flying parallel to the stern of Sea Base now.

"Raptor 10, Raptor 10; you okay?"

"No, I'm not okay. The right engine flamed out for a moment. I am in a turn to line up, but I'm not sure I have enough fuel to reach Sea Base." He turned the stick slightly to the right, and let out a sigh of relief when the aircraft eased into its turn again.

Off to his left, motion drew his attention to a helicopter hovering a couple of miles from Sea Base. At least he wouldn't be in the water long, but then his thoughts went to the swarm of sharks that had taken up residence beneath Sea Base. The closer he got to Sea Base, the slimmer his chances of being picked up by the helicopter before the sharks picked him up. The alternative was to turn away, put some distance between him and Sea Base, so the rescue would be safer. Even as these thoughts passed, Walters continued the slow turn toward Sea Base, knowing he was going to bring the Raptor on board.

He fought an urge to jerk the F-22A Raptor into a hard turn, hit the throttle, and dive for the safety of the floating island. But to do so might take away the slim control he had on the aircraft now and send him into the ocean before he could eject. He took a deep breath. Fear seemed to fade away as confidence in his ability rose to the top. This was his aircraft and as long as he had fuel to fly it and an engine that would stay lit, he could do it.

Walters came out of the turn. He eased the aircraft farther right slightly, feeling the strong pull of the lone engine as he maneuvered to line the fighter up with the stern of Sea Base. He would land slightly skewed to the left of the end of the runway, and veer left away from the damaged portion near the center. He glanced through the cockpit at the smoke rolling upward from the front of the burning Y-8. He squinted. It looked as if the ramp was halfway down on the rear of the bandit.

He touched the pedals slightly, righting the aircraft. The Raptor vibrated and for a fraction of a second, he lost control. He took a deep breath, blinking several times to clear the sweat, and mumbled, "Mary, Mother of God . . ."

Walters had heard of Raptor pilots who had lost control and used the engine nozzles to land. The F-22A Pratt and Whitney engines had nozzles that allowed the pilot to change the direction of exhaust two-zero degrees upward or downward. This gave the Raptor an immediate change in the angle of attack when engaged. Something no other fighter aircraft in the world could do. But right now it was landing that interested Walters the most.

Changing nozzle angle would allow him to compensate a little for loss of his ailerons and change the altitude of the aircraft. But without both engines, it would be nearly impossible to affect the direction of flight if he lost control of the rudder.

"Raptor 10, Raptor Haven; continue inbound. Be advised your kill is burning on starboard fore side."

Starboard fore—what in the hell does that mean? he asked himself before taking a deep breath and saying aloud, "Stay calm. Forward right side."

He looked ahead at Sea Base. Dashing across the front of the runway, a bright-yellow vehicle headed in the direction of the burning aircraft. He wondered briefly if the vehicle was prepositioning for his landing or fighting the fire of the burning aircraft. If Walters had the time, he would have been amazed at how a floating island the size of Sea Base continued flight operations while fighting a fire on deck and other enemy aircraft inbound. On land, Walters would have understood how they could do it, but to do it at sea was something else altogether. If he was ever asked, the Navy could have its carriers.

"OKAY!" Willard shouted. "The rest of you get your asses over there and get Lieutenant Franklin's aircraft ready for launch. Let the sailors take care of the fire on the other side."

He walked behind the running ground crew, confident in their ability to get Raptor 20 refueled and ready for launch. His breathing was rapid and for a fraction of a second, Willard thought he was going to cry! Him! He shook his head. *Stupid emotions,* he thought. He glanced at Nolan. Ten minutes ago, he would have said the officer was destined for a short career, but now Nolan and the other officer, Sipes, were hunched over, running beneath the stalled Raptor, helping the ground crew with the chocks.

Nolan ran to the left side of the Raptor. "Blackman, you okay?"

Franklin stood up in his cockpit, looking over the edge as if contemplating whether to remain where he was or climb down. "I'm fine, Cat," he said, surprised to find his voice steady. His legs didn't feel that way.

Willard walked up beside Nolan. "Captain Franklin, welcome back, sir. If you want to come down, we'll be a few minutes before we have the aircraft ready to take off."

"Thanks, Chief."

Franklin climbed down. When he was halfway down, Nolan spoke up. "Blackman, I'll be taking your aircraft up. You've had your fun for today."

Franklin jumped onto the flight deck, landing with his knees bent. He quickly straightened. "Bullshit, Cat. This is my aircraft, and besides, as soon as Fast Pace gets his sorry ass down here and has had a few bows, then we'll both take back off."

Sergeant Thomas rushed behind Franklin and scrambled up to the cockpit, where he leaned into it, his hands doing something out of sight.

Nolan opened his mouth to say something, thought a moment, and then replied, "Let's get you some water and have a talk."

Willard watched the two men move their conversation toward the rear of the aircraft. Sipes walked up to the two men, wiping his hands on his handkerchief. *Lord forbid you should get your hands dirty,* Willard thought, shaking his head. *Officers! It takes a shrink and their parents to really understand and love them. Who in their right mind would be fighting over the chance to die?*

"Chief," Thomas said, peering down from above. "We got a full weapons load-out. Diagnostics are running. No fuel, and when I say no fuel, I mean even the fumes are gone." Without waiting for a reply, the tech sergeant took off.

Willard looked around the aircraft. It wasn't in an approved parking spot, so where was the nearest hospitality spot? Flush with the deck, you had to look for the yellow and black slanted stripes. The nearest one was a good fifty feet from the aircraft. Snaggles Cole, his young airman from Chicago, was already unlatching the cover. Willard gave a weak smile to his self-acknowledgment that his people knew their job.

Thomas scrambled down the ladder and looked in the same direction as Willard. "Chief, you think the hose is going to be long enough?"

Willard shrugged. "Won't know until we unwind it." He looked around for Sergeant Thomas. "Lou," he said, seeing his number two on the other side of the front wheel. "Send a couple of them back to the apron and wheel one of those fire canisters over here."

"Not much to burn, Chief," Thomas said. "No fuel."

"Not much isn't the same as nothing, Lou. Now, do it," he said, his voice low, but in a tone that stopped any further argument.

"WOW! Did you see that?" Taleb asked, reaching over with his fingers and pushing Kiang's shoulder. "Wow! I never thought I'd be in a place where you could watch every action like this and not wet your pants."

Kiang ignored the young boatswain mate, continuing to snap pictures. He had already filled one file, flicked it out, and stuffed the disc into his shirt pocket. This was his second digital set. His heart pounded, audible in his ears each time he lifted the camera or binoculars to his eyes. Was that fear or anxiety or the natural reaction of the body to adrenaline when it hits the bloodstream? Like most PhDs, he was prone to analysis even when it was about how his own body reacted. He had done it when the colonel left him lying in his own body wastes for weeks. His breaths came in deep, steady draughts. He shut his eyes for a second and asked himself how much mileage he might get from his handler for these photographs. Even as he thought about how much he could make from CNN.

Maybe this might be the exit price to free his parents. He grunted at the thought, knowing there would never be an exit price. They couldn't allow him to live, but his parents were innocent pawns. As long as he was doing what they wanted, his parents lived. If his parents should die, he would never know because his life was one of continuous servitude.

"The ramp is coming down," Taleb said, pointing at where Kiang's camera was aimed. "I want some of those photographs when you develop them," the young sailor added softly.

Kiang dropped his camera and lifted his binoculars. He focused on the rear ramp. Smoke roiled out of the top portion of where the ramp had separated from the aircraft, and for a fraction of a second, he thought he saw movement near the spreading opening along the bottom of the ramp.

"RAPTOR Haven, this is Black Leader," came the British accent over the tactical air frequency from the overhead speaker in Combat.

"Who's that?" Garcia asked.

"Black Leader, this is Raptor Haven; please identify yourself."

"Roger, Raptor Haven; we are two Foxtrot thirty-fives inbound your location from His Majesty's Ship *Elizabeth*. Request instructions."

"Raptor Haven, this is Raptor Leader; Fox two by Raptor 50 on second bandit. First Sidewinder missed."

Garcia recognized the voice as Major "Tight End" Crawford. He also recognized the disbelief in the fighter pilot's voice.

"I am past the second inbound," said Crawford. "I have two unidentified friendlies about fifteen miles in front and above me. I also have the third bandit on radar."

Garcia had once taken a ride in the F-22A with Crawford, and listened to the junior officer extol the virtues of the world's most technologically capable fighter aircraft. But then, when fighter pilots were talking about their aircraft, whichever aircraft they were flying was the world's best. He recalled Crawford saying several times that the F-22A had a "first-shot first-kill" capability, so maybe that was why the major's voice showed disbelief over the miss. Navy pilots believed in "Fire one; wait; then, fire the second." By the time the enemy knew the first missile was inbound and taking countermeasures against it, the second was on its way with the tactical belief it would dodge through the decaying value of the countermeasures.

"Commander Stapler," Garcia said. "Do we have fire control on the second bandit inbound?" He stood with his feet at a forty-five-degree angle and legs slightly spread. His closed lips hid teeth knocking together from the slight shaking of his jaws. What in the hell was he doing out here? He thought of his wife, his young son, and daughter. Then, he quickly banished the diversion from his mind. *Stay focused on the events. Handle one at a time. Do the things they teach you in Navy schools and do the things you've learned having been a captain at sea for over eight years.*

"Am giving firing parameters to the starboard rail gun, sir."

"How close is the rail gun to the burning aircraft?" Garcia asked, refocused and reengaged.

"About a hundred fifty yards, sir."

He nodded. If the aircraft blew, there'd be nothing to stop the second aircraft. *If the inbound aircraft reached Sea Base before that happened, then worry.* "Can you turn Raptor 50 around to take out the second bandit before it reaches Sea Base?"

"I thought of that, Captain, but by the time we could turn him, the number two bandit would be overhead and the remaining bandit would be close behind him. Recommend we keep him on course to the last bandit."

"How about Raptor 10?"

"Raptor 10 is in extremis. He has lost an engine and we're trying to get him back aboard Sea Base before he hits the drink."

"Raptor Haven, Black Leader here; be advised, we have both remaining bandits in our field of fire. Request engagement guidance."

Garcia and Stapler looked at the speaker. Without discussion, Stapler stepped quickly to the Air Intercept Controller, bent down, and gave new instructions.

"Black Formation, this is Raptor Haven; you are cleared for the far target from you, nearest one to Sea Base. Be advised we have one F-22A Raptor at angels two closing third bandit."

Several seconds passed before the British leader responded. "Raptor Haven, this is Commander Lester Tyler-Cole. Be advised we only have two bandits on our screens. Please advise where third is."

"Black Leader, original enemy formation composed of three heavies. First heavy splashed by Raptor beneath you. Remaining two continue inbound—fifteen miles—toward Sea Base. You have weapons free on the lead heavy."

"Roger, Raptor Haven. We have Raptor 50 Formation and Raptor Leader overhead on scope. Bandits identified. I am linking with you at this time. Request confirm we both have same target in mind."

On the Naval Tactical Data System, the top half-diamond symbol flashed. The operations specialist hooked on it. A readout showed the Royal Navy fighter with lock-on on the lead bandit.

Stapler nodded. "Tell him take it out."

"Black Leader, we confirm target. You are cleared for attack. Raptor 50 is in descent against last bandit—"

"Raptor 50 is clear of my weapons system," Tyler-Cole interrupted.

"Black Two, Black Leader; rear hemisphere attack. Launch one missile. We'll follow them to the target. Wait one, let's give the American fighter a wee bit more separation."

Garcia walked over beside Stapler, the two men watching the video returns on the Air Intercept Controller's console. The two F-35 Joint Strike Fighters flew overhead of Raptor 50.

"Raptor Haven, Raptor 50; I have the two Brits on my screen."

"Sir," the sound-powered phone talker interrupted. "Commander Stapler, the topside watch reports visual on an approaching aircraft."

"That will be the Y-8 or AN-12. It will be the enemy transport, sir."

"Tell them to take that aircraft out," Garcia said harshly.

Stapler nodded at the Air Intercept Controller, who pressed the talk button, "Black Leader, Raptor Haven; request engage target immediately. Target is within visual range of Sea Base."

"Roger, Raptor Haven; we understand. Black Two, tallyho!" Tyler-Cole broadcast.

"Raptor Haven; Fox one!" cried Zimmerman. The whoosh sound of the Sidewinder leaving its cradle filled the background of his announcement.

"Following missiles with guns," Fairwell added. "Raptor 50, Raptor 60; follow me in."

The sound of the 20mm cannons replaced the whoosh for a moment before the broadcast button was released. In Combat, the vision of the missile heading toward the target with 20mm shells racing behind it like angry wingmen filled Garcia's mind. No way the third target was going to get away.

"Fox one," said Tyler-Cole calmly.

"Fox two," Black Two added.

"I think this calls for cannon, Black Two." The sound of 25mm shells accompanying the missiles toward the target came over the speaker, drowning out the broadcast of Black Two. Sounded to Garcia as if the pilot was only acknowledging Black Leader's command. The British sounded a lot calmer than his pilots, but then it could be the accent.

"The missile is skewing away from target!" Crawford broadcast from his vantage point overhead the action.

"Which missile?" Garcia asked.

"Must have some sort of electronic warfare device on these birds," Stapler said to Garcia.

"Confirm Raptor 50 observation," Tyler-Cole echoed. "Our missiles have been decoyed. Flares are being expended from the rear of the bandit. My ECM detector shows no discernible devices. But," he said with a laugh, "hard to decoy bullets. We are stitching up the side of the bandit. Tallyho!"

"Confirm same," Fairwell said. "Angel and my shells are hitting the bandit."

The sound of an explosion echoed through Combat from the tactical air speaker.

"What was that?" Garcia asked.

"Raptor 50, Raptor Haven; do you read me?"

Seconds passed with no answer until suddenly Crawford's voice broke the tense silence. "Splash bandit number three. Bandit is spiraling . . . Forget it. Bandit is in the drink and burning. Heavy smoke marks the spot."

"Black Leader, Raptor Haven; I show your target in a right-hand turn."

"You are correct, Raptor Haven. That's because his number-four engine is burning and he has several large holes in his transport section."

Garcia's lips curled in a tight smile. The North Korean attack had failed. One aircraft burned on his deck. He was confident the fire teams would quickly bring that under control. Two were in the drink and the remaining one the British were taking out. The four-formation attack was kaput.

"Raptor Haven, Black Leader; belay my last. That puff of smoke on the horizon is the bandit. He just exploded. Looks like bits and pieces now."

"Roger, I copy bandit is gone."

"Black Two; one flyby, then we'll go around to make sure our bandit isn't hiding in that smoke cloud."

"TAO!" the electronic warfare operator shouted. "I have a missile inbound! Sidewinder. Am hitting countermeasures. Make that two missiles."

"It's from Black Formation!" Stapler shouted.

The British missiles decoyed by the flares would revert to active search mode once they lost an infrared signature. Garcia dropped his head to his chest for a moment before reaching for his coffee cup. The nearest large target was Sea Base. He was surprised his hand seemed steady.

On the AN/SLQ-32 electronic warfare console the operator hit the automatic-countermeasures switch. Unseen electronic waves swept toward the inbound American-made missiles. Was it possible to become immune to fear, or could the body only handle so much excitement before that became the norm and the body adjusted? What he did know was he needed to make a head call. He looked toward the hatch leading to the passageway where the heads were located. He took a deep breath and turned back to the action in front of him. He could wait a few minutes longer.

The Sidewinder was essentially an infrared missile, hunting for the hottest signature in front of it. It had first been fired in 1954, and technology had transformed the Sidewinder over decades of use. Around the world, over twenty-seven nations used the American missile. It was the least expensive but most widely used short-range air-to-air missile in the modern fighter inventory. Growth in technology eventually gave it an active optical mode to enhance heads-on attack, and within the past ten years had added an active digital seeker that activated when the heat signature was lost. Every advantage had been given to ensuring the Sidewinder hit something.

And the Sidewinder's technology didn't care if what it hit was friendly or hostile, as long it hit something hard. Similar to the logic heads of the American torpedoes, infrared seekers were nearly impossible to decoy and impossible to detect. A target either took advantage of the maneuver limitations of the missile to exploit its envelope, or dropped flares with fingers crossed in the hope of fooling the infrared seeker. The North Korean transport had used the flares and been successful against the British rear hemispheric attack.

It was something for García's after-action report. He turned to the second-class operations specialist manning the telephones and speakers and motioned the young sailor to him. Garcia took a few seconds to tell the sailor what to write down. He could tell the young woman was distracted by the action ongoing as Combat dealt with the inbound missiles. Intuitively, he glanced where normally her right pocket would be with her name embossed on it, but the life vest covered it. He prided himself on using the names of his sailors when he talked to them.

But this tidbit about the decoying of the missiles was more important than knowing the name of the sailor in front of him. Office of Naval Intelligence would figure out what it was; he'd just tell them how it acted.

Garcia held up his hand to the sailor, motioning for her to wait. He turned to Stapler. "Commander, have EW save her recordings. Don't overwrite them."

Stapler passed the instructions while Garcia continued his dictation to the second-class petty officer. When he finished, he asked, "You have all that, Petty Officer? Understand what you're to do?"

"Yes, sir," the sailor replied, nodding, her eyes glancing toward the far EW console and to Stapler, who was standing near the weapons control console.

"Not to worry," Garcia said, truly believing it. "It'll be over soon." He turned away from the sailor and back to the action surrounding him, clasping his hands behind him. If Holman were here, he'd have lit his cigar by now, Garcia thought, a slight smile crossing his lips.

"WHAT did the Skipper want?" the sound-powered phone talker asked the OS, his voice shaking.

The OS shook her head. "Man, he is one cool dude. You know, he asked me to write down something about those inbounds being able to decoy the air-to-air missiles."

"He what?"

"Yeah. Look at him," the sailor said, nodding toward Garcia's back where he stood with both hands clasped behind him. "He's smiling. We got missiles inbound, a fire on deck, and he smiles!"

The sound-powered phone talker shook his head slightly, the heavy weight of the helmet stopping most movement. "I don't know how he does it. I'm about ready to pee my pants and he stands there like it's a day at the races."

The OS picked up a pad of paper. "Yeah, we got one cool dude for our skipper. Go figure!" She started writing.

WITHOUT a hot signature in front of it, the two Sidewinder missiles continued on trajectory, the active digital seeker searching for another target. The EW operator knew that once the radar signal disappeared, it meant either the missile had run out of fuel and fallen from the sky, or it had locked on another heat source.

Too many targets for it to fall from the sky.

THIRTEEN

"Showdernitzel! Grab the hose!" Jacobs shouted.

Water raced through the deployed hose, pressure filling the two-and-a-half-inch hose—whipping the flat, loose S lying on the deck of Sea Base to a hard, near-straight thing of strength waiting impatiently to be released.

Jacobs gripped the nozzle tightly, pointing it at the cockpit. He spread his legs, bent his knees, ready for the fight. He glanced behind him. Showdernitzel and Potts were not ready.

The slight wind across the deck cleared the smoke obscuring the cockpit. Jacobs stumbled backward a step. The eerie black silhouettes of the pilot and copilot sat motionless at their controls, enveloped in flames like candles from hell.

Showdernitzel gripped the hose behind Jacobs. "Got it, Boss," she said looking at the hose. Her shoulder bumped Jacobs. The bump shook Jacobs's stare away from the sight above him.

Potts stood close behind her, his hands flexing as he fought for a good grip on the hose.

"This is going to be rough, you two. Whatever you do, don't let go! You hear me?" Jacobs shouted. His voice sounded shaken to him.

"Yes, Master Chief," the two said in unison.

Jacobs had seen what a two-and-a-half-inch could do if a fire team lost control of it. He licked his lips. Once he pulled the toggle back freeing the water, the three of them were going to have a rough time keeping control of the hose. You needed a minimum of five to control the hose: a nozzle man and four tenders. Here he had three.

He reached forward and grabbed the handle, wriggling his fingers for a moment before gripping it tightly. Once he pulled it back, the water pressure pouring through this hose would be tremendous. If he lost his grip, the hose would whip around the deck like a mad snake, knocking down anyone and anything in its wild path. If they lost control and it got away from them, the hose would leap into the air, breaking flesh and bones until someone turned off the water. Jacobs glanced at the brass nozzle. It would become a battering ram, killing and breaking anyone and anything in its path.

A sailor from the rail gun ran up between Showdernitzel and Potts, grabbing the hose. "Chief said you could probably use some help, Master Chief!" the sailor shouted breathlessly.

Jacobs nodded in acknowledgment and jerked the handle back. Then he pulled the toggle switch back. The hose jerked, nearly knocking the four down with its initial leap. Water bore in a near-straight line from the vari-nozzle, jetting through the center of the flames roiling through the shattered cockpit windows. Jacobs twisted the settings slightly, giving the water a wider spread, forcing the fire down.

The water pressure wrenched them back and forth in small steps like a wild animal fighting to wrest itself from their grips, pushing and pulling as if searching for a lax second, a lost grip, for a jump to freedom. Jacobs shifted his weight from one leg to the other, fighting to keep his footing as he kept the water trained on the cockpit.

Five minutes, Jacobs told himself. Five minutes and the real damage-control teams would be here as well as the P-25 truck. He could hear shouting, and knew the voices came from fire teams racing across the deck toward the conflagration.

A muffled explosion drew his attention toward the horizon off the bow of Sea Base. A black ring of smoke cascaded away from a flash of silver. To the right of the explosion, two swirling contrails trailed something heading their way, but in the gaze of seconds Jacobs took away from fighting the fire, he failed to see the Sidewinder missiles from whence the contrails came.

Jacobs turned his attention back to the cockpit, directing the steady flow of water over it, showering the fire, praying through clenched teeth that they'd snuff it out before it reached the fuel tanks. Once it reached the fuel tanks, water would be ineffective. He and his ad-hoc fire team would not have to worry about it, because a fuel explosion at this range would take the four of them with it.

Bending his knees further, Jacobs took a step forward. The three sailors behind him lifted and pulled the hose in the direction Jacobs moved. He was the nozzle man. He directed the flow while those holding the hose had the responsibility of moving it wherever the nozzle man led.

Jacobs wanted to shift nearer the front of the aircraft so the water could cover both sides of the inferno. While he had the left-hand side of the Y-8 covered, he couldn't see where the right wing connected with the aircraft. Both wings held fuel tanks. He had to keep the fire away from both wings.

A loud clang of metal hitting metal drew his attention to the rear of the aircraft. The ramp had finally given way, falling twenty feet to hit the deck. It bounced once before coming to a stop in the slight indentation made in the deck. A large cloud of smoke puffed once from the rear before returning to roiling out along the edges of the top.

Jacobs's attention returned to the cockpit, making sure the water was staying on top of the fire. Flames burst upward in the cockpit, the air from the open ramp feeding them like a damper freshly turned.

Motion at the rear of the burning Y-8 drew his attention. Armed uniformed men stumbled out of the rear of the transport, coughing and wiping their eyes. Several fell to the deck, with others grabbing the arms of their comrades, tugging them out and away.

"Jesus Christ!" he said.

"Shit, Master Chief. They're . . ."

Army! Troops! North Koreans! emerged as one thought even as he kept the hose trained on the cockpit. *The transport carried troops! That explained the other three aircraft inbound.*

One of the North Korean soldiers, wiping his eyes, shouted

something, and pointed at Jacobs. He lifted his weapon toward them.

THE flash of the explosion on MacPherson's screen startled Agazzi and Keyland, who were looking over the sailor's shoulder.

"What the hell was that?" Bernardo shouted, ripping his earphones off and sticking his finger in his right ear. "I've got an explosion in the water, Boss! Bearing two-two-zero degrees!" Bernardo shouted as he twisted the finger in his ear a couple of times. Staring directly at the console, he slipped the earphones on again and leaned toward it. "Christ, that hurt."

On the AN/SQR-25 passive sonar console, the ripples of the explosion disrupted the steady digital flow running from top to bottom. Multiple white traces of varying amplitudes tore through the screen, obscuring any noise signatures that might be in the water.

"It'll take a few seconds for the pattern to settle down again," Bernardo added when he saw Agazzi and Keyland looking in his direction.

Agazzi turned to Calvins, who was trying to balance the large sound-powered phone helmet straight on his head. "Calvins, ask Combat if one of those helicopters dropped a torpedo."

"I've lost my UUV," MacPherson said, bewildered. "One moment it was there, and the next it was gone. I got no data link, no picture. Nada."

"Gentron, how far away are you?" Agazzi asked.

"About a mile and a half, Senior Chief."

"It might still be out there," MacPherson said softly. "Maybe the explosion damaged her."

"Gentron, kick your UUV up to twelve knots and get in there. I want to know what . . ."

"I've lost contact with the submarine!" Bernardo shouted, looking at Agazzi and tapping his screen. "It's gone."

"Twelve knots, aye," Gentron replied.

Agazzi shuffled a couple of steps to the passive sonar display. Where seconds earlier a thin line denoting the slight noise of the enemy submarine had trailed down the digital rainfall, now there was nothing. Like bushes closing behind an animal crawling through them, the digital bits were smoothing out across the screen, creating a single opaque rainfall. Then, in a different area of the screen, a slight trace appeared.

"What's that?"

Bernardo hurriedly slid the cursor on top of the new noise spike. He reached up and with both hands pressed his earpieces down hard against his head, his eyes squinting tightly as he concentrated on the faint sound.

"What is it?" Agazzi asked.

Bernardo didn't answer. His eyes closed as he leaned closer to the console. His tongue flicked out for a second and touched his upper lip. Then he leaped back in his seat. Wide-eyed, Bernardo looked at the Senior Chief. "We've got a torpedo inbound. It's a mutha-f'ing torpedo, Senior Chief!" he shouted, his words running together with emotion.

"Calvins, tell Combat we have a torpedo in the water . . ."

"It's coming this way!" Bernardo added.

". . . inbound," Agazzi finished.

"Distance?" Keyland asked. "You got any range? What is the bearing?"

"It's bearing two-zero-zero. Same as the North Korean sub."

"My UUV was at thirteen nautical miles. If it fired torpedoes, then the UUV must have taken the hits. That must have caused the explosion?"

The trace on the passive sonar display steadied and became clearer as the effects of the underwater explosion dissipated. The torpedo was steady on bearing 220. At fifteen nautical miles, this was a long-range firing. What was the speed? A long-range torpedo usually went slower than the normal forty knots of a short-range firing. But even a slow torpedo was a fast one. This submarine skipper meant to live through his action. But there was another reason for a long-range firing.

"Time to impact?" he asked.

Keyland spoke from behind him. "I'm working it now, Senior Chief," he said. In his hand, he held a calculator.

"Estimated speed?" Keyland asked Bernardo.

Bernardo shrugged. "I don't know."

"Yes, you do," Keyland said. "Use your database, Bernardo."

"Okay, everyone," Agazzi said. "Treat it like you trained. Take a deep breath and work through the problem."

"Senior Chief, we still have Gentron's UUV. We could use it to intercept the torpedo."

"Bernardo, you got the UUV on your console?" Agazzi asked, never taking his eyes off Gentron's screen.

"Sure, Boss. I got it. I hold it bearing about one degree off the torpedo trace."

"Okay, Petty Officer MacPherson?" Agazzi asked, hoping MacPherson said the right thing. This wasn't the time to be too active in training his team.

"Send the UUV at the torpedo." MacPherson looked at Bernardo. "You only got one torpedo, right?"

Bernardo nodded. "Only one torpedo. Only thing I have on my screen . . ."

"Then, we send the UUV at the torpedo. We have the capability to simulate a large ship. If it's any sort of sophisticated torpedo with any kind of modern homing device, it'll lock on the UUV and we can guide it out to sea."

"Or it can hit . . ."

"We got about four-and-a-half minutes until it reaches Sea Base," Keyland interrupted sharply.

"Plenty of time. MacPherson, you and Gentron make it happen," Agazzi said, hoping his voice was more confident than he felt. His eyes rolled slightly in the blue-lighted space as he took a deep breath. In combat four-and-a-half minutes was a long time. The last thirty seconds were the "Hail Mary, cross your fingers" moments.

MacPherson leaped from his seat. Leaning over the young sailor's shoulders, the second-class petty officer started giving directions.

"I have the UUV in a turn," Bernardo said. He reached up and pressed his earphones closer. "I have a new sound in the water!"

MacPherson leaned back, looked at Agazzi and the others. "That's us! We're simulating a large ship."

"It's not working. The torpedo is still inbound. No change of course."

"We got to get within its detection window. Gentron, increase speed to fifty knots."

"Fifty knots!" Bernardo said incredulously. "Don't you think . . ."

"The torpedo has to be doing nearly forty knots," MacPherson interrupted. "If we want to guide it away, we got to get in front of it."

"Forty knots!" Agazzi said, his eyes squinting. "Too far out for a forty-knot torpedo."

MacPherson shook his head without turning around. "It could be slower, Senior Chief, but if it is, then we'll know when we pass it."

"Or, at least close enough so the angle of its logic head detects the noise we're generating," Gentron added.

"YES, Admiral. Not much we can do to avoid the inbound torpedo. We have to rely on our ASW team to stop it. We estimate four . . ."

"Skipper! Skipper!" the sound-powered phone talker shouted. "We got North Korean soldiers coming out of the burning aircraft!"

"What was that?" Holman shouted through the headset.

Garcia moved the headset away.

"Say that again!" Stapler shouted.

"I said the topside watch is reporting enemy soldiers coming out of the rear of the burning airplane."

Garcia lifted the headset. "You hear that, Admiral?"

"I heard. The helicopters with the Marines I promised you are already airborne. The two helicopters should be there in minutes. We'll take care of alerting them to their change of mission."

"Admiral, if we land them with the torpedo inbound and it hits, then it won't matter whether we have North Korean troops on board Sea Base or not."

"Hank! You told me you'd take care of the torpedo. So the torpedo is your problem. Do it. Meanwhile, we're going to take care of those troops that have landed on American soil . . . or metal . . . or whatever you want to call that floating bucket of bolts of yours."

"Aye, sir," Garcia replied, but Admiral Holman had already left the link. He handed the handset to the sailor, who placed it back in its cradle.

Behind Garcia's back, the sailor started to flick the chrome metal latch to secure the handset, but then shook his head. He knew it would be only a minute or two before it rang again, so he mumbled, "Naw," and left the handset unsecured.

"Commander Stapler, tell the battle group of our situation,"

Garcia ordered. He clasped his hands behind his back, wondering if he should be doing anything else. He probably should, but he couldn't think of anything to say or do that would help what those involved were already doing. All he could do was distract them, so he kept quiet, listening to the low murmur of Combat as the sailors and officers manning the weapons and radars worked through the numbers as the situation deteriorated.

Stapler lifted the microphone. Moments later, he handed it back to the LPO, who secured it. Across a secure tactical common frequency audible to every Combat Information Center and every airborne fighter aircraft assigned to his Task Force, the news of the burning aircraft and the presence of North Korean troops on Sea Base was being reported.

"Sir, we do have the British F-35s off our port bow, entering the landing circuit," Stapler offered.

"HE is one cool cookie—our Skipper," the leading petty officer said to the second-class standing near him. "Stapler shouting his head off. The admiral demanding an update every few seconds. An enemy aircraft burning on the deck, and old ironman himself stands there as if he doesn't have a worry in the world."

"Damn good thing, too," the second-class said, her voice shaking. "It's probably the only thing keeping me from shitting my pants."

"Cooley, you're one gross dude, girl." The LPO nodded toward Garcia. "But he's one cool dude." He let out a deep breath. "We ought to be thanking our lucky stars the Captain knows what the hell he's doing."

"If we're not swimming in the next few minutes, then I'll thank our lucky stars," she said, her voice trembling.

"WHEELS down and locked," Walters said, breathing a sigh of relief.

"Roger, Raptor 10; I hold you three miles from touchdown."

Walters acknowledged the broadcast, his eyes glancing across the control panel before returning to watch the approach of Sea Base.

A cloudburst of black smoke exploded on the horizon ahead of Sea Base. He looked at his radar. Two high-speed contacts near the explosion blinked on the heads-up screen. The system automatically identified the two airborne contacts as F-35 fighters. *Looks as if the British have arrived.*

Suddenly, the automated electronic warfare system alarmed. "Jesus, what now?" he asked softly. The readout flashed. Two inbound Sidewinder missiles off his nose in the direction of the explosion. Automatically he looked at his range to Sea Base: 1.5 miles.

"Raptor Haven, Raptor 10; be advised I am reflecting Sidewinder missiles off my nose."

"Raptor 10, those would be the British Sidewinders—they're friendly."

"Friendly! There isn't such a damn thing as a friendly missile when its fire control is painting your aircraft!" he shouted over the circuit, surprised at his own ire.

"Roger, Raptor 10; wait one."

Walters shifted the pedals slightly, correcting the push to the right, fighting to keep the aircraft aligned with the runway. Once he touched down, he was going to have to skew the F-22A to the left, away from the center of the marked runway. He started going through the actions he needed to take, thinking about what-ifs and what he would need to do. What if he lost power? What if a landing gear collapsed? What if he couldn't steer it once he was on the deck?

He touched the pedals again. The right engine stopped for a second before reigniting. The aircraft dropped a few feet. The control panel was flashing, every light on it, but he still had control.

"Raptor 10, be advised topside watch is reporting your left engine is smoking."

He pushed the talk button, then released it. Taking a deep breath, he said with forced calmness, "Raptor Haven, that's what I said earlier. My left engine has FOD damage. I have a fire-warning light on and now I have an EW warning light on. What is the status of those missiles?"

"Roger, Raptor 10; just wanted to pass along what we are seeing from the deck. Our EW is jamming the missiles. The topside watch says he can see flames from your left engine; were you aware of that?"

"No, I wasn't, thanks," he said. *So, what do I do now?* he asked himself. He glanced at the distance to Sea Base and safety. Less than a mile. Smoke was one thing. Flames were another, and he had exhausted the extinguishers.

"He says the flames are jetting out about twenty or thirty feet behind you."

"Roger," Walters replied. *Just keep piling on the good news.* If the flames were straight out, then maybe the wind speed was keeping the heat of the fire away from the fuel lines. Must be, or otherwise he'd be vapor now. What was going to happen when he touched down and air speed slowed to nil?

The EW alarm went quiet. *Thank God for small pleasures.*

"SIR," Stapler said. "EW has lost the Sidewinder."

Garcia turned to the sound-powered phone talker. "Ask the topside watch if he has a visual on the missiles."

TWO miles in front of Sea Base, the infrared seekers of the two Sidewinder missiles acquired two heat signatures. A faint one, barely detectable, flickered left. The other heat signature was nearer the center of the infrared sensor, so the two missiles changed course slightly to fully center on the stronger heat signature.

Ahead of them, Raptor 10 continued its descent to Sea Base, flames trailing from the burning left engine.

WALTERS looked up. The spiral contrails were on a constant bearing. Meant only one thing—those missiles were locked on his heat.

He pushed his talk button. "Raptor Haven, I have the missiles visual and they are dead ahead, coming at me."

"RAPTOR Haven, I have the missiles visual and they are dead ahead, coming at me," came the broadcast from the speaker overhead.

Garcia glanced up at the speaker. Only seconds until the missiles hit Raptor 10. Wasn't a thing he could do to save the pilot. He turned his attention back to Combat, drowning the thoughts of helplessness with the low ebb and flow of the murmur-level conversation drifting over banks of electronics glowing varied colors of green, gray, black, and red in the shadowy world of blue light. He took a deep breath, crossing his arms. The smell of sweat mingled with stale half-drunk coffee sitting on nearby consoles, mixing with the background odors of fuel and grease, layered with the sharp ozone tang that took residence in shipboard areas where large amounts of electricity were required.

"Fire the rail gun!" Garcia commanded.

WALTERS hit the flare dispenser, touching the stick and pulling the aircraft slightly right, breaking his alignment with the runway. The maneuver opened up the heat of the burning engine. The powered right engine was less exposed. Raptor Haven told him he had flames jetting out from the left engine. Then the flames—*How far out are they flaming? Twenty-thirty feet. Let's hope the information is right.* The flames and the flares might be enough to decoy the missiles away from the fuselage and behind him. He'd know in seconds if it worked. He'd never know if it didn't.

"Raptor 10, you're off course for landing."

Walters ignored the Air Traffic Controller. What the hell did they expect him to do? Land? Did they think landing would negate the logic head of the Sidewinders? Not a snowball's chance. The missiles would just double back and take him out on the runway.

Two quick motions, one after the other, erupted from the rail gun off the left side of his nose. If it was firing at the missiles, it was too little, too late, no effect.

"Raptor 10, Raptor 30 here; Fast Pace, don't be stupid. Eject!" Major Johnson shouted over the formation frequency.

Walters ignored her order, too. She was two hundred miles away and had no idea what his situation was. She only had the transmissions and the aircraft data link to go on. This was his decision. Even *"Pickles"* should know that. If he made a bad one, she'd have no one to shout at, and if he was right, then when she started unloading on him, he'd have the pleasure of being alive while he stood at attention in front of her.

He glanced out the left side of the cockpit. The contrails showed the missiles changing course slightly. He watched the missiles cross the bow of Sea Base. It was a matter of seconds now. Too late to eject. A smart pilot would have ejected by now, he told himself, but then he wasn't all that smart if you listened to his flight instructors. Where were they when things went to hell? Back in their offices, drinking coffee, and waiting for the next set of students. "I want that job," he whined, surprising himself over how shaky his voice seemed.

Walters put the aircraft into a shallow dive and headed toward the burning wreckage on deck.

JACOBS turned the nozzle toward the North Korean soldier; the blast of the water knocked the man backward into other soldiers, sending them sprawling across the deck like a set of bowling pins. The weapon fired, its bullets going into the air. Several guns scattered across the deck from the flailing figures. The weapons spun toward the edge of the spray.

Jacobs glanced over his shoulder. The fire team heading his way had turned around and was running for cover. The sound of gunfire came, with bullets whipping past his head. Jacobs instinctively crouched, but he kept the water aimed toward the soldiers. Beneath the aircraft, he saw feet running toward the front on the other side. Shit! Seconds before they outflanked him.

"Back up! Back up!" he shouted, feeling the tugging of the hose as the three sailors followed his orders. He never doubted they'd stay with him, not run like the fire team. Showdernitzel bumped into him. "Not so close!"

"No way, Master Chief!"

Without the water damping the flames in the cockpit, the fire regained power, leaping into the air. Nothing he could do now but put as much distance as he could between them, the North Koreans, and the burning aircraft. Which would kill them first? he wondered. The explosion of the aircraft—*does it have a bomb on board*? Or the North Korean soldiers? All he had was the fire hose and three sailors using his body as a shield. And an immense amount of waterpower, but in this situation waterpower lacked the destructive force of a well-placed bullet.

He glanced right and left. Their shotguns were fifty feet to his right. Motion caught his attention. The rail gun was swirling on automatic, its sensors guiding the weapon toward a target. *God! Let's hope they don't intend to fire that thing di-*

rectly at the aircraft! Shit! It'd kill the NORCOMs all right. It'd also blow up the aircraft, kill him and the others, and destroy the rail gun.

"Move toward our weapons!" he shouted, shuffling to the right while still backing up.

"Front of the aircraft, Master Chief!" Showdernitzel shouted.

"Front of the aircraft!" Potts repeated.

The hose kicked as if the pressure had picked up. He tightened his grip and turned the water toward the front of the aircraft just as two North Korean soldiers appeared around the edge. The water knocked the lead one down, sending him skidding across the deck. Jacobs hoped the rough non-skid on the deck ripped the man's skin off. The second soldier pulled back behind the nose, but not before the water knocked the weapon from his hand. Several soldiers at the rear took the opportunity to regain their weapons, throwing themselves down on the deck. He aimed the water at them, obscuring their vision and knocking several of them backward before they could get a good aim. Bullets ripped by Jacobs and the others, but missed.

The hose jerked again, nearly lifting him off his feet, forcing his attention fully on keeping the North Koreans dancing. "What the . . . !" Jacobs looked behind him. Only Showdernitzel and Potts held the hose. He looked the other way. The sailor from the rail gun was running toward the shotguns. Bullets stitched up the deck, ripping through the man. Jacobs watched mesmerized as the young man tumbled forward. At the last second before the sailor hit the deck, their eyes met. Jacobs's eyes clenched and anger tore through his body. He shouted—a long, agonizing, wild cry of someone ready to die, someone willing to take every enemy, every person who ever deserved to die with him.

"Boatswain mates!" he shouted when he finished the cry. "We're going into the maelstrom! Follow me!"

"Master Chief, no! Don't do it. Keep backing up!" Showdernitzel shouted. "They'll kill us!"

He started forward, ignoring Showdernitzel, knowing she was right, but this was his "by God" ship—or whatever it was—and no Gawl-damned bunch of Commie muthafuckers were going to take it without a fight. Jacobs moved as fast as the fire hose would allow them. Charging the North Koreans like a group of Keystone Cops. Forcing them away from the burning aircraft, into the open, and toward the deck edge of Sea Base. The water ripped from side to side. Bullets barely missed, the high-pitched whistles telling him one was going to find its mark. But he felt invincible. The feeling quickly evaporated when the water pressure started dropping.

The rail gun fired, the concussion from the shell shaking the aircraft and knocking several of the North Korean soldiers off their feet. The second round nearly caused Jacobs to lose his grip on the fire hose. He glanced in the direction the gun had fired, seeing two contrails approaching the bow of Sea Base.

"Master Chief!" Showdernitzel shouted. "They got the hose! Will you listen now? We gotta run!"

Jacobs looked back. In several places bullets from the fray had pierced the two-and-a-half-inch hose. Water sprayed out like a fountain shower from places where bullets had penetrated.

Showdernitzel was right for once in her life.

"Haul ass!" he shouted, dropping the hose and running. The hose slid back and forth, whipping the brass nozzle across the non-skid of the deck.

Showdernitzel and Potts did not need to be told twice. They led the way.

They had seconds before the damage caused the pressure to drop low enough for the hose to stop its twisting death throes. The water spraying from the holes and the slow whipping of the open nozzle back and forth across the deck helped obscure them from the North Korean soldiers.

Behind Jacobs, the sound of gunfire made his shoulder blades twitch as he expected any moment to feel bullets ripping through him. He put on an unexpected burst of speed, but the two sailors were still outdistancing him. In the angst of survival, the thought of the joke where two men are running from an angry grizzly bear crossed his mind. When the man running behind asked the man running ahead if he thought they could outrun the grizzly, the one in front shouted over his shoulder that he didn't have to worry about outrunning the bear. All he had to do was outrun his friend. Jacobs was the third person in this race.

ONE Sidewinder swerved left, away from Walters. His eyes widened. The other Sidewinder remained heading his way. Walters twisted the F-22A left, into the missile. An instant later the missile disappeared from sight, toward the rear of the fighter. His body tensed and he shut his eyes at the last second, expecting never to open them. When nothing happened, Walters opened his eyes.

The missile was gone. He quickly jumped around from side to side, trying to spot the missile that had just gone by him, but he couldn't see it. It was out there somewhere. Sidewinders didn't just disappear and go away. They kept after their target until they won the battle of maneuver or ran out of gas. His EW system reflected nothing, but then on infrared it wouldn't.

His aircraft flew past the bow of Sea Base. A quick movement out of the corner of his eye caught his attention. The other Sidewinder drove into the burning aircraft on the deck. A huge explosion rose into the air on his right, shaking the Raptor as he headed out to sea. He breathed a sigh of relief. Only one Sidewinder still active, and with the conflagration on Sea Base, Walters knew the chances of it following him were small.

"Raptor 10, Raptor Haven; what was that?" the ATC exclaimed.

"Raptor Haven, second missile hit the burning Y-8 on the . . . on the . . . on the airfield. You got a major fire." *What do you call an airfield at sea? An aircraft carrier, but Sea Base is more than that.*

"Roger, Raptor 10; report status, please."

"Status? You want status?" he asked in a shaking voice. "Status . . . status . . . status . . ." he mumbled aloud to himself, looking over the control panel. The fuel-warning light was steady now. He was definitely on fumes. The fire-warning light continued to blink its constant warning.

"Raptor 10, this is Pickles. Report status!" she shouted.

He ignored her command. Get it together, he told himself. "Raptor Haven, Raptor 10; I am declaring an in-flight emergency and request permission for immediate landing."

"Raptor 10, you have already declared an in-flight emergency and you have been cleared for immediate landing. You have overshot the runway. Be advised the enemy aircraft has exploded, so starboard side of Sea Base is closed."

"Yep, Raptor Haven," he acknowledged. That's what he'd just told him. He realized he was breathing too rapidly, and mentally slowed his breathing down. Those sailors entombed in that tower fighting Sea Base were probably more scared than him. At least, he could see death coming at him.

"Raptor 10, you are going to have to go around again and line up with runway. You will have to veer to the left once you have touched down. This will limit the length of runway you will have to land. Do you understand?"

"Raptor Haven, copy all." In his other ear, Major Johnson demanded he talk to her. He ignored her. Walters had to get the aircraft down. "Raptor Haven, I don't know how much fuel I have remaining."

"Raptor 10, topside watch reports no flames from your left engine. He says a missile exploded behind you while over Sea Base. We are assessing missile to be a Sidewinder fired by Black Leader against another . . ."

"Raptor Haven, I don't have enough fuel to do another landing pattern. I'm going to come around best way I can and come right in," Walters interrupted. Expecting to hear an argument from the ATC, Walters eased the aircraft left, lining up with Sea Base.

"Roger, Raptor 10; cleared for landing."

His eyes rose slightly, surprised the Navy Air Traffic Controller had acquiesced. "Thanks," he replied softly.

Walters touched the controls, aiming the nozzle upward twenty degrees, taking the aircraft up—gaining altitude. If his right engine quit, then he wanted sufficient height to make the ejection safer.

"Raptor Haven, Raptor 10; am turning; ascending. Intentions are to line up with Sea Base regardless of where my nose is when that occurs and come in. I still have an engine fire-warning light on."

"Raptor 10, you are . . ." the Air Traffic Controller started to command, but as if someone stopped her, she paused and then continued. "Raptor 10, be aware starboard side of Sea Base is crowded with emergency personnel and equipment. We have firefighting stuff ready for your landing. You will have to land in such an angle that you transverse Sea Base either bow to stern or stern to bow. Then, you have to steer to port side of Sea Base. Do not, I repeat, do not steer to starboard side."

"I understand, Raptor Haven. I have clear field of vision. Please notify my ground crew of my condition." *Hope that "firefighting stuff" has rescue personnel and foam-fighting "stuff" with it.*

"They are aware, sir. Chief Willard says they are ready." She paused, then added, "He also says, 'Be careful.' "

"Tell the chief he picked a hell of a time to tell me to 'be careful.'"

On the deck of Sea Base, Walters watched Franklin's Raptor start to taxi, heading toward the far side of Sea Base, clearing additional landing room. Is this a dumb thing to do, or should he eject and let the aircraft head toward the dark Pacific? The moment of indecision passed. An Air Force fighter pilot's duty was to bring the plane home unless no other option existed. At this time, he had the option of landing. Sea Base looked awfully small even from one thousand feet, but maybe that was because he was used to landing where if you missed the runway, you still had thousands of miles to find an alternate runway or a cornfield to plant those wheels. His instructor had told him thick cornfields were the best if you intended to "Billy Mitchell" the plane.

"SENIOR Chief!" Bernardo shouted. "I have crushing. Below the layer. I've got the enemy submarine and it's heading down."

Everyone turned to Bernardo. Every thought inside the ASW Command Center was of the sailors trapped inside the long man-made tube that once had been a functioning submarine. The explosion near the torpedo tubes of the submarine must have blown away the bow of the submarine, opening it to the sea. The water would have quickly filled the front of the North Korean Golf class, killing everyone in the forward half. Then, acting much like an anchor, the heavy weight of the flooded compartment would have started pulling the submarine downward. Trapped in the aft portion would be the few survivors, who would know mind-numbing terror as their submarine picked up speed on its one-way trip toward the dark Pacific.

Long before it reached the bottom miles below, the water pressure would cave in the sides of the submarine. The crushing sounds Bernardo reported were coming from the submarine reaching that depth.

Bernardo removed his earphones and shut his eyes.

Agazzi understood. No one wanted to hear the end of a sinking submarine even when the submarine had just tried to sink Sea Base. He glanced at the control lights above Bernardo's console. The automatic recording device was on. It would record the death of the submarine. The people at the Office of Naval Intelligence would be dancing in the hallways when they played it back, but then they were not responsible for sinking it.

Agazzi turned back to MacPherson and Gentron. "How much longer until we reach the right angle for the torpedo logic head to detect your noise?"

"One minute, Senior Chief," Gentron said.

"How long until impact?"

"One minute, thirty-five seconds," MacPherson answered.

"What if we're wrong?" Keyland asked. "What if the North Korean torpedo is a fire-and-forget torpedo? No logic head; just a warhead and a heading."

Agazzi looked at him. Some of the older torpedoes were like that. The Golf was an ancient submarine compared to most of the ones patrolling the oceans today. But that ancient submarine had sunk a modern Chinese submarine.

"It has to have a logic head," MacPherson said. He pointed at Bernardo. "When the submarine sank the Chinese submarine, the Chinese tried to outmaneuver it, but the torpedo twisted and turned with it."

"That's right," Bernardo agreed.

"I'm not saying it isn't," Keyland replied defensively. "I'm just saying we should think about what to do if we can't decoy it away from Sea Base."

Agazzi looked at MacPherson and then at Keyland, but said nothing. *What if Keyland is right? It might be too late to do anything else.*

"Forty seconds until we're within range," Gentron said, breaking the few seconds of silence.

MacPherson looked at Agazzi. "We can switch from noise generation to active pinging and see if we can pinpoint the torpedo. We can then intercept the torpedo. Ram it."

"What's the odds of doing that?"

"I don't know, Senior Chief." MacPherson nodded at Gentron's console. "Everything we are doing now is new. Everything we are trying is new technology. If it doesn't work"—he shrugged—"then most likely no one will ever know."

"Twenty seconds until we're within range," Gentron said.

"That means when we reach range, the torpedo will be thirty seconds from Sea Base," Keyland added. "Which ship will it hit?"

"It could be *Regulus, Altair,* or *Pollux,* depending on which one it locks on when it reaches this area," Agazzi said. "If it has a logic head."

Behind him, he heard Calvins softly relaying the information to the other sound-powered phone talker in Combat.

"If it doesn't?"

"Then it could still hit any of them."

"I think we should try to intercept the torpedo," Keyland said.

"We should try—"

"Listen to me, Senior Chief," Keyland said emphatically. "Even if the logic head of the torpedo falls for the noise decoy and twists toward the UUV, it is going to be so close to Sea Base that it will have other targets out there that could distract it. If it is distracted only once"—he held up one finger—"from the UUV, then it's going to hit one of the ships."

Agazzi let out a deep breath. "Petty Officer Keyland, even if it hits one of the Fast Sealift Ships, it's going to be like hitting a vintage Volvo-850 on the beltway. It's going to shake the ship for a moment, but it's not going to do much damage."

"If it's only TNT," Gentron said. "Ten seconds to logic angle."

"What do you mean?"

"The North Koreans have nukes. What if it's a nuke? Nuclear torpedoes have to be fired from long range. They don't need logic heads. They're fire-and-forget torpedoes."

"But the submarine used a torpedo with a logic fire control to sink the Chinese!" Bernardo exclaimed.

"We're within angle range."

"Senior Chief, I show no joy. The torpedo isn't changing course."

He turned from Keyland and pointed his index finger at MacPherson, "Ping it!"

MacPherson squatted beside Gentron, two motions, and the UUV was now an active seeker.

"I've got it!" Gentron said.

"Ram it!" Agazzi ordered.

"I'm a half mile from it. Bringing UUV up to maximum speed."

"Forty seconds until impact."

"If it's a nuke and you hit it, will it explode?" Calvins asked from above, his young voice shaking.

"I wouldn't worry about it," Bernardo said.

Yeah, Agazzi thought. *We'd never know.*

"Just keep telling Combat what we're doing," Keyland said, his voice soft.

"But I am worried," Calvins mumbled.

Bernardo looked at his rainfall. Seeing no sign of the submarine, he slipped his headphones on.

"If we hit the rear of the torpedo, it shouldn't explode, and even if we hit it dead on, there is a chance it won't explode," MacPherson said.

"Hey, it's changing course!" Bernardo said. "The torpedo is heading toward you, Gentron! I have the torpedo in a turn." He laughed. Bernardo leaned forward and kissed his console. "Love, love, love."

"What's happening?" Agazzi asked.

"The torpedo has a logic head, Senior Chief. Must have a sensor code that specifically locks on sonar. A chance to take out a major warship."

"So, it's not a nuke?" Calvins asked.

"Don't know," Keyland answered.

"Most likely not," MacPherson added.

"Unless it's a specialty torpedo for aircraft carriers."

"MacPherson, take the torpedo out to sea," Agazzi ordered. "Calvins, tell Combat it looks as if we may have decoyed the torpedo. It is turning out to sea. . . ." He looked at Keyland. "Best direction?"

"Take it southwest of us, Senior Chief. We have *Boxer* to our west, *Gearing* northwest, and the cruiser *Anzio* a hundred miles ahead of us."

"Slow it down to the speed of the torpedo," Agazzi said. "We don't want to outdistance it."

"What is the speed?"

"I'd say forty knots," Gentron offered. "That's what we were discussing earlier as the most common speed for a long-range torpedo."

"That's really not the most common speed."

"What is it, then?" Agazzi asked.

"More like twenty-five knots."

"This thing is moving faster than that," MacPherson said.

"Bring it down to around thirty knots," Agazzi said. "Bernardo, you watch the two noise signatures and tell me when they're closing."

Bernardo ripped his headset off and tossed them on the counter, leaning back as if they had scalded him. He looked at the senior chief. "The submarine just imploded." He started breathing rapidly.

Keyland reached over and slapped him upside the back of the head. "Stop that!"

Bernardo looked at the LPO for a few seconds. He nodded, took a deep breath, held it, and then let it out. "Sorry. I wasn't expecting to hear that."

"I'm turning the UUV on a course of one-nine-zero true." Ships at sea used two types of compass direction. True direction was based on a compass reading. Relative direction used the bow of the ship as bearing zero-zero-zero; everything was then relative to the bow. On Sea Base, it was hard to determine the bow.

"Make it a shallow turn," Agazzi said. "We don't want it to lose contact."

"Shallow turn, aye," MacPherson acknowledged.

FOURTEEN

"Can we get a visual?" Keyland asked.

"I can turn the cameras so they're pointed toward the torpedo. But at this speed, unless the torpedo is very close, most likely all we're going to get is bubbles," MacPherson answered.

"Another thing," Gentron added. "If we try to turn the cameras at this speed, we run the risk of affecting the UUV maneuverability while they're being reset."

"We also run the risk of them being ripped off."

"Oh," Keyland replied with a nod. "But you're guessing about the risks, right?"

No one replied. Everyone quietly watched the UUV path on Gentron's console.

Agazzi periodically glanced at Bernardo's passive sonar display, watching the two weapons close the distance between them.

"I asked if you could shift the cameras at this speed," Keyland said firmly.

MacPherson nodded and touched Gentron's shoulder. Gentron's hand rolled the mouse, placing the cursor over the correct icon. With a couple of clicks, a small box appeared on the lower left-hand corner of his screen. Several clicks later, the box turned to a small viewing screen. After a few seconds, he said, "It's turning. I'll turn it on once it's locked in place."

"I'm just guessing, you know, from watching the noise signatures, but I would say the torpedo is less than two, maybe three hundred feet behind your UUV," Bernardo offered.

ONE moment he was running, the next he was flat on his face opening his eyes. Pain rocketed up his left side. Jacobs reached back and touched his lower left side; his hand came away wet with blood. *So, one of those sons of a bitch actually can aim,* he thought. He shut his eyes. Suddenly, he was so tired, a tiredness that overrode the pain racking his body.

"Master Chief, Master Chief, don't you die on me, you son of a bitch!"

"Showdernitzel, that's no way to talk to your master chief," he mumbled, his head lying flat on the deck. He opened his eyes for a moment. *Must be fog across the deck; she's hard to see.* He let his eyes close. He just needed some sleep. "Let me sleep," he slurred.

"Screw you," Showdernitzel said. "We've worked too long training you the way we want you. Potts! Grab his arm. We got to get him away from here."

Jacobs was lifted by the armpits and pulled. His feet dragged across the rough non-skid covering of the deck. This was really going to screw up his shine. He smiled. *Shine, hell. I wear Corfam shoes; you don't need to shine them.*

"Stop the grinning, Master Chief. You think this is funny? Shit! You gotta bullet in you and you're still laughing at something? You're one screwed-up master chief, Master Chief."

He opened his mouth to say something, but he couldn't quite remember what it was he was going to say. What was Showdernitzel bitching about? She was always bitching about something. Whatever it was, it was something he could take care of later. Something pushed against them like a wave. He opened his eyes.

"Jesu—!" Potts screamed.

The explosion sent them flying. The last thing he recalled before darkness dropped over him was Showdernitzel, legs and arms spread, tumbling head over heels like an overweight circus acrobat. He would have laughed, but he was having a rough time comprehending what he was seeing.

* * *

WALTERS reached down and hit the console switch. He released his breath as the wheels lowered. The slight sound of hydraulics filled the cockpit. A moment later, the console showed the wheels down and locked. The maneuverability of the aircraft changed slightly. Ahead of him, filling the front of the cockpit window, was Sea Base. Only a mile and he'd be safe.

He eased the throttle back, reducing speed, and pushed the stick forward slightly. The F-22A lined up with flight deck. In his ear, the Air Traffic Controller told him about a slight crosswind, pushing from the left rear side. Not the best wind for landing even if he had both engines. For a fraction of a second, Walters thought about taking a chance by flying over Sea Base and landing from the other direction. The right engine coughed twice and stopped.

The console lights flashed a couple of times and went dark. On the heads-up display, the Stand-by Flight Group remained lit. The Stand-by Flight Group was connected to the last bit of power in the F-22A, so regardless of what happened, the pilot could still fly the aircraft. Of course, without fuel, all Walters could do was glance at the altimeter.

The fire-warning light flashed back into operation, followed a short moment later with parts of the integrated control panel. If he made it back to Sea Base, he'd make sure everyone knew the Stand-by Flight Group operated like it should.

Meanwhile, the fire-warning light flashed at a constant rate as if it had a life of its own. Flashing through the hiccup of losing the right engine. Laughing at him as if shouting, "You may have no fuel, asshole, but your fire is still here and I'll keep you company into the dark Pacific." The fuel gauge read zero. Even so, zero wasn't really zero, Walters told himself. There had to be a drop or two somewhere.

The F-22A edged over, the nose dropping downward. He recalled Blackman's comment about the Raptor gliding like a rock. Walters pulled back on the stick, feeling the air pressure from the drop-rate lift the nose. The landing field on Sea Base was dropping too rapidly. Without a few more feet of altitude, he'd be flying beneath the Sea Base canopy, right into the field of sharks and gray behemoths of ships holding Sea Base aloft. Any ejection would splatter him on the underside of Sea Base. An impulse nearly had him reaching for the ejection handle.

"Raptor Haven, Raptor 10; I have lost both engines. One mile until touchdown."

The fire-warning light kept drawing his attention. Walters looked at the light for several seconds; something tugged at the edge of his mind. He looked at the nozzle angle and saw it was level. His fingers twitched on the control, his mind telling him how stupid to even think it, but when all else fails, even something stupid can be better than doing nothing. He lowered the nozzle angle to 10 degrees upward. He still had flames and smoke coming out of the left engine, and some air had to transverse through the right.

The nose of the Raptor steadied, bringing the aircraft level though it was still in a free fall. He gritted his teeth together. It was going to be close. The edge of the runway jutted out one thousand feet ahead of the main Sea Base body. Holding up that first one thousand feet was the Fast Sealift Ship USNS *Altair*. If he miscalculated and hit *Altair*, the whole of Sea Base would sail over the ship and the debris, sinking everyone. Beneath the runway, the bow of the ship was barely visible.

"Fast Pace, this is Pickles. I don't care about the aircraft. You eject. You hear me; eject."

Walters sighed and pushed the talk button. "Major Johnson, Captain Walters; I am quarter mile to touchdown. Too high of a speed," he lied, "to eject safely. Am committed." He switched off the formation frequency. If something happened and he didn't make it, no reason for his fellow Air Force fighter pilots to hear him cry.

Bullshit! What the hell am I doing? He sucked in a deep breath of air and raised his head. No way he was going to lose his aircraft. He was a by-God United States Air Force fighter pilot and, by God, he was going to bring his fighter back to earth. Or metal, or whatever those Navy flyboys called a floating flight line.

Ahead of him, he spotted the ground crew gathering around Willard. Easy to spot the tall chief even from this low altitude. His height dwarfed most everyone around him.

The aircraft shot upward a few feet. The muffled explosion ripped through the cockpit. "Jesus Christ!" Walters exclaimed. "What in the hell was that?"

He glanced out the right side of the aircraft, his first thoughts being the right engine had exploded, even though the aircraft had rocked from the left. He still had some control. Control that would have been lost with an engine explosion. Walters twisted to the left. On the deck of Sea Base, a second massive cloud of roiling smoke, flames, and debris rose from where the enemy transport had been burning. People ran from the vicinity of the aircraft, flames encompassing them, turning them into human pyres. Walters shuddered at the vision and wondered briefly if his own near future could . . . He shook the idea away and glanced at the altimeter.

The concussion of the explosion had given Walters a few more feet of altitude. Out front, the bow of the *Altair* disappeared.

He was coming in fast with no control to change the angle. His nose wheel touched down hard, slamming onto the curved bitter end of the flight deck. Momentum carried the wheels up and over the edge onto the flight deck. The landing shoved Walters violently downward against his seat for a brief moment before reaction tossed him upward against his seat straps. He felt blood in his mouth where he had bitten his tongue.

He pushed forward on the brakes, the scream of rubber and metal filling the cockpit. The fighter wobbled left, bringing the right wheel off the deck. The aircraft pulled leftward for a moment before the right wheel slammed back onto the deck, heading straight down the runway.

The Raptor was no stealth when it came to noise. Ahead of him, coming fast, were holes his own shells had created minutes earlier. Walters twisted the stick to the right, trying to take the aircraft away from the holes ahead, but the aircraft remained straight, heading toward the holes.

The left wheel hit an unseen hole first, jerking the aircraft left. At least he was heading off the runway away from the bigger holes, even if it was toward the wrong side.

He leaned forward, looking at the flight deck. His eyes widened. A bigger hole than the one he'd just missed was directly ahead of the front wheel. It was too late to avoid. The wheel hit the hole, collapsing the strut. One moment, Walters was riding level, high in the aircraft, and the next, he was skidding along the flight deck with sparks and metal cascading around the cockpit, blinding him.

Instinctively, he closed his eyes. In his earphones he heard Raptor Haven shouting something, but in the fear of the moment he failed to understand the shouts to eject. It was the last thing he heard before the concussion knocked him out.

"THE pickup!" shouted Willard. "Get in the pickup!" Willard jumped in the cab of the Air Force light blue pickup, glancing behind him to see the two officers and part of the ground crew jump into it also.

He hit the gas, sending the pickup speeding forward, heading toward Major Walters's aircraft on the other side of the runway. Flames encompassed the aircraft.

Willard twisted the wheel roughly to the right, avoiding a crater in the runway, then turned back to the left. Never losing sight of the aircraft. Willard grabbed the microphone. "Combat, this is Chief Willard. We got a Raptor on fire near center left side of runway. We need firefighting response. I repeat, we need firefighting response. I have a pilot trapped inside."

"Roger, Air Force, we copy."

Willard glanced at where the Y-8 transport had been, the flames leaping and roaring into the sky. The P-25 firefighting truck was upwind of the enemy transport, pouring AFFF foam over the conflagration. It seemed to him in that split second of watching that the firefighting foam was having little effect. The P-25 was only a couple hundred yards from the F-22. Any moment, he expected to see it turn toward the burning fighter.

He swerved to the left, avoiding another crater, before jerking the wheel back to the right toward the Raptor. In the back of the pickup were some small extinguishers. From the other side of Sea Base, Willard saw a Navy firefighting team running toward the burning Raptor. He licked his lips, leaning forward, pushing his gas pedal to the floor, but the governor on the truck limited the speed to twenty-five. The flames pulled back from the aircraft. Maybe lack of flammable material would cause the fire to stop, but even through this hope Willard knew the fire would kill Walters before it ran out of flammable material. The cockpit was still closed. He didn't know if that was good or bad.

Where was Fast Pace? *Eject, you young shit! Eject! He slammed the palm of his hand down on the steering wheel a couple of times. Eject!*

Willard twisted the steering wheel to the right, avoiding another crater on the flight deck, and then he was quickly across the runway. He hit the brakes, squealing to a halt. Everyone in back fell toward the cab of the pickup. They quickly righted themselves and leaped out, pulling fire extinguishers with them, running toward the aircraft about sixty feet away, ignoring the possibility of another explosion. The right strut had collapsed, the right wing crushed at the end of it. Flames roared around the edges of the wing like a predator tasting the flesh of its prey before ripping it apart.

Without hesitation, Willard ran toward the right wing. A tongue of flame leaped toward him, barely touching his flight suit. He raised his arm to keep the heat from his face. Bursts of CO2 enveloped him. He leaped onto the right wing and steadied his feet as he fought through the flames to the slippery slope of the wing. He'd hit the wing running, thankful his flight boots gripped the surface enough so he was able to quickly reach the cockpit.

Light smoke filled the cockpit. Willard draped his arm over the fuselage behind the cockpit to keep himself from sliding down the wing. With his right hand, he reached down and hit the emergency release switches. He heard the click of the release, but the cockpit failed to rise.

Flames leaped up from the other side, brushing his face, searing away eyebrows and mustache. He felt the blisters on his face and hands rise, but ignored the pain. He could see Walters through the cockpit window, leaning over, his torso held upright by the straps. He didn't know if the man was dead or alive. Willard let go with his left hand, grabbing the edge of the cockpit with both hands.

Beside him appeared Captain Nolan.

"Together, Chief." Nolan grabbed the edges of the cockpit.

The two men put their hands and shoulders against the cockpit window. Grunting, they pushed upward, their flight boots slipping once on the wing, threatening to send them cascading down it. If that happened, Walters was dead.

Suddenly, the cockpit broke the pressure seal and lifted away. Willard reached inside and unbuckled the young officer, burning his hands on the metal. He thought he heard a groan.

"He's alive!" he shouted, his words slurred through blistered lips.

Nolan reached into the cockpit. "Come on, Chief. I don't know how much time we have."

They pulled Walters out, the pilot's feet catching on the seat. Nolan reached in and freed them. He noticed skin from his fingers coming off on the seat.

Nolan held onto the edge of the cockpit as they pulled Walters out.

"Grab him on your side, Chief. We gotta get out of here."

Willard grabbed the edge of the cockpit with one hand, feeling inordinate pain preventing him from firmly gripping the edge. With his free hand, he and Nolan grabbed Walters beneath the arms.

"Time to let go, Chief."

Willard nodded, and the two men released their hold on the cockpit edge. One moment they were at the top of the wing and the next, they were sliding down it, Walters riding between them. They reached the end. CO2 extinguishers covered the three men.

Sailors wearing white hats with red crosses on them pulled Walters from the two men, laying him down on the deck.

"We're too near the aircraft," Willard mumbled.

One of the sailors replied, "You're right, but if we don't get his mask off, he's going to suffocate." The sailor looked up. "Jesus Christ! You're burned."

The sailor looked back down. Two quick moves and the mask flipped away.

"He's not breathing," one of the corpsman said.

The other one started pushing on the chest, while the first spread-eagled Walters's legs and arms. Then, the sailor crawled back to Walters's head and started mouth-to-mouth on him while the other did the chest compressions.

Willard and Nolan watched helplessly as the corpsmen did their job. Between breaths, the corpsman near the head pulled out a walkie-talkie and shouted their emergency into it. Within minutes a four-man stretcher team arrived along with a CPR machine.

A couple of seconds later, the medical team had Walters on a stretcher, racing across the deck to the far port side of Sea Base where medical was setting up a triage position. Nolan and Willard looked at each other.

"You go with him, sir," Willard said. "I'll stay here with the others."

Nolan grabbed Willard's wrists. "Bullshit, Chief. Look at

those hands. You heard the Navy doc. You get your ass over to medical. We can handle this," Nolan ordered.

Franklin came running up. "Fast Pace, where is he?" he shouted.

Nolan pointed at the stretcher-bearers, running toward the open hatch on the starboard aft side of Sea Base.

Without a word, Walters's wingman took off chasing the stretcher.

"Chief, you go with Captain Franklin. He'll see you get taken care of."

Willard nodded. "Thank you, Captain. Tomorrow, you and I both are going to feel like shit, sir. Captain Franklin can ensure Captain Walters is taken care of." He held up both hands, noticing small pieces of skin dangling loose in several places. "Looks worse than it feels," he lied.

A different corpsman walked over to Willard and slapped a tube of medicine into Nolan's hand. The corpsman looked at Nolan. "You two have some bad burns, sirs. Put this on your face until someone can look at them." He looked at Willard. "Sir, you need to have those burns looked at now."

"I'll do it later," Willard said, nodding toward the aircraft where Navy firefighters had succeeded in dampening the fire. Only smoke rose from the Raptor carcass.

The corpsman shrugged. "Then, sir, don't wash it. Some of that burn"—he nodded toward Willard's hands—"looks like third-degree burns and all that will do is peel the skin away. You need to get over there"—the corpsman jerked his thumb toward the triage area—"so someone can look at them, unless you don't like the idea of having hands."

"I'm not a sir," Willard said. "I'm a chief."

The corpsman picked up his medical case. "It figures," the Corpsman said, walking away, leaving the two injured men alone. The corpsman looked back over his shoulder. "I said get your ass over to the triage area."

The ground crew pulled back from the burning Raptor as the Navy firefighting team took over the firefighting effort.

"Major Johnson is not going to be happy," Willard said.

Grossman nodded. "There is always something positive about everything, Chief."

* * *

"SKIPPER, the North Koreans have disappeared from the scope," Stapler said.

The sound-powered phone talker inched forward, reaching up nonchalantly to slide his helmet away from his right ear, hoping to hear the conversation.

Garcia nodded.

"Sir, the damage-control assistant reports the fire is under control," the leading petty officer interrupted.

"Which fire?"

The LPO's eyes widened and he took a deep breath, motioning the sound-powered phone talker on the far side of the chart table to ask the right question.

"They have left the scope," Stapler added. "As far as we and the *Boxer* can tell, they've gone home."

"How do we know they're not heading this way like the transports?" Garcia asked.

The eavesdropping sailor smiled. The Skipper was no fool. He was the iron spine during all of this.

Stapler shrugged. "Don't really, sir, but our fighters need to return and refuel. I have talked with the air boss or whatever he calls himself on His Majesty's Ship *Elizabeth*. They have launched four additional F-35 fighters to take the place of the F-22s on station. That'll give them a chance to land, tank up, and if necessary, take back off."

Garcia thought for a moment. Was this the right thing to do? The North Koreans had been smart enough to draw their attention to their fighter aircraft while four aging transport aircraft filled with what? Troops and bombs? Or just troops? What if all four of those transports had made it to Sea Base? They'd be swarming in hungry little Commies trying to kill everyone. Of course, he could have thrown food at them and that would have kept them occupied for a while. He smiled at the thought.

The sailors saw the smile, exchanging sideways looks at each other. Their old man was one calm son of a bitch. Most of them were ready to wet their pants. Or, as Bad Ass McGufie said, "Damn, if I had teeth in my ass, I'd a chewed a hole through my seat this past hour."

"The two CH-53 helos with the Marines are landing. I have given them carte blanche to secure the topside of Sea Base. Our MAA forces have several North Korean soldiers as prisoners.

Most were killed in the blast. Those in custody, most are burned."

"How about our casualties?"

Stapler's lower lip pushed against his upper. "Sir, I don't have a total picture yet. We have at least two dead, some wounded. The pilot of the fighter aircraft is in sick bay with third-degree burns over his hands and chin, but the doctor said he'd survive. Some of the rescue party for the pilot are burned, but are refusing treatment so it can't be too bad."

The red phone rang. Garcia's smile disappeared immediately. He nodded at Stapler. "Go ahead and bring our fighters back, Commander. Remind me later to thank the Skipper of the *Elizabeth* for their support."

"Aye aye, sir," Stapler said, turning.

"Commander," Garcia said, touching the slightly taller commander on the shoulder. Stapler turned his head. "Good job, Stan. Couldn't have done this without you."

The taciturn Stapler's eyes widened slightly before dropping. Garcia was sure the man blushed. People such as Stapler were unused to compliments.

"Thank you, Captain," he stuttered before hurrying away to bring the fighters home.

The LPO handed the handset to Garcia. Garcia cocked his head at the first-class petty officer. "Well?"

"Both fires are under control, sir. Fire teams still on scene."

"Get me the casualty report, Petty Officer Owens, and tell the DCA when circumstances permit for him to report to me."

"Aye, sir."

Garcia raised the handset to his ear. "Charlie Oscar here, Admiral."

"Hank, what's your situation?"

Garcia spent the next five minutes bringing Admiral Holman up to date on the awry Sidewinder that destroyed the Y-8, the crash landing of Captain Walters's F-22A, and the securing of Sea Base from the attempted boarding.

When he hung up, it was with the unexpected invitation to Holman to fly over to see for himself. One thing about Holman, he wasn't afraid to offer his advice and become part of the action. On the other hand, if the old warrior had not been on *Boxer,* no telling how Garcia would have screwed up this action. A wave of relief swept over him at the thought. This was combat action, he told himself. And for the years he'd been in the Navy, it was the first combat action he'd ever seen. Looking up, he saw most of the eyes in Combat trained on him: sailors, junior officers, and even Commander Stapler, without whom the defense of Sea Base would have been impossible. Simultaneously, he realized that what had just happened to them was the first attempt to board and capture a United States warship since the North Koreans boarded and captured the USS *Pueblo*.

He smiled and in a loud voice said, "Well done, everyone."

The applause started with a single clap from an unseen someone in the dark of the Combat spaces and rapidly spread throughout, until everyone was on their feet looking at him. Garcia was shocked. He had been useless through these past few hours and they were applauding him, including Commander Stapler. Him: Henry "Hank" Garcia. He pushed his lips together, putting pressure on them so they stopped shaking.

Taking a deep breath, he motioned the applause down. "You deserve congratulations for what you have done, but we still have work to do. The battle is not over." He turned to Stapler. "We still have a torpedo out there, don't we, Commander Stapler?" He looked around Combat. "And we have dead and injured on the deck. We can congratulate each other later for safely defending our ship."

As if on cue, the sound-powered telephone talker announced a warning that the torpedo and the UUV were about to collide southwest of Sea Base at a distance of twelve nautical miles.

Garcia nodded. "Commander, alert the battle group."

Then the sound-powered telephone talker added, "Senior Chief Agazzi said to tell you that he doesn't know if the warhead is conventional or a nuke."

"SENIOR Chief!" MacPherson shouted. "I think we can see the torpedo." The second-class petty officer pointed at the UUV picture, small-sized on the bottom left-hand side of Gentron's console.

Keyland stepped up. "Taylor says he has reloaded the UUV firing cartridge if we want to launch another one."

Agazzi squinted, trying to see what MacPherson was seeing in the small box. "I can't see it, Petty Officer MacPherson."

"I can't make it bigger," Gentron objected before anyone

asked him. "If I do, it will fill the screen and I will be steering the UUV blind."

"I thought you were already doing that," Bernardo said with an embarrassed laugh.

"No, don't make it bigger," Agazzi agreed, leaning back.

"Senior Chief, Taylor says . . ."

"I heard, Petty Officer Keyland. Petty Officer MacPherson, what do you think? Should we launch another one?"

MacPherson straightened, turning to look at both Agazzi and Keyland. "I don't know, Senior Chief."

Agazzi waited. There was no correct answer, but it was important his men knew how to reach the best one.

"Tell me what you think," he said softly.

MacPherson shrugged, looked at Keyland for a moment, then answered, "I don't think we have another submarine out there. If we think there might be one, then we should. If not, we should play this out."

"Why?"

MacPherson's eyebrows arched inward and he licked his lips. "Cost?"

"Cost is always a factor, but safety of ship is paramount."

"Then, I would launch one."

"Why?"

"Worst case is that there is another submarine out there, farther away, waiting like we are to see what happens."

Agazzi nodded. "Then, let's launch another one."

MacPherson looked at Gentron. "Senior Chief, I'd have to do it from my console."

"Seaman Gentron is doing okay and you're sitting beside him. Besides, Petty Officer Keyland is here."

MacPherson slid into his seat.

"The torpedo is less than one hundred feet behind me," Gentron said.

Keyland moved around Agazzi and stood to the right of Gentron.

Three minutes passed before MacPherson announced the launch of another UUV and asked where to position it. The ASW team discussed it for about a minute before Agazzi gave the order to move the UUV out in the direction of the last submarine. "Keep it away from the torpedo. We don't want it changing its target now."

Agazzi was also thinking that if the ancient Golf class was traveling as a pair, the two would have been able to exchange underwater communications. Underwater comms were short-range.

"I'm reaching critical fuel status on the UUV, Senior Chief."

"How much longer?"

"Combat reports the North Korean fighters have disappeared from radar. They think they've returned home for the night," Calvins announced from the upper level.

"It's night?" Bernardo asked.

Keyland looked at the clock. "It's only five o'clock. It just seems night because we're down on the lowest level of *Algol* and we're in a darkened space."

"They're bringing our 22's back to refuel," Calvins added.

Agazzi nodded. The air battle wasn't his problem. "Thanks." He touched Gentron on the shoulder. "How far away from Sea Base are we?"

Gentron slid the cursor to an icon on the far left side. A small box leaped up over the television picture from the UUV cameras. "About twelve miles."

"Time to let it hit," Keyland suggested.

Agazzi nodded. He touched MacPherson. "Location?"

"UUV is outside the perimeter of Sea Base, Senior Chief. I have it loitering about one mile away on a north-south pattern. I have nothing on my sensors."

"Bernardo?"

"Senior Chief, I only have Gentron's UUV and the torpedo. Both noise signatures are decreasing in noise. I don't show Jenkins' UUV yet."

"Okay, Gentron, how do you want to do this?"

"I could start a series of maneuvers—like undersea combat . . ."

"No!" MacPherson shouted. "Let it hit. If you start turning and churning, we run the risk of it losing contact and reengaging Sea Base."

"It'd probably run out of fuel before . . ."

"Probably!"

"Petty Officer MacPherson is right, Seaman Gentron. So, how do you want to let it hit?"

"Slow up so we can watch it all the way to impact?"

Agazzi turned to Calvins, telling him to warn Combat. They

needed to know about the coming explosion so other ships in the area would be aware. They also needed to know that ASW was unable to tell them whether this was a conventional warhead or not. Listening to Calvins with one ear and watching MacPherson guide his UUV while Gentron started to slow his, he heard Calvins use the word "nuclear."

Agazzi turned quickly. "What did you say?" he asked sharply, startling everyone.

Taken aback, Calvins said quietly, "I told them we were fixing to collide the UUV and the torpedo."

"No, I mean you used the word 'nuclear.' "

Calvins licked his lips. "I told them you weren't sure if the warhead was conventional or a nuke."

Agazzi pointed at the young seaman. "Quickly, you tell Combat we can't tell them if the warhead is—"

"Jesus Christ!" Gentron shouted. "There it is! It's going to hit!"

Agazzi turned back in time to see the nose of the torpedo a second before it hit the UUV; then the small television screen went dark. The control parameters that a moment ago lit up the bulk of Gentron's screen were now blank.

Fifteen seconds passed. Everyone remained quiet, waiting for the concussion.

"It was a conventional," Bernardo said, tapping the rainfall display on the AN SQR-25. "Barely audible, but still audible."

Agazzi let out his breath. "Tell Combat the torpedo has been destroyed. Tell them also it was conventional. And for everyone here, we don't use the word 'nuke,' 'nuclear,' or even 'atomic' to describe a warhead unless we are damn certain. The terms are conventional and nonconventional. Let the officers decide the specifics. That's why they get the big bucks."

Everyone started laughing. Agazzi thought he saw a tear on Bernardo's cheek. MacPherson slapped Gentron on the back, hard, drawing coughing from the young sailor. "Great job."

Keyland did the same. The tension dissipated quickly in the need to touch a fellow human being, as if ensuring each other they were alive. Even Agazzi felt his throat constrict for a moment. He took a deep breath and let it out. Never again did he want to go through something such as this.

* * *

TALEB pushed his headset back. "What do you think, Dr. Zheng? Did you get a lot of good pictures?"

Kiang nodded and let out a long breath. "I think I am going down."

Taleb took off his helmet and started storing it.

"They're securing from general quarters?"

Taleb shook his head. "Naw, they're setting modified GQ for a few minutes to allow everyone a chance to stretch and make a head call. Then, they'll reset it."

Kiang didn't bother to check Taleb's story. He just nodded and started down from the height of the main mast. His master was going . . . Master? He didn't like it when he thought of the colonel as his master. He tried to put the best face on what he was doing, referring to the torturer as his handler. In the back of his mind was a small glimmer of hope that one day his parents would be released and the Chinese would tire of using him. By the time he reached the deck, he once again faced the truth that his service to his parents' homeland was something that would carry him into his old age and eventually death. Regardless of what happened to his parents, they would never let him go.

He stood for a moment at the bottom of the ladder until Taleb shouted for him to step aside so he could reach the bottom also.

Kiang started away from the side of the building, turning the corner to come face-to-face with the NCIS Agents Zeichner and Gainer. The three men stared at each other for several seconds. Kiang saw the recognition in their faces.

"Come on, Dr. Zheng," Taleb said as he reached the tableau. He grabbed Kiang's arm. "Let's go have a cup of coffee and you can show me those photographs you took."

Kiang nodded at Zeichner and Gainer, stepped around them, and allowed the boatswain mate from the crow's nest to guide him toward the nearest exit.

FIFTEEN

Through half-opened eyes, the first thing Jacobs saw was his feet sticking off the end of a cot bed on the open deck. Looking up, he saw the sun lighting up the top of a canvas tent covering the space where the cots were aligned row upon row. He glanced around him as the flow of returning consciousness brought understanding to what he was seeing. The cots extended as far as he could see without raising his head. Each had a person on it. Some people were sitting up talking, swathed in bandages; some were motionless; and others were prone like he was. *What the hell happened?* Strolling among the tableau of injured were men and women in white smocks reaching to a few inches below their knees. Khaki trousers emerged along the bottom edges to identify them as active-duty Navy.

Jacobs lifted his left arm a few inches before something stopped the movement. He wanted to touch his left side. His eyes widened. The left side! He recalled his hand covered in blood. The pain still radiated from the left side. *What if they've amputated my left side?* he thought, before quickly dismissing the thought as irrational. He just wanted to see if blood was still there. He tried to lift his arm once again and realized something was holding it down.

It was painful, but he raised his head and looked down at his left hand. A tube ran from beneath a bandage on his wrist to a metal stand, holding a plastic bag with clear liquid in it. "Guess I'm still alive," he mumbled. "The Navy wouldn't waste good medicine on a dead sailor."

"Won't be a live sailor once Helen gets ahold of you," a voice from the right warned.

Jacobs turned. Agazzi sat there on the deck, playing solitaire. His best shipmate's head was nearly level with his.

"How long have I been out? And has anyone told her?"

Agazzi shoved the cards together, destroying the game and gathering the cards into a single deck. He kept quiet as he did it.

Jacobs raised his head slightly. What happened? More thoughts of events became clear as he struggled to recall. One moment he was being pulled across the deck, and the next he was regaining consciousness on a cot. His head turned slowly from right to left. He glanced over his shoulder, but pain ripped through him.

"I wouldn't try to move too much, Jerry."

"What's happening to me?"

Beside them, one of the chief corpsmen walked up. "Master Chief, glad to see you're back with the living," the chief petty officer said. "We're going to be flying you over to the *Boxer* later this afternoon. I'll have the doctor come by to see you now that you're regained consciousness. So, just lay there until we can get you over to the *Boxer*."

A young second-class petty officer checked Jacobs's drip and then lifted the sheet over him. Jacobs looked beneath the sheet also. A huge, thick bandage was wrapped around his left side. "What's that?" he asked weakly.

"That, Master Chief Jerry 'Dumb-shit' Jacobs, is your Purple Heart," Agazzi said.

"I got wounded?" he asked with amazement. He touched his upper lip with his tongue. "I got shot? Or was I bombed?"

Agazzi nodded. "Yes to all three questions."

Jacobs's head fell back against the padding making up this makeshift bed. "Helen's going to kill me." His wife was already pissed at him for sneaking away on this deployment. He had barely made it out of Pearl Harbor, and then only by promising to retire. She'd march him down to personnel and do it herself if he didn't.

The corpsman straightened. Then patted Jacobs on the shoulder. "Well done, Master Chief. You're quite the hero."

"Where are my two boatswain mates?" he asked, his gaze traveling from the chief corpsman, across the second-class, to Agazzi.

The second-class shook his head. The chief answered with a puzzled look on his face. "Boatswain mates, Master Chief? I don't know what you're talking about."

Jacobs looked back at the chief.

"There were two others with me. Are they here?"

"Master Chief," he replied, shaking his head, "I wouldn't know. I just got here thirty minutes ago. You've been here two days."

"Alistair . . ."

"There is a Petty Officer Potts somewhere over there, but otherwise, I think your boatswain mates are okay," said Agazzi. "And I think every one of them has managed to make their way over to check on you."

"Must have been scared I was going to live," Jacobs said with irony.

"No, I wouldn't say that," the chief said. The corpsman turned to the second-class. "Come on, Simmons, we have others to see." He looked down at Jacobs. "Master Chief, you take care, my man." He shook his head, smiling. "I don't think I could have done what you did."

The two corpsmen walked away, taking their small bag with them and moving to nearby cots.

Agazzi laughed. "I think your boatswain mates were truly worried about you. Unfortunately, because of their concern, I do have some bad news for you."

"What's that?" Jacobs asked, trying to prepare himself for the worst.

"I think they all think of you as a father figure, or more likely a grandfather figure. Guess when I reach your age . . ."

Jacobs grinned, wrenching from the effort. "Shit, man, you're only three years younger than me," he gasped. He let his head flop back on the small pillow. Several seconds passed. "What happened?"

Agazzi pulled his knees up, wrapping his arms around them, trying not to lean back against another cot with an unconscious soul in it. Then he started talking, bringing Jacobs up to date on the action that had occurred in a few hours of the afternoon two days ago. What a difference forty-eight hours made.

"... and as they were pulling you across the deck away from the firing North Koreans, apparently a British missile hit their transport aircraft—"

"A British missile? Tell me we aren't at war with them."

Agazzi shook his head. "Oh, I forgot to mention that the British aircraft carrier HMS *Elizabeth* launched her fighters to help us. Two of those fighters attacked the approaching enemy aircraft firing missiles. I think they only fired two, but both missiles missed the aircraft, approaching Sea Base from the front."

"Then they fired at Sea Base?"

"Nope. The missiles needed something to lock on to, so the heat from the fire of the burning aircraft on the deck drew one of them to it. When it struck, the explosion sent you and the two people dragging you head over heels toward perdition."

"What's the frame number for perdition?" Jacobs interrupted, without raising his head.

"I'll find out for you."

"What happened to Potts? And to Showdernitzel?"

"As the chief said, Potts is on one of the far cots. He's okay, more scraped up by the non-skid than anything else. Isn't Showder . . . *what's her name?* She's the one you've griped about since we set sail? The female Amazon?"

"Yes, but she was with Potts pulling me away after being shot." Jacobs looked at Agazzi. "That's right. I was shot, wasn't I?'

"Among other things, Jerry."

"She's not among the wounded?"

"She must be okay, Jerry. If she wasn't, she'd be on the list stapled to the bulletin board medical put up near the entrance."

Jacobs turned his head from side to side. Every movement hurt. It seemed every bone and muscle in his body had been beaten with a baseball bat.

"Would you check the list again? Just want to make sure she's okay."

"Of course."

The huge medical tent was open on all four sides, allowing the soft warm breeze off the Sea of Japan to whiff through the triage area.

"Looks to me as if everywhere is an entrance."

"Naw, that's just a boatswain mate's perspective. Everything has an entrance."

"Don't pull that philosophical bullshit on me, Alistair. I barely can remember my name." He twisted his neck, trying to look on the deck around his cot. "Can a man get some water around here?"

Agazzi reached beneath the cot and pulled out a plastic water bottle, breaking the seal, and handing it to Jacobs.

Jacobs took the water, raised his head, and gulped it down, pausing once before he finished the bottle.

"I got to go to the head," Jacobs said as he handed the empty bottle to Agazzi.

"Well, don't expect me to help you there. Besides, lift the sheet. I think you'll see they've already taken care of the problem."

Jacobs lifted the sheet. "A tube. They stuck a tube up my pecker! What in the hell kind of perverts are they?"

"Well, they did have a crowd around watching," Agazzi lied.

"Watching?"

"Yeah, lots of talk while the nurse . . ."

"Nurse?"

". . . was pushing it up through that small hole to reach your bladder."

"Not right having a crowd when they do that shit."

"Well, at least you helped kill some Navy lore for a lot of young sailors."

"What d'you mean?"

"They now know that master chiefs do have balls and aren't peckerless. But look on the good side."

"What good side?"

"You don't have to get up."

"Get up? I don't even know how to use it."

"You were doing okay when you were unconscious."

"But I ain't unconscious now." He looked under the sheet again. "Do I grab it and pretend I'm at a urinal."

Agazzi's left lower lip curled up. "Look, Jerry, I may be your best friend, but sitting here talking about your peeing problems isn't in the agreement."

"Look, I'm the injured war hero, you prick, and you're suppose to be my best . . ."

* * *

"IS that the man?" Holman asked Garcia as they moved between the cots, pointing toward Jacobs and Agazzi.

Garcia nodded. "That's him. Looks as if he has a visitor."

"I would like to meet him. He was unconscious yesterday."

"Doctor said he lost a lot of blood before they were able to stop the loss. He's lucky the bullet went in one side and out the other without exploding inside him or hitting anything major."

Holman and Garcia stopped near the foot of Jacobs's cot.

Agazzi leaped to attention, nearly falling on top of Jacobs. His eyes widened at the sound of urine flowing into the metal container. He glanced down at Jacobs, who had his eyes shut.

"Wow! That feels good."

"Stand at ease, Senior Chief."

Jacobs's eyes opened. "Jesus!" The sound from beneath the cot stopped abruptly. With his right hand, he pushed on the cot as if trying to get up.

"Stay put, Master Chief. It is I who should stand at attention, not you," Holman said.

A puzzled look crossed Jacobs's face. *What is the admiral talking about?* he asked himself.

"What you did was heroic and in the highest tradition of the Naval service. It is indeed an honor to know how blessed our Navy is to have service people of your caliber leading our junior officers and our young sailors. You are definitely the talk of the fleet."

"Thank you, sir," Jacobs answered, wondering, *What in the hell are they saying about me out in the fleet? Better not be a lot of bullshit.*

"Well done, Master Chief," Garcia added. "We are all very proud of you."

Holman bent down and took Jacobs's right hand. "Yes, well done, Master Chief."

While Garcia also shook Jacobs's hand, Holman added, "The press has been demanding an opportunity to talk with you. All of America wants to meet you."

Jacobs's eyes widened. "Admiral, does my wife know?" he asked weakly.

"Why, of course, Master Chief. I know she has been trying to get ahold of you since yesterday. We have reassured her that you are okay, but I think she wants to hear it directly from you. She has asked to speak to you directly. In fact, she's been very insistent about it, and we promised her she could as soon as possible. We didn't tell her how badly you were wounded. Didn't want to worry her too much since the doctors said you were going to be all right." Holman looked at Garcia. "I'm sure the Skipper will make arrangements."

"They're moving the master chief to your flagship soon, Admiral," Garcia added. "Might be better communications facilities on the *Boxer* than here."

Holman nodded. "Master Chief, as soon as they get you settled on board the USS *Boxer,* I'll have the communications officer set up the telephone call." He glanced at his watch. "Besides, it's oh-dark-thirty in Hawaii."

AGAZZI and Jacobs watched the two senior officers leave.

"See, told you Helen would be more worried than angry."

"Right! Probably can fry an egg on her forehead right now." He looked at Agazzi pleadingly. "Why did they have to tell her I was all right? Helen isn't going to feel any sympathy in reaching through the telephone and throttling me." He laid his head back. "You gotta help me, shipmate."

Agazzi stuck his palm out toward Jacobs. "No way, my friend. I'm not talking to Helen. That's your joy."

"You think she is going to be angry?"

"Angry? Who? Helen?" he asked with a laugh. "You wait to the day before you're leaving for a six-month cruise for her to find out from the other women that you're going again, and you wonder if she is going to be angry over you getting yourself shot and peppered with shrapnel?" Agazzi shook his head. "Un-uh. Methinks you won't have to worry about your promise to retire when you get back to Pearl; methinks they'll be putting you out on a medical when she finishes with you."

"Look! I don't need you to talk to her. I need you to get the senior chief from the personnel office up here with some blank retirement papers."

The smile left Agazzi's lips. "You're going to retire?"

"What do you think?"

"I think you got something up your sleeve."

"I told Helen I would fill out the papers. I'm going to fill out the papers."

"Then?"

Jacobs shut his eyes. "Then I can tell her I've filled out the papers. I didn't say when I would put them in."

Agazzi crossed his arms. "I wouldn't worry about a medical discharge if you pull that shit. I'd worry more about her collecting your Servicemen's Group Life Insurance after they free her for justified homicide."

Jacobs didn't answer. After a minute, Agazzi thought his friend had passed into sleep. He was turning to leave when Jacobs spoke. "What was the admiral talking about this 'hero' crap?"

"Oh, you know: standing out there in broad daylight with a less-than-full fire team fighting a bunch of North Korean soldiers firing guns at you. You stood there like the Rock of Gibraltar fighting them with a fire hose. You should see the cartoon in the *Stars and Stripes* newspaper."

"Well, then they didn't check my skivvies."

Agazzi chuckled. "Yeah, you are quite the hero, my friend. I wouldn't be surprised if the President doesn't invite you to the White House for tea and crumpets."

Jacobs's head made a slight nod. "Good, because I'll need a place to live. She's gonna kill me," he mumbled, the words tapering off as Jacobs's visit to the real world descended into sleep.

Agazzi watched for a few minutes, wiped his eyes with a sense of relief, and turned to go find the senior chief petty officer in charge of personnel. Wasn't his job to question the tactical maneuvers of a master chief more worried about his wife than facing the North Korean soldiers. But then, of course, most had never met Helen.

"I'M telling you, Kevin," Zeichner said. "Dr. Zheng is our spy. What was he doing up in the crow's nest during all this time?"

Gainer leaned back against the bulkhead of the small NCIS office. "I checked, Boss. As I said, he's the head of the Institute and those antennas are part of their product lines. According to the boatswain mate up there with him, the man just watched the action, and periodically tested the equipment to make sure it was functioning."

"Something doesn't ring quite true, Kevin. The good doctor had binoculars and a camera with him. Why in the hell would he have a camera up there?" Zeichner leaned back in his deck chair, his knees wedged beneath the metal middle drawer of the government-issue desk. He shook his head. "I'm telling you, he took photographs from up there."

"No law against it . . ."

"There is if he is spying," Zeichner interrupted. "I want the truth, and I know he is working for someone other than this nonprofit Institute." He leaned forward, putting both elbows on the desk. "We're going to get to the bottom of this." He lifted a message from his desk. "According to headquarters we are headed back to the original operations area. Between here and there, we are going to know more about Dr. Zheng than he knows about himself."

"But the sailor who was the phone talker up there said the man only used the binoculars, and then to watch the antennas."

"Why would the sailor lie?"

"I don't think he was."

"And I don't think Dr. Zheng was up there with a camera that stayed buttoned the whole time." Zeichner pushed his heavy frame up from the chair. "Kevin, go back to headquarters and ask them for everything we have on Dr. Zheng. I want copies of his last security clearance questionnaire and a copy of the polygraph assessment done when he got his compartmented clearances. I want to know what makes the man tick."

"We could always bug his room."

Zeichner put both hands on his hips and cocked his head to the side. "Kevin, if he is what I think he is, he'll find anything we plant in his stateroom. He knows we've searched it once." He dropped his hands. "You saw the look on his face when we turned the corner of the tower and nearly knocked him down. He knew who we were. You could see the shock on his face." Zeichner worked his way around the edge of his desk toward the door.

"I was shocked," Gainer said. "I didn't realize he was there. In fact, I wasn't even thinking of him."

"He wasn't aware we were there or if he was, he didn't think he was going to bump into us. I'm glad we did. If I needed confirmation that he was up to no good, his countenance was proof enough. For a fraction of second there, Zheng was going to run. He was going to take off sprinting across the deck." Zeichner shook his head. "Nope, he's our guy. He knows we know and when we tie back up in Pearl, we are going to know who his handlers are. And he is going to be in chains somewhere in the bowels of the bilges."

"What if he's innocent?"

Zeichner rolled his eyes. "He's guilty of something. Everyone is guilty of something. If he's not a traitor, then he's done something to make himself feel guilty and I'm going to know what it is before we disembark in Pearl. Besides, we don't need concrete proof to arrest him and hold him. We can call him a terrorist and keep him for the remainder of the voyage and when we get back to Pearl Harbor let headquarters decide if they want to take him before a judge or not."

Gainer agreed. "I'll go take care of asking headquarters for what you want."

"Good," Zeichner said, walking through the door. He looked at his watch. Two o'clock in the afternoon. The fresh pastries would be coming out of the oven on board the *Denebola*.

HOLMAN and Garcia emerged from under the huge tent, walking toward the tower, Garcia on Holman's left. Near the tower, the blades of a CH-53 helicopter turned slowly.

"I think it's the airdale way of urging me to return to my flagship," Holman said, pointing at the helicopter.

Garcia smiled. "Most airdales aren't that tactful."

Holman smiled. "Thanks."

"With you as the exception, of course, Admiral."

"Hank, you did a good job in this action," Holman added, keeping quiet his initial misgivings about the four-striper.

"Thank you, Admiral, but I think a lot of it was blind luck."

"Sometimes luck is better than skill. What's the status of the Air Force pilot who got burned when he crashed on the deck?"

"Critical. We flew him off on a C-130 the next day. Last SITREP I received showed he was en route to the burn unit in San Antonio. They'll send a SITREP once they have him admitted and let us know his status. The chief master sergeant and the other Air Force captain named Nolan had some burns on their hands and face, but we are treating them on board. Doctors said they'd recover, but the chief will have some scars on his hands."

Holman nodded, his lips pushed together. "Fire is a terrible scourge of the sea. We have little choice but to fight it when it happens. Not like flooding, where we can always pump out the water and recover the spaces. Fire destroys and kills and when you're at sea, you have no choice but to win against it."

Garcia saw the familiar two gold epaulets on the left shoulder of the admiral's executive aide walking toward them. It was those who took those types of jobs who made flag. Of course, there were also those who took the job of EA and tried to wear their admiral's stars, pissing off other senior officers, and then were surprised when they never made another rank. Admirals tend to retire long before their EA's do.

Garcia had never been anything other than a surface warfare officer who jumped from one easy assignment to another, always shocked when he was promoted, and always thankful when his time at sea was short. Unlike others, he had not purchased any future epaulets or stars that might indicate an ambition to become an admiral. After this deployment, he was seriously considering retiring.

"Hank, you listening to me?"

"Sorry, Admiral, my mind wandered for a moment."

"I said, I think my shadow is coming to tell me that it's time to go."

Motion across the bow of Sea Base caught their attention, causing both men to stop. The Royal Navy aircraft carrier CVA-1 HMS *Elizabeth* steamed along at a nice brisk speed, crossing the bow of Sea Base from starboard to port. Aircraft topside were parked tightly along her port side, the symmetry interrupted by the forecastle.

"She's magnificent, isn't she?" Holman asked, more of a statement than a question.

"Without her, we might be fighting hand-to-hand to recapture Sea Base from the North Koreans."

"The good news is we are moving out of the Sea of Japan and going back out to sea. With the North Koreans ramping down from their muscle-flexing and knowing their one opportunity to make us look bad failed, they exhausted what little resources they had. It will be a while before they can reach a point to try this again."

From the bow of the *Elizabeth* a F-35 Joint Strike Fighter took off, flying straight ahead. Garcia knew the pattern. The carrier would have coordinated the launch with his Combat Information Center. They would have known that Sea Base had no flight operations scheduled for today except for the daily C-130 mail flight due later in the afternoon.

"Wish we had some new carriers," Holman observed.

"Eight going down to six," Garcia said.

"With Congress promising to use the savings to build six new ones in the future."

Commander Albright saluted as he approached the two men, with Holman and Garcia returning it.

"And what does my EA want?"

"Admiral, I have this message that just arrived," Holman's EA said, handing him the folder he was carrying.

Garcia and Albright stood quietly while Holman read the message. The admiral's eyebrows furrowed as he read, his lower lip pushing into the upper. He grunted several times as he read. Closing the folder, he handed it back to Commander Albright.

"Well, Hank, looks as if the Chinese accuse us of sinking one of their submarines. That, along with the recent vote by Taiwan for independence, seems to have caused them to feel froggy. They are amassing along the coast with their Navy units sailing toward the Taiwan Strait." He slapped the message in his hand. "This is secret, but their ambassador has warned our State Department that the United States should stand clear or risk war with China."

A slight chill wrapped around Garcia, for the only American force anywhere near Taiwan was Sea Base.

"And?" Garcia asked.

"We have been ordered to take position northeast of Taiwan; near the original Sea Base operations area."

"When?"

"We shift colors and start moving southward today."

"I'll make preparations for shifting Sea Base immediately."

"Hank, on the positive side is that HMS *Elizabeth* is to become part of our battle group. Seems the Chinese blame the British for the sinking and have issued them a similar warning."

Garcia shook his head. "There is no way they can believe we sank their sub. We have proof the North Koreans did it."

"Proof and fact are only useful if it supports a political will. We all knew the time would come when either"—he held up one finger—"one: Taiwan would acquiesce and become a part of the mainland, or"—he held up a second finger—"two: China decided enough was enough and would use force to take the island."

"I never thought they'd use force. Always thought their desire to keep becoming an economic powerhouse would offset this bluster."

Holman shrugged. "Might be a bluster this time. Every now and again a nation has to show it's ready and willing to fight for a principle even if it leaves you scratching your head wondering why."

The jet blasts of a second F-35 leaving the deck of *Elizabeth* drew their attention.

"Let's hope we can find an aircraft carrier to help the *Elizabeth*. She only carries fifty fighters. Not much of a match against the entire Chinese Air Force."

"Never thought the British would ever build a carrier such as that. Thought they'd stick with the smaller vertical-takeoff-and-landings types. This one has a catapult and functions a lot like ours."

Holman chuckled. "You know, empires and nations have risen and fallen throughout history. England at one time was the greatest military power in the world. Then, we took over for a while, but our time in the sun may be coming to an end. We're reducing our military by leaps and bounds every year while England is starting to grow its maritime strength once again. Maybe we are witnessing the return of the baton."

The hammer clicked on an empty cylinder. Andrew jumped. His eyes flew open. Beads of sweat raced down his cheeks. His breaths were short, rapid, and panicky with relief. The steady outward appearance of calm moments earlier vanished. His body shook and he nearly tumbled off his knees. He closed his eyes and bowed his head slightly, knowing those watching believed him to be praying. Andrew fought to stop the trembling, slow his breathing. He recalled his father's warning about how he should act once the selection process finished, but it was easy for his dad to tell him because his dad never had to do this.

The pressure of the barrel shifted off his temple. When the handler pulled the pistol up, the cool air circulating through the shadows of the barn brushed a like a circle of ice across the red pressure spot on his temple. His eyes followed the pistol as the man placed it in the case carried by another man.

"It is God's will," the crowd said in unison.

"Like his brother," someone said.

"The pistol!" one of the deacons shouted.

"The pistol!" the crowd took up the cry.

The man, who moments earlier had pulled the trigger while the gun was against Andrew's temple, reopened the case and took the gun out. He pointed it upward and pulled the trigger.

The gun fired. The bullet shattered old wood shingles as it penetrated the roof. Andrew jumped at the noise. The smell of cordite drifted across his face. Small splinters drifted down onto the crowd.

"Amen," came a smaller chorus from the deacons surrounding the pit. "Praise the Lord."

Four more shots followed the first one. More small pieces of wood rained on the crowd.

The congregation went wild with cries, prayer, and shouts of praises for God's grace on Andrew.

The pistol was laid reverently back in the case. The man locked the case and nodded at the man holding the case. Then the crowd watched as the person carrying the case walked up the steps leading from the pit. Andrew watched along with everyone else until the case disappeared within the crowd, the man carrying it heading toward the area where earlier Andrew had hugged and left his father.

Two pairs of hands grabbed Andrew under the arms, pulling him to his feet. He opened his eyes and glanced at the two men. Their lips moved. They were speaking, broad grins stretching their faces. He smiled. He knew they were praising him, shouting thanks to the Lord. But the words flowed around him in a bubbling stream, failing to penetrate the frightful haze still enveloping him.

His knees buckled, their hands tightened. He was numb from kneeling so long—while the congregation prayed for divine intervention. Upright, he was a good six inches taller than either of the two men holding him. His weak smile faded, removing all expression from his face.

The hands tightened slightly and the two men turned him toward the steps. He took a deep breath. A few tears edged from the corners of his brown eyes, trickling down across his day-old growth of dark stubble. He wanted to fall back onto his knees. Take more time to regain control of his body; show his composure; impress the congregation—not disgrace his father.

Andrew shut his eyes for a brief moment when he reached the first step, causing him to trip slightly on the rough rise of the concrete pit. The pressure from their grasp increased enough for him to regain his footing. They kept him from falling, as if they knew he had no energy to stop anything that might happen now. When God pulls you back from the abyss of death there is a great weakness surrounding the body in the knowledge of His power, Andrew thought.

Three slow steps later he stood at the top of the pit. Gradually, they let him go. He swayed to the right. The man there touched Andrew briefly on the shoulder, steadying him. Andrew grimaced, bending his knees slightly to relieve the itch and pain of blood flowing into the numbness. He turned slowly, testing his feet, prepared to fall, even though the two handlers remained alongside him.

He turned and looked down at the pit behind him. Ten feet from one side to the other, the ancient pit canted toward the far side, where drainage ran across a rusty wire grating covering a twelve-inch iron pipe that carried the blood and run off of the old slaughter pit from the barn.

As a lad, Andrew had followed the course of the pipe. It ran under the nearby dirt road to an overgrown drainage field created by the runoff from it and the septic tank of the nearby abandoned farmhouse. The stamped, ancient straw stomped into the bottom of the pit was soaked in fresh blood. Andrew looked at the drain cover at the far end where earlier in the day four other disciples had preceded him. Pieces of white flesh hung on the crated edges of the drain cover.

God had not intervened in His display of love and worship for the four who had preceded him.

He stared for a moment, looking at the imprint in the blood-soaked straw upon which he had knelt for what seemed hours. He stopped a quick impulse to look at the knees of his blue jeans to see if the blood of his fellow believers had soaked into them. He knew it had, he didn't need to look.

He turned away, nearly falling, but his handlers took him gently by the arms, softly offering gratitude to God. He was too unsteady. He'd fall or the handlers would grab him again. The travail wasn't over. He had to accept this as God's will.

The gun had five bullets along with an empty chamber. Holding the pistol by his side the handler had kept turning the cylinder throughout the hour of prayer—one spin after the other; over and over again—never looking to see where the unloaded chamber came to rest. The sound of the spin, the smooth clicking imprinting itself in Andrew's memory, drawing his attention to the cylinder and away from his prayers, and still God had intervened to choose him.

Without warning, his father had volunteered Andrew. He should have known that eventually he would be chosen to go through the selection. His father had taken him for a walk this morning talking about God's will and how the Bible many times required God's followers to demonstrate their faith through sacrifice. He should have figured it out, but his father was forever sharing his thoughts with Andrew during their many walks. It was good he hadn't fully shared this one.

A clear insight rushed through Andrew. His father had had little choice, but to send him into the pit. The past few weeks had been a jumble of pastoral maneuverings his father believed were leading those who opposed him into replacing him with another. When mumbling turns to whispers the leader has little choice but offer a sign of his faith before the whispers become shouts and fist-waving demands.

Andrew was that sign. As others in the Bible had offered up their first born as a sign of their love for God, so his father did with him. His father preached to all to never worry that God would be with them always.

But, his father hadn't been the one on his knees hearing the spin of the chamber or surviving the click of the hammer. Suddenly, his bladder was full and Andrew had an overwhelming urge to pee. He tightened, forcing the urge down. Joshua, his brother, probably had had no doubt he would survive the selection process.

Now, as the Lord's chosen one, his father's leadership would not be challenged for a long time.

He looked at the crowd chanting his name. There was more than a hundred crowded into the huge barn in the woods of eastern West Virginia. Andrew breathed deeply, fear dissipating quicker as the joy of being alive raced through his body. A few tears escaped from his eyes. His brother had not cried. The chanting increased in intensity.

"The purity," someone said and he knew they were referring to his tears.

"Holy."

"Acceptance of God's will."

Andrew nodded at his handlers, standing near him, ready to grab him if he faltered. If he fell, no one would think ill of him, for God had chosen him. But if he regained his composure and walked with confidence, then when his father fell, he'd assume the mantle of God's Army. The thought of replacing his father had never entered his thoughts until now. There was only one more trial to face and then, God's Army would be his. But, not until his father, whom he loved and worshipped, passed into God's arms.

Andrew raised his arms wide, feeling the joy of his name being chanted louder and louder as the congregation swayed in unison to the love of God. His arms felt heavy as he held them aloft and he fought the momentary urge to lower them; holding them in this position for a few minutes before bringing them down.

Andrew's eyes roved the crowd, stopping when he saw his father standing in the rear. His father's thick trademark dark beard traced with streaks of white hair running down from each side of the chin, tracing a path like a waterfall to the beard's very edge that rested on the second button on the white shirt. Ezekiel's eyes were hidden beneath thick eyebrows that were forever brooding.

Looking at the old man's face, Andrew wondered if this man he called Father cared whether he survived the selection or if he was willing to chance Andrew's survival as the only option of maintaining sole control of the people. It may not have been his only chance, but it was a quick one if Andrew survived—and survive he did.

"Sir . . ." one of the handler's whispered. "The Bishop waits."

The Bishop waits. His father would never willingly give up the title of Bishop. His father communed with God. He spoke with Jesus. Ask his father, he'll tell you. His father preached the righteousness of his faith. A faith grown from the tens it was when his father started God's Army to encompassing nearly six thousand in less than eight years; dedicated to whatever his father wanted. Within that six thousand were the core one hundred who plotted and planned the coming Armageddon. The core one hundred who sent followers across the globe to start the world toward Armageddon.

The Bishop preached and they all believed that with anarchy and the growing radicalism of Islam, the return of the Messiah would occur sooner, wiping bogus religions from the face of the earth and bringing peace for a thousand years. Ezekiel preached that the key to release the demons of Revelations was to rain destruction upon the world. The explosions at North Korean embassies in Canada, New York, and London nearly achieved that goal. Alert police in France and across Europe stopped the others—others who now languished in jails around the world, but who would die rather than betray God's Army. They knew when Armageddon came their freedom would be assured.

If this first march toward anarchy had been successful, God's Army would have led the people of America toward salvation as they waited for the return of the Lord.

A handler touched him slightly. Andrew nodded and started forward. The crowd shuffled apart, creating a path through which Andrew and the two men walked abreast. Someone tossed a small bouquet of flowers into the path. As Andrew passed worshippers fell to their knees, giving thanks to God. God looking down who had taken His finger and touched Andrew as the most faithful, most pure of the five men.

The scuffing of shoes disturbed the mildewed straw, stirring dust long idle, years of dried manure crumbled, joining the sharp-mixed coppery odor of blood rising through the lantern-lit barn. It was the smell of God's creation, which was why his father liked this abandoned and long-forgotten farm. *Blood and manure—the beginning and the end, the Alpha and the Omega, the Ying and the Yang—for every start there is a finish.*

Each step brought more confidence. Andrew's pace quickened to a normal gait. His smile broadened and his tears stopped; only moist streaks remained down his dust-covered face. He raised his right hand as if blessing those who kneeled in honor of God who had chosen him.

A few feet from his father, he met the old man's eyes, and saw anger in them. His knees weakened for a moment and then coursing through his body was the realization that with the click of the hammer he had both become his father's successor and his father's adversary. Only hours earlier Andrew had been the Bishop's eldest son. He thought of Joshua for a moment—now he was his father's only son.

His father reached out and touched Andrew's shoulder with his right hand. Even through the light shirt, the calluses on the hand were rough against his skin. Calluses that told of the hard labor of many years put into the fields of the farm and the cotton mills of the south. The Bishop looked upward, lifting his left hand, waiting for the prayers and chanting to stop.

Keeping his hand on Andrew, Ezekiel stood. He looked down

at Andrew, their eyes meeting briefly. "My son, I am proud of your goodness and faith." His father looked at the congregation and continued. "Pride is something God forbids in the faithful and for that pride I accept the small sin for what I feel for my son. God has reached down." He looked at Andrew. "He has touched you with His spirit and He has returned the son I offered as a sign of my faith and love."

Andrew dropped his gaze. His father dropped his hand. Andrew cut his eyes upward, watching his father. His father's head turned slowly as the old man surveyed his loyal followers. In a loud voice—his pastor's voice, his father took a deep breath and addressed the crowd, "This is a sign. It is a sign that God's Army continues on the right path. I offered my son to the Lord to prove my faithfulness to Him—and to those who think that God's Army needs a new Bishop; that God's Army is moving too fast or too slow to hasten Armageddon; that our direction is too radical for a country founded on the Bible. Let me say and ask each of you to carry this story forth. Carry it to your own congregations. Let it be known that Bishop Ezekiel offered God his remaining son, and God, through His benevolence, rewarded my faithfulness by sparing Andrew."

"God shows His love," the congregation said in unison.

He patted Andrew a couple of times on the shoulder while never taking his eye off the people surrounding him. "We will do what God has approved today. We will destroy the evil taking hold of this country—the evil growing in our enemies around the world. We will see the prophecy fulfilled and my son, through His selection, has become a Holy weapon for this fulfillment. For without God's intervention, Andrew would be dead, so his life now belongs to God. He must prove worthy of this selection. . . ."

Prove worthy? Andrew would have laughed, if he had had the energy. He tucked his chin deeper into his chest and shut his eyes, knowing those nearby watched. He kept the small smile frozen on his face as he lifted his head and turned to face the congregation. *Never underestimate the old man.* His father didn't create this biblical following by being ignorant or stupid. His father would never allow anyone to replace him, least of all his son. When his father was ready to lay down the mantle of the Lord or the Lord laid it down for him, Andrew would be there to step up. To grab the reins of God's Army and continue the Lord's march to anarchy and a thousand years of peace and love.

This day, he knew this. He could and he would wait with patience for the path. His wearing of the mantle would wait until his father drew his last breath. And when that last breath expelled, Andrew knew his father would die without ever identifying a successor for his father believed God would never allow him to die. But, he would die. Everyone dies.

Andrew raised his face high, looking upward as if seeing something others in the congregation couldn't. Other eyes followed his, staring at the roof of the barn, seeing the stars poke through the holes weathered through the aged wood or scattered by the numerous bullet holes. Eyes turned away from his father to follow Andrew's unspoken bidding.

Andrew's smile broadened. He hoped his countenance shined in the faint light. Strength was growing with each passing second. He was the chosen one. He detected a slight disruption—a slight hesitation in his father's words. It was small—barely detectable—but it was there. And he had caused it.

His father could preach for hours, so he stood listening to his father explain that he—not Andrew—was the beneficent of today's miracle. Swaying those who whispered for a new Bishop. Swaying them back to the continuing leadership of the founder.

He had never had so many epiphanies at one time. God truly reached down and touched him. The people. His father. Everyone's true purpose glowed in clarity.

Andrew turned and looked up at his father, knowing his face reflected love and respect for everyone to see, even as he thought through the idea of how his father had miscalculated.

It was the anger Andrew saw earlier when he had approached his father that had revealed to him that his father had also fully understood what had happened. Throwing his son into the selection—watching his son nearly fall from fear as he was led into the pit—all to chance God's mercy so his father could keep leadership. In doing so, his father had unwittingly allowed God to identify his successor. It was as if those maneuvering to replace his father down one path had been stopped because God had chosen a quicker, easier one.

* * *

"ANDREW, sit down," Ezekiel said, motioning him to the couch. Even in the small living room his father's deep bass voice resonated.

Across from his father, on the other side of the unlit fireplace, Thomas Bucket sat in the straight-back chair brought from the dining room. Bucket's legs firmly together, his unsmiling face and dark eyes followed Andrew as he crossed the room. Andrew was uncomfortable around Bucket. The man seldom spoke unless asked a question. Usually the answer was a monotone "yes" or "no." If more was expected, Bucket would fold onto his knees and entice you to join him as you both asked for God's guidance.

It wasn't the taciturn nature of the man that made Andrew uncomfortable. The man killed at the whim of his father. Bucket was the most loyal of Ezekiel's disciples, willing to prove his loyalty and worship for the old man whenever asked. If Bucket thought Andrew was other than the loyal, loving son of Ezekiel, Bucket would wrap his large, work-strong hands around his neck and with the strength of those sinewy arms, snap his neck with as little emotion as a chicken chosen for dinner.

"Andrew, God bless," Scott Temple said as Andrew walked by the heavyset man sitting on the right side of the couch.

"God bless," he replied.

Scott Temple sprawled on the right side of the couch. The rich black beard of the forty-something disciple failed to mask the smile lines of a man happy with himself and happy with his God. Like Bucket, Temple would execute Ezekiel's words without question. These two men were the power behind the throne. He wondered briefly as he sat down, what were the last thoughts of those whom these two disciples had dispatched to God's kingdom on the whim of his father.

"Thanks be to God," his father said, remaining seated.

Andrew joined the other two men on his knees and as his father led the mantra of God's Army, he repeated it along with Bucket and Temple. The words so ingrained in his mind, they came easily as he thought of other things, relived the near-death experience of earlier.

In the background, as the men prayed, Andrew's mother talked softly to their wives in the kitchen. The sound of a knife slicing through something on the carving board came faintly from that direction. Making sandwiches, he told himself, causing him to realize how hungry he was. His stomach rumbled.

He had refused breakfast this morning, knowing his father had called for a selection. He never ate when his father called for a selection. Andrew was a creature of routine. He washed before going to bed at night and again showered when he arose. His pants hung in the closet on the left side and his shirts on the right. Coats and suits hung in the hallway closet of the small three-bedroom farmhouse. Andrew expected his mom to have coffee ready by the time he dressed. He only expected it because his father demanded it. His underwear was divided into briefs on the left and undershirts on the right. Everything had a time and a place, his father taught. Andrew had yet to reach the age where such meticulous attention had turned into a full-blown phobia.

Selections were emotional days. Someone always died. The selections disturbed Andrew's sense of order. So, this morning like others, Andrew took the obligatory solitary walk of his developing phobia along the path leading from the house, past the barn, listening to the chickens rising, the clucks announcing fresh eggs filling the nests. Two roosters parried in the corner for the position of master of the roost as he passed. Life was a cascading waterfall of complexities. His twin sisters were already gathering the eggs, waving at him as he passed by.

From behind the barn, Juan had emerged. Andrew had waved at Juan as the hired hand led the two cows into the barn, their bells parading tones in front of them. He could almost feel the man's rough hands on the teats pulling forth God's bounty. This smell of the fresh morning air mixed with the rich odor of manure, and the faint rustle of the dark leaves of the nearby wood accompanied him, surrounding his solitude of thought, as he walked to the spot above the stream. The heat and humidity of the summer morning had already stained the underarms of his shirt.

"Amen," his father said, bringing Andrew's thoughts back to the living room.

Andrew repeated the word with the others. He took a deep breath, finding ease in the situation as he leaned back onto the couch. His father was speaking, but Andrew's thoughts returned to his walk.

He recalled how, upon reaching the huge rock jutting out

over the stream, he had bent down and ran his hands over it feeling the moisture blanketing the moss that covered it. Andrew and his brother had played many times on this huge rock, playing Cowboys and Indians as children. Scaring each other with tales of gore and wild animals when they camped upon it. It was here he had fell, gashing his forehead. He touched the faint scar above his eyebrows, feeling the long indentation that ran from above the left eyebrow to the top of his forehead on the right. The thin line blended with his face except when he was sunburned. Then the scar glowed in brilliance across his forehead, drawing pitying comments from his mother. His brother and he had fished, swam, and camped on this huge rock, scraping their initials in it. It was here while camping one night that his brother taught him the fine art of masturbation.

"Andrew, you listening, Son?"

Andrew shook his head, shooing away his thoughts and bringing his attention back to his father. "Sorry, Father. I was thinking of Joshua."

His father nodded. "Not a day goes by that I don't thank the Lord for the time He allowed us to have your big brother." He sighed.

Andrew had walked his life in the shadow of his older brother. Joshua's death while in the Navy had devastated Ezekiel. Andrew never understood why Ezekiel sent Joshua into the Navy.

He looked across the room at Mr. Temple. Then, his eyes rested for a brief second on his father before shifting to Mr. Bucket. He was surprised to see Bucket returning his gaze. Their eyes locked for only a moment before Andrew quickly lowered his in deference to the older man. There was coldness in the man's eyes as if he enjoyed the tasks he performed for his father for more than the purpose of the task.

These three men had a plan to hasten Armageddon; to bring God's kingdom to Earth during their lifetimes. Many a night, as a young lad, Andrew had fell asleep listening to the men dissect Revelations, fighting to understand the meaning. To find the secret that was intertwined in this Holiest of Holy within the Bible. Along with the theological discussions had gone hours of prayer until one night as he lay in bed listening to the men begin their studies, his father announced that God had visited him.

Andrew laid in bed listening to his father tell the story of how a few hours earlier God had seized him in the barn and when he revived hours later, the vision had been given him. The prayers had been quite loud that night as if the three wanted to ensure God was aware of their faith and love. Andrew had quietly joined them, muffling his voice with his pillow. He had peeked several times from beneath his pillow to glance at the moon, afraid each time it would be a bright red, the sign of the Lord's imminent arrival. He loved the Lord, but he wanted more time on Earth before joining the heavenly Father.

The morning after his father's vision, the three men packed their camping gear and disappeared along the Appalachian Trail. For two months they vanished, sending his mother into a panic. When they returned, they were surprised to discover how long they had been gone. It had been their trek into the wilderness to understand God's message and His love.

For Andrew, Joshua, his mother, and his twin sisters, Mary and Charlemagne, it had been a time of deep sadness and loss. It was as if they had no path to follow. It had been the time when Joshua discovered how to comfort his sisters and watched as he brought Andrew into the comforting.

The day of his return, his father dismissed with a wave and impatience the family's concern. Ezekiel and his two disciples had sat down at the kitchen table as if they had been outside for only minutes instead of being gone for two months. The light in his father's eyes that day seared a spot in Andrew's memory for as his mother rushed around the kitchen making food and coffee, Ezekiel announced that they carried the plan to fulfill the prophecy of God's return—a prophecy given to his father in the vision. A prophecy refined with his two trusted disciples. A prophecy burst forth in glory and vision during the wilderness months in the Appalachians.

Andrew blinked a couple of times, realizing his father was speaking to him. His thoughts returned to the living room.

"Andrew, I *said* you need to listen and pay attention to what we are going to share with you. You understand?"

"I always understand, Father."

Ezekiel's eyes narrowed. "You do not fully understand, Son. It is your youth speaking. Do you understand the vision?"

Andrew bent his head in deference. "Yes, Father."

Ezekiel shook his head. "No one but the three of us, and now, you, will understand the vision. A vision entrusted to me by

God Almighty. A vision only myself, Thomas, and Scott fully understand." The Bishop leaned forward in his chair, his elbow knocking the empty glass off.

"Sophie!" his father shouted.

His mother appeared in the doorway, wiping her hands on a kitchen towel. "Yes, Father."

"I've been a clumsy fool again, dear."

His mother saw the ice on the carpet. She smiled. "No bother, Nate . . . I mean, Ezekiel," she said, hurrying over to the spill, squatting to use the towel to push the ice cubes back into the glass.

Andrew saw the moment of fear wash across her face, but his father only nodded.

"We will speak shortly," his father said to him and the two deacons.

"There," his mother announced as she stood up. "Spic and span again."

His father reached over and patted her hand. "Thank you, my dear."

His mother's face glowed. Andrew could count on his hands the number of times he'd seen his father show his mother affection. "Affection" was a word Andrew doubted the old man truly understood. "Loyalty" was something he truly understood and demanded.

At the door his mother turned her head and said in a bubbly tone, "We'll have sandwiches shortly, gentlemen." She looked at Andrew just before disappearing from sight, mouthing the words, *Love you.*

"My apologies for my clumsiness," his father said. He leaned forward in his chair. "Andrew, today is the day you become a sharer of the prophecy of the vision. There are things within the prophecy that must be fulfilled for God. He is counting on us to do that."

"Yes, Father," Andrew said, his voice respectful. He uncrossed his legs and sat up straight. The vision was what guided God's Army. It was delivered to Ezekiel directly from the lips of God. While everyone knew of the vision, lived the vision, and believed with their hearts and souls it was divine guidance necessary to bring God back to Earth. Everyone also knew that parts of the vision were secret. The secrets were designed to keep the unbelievers from disrupting the prophecy. Only two leaders were privy to Ezekiel's secrets within the vision and they sat in this room alongside Andrew.

Andrew had become more than the Bishop's son. Today, he had become a pawn in the vision.